MAN
OF THE
CENTURY

MAN
OF THE
CENTURY

JAMES THAYER

DONALD I. FINE BOOKS
New York

Donald I. Fine Books
Published by the Penguin Group
Penguin Books USA Inc., 375 Hudson Street,
New York, New York 10014, U.S.A.
Penguin Books Ltd, 27 Wrights Lane,
London W8 5TZ, England
Penguin Books Australia Ltd, Ringwood,
Victoria, Australia
Penguin Books Canada Ltd, 10 Alcorn Avenue,
Toronto, Ontario, Canada M4V 3B2
Penguin Books (N.Z.) Ltd, 182–190 Wairau Road,
Auckland 10, New Zealand

Penguin Books Ltd, Registered Offices:
Harmondsworth, Middlesex, England

First published by Donald I. Fine Books,
an imprint of Penguin Books USA Inc.

First Printing, October, 1997
10 9 8 7 6 5 4 3 2 1

Library of Congress Cataloging-in-Publication Data
Thayer, James Stewart.
Man of the century / James Thayer.
p.   cm.
ISBN 1-55611-512-1
I. Title
PS3570.H347M36   1997
813'.54—dc21   96-49457
CIP

Printed in the United States of America
Set in 11/14 Goudy

To my beloved wife
Patricia Wallace Thayer

My life is but a wind
Which passeth by,
and leaves no print behind.
—GEORGE SANDYS

Foreword by an Unjustly Obscure Historian

"I AM THE spy of the century," were Woodrow Lowe's first words when I finally found him. They were hardly words, more the sound of a carpenter's rasp applied with vigor to a stubborn bit of wood.

Pinched and lifted by age, that voice went on, "I was also a white slave, a heavyweight contender, the ruler of China, and the man who started World War One, and if you don't believe me, you can get out of my house."

When I began the interview, Woodrow Lowe was 108 years old, as ancient and withered a husk as I had ever come across. I would have taken his pronouncements as those of a liar or madman had I not over the prior few years collected unimpeachable evidence of his feats. An account of how I came to find Woodrow Lowe and obtain his remarkable memoir is in order.

The United States government pays me to examine photographs. I work for the National Archives in Washington, D.C., in the resplendent archives building, with its seventy-two Corinthian columns of Indiana limestone and its two bronze doors at the Constitution Avenue entrance, each six and a half tons, the largest in the world.

My office is considerably and undeservedly less grand. Located in the subbasement—twenty-seven feet below street level and 19.38 feet below the Potomac River's mean high tide—my office originally was an electric fuse closet, and has the approximate dimensions of a human body. Actually, a small desk, chair, and file cabinet have been pried into it, but on the rare occasion I am visited by a coworker, that person must stand in

1

the musty hallway and speak through the door, because two people cannot fit into my cubicle at once.

I refer to myself as a historian, not an archivist, the former term having a more noble ring. I examine, analyze, and catalogue photographs, approximately 600,000 in my career. My title at the National Archives is senior research assistant, and my discovery of Woodrow Lowe may help realize my ambition of being promoted to assistant director of the Special Records Division.

One day in 1964 I was assisting the Smithsonian assemble a retrospective of the life of Theodore Roosevelt. I was working on his early years, including those he spent in the Dakota Territories. I had leafed through photographs of his Elkhorn Ranch and the neighboring communities and ranches when I came to a photo of a boxing match. The caption said the event had occurred in 1886 in Dickinson, Dakota Territory, where Roosevelt had visited several times. The caption identified one of the fighters as the legendary bareknuckler John L. Sullivan. Judging from the subject matter and the set-up—taken from an elevated dais undoubtedly with a wet-plate camera—the photographer was probably Julian Hatter, noted frontier sports photographer.

Sullivan's opponent was unnamed, but from the looks of his face was taking a beating. The anonymous fighter was a blond, with a flared (and bleeding) nose, and wide eyes reflecting his pain and perhaps bafflement. His face was not blurred in the photograph, indicating the boxer was too damaged to move. His brows were swollen, and a gash had opened above an eye. But what attracted me to the photograph was the fighter's ear, which was filled with a mound of tissue. A cauliflower ear is a classic mark of a boxer, but this was a singular specimen, with tucks and lumps of skin that looked as if they had been dabbed onto the side of his head with a plaster trowel.

That ear nudged my memory. I reached across my desk for a pile of Roosevelt photographs I had sorted earlier in the day. I dealt photos from the top of the stack until I came to one with an inscription in pencil on the white margin below the print, SECOND INAUGURATION, 1905. In black robes, Supreme Court Chief Justice Melville W. Fuller was holding a Bible. (I may be the only person alive who can recognize Melville W. Fuller on sight.) Next to the chief justice was Theodore Roosevelt, wearing a morning coat, a glint of light reflecting off his spectacles. One of Roosevelt's hands was on the Bible and the other was upraised for the oath-taking. Next to the president was his wife, Edith, wearing pearls and a fox stole.

And standing next to Edith was the man with the cauliflower ear.

I examined the photos side-by-side. John L. Sullivan's opponent and Theodore Roosevelt's honored guest at his second inauguration were the same man: blond hair (more sparse in the later photo), jut-jawed, rumpled nose, and mold-breaking cauliflower ear. The man had a scar not visible in the boxing shot, a deep diagonal slash across his left cheek, maybe new since the match with John L. Sullivan.

Perhaps this coincidence—that a frontier brawler would be on the podium at Roosevelt's second swearing-in twenty years later—was not as extraordinary as I had first thought. A number of Western toughs rose from squalid origins in those days. The caption did not identify the man.

My mother—a lovable stump of a woman—was present when I found another piece of the puzzle. This was three years later, in 1967. Mother was visiting from my hometown, Portland, Oregon, and after she had worn me out walking around the capital, we boarded the train at Union Station, headed for New York City. We eventually found ourselves in Chinatown, a place of narrow alleys, too much bustling about, murky aromas and mysterious foods. Mother charged right ahead, tasting this and that, and buying a few oddments. We went from shop to shop and finally entered Jo's House of China.

The proprietress, presumably Jo herself, was behind the counter, hidden among a vast array of tiny carved Buddhas, stylized dogs, each with paws resting on balls, plaster dragons, and bicycle nameplates. Mother tested several wind chimes, standing on her toes and blowing at them. I smiled at Jo and waited patiently.

My eyes drifted to the wall behind Jo, to an old cork bulletin board framed by an ornate wood carving of intertwined orchids. Pinned to the board were a dozen magazine photographs of the Chinese court, taken during the narrow span of time after the camera was invented but before China unburdened itself of royalty.

I have some knowledge of such photographs, having worked with the United States Army on its photographic exhibit on the Boxer Rebellion. I stepped closer to the counter and peered over Jo's head at the board. My breathing stopped.

One photograph was of China's empress dowager, Tz'u-hsi, taken when she was about sixty-five years old (her renowned dewlaps date her with precision), which would place the time of the photograph at the turn of the century. She was sitting in a low chair (not the throne) made of a dark wood, perhaps cherry, with feet carved to resemble the five-clawed dragon, a prerogative of the imperial court.

The empress was wearing a silk *haol,* a long dress split at the sides with narrow sleeves and fixed at the waist with a belt. A sleeveless jacket covered much of the robe. Although the photograph was in black and white, the robe was probably lemon yellow, the distinctive color of the royal family. On her head was an embroidered satin bonnet. Her feet were encased in slippers and were normal size because Manchu women—and she was a Manchu—do not bind their feet. Around her neck was her famous rope of pearls, many loops of pearls, each the size of a thumb.

The empress was looking blankly at the camera, her mouth giving the impression that it normally scowled but had been lifted at the corners with considerable effort for the occasion.

Sitting on the floor next to the empress' feet was a man in ceremonial clothing; a cap with a peacock feather tassel, a court-robe collar on which hung a *p'u fang* (a mandarin square showing a coat of arms) and a dragon robe with horse-hoof cuffs. His legs were crossed and his hands were at his sides.

The man was an Anglo and had a cauliflower ear. And a long scar on his left cheek.

I lunged across the counter, knocking over a box of brass camel bells. Jo dropped her pencil in fright. I ripped the photograph off the cork board and brought it to my eyes.

There he was—John L. Sullivan's opponent and Theodore Roosevelt's friend—draped in the clothes of a Mandarin prince and roosting next to the most powerful woman in the world. He was staring back at me, blithely unaware of the confounding mystery he would present me many years later.

Jo charged me twenty dollars for the magazine photograph, and I took it and mother back to Washington.

The pathway out of my dungeon to a window office overlooking the Washington Monument was abruptly and dazzlingly revealed to me; find this man's story and tell it to an astonished and grateful world.

This scarred witness to a tumultuous history, this feckless world jour-

neyer would escort me out of the maze of professional anonymity in which
I had been helplessly wandering for years. The man with the cauliflower
ear would be long in the grave, but he could not have passed through a life
filled with a legendary boxer, a Roosevelt, and a Chinese empress—as
twisted a course and as provocative a life as had ever been endured by one
man—without leaving a well-trampled trail. I would find it.

I took a six-month unpaid sabbatical from the archives to search for
my man. I waded into the Smithsonian, dug through the Library of
Congress, and sifted through one government and military records repos-
itory after another. Nothing escaped my scrutiny: late nineteenth-cen-
tury newspaper accounts of pugilists from sporting newspapers such as
the *National Police Gazette,* early issues of the Dickinson *Record,* Theodore Roosevelt's diaries and those of his wife and intimates, tons of
photographic plates by White House and Old West photographers. Increasingly desperate as my sabbatical neared an end, I traveled to the
University of Formosa on Taipei to examine records of the imperial
court, which were moved from the mainland just ahead of the Commu-
nists in 1949.

I found precisely zero, not one scintilla of evidence that the man with
the cauliflower ear had ever existed, not one molecule of information
about him. He had passed through his life without leaving the slightest
of marks, and apparently left life unmourned and unremembered. He
had been a phantom, captured in his mortal form only in three instants
of his life by three photographers.

He was taunting me. Each time I examined my precious photos again,
his mouth seemed ever so slightly more arched in a smile. Find me, if
you can, if you dare, he was saying to me. Search the world for me,
exhaust your life in this search, but I will come to you only in your three
photographs, and will forever remain your life's enigma.

I surrendered. Utterly defeated, angry at my passion, and distressed at
the prodigious waste of my time, I threw my photographs in a drawer at
home and returned to my electric-fuse closet in the archives building. I
would go on forever, one freight elevator and a football field to the
nearest coffee pot.

THE MAN WAS not done with me. One morning in 1972 while eating
breakfast I opened the *Post.* There, next to an article about some neigh-

borhood organizing committee, *was a photograph of the man with the cauli-flower ear.*

Yes, my great tormentor had surfaced alive! I trembled with joy.

The caption under the photo read, "President Nixon shakes the hand of Mr. Woodrow Lowe, 108 years old, of Newbury, Connecticut, last surviving Spanish-American War veteran. Mr. Lowe said later, 'I thought Nixon was reaching for my wristwatch.'"

In the photograph Mr. Lowe was sitting in a wheelchair in the Oval Office, wearing a shawl over his knees. His rumpled suit jacket was shiny with age and he wore a string tie with a lump of Indian turquoise at the neck. His bald head was slightly drooped. His arm, with sleeves too short, was extended toward the president. His wrist was as thin as a garden hose and his wristwatch hung on it like a bracelet. The ancient specimen—108 years old!—was wearing a rictus grin, a lipless slash above his chin revealing overlarge and unnaturally even teeth that could only be dentures. The scar on his cheek was black with age.

The president was keeping his distance as if the old man had a bad smell, and was bent at the waist to reach for Mr. Lowe's hand. Behind them was a yellow-tasseled United States flag on a pole.

My prey—now not just dry documents but a living, (barely) breathing man—would not escape me this time. I would find him, damn the trouble and expense. His story would be told to me, his Boswell, his confidant and confessor.

For a man who had apparently spent his long life insuring no record of him existed other than photographs, Mr. Lowe was remarkably easy to find. Newbury telephone information gave me his address over the phone.

One day later, July 10, 1972, I appeared uninvited and unannounced at Mr. Lowe's doorstep. Actually, I appeared at his gatehouse. I carried a tape recorder in my briefcase.

In the *Post* photograph, Mr. Lowe had the look of a beggared nursing-home cageling, as impoverished as he was infirm. In truth, he was anything but poor, as I was about to learn.

The gate, with wrought-iron scrolls, pickets and spear points, was mounted on wheels, and hung on the gatehouse. On the lawn was a discreet sign that read, ELEVEN DOWNING LANE. I pressed the button on a metal intercom box mounted on a post at the corner.

After a moment a woman's voice said through the intercom grating, "Yes?"

"My name is Truman Pease, ma'am. I'm here to see Mr. Lowe."

The metal in her voice was not caused entirely by the intercom speaker. "Mr. Lowe is not receiving today."

"Tell him I've come a long way, will you? And that I just want to ask him a few questions."

"I'm sorry. Mr. Lowe is unavailable." The intercom clicked off.

I jabbed my finger at the button. "Madam, I insist on an audience with Mr. Lowe."

Silence from the box. I was fearful, and suddenly seething. My ambitions, all my dreams, were about to be thwarted by a disembodied, tinny female voice, by some uncaring palace guard.

Again I stabbed the button. "Tell him I found the photographs of him in Dickinson and with the dowager empress."

Nothing from the intercom.

"And at Teddy Roosevelt's inauguration. Tell him about the photographs." I grabbed the iron gate and shouted, "Please, tell him."

A moment passed. Then another. Tears welling in my eyes, I stepped away from the gate and turned to go.

Then the lock snapped. A motor in the gatehouse hummed. The iron gate slowly swung open.

I quickly walked through the gate. The mechanism whirred behind me, and the gate rolled shut, securing itself with a loud clang. A moment of panic passed, replaced by my implacable desire to meet Woodrow Lowe. I walked up the drive, which was framed on both sides by rose bushes with pink flowers. Overhead, old oak trees dappled the sky. The trees finally ended, and the house stood revealed.

Not a house, but a baronial manor of at least thirty rooms, with turrets and gables and a half-dozen chimneys. White-trimmed windows made the red brick less ponderous. Balconies hung over the third floor, accessible by French doors. The second story was a series of bay windows.

The driveway circled around a pond where a statue of a boy peed into the water, a tinkle that blended merrily with the wind through the leaves. At the south end of the mansion was an attached Victorian sun room and at the north was a covered esplanade leading to a six-car garage. Massive cast-iron planters brimming with Martha Washington geraniums guarded the mansion's front door.

Four steps led up to an oak and iron door built to siege standards. I lifted a boar's-head knocker and let it drop several times. The door immediately opened. An eye flickered in the gap between door and frame. Behind the eye was darkness. That eye assessed me, then my briefcase. Apparently deciding I was harmless, the eye pulled open the door.

She was a nurse in white livery, as wide as she was tall with a football lineman's scowl and malevolent black eyes. She said in an uncharitable voice, "Mr. Lowe will see you."

She stepped away from the door and I entered a two-story foyer surmounted by Romanesque vaulting. Ahead was a staircase of travertine marble. I followed the nurse in a direction I guessed was south, through a library fitted in hand-carved walnut, then through a nameless room with velvet swags, wainscoting and a mural of a satyr leering at a dozen Rubenesque virgins. The nurse's abundant behind twitched left and right. Her hose scratched together like steel wool on a pipe with each of her steps. She was like a Mullingar heifer, beef to the heels.

She growled over her shoulder, "You will have five minutes with Mr. Lowe, and you are not to accede to any demand he may make for coffee."

We passed through a kitchen, redone in that year's appliance colors, orange and avocado, then finally through a door into the sun room.

The nurse turned her bulk toward me, her mammoth breasts swinging as if on a turret, almost toppling me. She made a production of looking at her watch. Her voice sounded like a truck engine cranking over. "Five minutes, no more."

She retreated. The sun room was overgrown with tropical plants and flowers that blocked out much of the window light. The air was redolent with the cloying scents of lilies, orchids and freesias, so syrupy that they carried the aftertaste of rot.

I stepped along the flagstone path through the overhanging and reaching leaves and tendrils and vines. I expected at any moment to hear the shriek of a gibbon or the trill of a Malayan moon rat. I turned a corner of the path, then another.

The moment held an undeniable grandeur, with me forging ahead through untamed foliage, another David Livingstone or Sir Richard Francis Burton. The splendor ended when I came to a clearing. There, framed by three palm trees and a tangle of bougainvillea, was my quarry, Mr. Woodrow Lowe.

Too late, was my first thought. He was sitting in his wheelchair as immobile as a stone, his eyes half open, as wasted away as an apple left for a summer in the sun, dead of terminal decrepitude.

I tiptoed into the clearing, approaching him straight on and unflinching, until I reached the footrests of his wheelchair. I loudly cleared my throat. No reaction. I waved my hand in front of his eyes as one does to the blind to see if they might be fooling. Still nothing.

I crouched next to him and sniffed hugely to detect the putrescence of the dead. My nose again filled with the sunroom's fetid tropical odor and the scent of mothballs, probably from the blanket over his lap. I glanced over my shoulder, about to call the nurse.

"I am the spy of the century."

Startled, I jumped back, catching a heel on a flagstone and almost twisting my knee. The dotard had miraculously sprung to life.

His eyes—hazel irises in the urine-yellow orbs of one suffering liver failure—rolled in their sockets toward me. He continued with the words set forth earlier in this account, ending with the testy remark about getting out of his presence.

"Mr. Lowe, my name is Truman Pease and I would . . ."

He began breathing coarsely, gulping for air. His sallow complexion darkened. I was alarmed.

"Do you need a doctor, Mr. Lowe?"

"My doctor is dead."

His breathing settled after a moment. The temperature in the sunroom must have been above ninety. I was perspiring, and the heady mix of blossoms, mothballs and debility had begun to nauseate me.

Swallowing quickly against the rising bile, I managed, "Mr. Lowe, I have come across three photographs of you from when you were a young man and—"

He waved one of his claws. "Only three photographs of me exist, I thought. But the three you found are not the three I know about. So there must be four photos."

This might have been a compliment. I was encouraged. "The life you must have led," I said in a laudatory way.

"I'm still leading it, despite appearances."

Mr. Lowe's face was an ocher color and flaked like a paper bag that had been wetted and dried many times. Perhaps mummification had begun. The skin was so thin that the bones of his cheeks and forehead and chin were surfacing through the epidermis. His eyes were held in place by a labyrinthine web of bottomless wrinkles. His nose had drooped, so the bulbous tip was almost resting on his upper lip. The boxer's bulge on the bridge of his nose was even more evident than in the photographs because his skin had shrunk around it. His mouth was malleable and moist with a bit of spit at one corner. His tongue steadily rolled behind the fraud of the glittering dentures, and frequently extruded between the teeth as if he were a snake testing the air. He had no hair to speak of, just several long white wisps that flitted above his head like insects. The slash on his face began above his left cheekbone and continued at an angle almost to the corner of his mouth.

And the ear. The hillocks of tissue in my photos had also been shriveled and darkened by the years, and resembled a handful of raisins stuck onto the side of his head. White patches of fuzz grew between the folds of the ear, and the tissue was damp as if the ear were leaking. Not a place where my eyes wanted to linger.

Mr. Lowe was wearing the same luminous green jacket in which he had met the president. The jacket suffered an olive plaid in its weave. The lapels almost reached his shoulders. His white shirt had been laundered so many times that the collar was permanently stained yellow. The blanket over his lap was from the American Southwest, one of those eagle-patterned, peach-and-turquoise-colored extravaganzas.

In my photographs Mr. Lowe gave the impression of height and solidity and power. But time had wasted him away to almost nothing. The old man was a frayed coat on a stick.

The nurse appeared out of the undergrowth, four pill bottles in her hand.

Mr. Lowe pointed a talon at her. "Get away from me, you demon."

"Now, now, Mr. Lowe." Her voice had a hardhearted tone. "The trust has hired me to look after you."

"I set up that trust when I was only ninety-two, before I knew better. Now let me be."

"Mr. Lowe, your medicines require—"

His words were chopped with anger. "Nurse, arguing with you is like wiping my butt with a hoop; it's endless. Now leave me alone."

She shrugged and disappeared into the jungle. He turned his gnarled head to me. "You said Dickinson. I don't know about that photograph."

"The match with John L. Sullivan."

His limpid mouth pulled into a grin. "I didn't see the camera."

"It was probably on a stand built specially by the photographer, maybe forty yards from the ring."

"I was too afraid to look around, what with the Boston Strong Boy coming on."

"Will you tell me of your life, Mr. Lowe?"

"You a wagering man?"

I was determined to tell him whatever he wanted to hear. "Yes, on occasion." I wouldn't know poker from pinochle or a football pool from a pool table.

He wheezed, "I'll bet you twenty dollars that my cock hangs below my knees."

I would not have been more astonished had the musty fossil spat at me. "Mr. Lowe, such lewdness . . ."

"Twenty dollars says my cock hangs below my knees."

"That is a biological impossibility."

"Get out your cash and we'll see about that."

Motivated purely by professional inquisitiveness, I pulled my wallet from my pocket and held out a twenty-dollar bill.

He snorted with glee and reached with one of his bony hands to push aside the Indian blanket and lift up the right leg of his trousers, revealing a leg as thin as rebar.

On his calf was a faded red and blue tattoo of a rooster with a hangman's noose around its neck. Instead of eyes, the rooster had little Xs.

He snatched the twenty-dollar bill from my hand, accompanied by a particularly annoying chortle.

Flummoxed, I asked firmly, "Will you tell me your story, Mr. Lowe?"

"Whatever for?" He slipped the bill into his shirt pocket. "I've kept it to myself for all these years."

This was the critical moment of the interview, I knew. I could have replied that his life deserved long-overdue acclaim, or that the crucible of history demanded an accurate account from one of its great participants, some such drivel.

Instead, I blurted, "I am stuck in the basement of my building, forgotten and ignored. You can help me get out by making me a famous historian. Christ, I need your story."

He peered at me. "I like undisguised self-interest, boy. You may simper, but I like you anyway."

I was ecstatic. Was it going to be this easy? Pray God, yes.

He went on, "Now get out of my house."

Crushed and rattled, with the abyss of my obscurity abruptly opening again, I pleaded, "The crucible of history demands an accurate account from one of its great participants."

He eyed me like a widow at the butcher shop inspecting pork chops. "I also like a man who can talk through his hat, and you have a knack for that, too."

Did this mean yes? Dear Lord, bend this antediluvian relic to my will.

"Now get out of my house."

My shoulders sagging in defeat, I turned away from him. Three fathoms below Potomac high-tide level, forever.

I was at the edge of the clearing when he said, "You aren't going to last 108 years like me, boy. You aren't tough enough."

I sighed over my shoulder, "Life has taught me that lesson, if nothing else, Mr. Lowe. Goodbye."

"And you aren't persistent enough. Nothing suits us old-timers better than someone who grovels wretchedly before us."

I leaped back to his chair. My voice was a tremolo. "I'll grovel like you've never seen. I'll fawn and flatter and be the perfect sycophant. You'll tell me your story? China and Roosevelt and all the rest?"

His eyes lowered slowly and his chin fell to his chest.

"Mr. Lowe?"

He was asleep. I took the tape recorder from my briefcase and set it up on the table next to him, plugging the cord into an outlet on a support beam.

His eyes creaked open. He continued where he had left off. "If you'd have been in China with me, you'd know how to grovel properly, I'll guarantee you that. But if you've got the time, I'll fill your ears, all right."

I looked at him intently. "Mr. Lowe, would you mind telling me why, after so many years of apparently keeping it a secret, you are going to tell me your story?"

His gaze caught mine in a moment of shared understanding and sympathy. His voice carried infinite sadness. "Other than my wife, you are the first person ever to ask me about it."

A word about Mr. Lowe's voice: the transcription you are about to read cannot convey the scratchy, reedy squeak that was his voice at 108. Nor can it replicate his hardy Boston accent, which can test the tolerance of even the broad-minded. When he became excited with his narration, his voice gained the timbre of a dentist's drill and his mouth would slaver and dentures would snap. I caught it all on tape in sessions lasting the month of July, 1972.

And about his vocabulary. Woodrow Lowe came from the back streets of Boston, and he occasionally spoke with a tough's mangled grammar. But he also claimed to have attended Yale University—though I could find no record of it—and so he often came across as an educated man. In fact, he could sound both unlettered and refined in the same sentence. And he'd throw in Irish slang, cavalry and nautical expressions, some Spanish and Arabic, a smattering of Chinese. His words were a hodgepodge that at times sounded deliberately put on, and I once challenged him. He had just said, "Hand me them cookies, which are quite exquisite." I jumped up and exclaimed, "Mr. Lowe, nobody—utterly nobody—says 'them cookies' and 'quite exquisite' in the same sentence." He looked at me a moment, then said, "Well, you can't polish a turd, can you?" I'm not sure what he meant, or whether he was referring to himself or me, but I never brought up the odd mixture of his language again.

We were interrupted only by his frequent naps and by his menacing nurse, who eight or ten times a day would give him pills or injections and serve him porridge, toast, canned fruit, and oatmeal cookies, the only items his weary system could handle. She detested me as an interloper and charlatan.

I have subtracted nothing from the tapes, even his more coarse observations. Mr. Lowe had an opinion about everyone and everything. At times it seemed he was flailing me with them. I wish to distance myself from them. Specifically, because I may someday yet find employment in the history department at Harvard University, let me say that I disagree wholeheartedly with Mr. Lowe's claim that on Harvard University's student application appears the question "Are you a pansy?" and that applicants who answer "no" are eliminated from consideration. Now that I have conveyed this outrageous assertion, I'll eliminate it from the body of his narration. But all the rest is here just as he spoke it.

Woodrow Lowe passed away in August, 1972. So why did I not immediately release his story? Professional cowardice, and I'm not afraid to admit it.

I meticulously checked Mr. Lowe's account. Whenever he gave dates or geographic and personal names, his narrative was completely accurate. But *nowhere*, not in any record I could ever find, does his name appear. The White House must have known of him because they honored him as a Spanish-American War veteran, but the White House would not cooperate with me for security purposes, the spokesman claimed. Mr. Lowe moved through his life entirely unrecorded, save the photographs. I am particularly averse to making a fool of myself, and did not want to do so by releasing the chronicle of an old man who may have been nothing more than a windbag and fraud, a prevaricator of immense talent.

What prompts me now to finally release Woodrow Lowe's story? Because after all these years I have just found the fourth photograph.

Here is how it happened. Regulations forbade hotplates in the archives building, but the nearest coffee pot was, as I said, a freight elevator and the length of a football field away. The blaze ignited when a thumb tack holding my copy of Julia Margaret Cameron's 1869 photograph of Charles Darwin—a harshly lit profile showing the atavistic bulge of brow above his eyes—fell from the wall. Darwin dropped onto the hotplate, where he burst into flame.

Grabbing a handful of photographs off the nearest pile, I swatted at the fire, but that only fanned the blaze, which leapt onto my folded cardigan sweater. So I lifted stacks of photographs and threw them at the fire. My quick thinking and about a hundred pounds of photos eventually quenched the conflagration.

In my dispatch to extinguish the fire I knocked from my desk a book entitled *The Crisis Moments* that had been sent to me by the Washington *Post* for review. The book contained famous photographs of critical moments. It landed face-up, open to a middle page. I lifted the book, and was about to toss it back on my desk when my eyes caught the photo on the page. My hand abruptly stilled.

The photograph was famous, taken on June 28, 1914, a few moments after the assassination of Archduke Franz Ferdinand, heir to the throne of Austria-Hungary. The photo showed the Serbian police just after their capture of the assassin, a nineteen-year-old Bosnian student named Gavrilo Princip, who wore a sparse mustache. The murderer was being hauled along by two policemen while several Serbian soldiers kept the crowd away from him.

One policeman was wearing a uniform replete with immense brass buttons, a ceremonial sword in a scabbard, and a kepi with a braid above the brim. The other policeman was in plainclothes, a coarse wool suit and a peaked cap.

My gaze locked on that plainclothes policeman, on the one feature I had seen thrice before.

The policeman had a cauliflower ear. I squinted at the photograph. Could the scar tissue in fact be a blur caused by a flaw in the plate? No, that battered ear was no illusion. And he had the same square face with the granite eyebrows, the crook in the bridge of the nose, the sculpted, cruel mouth, and the cheek scar.

This was more than I could bear and destroyed my innate historian's caution. Thus, I deliver to the world the testament of Mr. Woodrow Lowe. Prudence be damned.

I will reappear in an epilogue for a few more comments about Mr. Lowe, and to tell how he won another twenty dollars from me.

ONE

Two Scourges

I MET THE two great scourges of my life on the same day. Beginning on a summer afternoon in 1879 them two folks would torment me for a total of seventy years, if you counted the years separately then added them up. Fortunately, they were plaguing me at the same time, thereby leaving the last part of my life in peace. I needed that time to recover.

The Lowes came to Boston from County Kilkenny during the Great Hunger. My father worked as a canal digger and street grader for the pioneer Irish contractor Timothy Hannon, filling in Back Bay swamps, leveling Fort Hill, and grading many of the city's boulevards.

My mother, born Annie Tighe, was a domestic for a Beacon Hill family where for an eighty-five-hour week she was paid $3.75 plus room and board, and where she worked herself to illness, and finally had to be admitted to Saint Joseph's Catholic Home for Sick and Destitute Servant Girls. My pa met her there one day while she was leaning against the fence and he was strolling by.

A week later they were married, my father promising she would never have to work again, which she didn't, if you don't count the hundred hours a week she cleaned our clothes, cooked our meals, swept the floors, and clipped dad's nose and ear hairs.

Mother was a squared-away, pious woman without an ounce of foolishness except when it came to her husband's hair. For as far back as my memory goes, mother would plant pa on a three-legged milking stool and labor over him with a pair of tweezers for ten minutes a night, every night including Sundays, searching for elusive nose and ear hairs, and any other hairs. My old man pleaded with her to allow him to grow a mustache but it was never to be.

She wanted me as her oldest son to become a priest, of course. But when I reached ten years of age mum no longer had the strength to wrestle me into a confessional, so my religious education ended and I have not been into a church since, save for a wedding or two, and to hear words intoned over some deceased friends and relatives, in fact, all my friends and relatives. The worst part of living more than ten decades is attending all the funerals, and they've been plenty, I'll guarantee you that. Now I keep company mostly with the dead.

When I reached fourteen years of age, I figured I had learned everything worth knowing so I quit the Dwight Grammar School on Springfield Street and went to work for my father, which almost shipped my dear mother to her grave.

My mum had a tongue that would clip a hedge, and she lived to ballyrag pa. They were married sixty-three years, and mum died from loneliness ten days after pa left this earth. I have never ceased to wonder at the enduring affection between them, given the sixty-three years of arguing they did.

The main dispute was the way my father earned his provender once he quit the shoveling profession, which he did one day when a hod carrier on a scaffold lost his load and sent sixty pounds of bricks to the ground on pa's shadow. Pa threw down his number two idiot stick—he never called it a shovel—borrowed three hundred dollars from his mortician brother, and purchased Lonnie's Hall of Relaxation on Lenox, near where Boston University used to be, in the Roxbury neighborhood. Pa renamed the place Joe Lowe's Museum and Sporting Palace.

Another activity my parents argued over was my father's habit on cold winter nights of opening the bedroom window of our third-floor apartment and taking a leak into the air, hot steam rising from the flow, rather than using the frigid one-holer down the hall. My mother never had the heart to tell Mrs. Shaw in apartment 2A why her window box petunias never did well. But I digress.

Joe Lowe's Museum and Sporting Palace was a saloon, a place where a man could find his pleasures. Now, this word "saloon" has been polished over the years by oldsters with hazier memories than mine, so my pa's establishment needs some context. Boston in 1879 was a place of ostrich plumes, horse manure, swinging doors, corsets, lima-bean sleeves, knick-knack cabinets, gas lamps, lancet windows, crooked streets, cholera, and cloth-topped shoes, a city of high collars and low tastes. Most of the low tastes could be found at Joe Lowe's Museum and Sporting Palace.

The east wall was dominated by a backbar of beveled mirrors, fluted walnut columns, and topped by elaborate moldings. By the time the woodcarver had reached the inscription on the burnished frieze he had run out of inspiration because it read in ornately carved Old English lettering, DRINK, DRINK, DRINK.

No chairs or stools were found in the saloon but a dozen spittoons lined the bar's brass rail. Although sputtering lamps were mounted on the walls the place was always dark, even at midday. Casks of whiskey crowded shelves on the backbar. The Irish flooded Roxbury beginning about 1858 when the horsecar line to the neighborhood was completed, but there were also Germans in the area and a number of their breweries. So pa served beer of a fine quality. Boys would "run the growler," coming into the saloon in the afternoon to fill their fathers' growlers with beer. Growlers were tin pails in which the navvies, canal diggers and coal heavers carried lunch and coffee to work in the morning. Some boys made a living with the growlers, "rushing the can" for the workers. Two industrious lads might tote a dozen growlers on a pole carried between them.

The whiskey—which my mother called potheen when she was railing against pa's business—was fiery and coarse, a boilermaker's delight. "No taste and all blast," my pa would counter proudly. No mixed drinks could be had at all, much less concoctions like the shandygaff, which was beer mixed with ginger ale and was drunk mostly by Harvard students when they were playing billiards at places like Young's Hotel.

Boxing was the theme at Joe Lowe's Museum and Sporting Palace. The walls were plastered with lithograph posters of fistiana's finest: Jack Slatt, the Norwich butcher who introduced the blow to the nape of the neck called the rabbit punch; Monsieur Petit, the first Frenchman to take up boxing, who was six feet six, two hundred twenty pounds, and was called, naturally, the Giant; and James Burke, "the Deaf 'Un," who fought the longest championship bout ever, ninety-nine rounds lasting three and a quarter hours, after which his opponent Simon Byrne keeled over and never rose again. The masterwork on the saloon's wall was a reproduction of Lord Byron's screen depicting battles for the English championship between Tom Johnson and Big Ben Brain in 1791, between Johnson and Daniel Mendoza in 1788, and many others.

At the rear of my pa's guzzlery was a boxing ring. Back then a ring did not have padded turnbuckles, aprons, or a canvas mat. Pa's had four ring posts holding two ropes, and nothing more. When a boxer fell, he hit hardwood floor.

I'll interrupt myself here to say that my father put "museum" into the name of his establishment to appease my mum. That notable buttinski Horace Greeley wrote about boxing, "The thing is whereby its natural gravity of baseness it stinks. It is in the grog-shops and the brothels and the low gaming hells." The stigma against prizefighting ran deep in most society, and deeper still in my mum. Not once in all the years pa's saloon survived did my mother visit the place. Pa never retired, so Joe Lowe's Museum and Sporting Palace lasted as long as he did.

The museum portion of the saloon was comprised of one large glass display case purchased used from Bendel's Dry Goods Store. The case sat against the wall under the portrait of Jack Slatt, and contained a wealth of important rarities. I stared for hours at the shrunken head from Dutch Guiana, the Lord's Prayer etched onto a grain of rice (displayed under a magnifying glass), Saint Eglactise's curled and mummified finger, two wild boar tusks, a two-headed kitten pickled in a canning jar, six hairs from Robert E. Lee's beard, and a medieval torturer's thumbscrew. Small wonder I didn't need no further schooling.

That summer my father said, "Woodrow, down at the museum you'll be doing the fluids." I didn't know what doing the fluids meant, but I hoped there might be tips involved.

There weren't. That fateful summer day when the two banes of my life found me, I was doing the fluids.

"Get ready, Mr. Fitzpatrick," I said, standing behind the bar with one hand on a whiskey barrel's bung. I was fifteen years old and still called people mister, even an old straddy like Michael Fitzpatrick. I haven't always looked like the 108-year-old flyblown carcass you see before you. Back then I had hair, and was the blondest boy in Roxbury. My nose was as true as a ruler. I picked up this kink in it as I went along. Same with my ear, which weren't clogged up with tissue yet. And I didn't have this big scar on my cheek. My eyes were green with brown and gold flecks, and bright with youth and innocence. There were none of these scars on my brow. I once had an actor's smile, a mouthful of fine, even teeth. But I dropped a few here and there over the years since. I weren't the handsomest boy in the neighborhood, but no mirror wailed in agony if I stood in front of it.

Already at fifteen my body had settled on its shape and size. I was a mite over six feet and had the strength and stamina of a rat terrier. I could stand flat-footed on the saloon floor and jump up to the bar, then down, then up, eight times in a row. Pa said he had never seen anybody do that before and surely would never again, which was the kindest thing he ever said to me.

I passed the rubber hose to Mr. Fitzpatrick. He inhaled hugely four or five times.

I shook my head. "The nickel first, please."

He smiled slyly and dug into his breeches for the coin. He slid it across the bar to me, then filled his lungs once again and stuck the rubber tube into his mouth. For the nickel he was entitled to siphon off as much whiskey through the hose as he could without taking another breath. It was my job to closely monitor the imbiber's breathing and shut off the flow the instant he gasped for air. A man with good lungs could get sizably drunk for five cents.

A touch of blue in his cheeks but still grinning, Mr. Fitzpatrick ambled off to find a place to collapse. Wheezing and burbling, Seamus McWherty took his turn at the rubber tube. The old gent had a touch of asthma, and I always let him have one breath between gulps. He wore a tattered coat despite the heat in the saloon. Old Mr. McWherty bathed himself once a year whether he needed it or not, and was so dirty that if you flung him against a wall, he'd stick.

So whiskey was one of the fluids I was in charge of. Tobacco juice was the second. My other duties at Joe Lowe's Museum and Sporting Palace were emptying cuspidors and sweeping the floor. I never shone at these tasks. A cigar butt tossed to the floor might still be there two weeks later. And emptying the spittoons weren't as much fun as it sounds, so I let them get filled to the brims before I lugged them out back. This provided sport to the patrons. They would jostle me and stick their legs out, hoping I'd spill the juice all over my hands and shirt. So I usually was wearing splashes of the brown murk before I reached the alley to toss the contents onto the dirt. You would think that, facing this gauntlet of whiskey-guzzling pranksters I would have learned to empty the spittoons when they weren't quite so full, thus avoiding the spills. But I never did, being a slow learner, which you'll note will become something of a motif to my story.

Blood was my third fluid. This was a Saturday afternoon, and the sports were already gathering. The saloon's walls had disappeared in the cigar and cigarette smoke. Pa was pulling the taps with no letup and sailing beer glasses along the bar. When he saw Tom Kelly enter the saloon, he turned the taps and barrels over to one of his bartenders and headed toward the ring. I followed, knowing my skills would soon be needed.

Tom Kelly was a local mallethead who had just taken up club fighting. He had a narrow face, not much of a target, and a moist mouth and doe eyes. He always looked afraid, but he had a long reach and some stamina. His hair was cropped short, a trademark of a club fighter. Grabbing hair was allowed by London Prize rules.

Kelly removed his trousers, revealing knee-length black tights held up by a maroon sash around his waist. On his feet were leather high-tops. London Prize fights were often bareknuckle, but pa insisted on two-ounce gloves to keep down the clean-up time after the fight. He disliked wiping blood off the back wall. Most work gloves had more padding than the ones I handed Kelly. The fingers were cut off at the top knuckles. Back then, boxing gloves were always white.

I stepped through the ropes and held my arms up to ward off blows from his fists and elbows. Kelly warmed up, lightly jabbing at me, not intending harm.

Suddenly the drinkers roared, and I knew John L. Sullivan had entered the saloon. The crowd parted before him and he stepped into the ring wearing his dead grin and a felt hat.

Kelly and I turned to look at him. Bony eyebrows roofed eyes of dark hazel, but in the overhead light of the ring his eyes were a flat black. His teeth were remarkably even, and I don't think he lost a one of them during his long career. In later years he wore a regal mustache, but never when he fought because a mustache was just another handle for an opponent. He had a lantern jaw—his foes often mistook it for a target—and jug ears. His hair was so short that it was nothing but bristle.

John L. was five feet ten and topped a scale at 190 pounds. He removed his plaid shirt, then his pants to reveal white tights and a green waist sash. He also donned fingerless white gloves. He produced a white silk handkerchief with a green border—green and white would become his famous colors—and tacked the hankie to a ring post. Staring morosely at his opponent, Kelly had forgotten the ritual, and quickly attached his maroon-and-white colors to his post. Sullivan pulled fifty dollars from his sash and handed it to me. Next I took Kelly's fifty. There was no prize, just the wager between fighters.

I held up my arms for Sullivan to warm up. I had often sparred with him in this ring, and because I was just a kid, he pulled his punches. They still felt like four-by-fours upside the head. John L. (never John or Jack or Sully) had the largest hands I ever saw on a man. When balled, each was only slightly smaller than his head. That was one of the biggest differences between John L. and me, and at least partly explains why his boxing career soared to the sky while mine sank to the sumphole. Whereas John L.'s hands were cudgels, mine were long-fingered and elegant, the kind meant to wrap around the ivory head of a walking stick. Now I see you gawking at my hands, and I admit they look like gnarled tree roots today. That's because I've broken my fingers and hands—or someone else broke them, despite my protests—six times in my life, usually when a good distance separated me from a doctor.

John L. wanted no warmup. He ordered in his bass voice, "To the woods with yah, Woodrow."

I stepped outside the ring. My father held up a cowbell. The crowd fell silent.

This particular fight lasted only two blows, so if I'm to say a few more things about John L. Sullivan and boxing, I'd better do it here. In 1879, John L. was twenty-one years old. He was a well-known Boston club fighter then, but his stardom lay ahead of him. Ten years later he would be the most famous man in America, save maybe the president and Thomas Edison. He would be called the Great Knocker-Out, the Great John L., the Boston Strong Boy, the Champion of Champions, and the Fistic Gladiator. A line from a song of the day went, "Let me shake the hand of the man who shook the hand of John L. Sullivan." Although he lost the Queensberry rules title to James Corbett in New Orleans in 1892, John L. would retire undefeated as bareknuckle champion.

Boxing was important to us Roxbury boys. There was no baseball league of significance (the National League had been founded three years before, but didn't pull much weight) and football was an oddity. Newspapers didn't even have sports pages. It was boxing or nothing.

Most boxers began as criminals and ended up dead. Yankee Sullivan was lynched in San Francisco in 1856. Penniless and alone, John Carmel Heenan died at a train depot at Green River Station in Wyoming in 1873. Joe Coburn had been in prison for years for attempted murder.

Mike McCoole killed another fighter with his fists, then spent the rest of his mean life hiding along the Mississippi. My mother knew all this and feared for me because I longed to become a fistic scientist.

John L. and his victim came to the scratch line. My father shook the bell. Kelly put up his fists.

John L. swung once, and he might have been using a pile driver. The blow knocked Kelly's own fist into his nose, snapping it. He sank to the floor.

Kelly had some bottom, which is what we called gumption back then. After a moment, he gathered his shaking legs under himself and crawled to his corner. Stools weren't allowed in the ring, so Seamus McWherty slipped through the ropes and squatted in the corner. Kelly sat on McWherty's knees. Sullivan sauntered to his corner, idly picking a morsel of lunch from a tooth with a fingernail and flicking it to the floor. As I recall, it was a bit of sauerkraut.

Blood poured from Kelly's nose. I bent over him, put my mouth over his broken nose, and sucked the blood from it. I spit the blood into a cup my father held out. As I said, blood was my third fluid. It beat tobacco spit, but not by much. Pa again rang the fighters to the line.

Kelly made scratch but John L. charged and struck again. This time Kelly's head hit the floor before any of the rest of him did. Eyes rolling and mouth drooling, he was dragged out of the ring. To whistles and applause, John L. pulled his pants and shirt back on, plucked the bills from my hand and climbed out of the ring.

On his way out of the saloon, he paused two or three times to throw back beers proffered by admirers. Never in his entire life did he dally longer than three seconds over a beer, so we made the saloon door in quick order.

I was one of the Roxbury youths who often tagged after the Boston Strong Boy, a mobile audience for his showmanship. He never refused a challenge. I once saw him drive a nail into a hitching rail with his forehead. Another time he opened up a horseshoe with his bare hands. And once I witnessed him win two dollars by eating a beer mug.

At the door, Seamus McWherty prodded, "You took care of Tom Kelly, who's nothing but a floor skidder. But you ain't never knocked out a horse, John L."

That brought the fisticator up short. During his career, John L. Sullivan earned one million dollars with his fists and not one dime with his wit. He growled, "Oh yeah? Says who?"

"Nobody ever coldcocked a horse with his hands," McWherty insisted, his wind squally in his throat.

"You got a ten-spot to back up your mouth?"

Seamus McWherty had never even seen a ten dollar bill, much less owned one. But this challenge held forth the prospect of splendid entertainment, so the sports passed a hat and soon collected the wager.

Seamus McWherty goaded, "All blow and no show is what I'm thinking, me lad."

John L. curled his mouth and bolted through the swinging doors, which slapped the siding so hard they broke two windowpanes. My father did not permit anyone under age fourteen into the saloon unless to fill a pail with beer, so half a dozen neighborhood boys were waiting on the walkway for John L., anxious to hear of his latest victory.

Now, you may have been supposing that John L. Sullivan was one of the scourges of my life I mentioned a while back. He weren't, although I'll warrant he would do me some damage in the future. But I was about to meet that scourge. She was a woman, curse my luck.

John L. was mad, and he had only one worse mood, which was drunk and mad. He sprinted onto Lenox Avenue. We tumbled through the doors after him. He seized the reins of the first horse he came to, yanked the animal's head around, and smashed his fist into his forehead.

Maybe John L. should have done some thinking on whose horse it was, but as he liked to say by way of understatement, "I don't make my living with my head."

The stallion was a dapple-gray pulling a hansom. Unfazed, the horse reared back in its traces and danced skyward, raking its hoof against John L.'s jaw. The harness rings and buckles clattered. Sitting high on the hansom, the coachman, a fellow with a hooked nose and wearing a gray uniform, shouted something I couldn't hear over the spectators' laughter.

The master of fisticuffs only knew one tactic, the charge. He lunged and shot his right fist into the gray's brisket. The horse, still on its back legs, neighed shrilly, its nose flapping. When it came down, its shoe cracked into John L.'s temple. The boxer staggered back into the arms of Mr. McWherty and me. He shook us off and stepped again to the horse, blood flowing from his head, his dukes up again.

"Hold there, you ruffian," came an iron voice.

All of us turned to the sound, even John L., who was a hard man to distract from his prey. This voice was as compelling as a policeman's, yet silky and faintly exotic.

The hansom's half-door was open. Glaring at John L., a young woman lowered her foot to the passenger step, then to the cobblestones. She was about my age, maybe a year or two older. The girl was as thin as a willow and was wearing a yellow chemise drawn in at the waist with a self-belt, and a long yellow skirt with a flounce at the calves. She had no hat, daring for the time. Her hair was as red as a blush, with gold flashes and bronze streaks, pulled loosely behind her head then hanging back down to her shoulders in a flowing ponytail. On a gold chain around her neck was a diamond pendant worth roughly what Joe Lowe's Museum and Sporting Palace took in during a good year.

Her eyes were dark blue, the color of first daylight. She had a flippant nose and a peaked upper lip. A spray of amber freckles crossed her cheeks and nose, as if carried there by a gentle wind. Her cheekbones were wide and high, and her cheeks were drawn sleekly in. She had a bit of a tuck in her chin.

An orchestra began a fanfare, joined by a choral tribute. A spotlight picked her up, highlighting her hair and backlighting her in an ethereal glow. John L., Mr. McWherty, the horse and hansom, and all of Roxbury fell off the edge of the earth, leaving only her in my sight. At least, so it seemed to me.

It weren't love, but immensely more than love and far less. Simply put, I had been poleaxed. The French have a word for it. I wish I knew what that word was. Ninety-three years have passed since my first sight of her, and I have not recovered yet. I'm beginning to think I never will.

She stood with unalloyed resolve and centuries of breeding, and waved a scolding finger at John L. "You Irish hooligans leave that horse alone."

No one had talked to John L. Sullivan in that tone since as a four-teen-month-old he had blackened his aunt's eye.

"Oh yeah?" he riposted brilliantly. "Says who?"

"My name is Amy Balfour, and if you aren't afraid of my daddy, you should be."

The crowd whooped at her effrontery. Her driver, sitting in a seat called a dickey above and behind the cab, cast a nervous glance at the throng, but made no move to climb down from the dickey. Irish mobs had caused incalculable trouble in history.

John L. sneered, "You hunting the elephant, missy?" Slang for slumming.

"I don't talk to guttersnipes loitering outside a saloon," she sniffed. "Now you get out of my hansom's way."

John L. waved her away. "Just as soon as I win my dime-note."

He cranked back with his ham-hock fist and was about to let loose at the gray again when I jumped forward and latched onto his gun arm with both hands. His swing followed through but with my added weight was thrown off course. His fist weakly struck the animal's jugular groove.

"What in hell?" John L. bellowed. He tried to scrape me off with his other hand. "Have you gone off your nut, Woodrow?"

"Leave her horse alone, John L.," I squeaked in terror. I clung to his arm like a dog on a bone. He held me up, entirely off the ground, like a prize. The crowd laughed and applauded. Then he threw me on the cobblestones and stepped on my belly to peel my hands off him.

"You're a mootch and a frailey, Woodrow." The words were old Irish for dimwit and child. They stung.

The girl must have tamed him, though, because he said to me, "I'm bored with you and this horse, so I'm granting you both a pardon."

He pulled a black cigar from his shirt. Seamus McWherty scratched a sulfur match against his pants and held it up. His huge chest pumping, John L. filled the street with cigar smoke within seconds.

With gilded dignity, I rose from the stones and brushed my shirt. I turned to Amy Balfour, ready to bend my knee for my Order of the Garter.

She had already entered the hansom and had drawn the curtains across the windows. The coachman lifted the traces from the rein guide and clicked the horse backward. When the gray was clear of the crowd, the driver snapped his quirt. The horse gave a last doleful look at John L., and took my love down Lenox Avenue.

John L. and his partisans returned to their drinking through the swinging doors. Some patted me on the shoulders and said, "That's eight lives left, cat," and "You're lucky you caught the Strong Boy smiling," and such like. My eyes damp from the humiliation and loss, I watched the cab disappear.

I would not lay my eyes on Amy Balfour again for ten more years. But she would cause me untold trouble in that time.

As ROUGH A place as Joe Lowe's Museum and Sporting Palace was during the afternoon, it got worse at night. Though my mother was resigned to my spending my life as an ignoramus, she didn't want me in the saloon after dusk. She had found me a job behind a broom three nights a week over in Cambridge, at Harvard's new Hemenway Gym. I suppose she hoped the college atmosphere might neutralize the time I spent at pa's saloon.

Hemenway Gymnasium was a brick structure with sandstone trim and a bell tower towering over a slate roof. The building resembled a church. That night I climbed to the porch on the Kirkland Street side and entered the vestibule under the vaulted brick ceiling. I picked up my broom from a closet off the main hall. The hall was one hundred twenty feet long and eighty feet wide, the largest gymnasium in the country at the time. A running track passed entirely around the main hall.

I followed my broom around vaulting horses, hydraulic rowing weights, and a badminton net. Not to cast aspersions, but if a Roxbury boy had been caught with a badminton racket in his hand, he would've been strapped to an Inner Harbor channel marker and forgotten.

Rich folks don't trail as much dirt behind them as us Irish do, so this was easy work. For three hours a night, three times a week, the gymnasium floor pretended to have some dust on it and I pretended to sweep. That night I pushed the broom blindly. Amy Balfour was so branded on my memory that she still seemed standing in front of me.

Five minutes or two hours might have passed, when a sibilant, explosive hiss cracked my tender reverie. My head jerked up. I was standing next to the gym's boxing ring. Inside the ropes were two Harvard students, each wearing sixteen-ounce gloves.

One of the boxers was acting like a circus ringmaster. He enticed his opponent by waving his gloves and dancing around in an exaggerated way. He laughed and cajoled and generally carried on like a horse's butt. His voice was like escaping steam. It was an extraordinary voice, and I've never heard one like it since. He bit off his words and his oversized teeth clacked together. The sounds burst forth and were then chopped off, a ragtime syncopation of words.

His opponent jabbed a few times, but the ringmaster flicked the gloves away harmlessly and pranced in a circle, launching jabs and crosses, smacking around his hapless opponent.

Five other Harvard students were at ringside, whistling and laughing. The spectators wore dapper knickerbockers and yachting sweaters despite the heat. The cant of their heads, the thrust of their jaws, and every compressed gesture spoke of their affluence and gentility. These young richlings were as foreign to me as the king of Siam.

One yelled, "Put him away, Teddy."

Another hooted, "Beanie, you'd better toss in your sponge."

The boxer named Teddy shuffled his feet in tiny steps, imitating an old man, bringing a clamor of appreciation from his ringside friends. Beanie jabbed in a dispirited way. Teddy closed in and poked his nose, to the cheers of his mates. One of the spectators held a pair of spectacles in his hand.

I leaned on the broom handle to watch this sorry spectacle. Two bluebloods swatting at each other with pillows on their fists, mincing around a ring pretending they knew prizefighting.

"Beanie, my boy," Teddy called as he cavorted, "you'd best stick to darts."

More boffolas from his friends.

I suddenly realized why Amy Balfour's voice had sounded exotic. Her suave accent was similar to these Harvard students'. It was the tenor of old money, of folks of independent means. These were the voices from the other side of the gate. I was potatoes and she was pearls, and it would always be that way.

I was abruptly enraged, and when that happens my mouth is my enemy. I said loudly, "That ain't real boxing, for God's sake."

Teddy's back stiffened as if water had been thrown on him. He lowered his gloves and turned to me. Actually, he turned past me, then back again, as if he couldn't see me. I was standing fifteen feet away in good light.

"Hold there, my man," he said magisterially. "What's that now?"

I leaned insolently on the broom. "Where I'm from, this kind of flouncing around don't hold much water."

Teddy grabbed the spectacles from his friend and wrapped them around his face, left ear to right. His gaze found me.

"So you say, do you, whipster?" He grinned with huge, dazzling, hang-

and-rattle teeth. Them choppers were made to hold onto anything once they closed upon it. Years later his face became so famous that envelopes with only teeth and spectacles drawn on them would be delivered to the White House. "Why don't you come into the ring and show your stuff, then?"

He waved at me with both hands as if gathering me to him in the ring. Glad for the diversion, Beanie slid through the ropes. He was handed a towel. The other students tittered at their sudden good fortune. They'd be able to witness their champion humble an outsider.

I dropped the broom handle and slipped between the ropes into the ring. Teddy's head was large, with stiff hair clipped shorter than the mode of the day. His ears were tiny, the size of coat buttons. His eyes were widely spaced and were cornflower blue. His fashionable muttonchops had drops of sweat in them. He was about five years older than me, maybe twenty, and was muscular under his white skivvy. He was also wearing white swimming pants, not the tights seen in the clubs. He had bandy legs, and most of his height was in his trunk.

I drew myself up, three inches taller than Teddy, and said acidly, "You ever visit a Boston boxing club, leave them gloves behind or you'll be laughed all the way back to your rich daddy's knee."

The spectators cheered my cheekiness.

Teddy hesitated one second, the only time in my long association with him that he ever revealed an instant of doubt. And it was for only one second.

Then he piped, "A bareknuckler, are you? Grand, just grand. P.J., help me off with these gloves."

P.J. worked the laces, then pulled the gloves from his friend's hands. Teddy gave his spectacles back to P.J., then spun away from the ropes and skipped toward me, his bare fists up.

Before I relate what happened next, let me put things in perspective. When sparring with John L. Sullivan as I had been doing for several years I couldn't help but learn a few things, other than how many ways there are to hurt. John L. always lightened his punches with me, sure, but he still came on: jab, right cross, uppercut, head butt, smash to the solar plexus, elbow strike, always so close you could smell the old cigars on his breath, which he'd been smoking since he was eight years old.

Other times, he would hold his hands behind his back and I would take after him, hitting him on his face and neck and chin, anywhere I could reach. He was utterly impervious to me flailing away. Once in a while we would hang a hundred-pound gunnysack of sand from the saloon's ceiling. I would stand behind the bag to steady it while he labored away. The sack would crash into me again and again, and for a week my lungs would feel ruptured. My Roxbury friends and I held our own matches, emulating the Boston Strong Boy. John L. coached us.

So while I was no John L. Sullivan I was no chump in a ring. I would guess I had 30 percent of John L.'s skills, which meant I had three times the boxing talent of anyone on a Harvard boxing club.

Teddy jabbed daintily at my chin and found only air. I slipped inside and sank my right fist so far into his stomach my knuckles bounced off his backbone. He doubled over like a hinge. Then a solid left hook to his temple knocked him to the mat.

The Harvard lads were silent as I returned to my broom. P.J. and Beanie entered the ring to tend to Teddy. Five minutes later, sweeping near a rack of medicine balls, I glanced again at the ring. Teddy had risen as far as his knees. His friends pushed him under the lower rope, then put his arms across their shoulders and helped him to the showers.

I wouldn't know Teddy's last name for another seven years, and then I'd learn it was Roosevelt. You'd think he'd forget a poor Irish lout in seven years. But he would not, and I'd suffer for his good memory. And that's how I met the second scourge of my life on that fateful day.

TWO

Yellow Chevrons

DICKINSON WAS A hard three-days' ride west of Fort Abraham Lincoln in the Dakota Territory. The Northern Pacific ran that route by then but our lieutenant said he didn't join the cavalry to ride the train, so his troops didn't ride the train either.

I wished it were otherwise because I detested horses and still do. In my life I have ridden asses, elephants, camels, dromedaries, oxen, yaks, and an ostrich, but only a horse has come close to killing me.

My unit was the 7th Cavalry, to which George Custer had brought fame and calamity. Custer had been dead nine years, remembered by all cavalry troops but mourned by considerably fewer. Our company rode into Dickinson the evening before Independence Day of 1886, with Lieutenant Smythe leading the procession and I, as company cook, bringing up the dusty rear in the chuckwagon, riding on the driver's box next to a teamster named Bo Latts. Behind me under the tarp, pots and pans and flatware jingled and clanked.

I couldn't cook, I loathed horses, and wide-open spaces made this city lad nervous, so how I ended up as a bull cook in the teeth-cracking cavalry on the Northern Plains is a tale I'll get to shortly.

Dickinson was a pull-water town which sprang to life five years before as a market for buffalo hides. By 1886, the buffalo had went the way of Custer, and Dickinson was shipping grain and wool and beef. The largest structure in the town was the Northern Pacific's water tank, next to the depot and the station eating house. We rode along the town's main street, which as I recall was called Villard, and passed a dry goods emporium, a lawyer's office, the Dickinson *Press*, half a dozen saloons, the sheriff's office, and a hotel. The undertaker's shop had a sign in its window: YOU PLUG 'EM, WE PLANT 'EM. Standing on boardwalks in front of

32

the stores, the citizens of Dickinson waved handkerchiefs and applauded our arrival.

Because I was preceded by one hundred twenty horses, by the time I got to any given point on the street, it was a carpet of manure. And the horse has flatulence down to an art. When ten dozen of the beasts march together, the sound is one long basso profundo roar, each blast timed to begin when the last ended. With all the scientific journals around, I don't know why nobody has written about this phenomenon before. John Philip Sousa was an old cavalry man. I have long suspected he got his inspiration for inventing the sousaphone by being stuck behind a spine-snapping cavalry company.

I had been through Dickinson several times but had never seen it so festive. The town was bedecked in red, white and blue bunting and streamers. American flags hung from telegraph poles and windows. We rode under a banner that read STATEHOOD FOR DAKOTA. Back then, Independence Day meant more to frontier folks than Christmas or Easter. Dickinson was going to do it up right.

Erected on both sides of the main street were grandstands, each about eight rows high. Between the stands and entirely blocking the road was a newly constructed boxing ring.

I was going to be half of the main attraction.

After seven years in the cavalry, I was the United States Army boxing champion. It had not come easily. I defeated the likes of Sgt. Will O'Donnell and Sgt. Ed "Stone" Hobbs. I'd had twelve other matches, winning them all. Because I struck a salt lick a hundred times every day, my knuckles had calluses the thickness of cowhide. Most of the blows sent my direction seemed to land on my right ear, which had scarred badly, permanently swelling and turning in on itself.

The term "cauliflower ear" didn't come into use until the turn of the century. Before then they were called nothing but ugly, and mine was. Sometimes at Fort Abraham Lincoln the camp children would stop in their tracks to gaze in wonderment at my ear. I always carried a pocketful of hard candy which I issued to the youngsters on condition they stare at something else. I look back now and surmise them tikes may have had a racket going.

Lieutenant Smythe issued orders I couldn't hear to Sergeant Rose. Rose was a small, nippy man. Years in the prairie sun had etched deep lines on his face, which looked like a cracked window. Sergeant Rose was a hellacious Indian fighter, by the way. You didn't want to leave your bedroll at night and go pee anywhere near his reclining form or he might suddenly wake up and ventilate you with his carbine. I know of one noisy private who got his leg lightened that way.

The decade of the 1880s was a fairly quiet time in the Indian wars. The Apaches caused some trouble in the Southwest in 1882 and Geronimo went on a rampage in 1885 but the tribes had been mostly whipped by then. The Indians have gained a sheen over the years, being portrayed as peaceable and frightened refugees. Sergeant Rose and the other lifers in my company knew otherwise and wore the scars to prove it.

My main recollection of Indians was their hunger. I never saw one who didn't show ribs. I'd often give them some grub, either from the mess at Fort Abraham Lincoln or from my wagon on the trail. In my years in the cavalry I never shot an Indian, but I might have poisoned some.

Given the choice between eating army victuals or eating the business end of a skunk, most folks would be hard pressed to decide. I routinely served beef that had been canned twenty-five years before during the Civil War. Loaves of bread had frequently been sitting in a depot five years, and would defeat any set of teeth unless soaked in coffee ten minutes. One time Sergeant Rose charged a loaf with his twenty-inch bayonet fixed on his Springfield, and couldn't break the crust. We were also issued enormous sausages that tasted as if their main ingredient was sawdust, and which all the troopers called horse cocks.

I dressed out and cooked whatever the troops brought in: pronghorns and blacktails, buffalo, prairie chickens, bighorns, gray wolves, anything. Some soldiers wouldn't eat prairie dogs, but if I added enough salt, they'd go down tolerably. So although we occasionally had fresh game, usual fare was army beef. The top layers were often green and had to be cut away.

One time Lieutenant Smythe sent his plate back with word that he wanted paprika on his beef. I checked around the mess and determined that paprika was a red spice, so I filed rust off a railroad spike and sprinkled it over his serving. On another occasion he demanded parsley. I crumpled up a handful of sagebrush and tossed it on his plate. One time we were out of salt so I boiled up an old McClellan saddle and cooked out enough salt left behind by soldiers' sweaty butts to make a salty stock for a stew. We all knew green vegetables were unhealthy, but most of the soldiers had Irish blood like me so we were accustomed to filling our bellies with potatoes. I prepared spuds and everything else the same way: burn it, then salt it. The food I served would have given a maggot some hesitation.

The lieutenant and Sergeant Rose rode back along the street at a trot. Smythe wore the standard-issue blue tunic and knee-high boots, but his troops weren't so well turned out. Some trousers were patched with canvas. A few troopers had coats of various issue from the Civil War. Others wore leather coats with buckskin fringes. Many had on black campaign caps, but others wore white- or gray-felt civilian hats or blue kepis. Some sported cartridge belts they had fashioned from rawhide. On our sleeves were the yellow chevrons of the cavalry, except for Sergeant Rose, who insisted on wearing artillery's scarlet. Above my chevron was sewn a little yellow chef's cap, if you can imagine how ridiculous that looked.

The lieutenant allowed this variation in uniform, but he was a stickler about weapons, and any soldier more than an arm's length away from his three weapons—the Springfield carbine, the Colt .45, and the saber—was in for a cold night of guard duty. The firearms were fine pieces of equipment, but the sabers were as useless as tits on a goat. I kept mine in the jockeybox under my rump.

Lieutenant Smythe and Sergeant Rose reined in at my wagon. Noble savages don't pester scalps with short hair, so the lieutenant and every other soldier in the company kept their curls as short as a pig's. Smythe had faded blue eyes. His pale skin never tanned, so was always a boiled red. In the summer his nose resembled a hot coal. He was a skilled cavalry officer. The lieutenant said, "Private Lowe, our man arrived in Dickinson on the morning Northern Pacific. He's at the Cut and Run. How're you feeling?"

"Up to snuff, sir."

"I'm putting a month's pay on you, private. And so's everyone else in the company."

"Yes, sir."

"You are relieved of mess duty tonight. Get some rest and don't do any drinking. We'll go to work on your opponent." He withdrew a dime from his uniform pocket and turned to the skinner. "Latts, there's a tub at the barber's. Here's ten cents to rent the water. Make sure you do."

Smythe jabbed his horse's flank with his heels and took off, the sergeant in tow.

Bo Latts was a civilian and as foul an excuse for a human being as I've ever come across. That man could have stunk a dog off a gut wagon. I always sat upwind of him and if the wagon trail wound around, I'd switch sides of the box as often as necessary to stay to windward. Latts always had a fist-size wad of tobacco in his cheek, giving him a lopsided look. The plug prevented him from fully closing his mouth, so he invariably had brown drool oozing down his chin. His hair hung to his shoulders, and was topped with a slouch hat.

He removed his hat and scratched his head. God only knew what species of vermin lived there. He said, "I weren't always a miserable mule skinner, Woodrow. When the beaver were still plenty along the plains rivers, I had some mighty high years. After the season, I'd take my pelt money and set myself up in a frilly St. Joe notchhouse called the Top of the Evening. I'd stay there until my cash-out was gone. Take me about a month."

Latts leaned over the side of the rig and spat a foot-long string onto the manure trail. "But it weren't the women that'd make my pecker really stand. It was them beaver pelts. They smell about the same, you know. Beaver pelts and women."

Following Bo Latts's conversation was a task because the giant tobacco ball robbed his words of consonants. Three citizens of Dickinson stood in front of a barbershop holding fistfuls of bills. Two shook hands and passed their money to the third. Another wager made on the fight.

Bo Latts went on, "Since me and my trapper friends killed all the beaver, we ain't had it so good. But I just traded some of the army's Winchesters for a bale of beaver skins caught up in Canada. I could stay my month at the Top of the Evening for that stack."

Most of the army payroll sent out from the Division of the Missouri's headquarters in St. Louis was going to be wagered on my performance. Soldiers from Fort Buford, up near the confluence of the Missouri and Yellowstone Rivers, and from Fort Yates and the Standing Rock Agency, both near the mouth of the Grand River, had also come to Dickinson for the fight.

"Woodrow, I love them beaver pelts more than most men love a woman, but I'm putting them on you."

I jumped down from the wagon. "I'm ready for him, Bo. Don't worry."

I maneuvered across the road, dodging horses and road apples. The boardwalk was crowded with soldiers, ranchers, and prospectors. I turned onto a side street and passed Donleavy's Dry Goods Store where tins of Woolson Mocha & Java coffee, Union Leader Cut Plug, and Heinz apple butter were piled high in the display window, along with a red Elgin National coffee grinder. I crossed an alley. A hanging sign indicated the Masons met up the side stairs.

While I'm thinking of it: if you like a good night's sleep, don't join the rump-rawing cavalry. Many nights you sleep under the stars, which is a happy way of saying on stones and cactus, and even when you are at your barracks, the army's thin, muslin-covered mattresses feel as if they are filled with fingernail parings. I still itch, thinking about them long nights.

I came next to the Cut and Run and pushed through a crowd lingering at the doors. The Independence Day celebration had begun in early earnest in the Cut and Run. Laughter and the clinks of glasses filled the place. A piano player banged out some tune, lost in the din of the crowd. The saloon was the largest in Dickinson, seating sixty in captain's chairs around tables. A hundred more patrons were bellied up to the bar, five deep. Six elk heads lined one wall and over the back door was a mounted cougar. Above the backbar was a line of stuffed pheasants. Kerosene lamps hung from the ceiling. The wallpaper was a dizzying pattern of orange floral medallions. A faro dealer at a table near the bar wore French cuffs and a string tie, and mechanically dealt cards and scooped up chips. Several patrons were bent over steaks. A door at the far end of the bar led to a kitchen.

The Cut and Run watered the whiskey, sanded the sugar, dusted the pepper, chicoried the coffee, and shaved the cards. I felt right at home.

Cribs were out the back door. A long line of grinning, cajoling 7th Cavalry troopers waited for the doorman to beckon them back one at a time. One of the girls staggered into the saloon for a breather. She was so slender she was little more than a shirt of bones. She wore a loose saffron chemise and two pounds of rouge that had been wiped around on her face. Smallpox had left pea-size craters along one cheek and were so filled with red rouge they seemed to glow. Her eyes were blackened by thick liner spread almost down to her cheekbones, giving her face the ghastly cast of a skull. Her professional smile faltered when she surveyed the host of rowdy cavalry bowlegs, many about to bring weeks of frontier celibacy to her bed.

A barman passed her a whiskey. She gulped it down, then bravely returned through the door accompanied by the soldiers' bawdy whistles and hoots. You'd think the first sight of that pocked, painted, cadaverous working girl would have taken the lead out of them troopers' pencils, but the cavalry always rose to the occasion.

One corner of the saloon was even louder than the rest, and because my opponent caused a stir wherever he traveled I knew he was over there occupying the seat of honor. I stared at the knot of revelers around the table until a few shifted and I caught my first glimpse of John L. Sullivan in seven years.

My heart sunk. The rumors must not have been true.

The Boston Strong Boy had held the world championship for four years, since February 7, 1882, when he beat Paddy Ryan in Mississippi City in a cruel ninety-round London Prize rules bout. From September 1883 in Baltimore to May 1884 in Toledo, John L. engaged in one of the great athletic feats in history, battling fifty-nine fighters and putting every one of them on the floor. The Great Knocking Out Tour had earned Sullivan a mantle of invincibility.

Now John L. was touring the country again, taking on anyone who would put up $500 for the pleasure of being pummeled into unconsciousness. Towns across America raised the money and sent forth their best man, usually the village blacksmith. To win the wager, the opponent had to be upright at the end of the fourth round. Marquess of Queensberry rules, so the rounds lasted three minutes each. Nobody had won John L.'s $500 yet.

Four rounds, three minutes each. All I had to do was fight him off for twelve minutes.

Before I saw him I thought I had a chance. Stories about John L.'s alcohol consumption were as prominent as tales of his ruthless ring performances. Sullivan had been drinking steadily for five years, with time out—usually very little time out—only for his fights. No man could dissipate himself with beer and whiskey every night, then relentlessly punish opponents in the ring the next day, day after day and week after week. He was undoubtedly weakened and slowed.

I had expected to see burst capillaries on his nose, puffiness under his eyes, pods of adipose tissue under the gray skin on his face, a glassy stare, maybe even an uncontrollable shaking of his hands. Yet the champion looked as hard as ever. Sitting under an antelope head, grinning idiotically and telling fight tales to the circle of Dickinson admirers, John L. with his oak arms and iron head reminded me of a sledgehammer. And my eyes seemed to be playing a trick on me, magnifying his hands to the size of sixteen-pound cannon shells.

I sidled along a wall, ducking under a set of antlers, keeping out of John L.'s line of sight, which weren't difficult because of the throng surrounding his table. Three bartenders dispensed beer and whiskey at a frantic pace. The Cut and Run smelled of boot leather, roll-your-owns, and old sweat.

An officer stepped into the saloon. Soldiers abruptly stood, followed more slowly by the civilians. I had heard that Brig. Thomas Townsend, commander of the 7th Cavalry, would be the ranking officer in Dickinson for the match, but the appearance of Little Phil Sheridan proved my information out of date.

The general marched straight toward John L.'s table. The drinkers gave way before him and fell silent. Little Phil was commanding general of the United States Army, thirteen rungs higher than my rank of private first class. We called him Little Phil because he barely came up to anyone else's Adam's apple.

Sheridan walked as if a ramrod had been stuffed down his uniform, and his boot heels slammed onto the wood floor with each step. I had seen in person some of the country's great Indian fighters—General Crook, who tamed Geronimo, Gen. Nelson Miles, who destroyed Crazy Horse's village, and Col. John Chivington of the Sand Creek Massacre—and their ferocious natures were revealed by their countenances. But with a rounded face, sparse hair, malleable chin, and gentle mouth, Phil Sheridan had the look of a bank clerk.

His docile face didn't fool anybody for long, particularly the enemy. What he lacked in physical stature, he also lacked in mercy. He had killed Confederates and then Indians in equal dollops. His famous message to President Lincoln after laying waste to the Shenandoah Valley was that even a crow flying over the place would have to carry its own rations. And his short treatise on Indian relations was this: "Kill or hang all warriors and bring back all women and children."

Sheridan was followed across the saloon by his aide-de-camp, an infantry major. An aide-de-camp is called a dog's body, always under foot and easy to kick. They stopped in front of John L.'s table. The aide straightaway produced two shotglasses of whiskey and passed one to the general and the other to the boxer.

Little Phil boomed, "Mr. Sullivan, I salute you and wish you the best of luck, except against my United States Army."

The congregation chuckled dutifully.

Without rising from his chair, John L. Sullivan replied in his bellowing voice, which made the general seem even smaller, "I don't know who you are, pal, but I'll drink your whiskey." He threw back the liquor and slapped the glass onto the table.

This thunderous impertinence to a lieutenant general—perhaps the second most powerful man in the United States—must have made Sheridan's whiskey bitter indeed, but he resolutely tossed it back, then turned on his heels and retreated. He surely understood his secondary importance in the saloon. For every person in any town in America who could have recognized General Sheridan, ten would have identified the Boston Strong Boy.

Now, John L. was not put on this earth to invent the calculus or to chart the motion of the planets, but even he should have suspected the plot against him when the aide-de-camp, who normally would have bustled after the retreating general, obtained two more shots of whiskey, gave one to John L., and offered his own toast.

"To your good fortune, Mr. Sullivan." The major raised his glass. "May you live long and well."

The aide and John L. quaffed their whiskies.

"Same to you, partner."

The major then rushed after Little Phil, passing Lieutenant Smythe at the saloon's door. The aide nodded conspiratorially at my lieutenant. Smythe waved at the bartender, and soon received two full shotglasses. He stepped up to John L.'s table and passed him a whiskey.

"Mr. Sullivan, the 7th Cavalry is proud you are visiting its territory. Here's to you."

"And here's mud in your eye, corporal." Sullivan drained his glass of the combustive liquid, then inhaled an enormous draught of air between his teeth to cool his tongue.

Lieutenant Smythe answered quietly, "It's lieutenant, Mr. Sullivan."

Sullivan waved him away. "Lieutenant, corporal, general, they're all the same to me."

Scowling, Smythe left the saloon. I stood to one side on the sawdust floor, unnoticed. I was going to star in the spectacle, but most folks in the saloon wouldn't have known me from Adam's off ox. By then everyone at the Cut and Run must have grasped the 7th Cavalry's strategy to gain fistic glory. One at a time we were going to drink John L. into a crapulous stupor. John L. would not even make his first scratch.

We knew we would succeed. First, not once in his life had John L. turned down a free drink. And second, he could not tolerate an unanswered challenge. The very combativeness that made him the most fearsome fighter in history would guarantee our victory.

Sergeant Rose appeared next, two glasses in hand. "A salute, Mr. Sullivan." Rose lifted a glass.

"Give me a moment, pal," John L. ordered, smiling sloppily. His chin dropped for an instant.

Sergeant Rose's eyebrows rose magnificently. "I heard you were always good for a toast, Mr. Sullivan. But perhaps I should come back later when you are up to it." Rose made a half-turn.

"About face, soldier boy," John L. barked, reaching across the table for the proffered whiskey glass. "Raise your shot."

Rose complied. "Your health, Mr. Sullivan."

Each man finished his whiskey in one swallow.

Unseen and increasingly confident, I remained under the elk for another thirty minutes. I witnessed John L. Sullivan drink fourteen shots of whiskey, each time in response to a toast from a cavalry trooper. When I left my post near the antlers, the Boston Strong Boy was still at his table, but tottering to his right, and taking a full five minutes before accepting another salute.

I stepped through the saloon's doors to see another half dozen of my cavalry mates lined up to post John L. to more rounds. They cuffed me on the shoulder and said, "No worry now," and "We got John L. where we want him."

Surely I would be able to stay in the ring for twelve minutes—*just twelve minutes*—against a man in a coma. The July 4 match was being won on July 3, the 7th Cavalry was seeing to that.

But, then, this was the outfit that had made the wrong turn at the Little Bighorn.

THREE

Four Strikes

BEFORE I TELL of my match against John L. Sullivan, let me report how I came to find myself in the pud-pounding cavalry. You can blame it all on Amy Balfour or on my own stupidity. I prefer to fault the former.

Amy Balfour. One look at her smote me to the ground, as you recall. Any other fifteen-year-old boy would have shaken off his pubescent passion and went on his meandering way. Not me. Given the opportunity to make myself out as a lunatic, I'm always game.

Finding her address was easy because all Boston knew the Balfour name. The next day I walked into the Balfour Building on Hanover Street, home of the Massachusetts State Bank, and saw her father's name, Lewis Balfour, under FOUNDER on a bronze plaque. On a wall was his portrait painted (I learned later) by John Singer Sargent during a Balfour family journey to Paris. I waited in the bank lobby until a fellow resembling the portrait emerged.

He boarded a horse-drawn cabriolet at the curb. I recognized the driver from my run-in with John L. outside pa's saloon, same hooked nose. And same gray horse that had clipped John L. The buggy sped away and I sprinted after it.

Four miles later the two-wheeler finally turned off a residential road through a gate onto a winding driveway. I was blowing like a rackabones horse and had to blink away sweat to glimpse the iron plate imprinted with the street address—428 SYCAMORE LANE.

The cabriolet traveled along the driveway under a steeple of low branches. Sunlight filtered through the leaves, dappling the buggy and driveway, blending them in the camouflage of half-light. The cabriolet stopped near a side door. Lewis Balfour emerged and quickly crossed the bricks into his home.

I walked along the iron fence until I could view the house. The state of Massachusetts had a smaller capitol building, I suspected. The mansion was a Greek Revival (I would learn these fancy terms much later in life) with six Corinthian columns holding up an arched porch roof. Orange bricks made up most of the building. Olive shutters were on both sides of all windows, except for two oculus windows under the porch. Far under the overhanging porch, the front door had leaded windows on both sides and a fan window above. White stone balustrades flanked the entryway, behind which was a verandah running the length of the building.

A flag with a red griffin on a yellow field hung from a thirty-foot pole to one side of the brick walkway. Beneath the balustrades were rows of radiant red-and-yellow marigolds in a combed garden. I didn't know precisely how many feet of billiard-felt lawn separated the sidewalk where I stood from the Balfour mansion, but I couldn't have thrown a rock that distance even if I was of such a mind.

Except for sojourns into Cambridge to drive my broom, I had never been in a neighborhood where a strip of grass lay between sidewalk and street, or where more trees lined the street than there were people on it. Or where the smells of cabbage, whiskey mash, and assorted offscourings didn't always fill the nose. Or where hordes of mewling brats weren't scurrying along the street. Or where I didn't have to step over the recumbent form of a drunk or two. My four-mile run had removed me from all that was familiar. Neither Sinbad nor Gulliver had ever discovered so foreign a place. My clothes were suddenly scratchy with their cheapness, my hands heavy with dirt and calluses, and my life utterly trivial.

The urge to flee seized me. Never one to resist that impulse, I lit out of there like a cat with turpentine on its ass.

My mother once told me, "Woodrow, you may have inherited your father's brains, which are hardly enough to keep his ears apart. So I want you to remember one thing: doggedness will always make up for dumbness."

Amy Balfour should have answered one of my six letters. That summer, waiting every day for mail that never arrived, I became convinced that her father was conspiring to keep us apart. My memory began to transfigure Lewis Balfour's portrait at the bank, giving his eyes a sinister glint and parting his lips as if he were cackling at me. I could not recall his hands in the painting, but my imagination had them rubbing together fiendishly.

Diabolical schemers would not defeat me. I would suborn the help.

Judging from the size of their home, the Balfours employed a dozen Irish domestics, calling all women servants "Bridget" and the men "O" followed by whatever came to mind, O'Flannery or O'Reilly or some other.

I became Tim Conner's bosom friend, which took me all of a week. Conner was the Balfour coachman I had encountered twice. One evening I waited in the alley behind the mansion and pretended to be strolling along just as he emerged from the carriage house to walk home.

At age fifteen there were still a number of things I had not done in this life. One was to speak to a Protestant, except maybe that Teddy fellow I had felled, but that weren't much of a conversation. Another was to determine what lay underneath a Roxbury girl's cottons and crinolines. And another was to drive a horse. I had never even been on a horse, but I knew "gelding" was a horse word.

As I caught up with him I enclosed one hand in another, grimaced theatrically, and said, "Damned gelding."

Tim Conner looked over his shoulder to find me. He had a bobbed, unstable chin over which hung his log-splitter nose. "Take a nip at your hand, eh?"

I nodded, waving my hand as if to shake away the pain. "I drive for the Madisons, and they've got a rough one." Madison was as moneyed a name as I could invent.

"Aw, that's nothing. Two months ago I was leaning over to pick up a trace and the gray got hold of my breeches and . . ."

Thus began a thirty-minute litany of complaints from Tim Conner, who, to listen to him, was the most persecuted man God ever put on this earth. He was a redoubtable whiner, and he took a liking to me because I had the only ear he ever found he couldn't wear out with his moaning. When I ventured the modest observation, "My rear end hurts after a day on that iron seat," he came back with "Aw, that's nothing," and supplied me with a story about his smarting backside. Or when I volunteered, "My pay isn't so much," he grumbled half an hour about his thankless servitude.

So I put up with his harping, walking home with him every day for a week, before getting around to my subject. At the end of a week I said bitterly, "The Madisons had me work seven days straight."

"Aw, that's nothing. The Balfours won't be satisfied until they break my back with work. Why, one time . . ."

I was adept by then at focusing so keenly on my memory of Amy Balfour that Tim Conner's voice shifted to the edge of my consciousness, no more noticed than the murmur of leaves rustled by the wind.

I let him wind down, which took two miles of steady walking, until I said, "You ever need a Saturday off, let me know. I'll drive for you."

"The Madisons give you Saturdays? Why, I've had to . . ."

He railed against his martyrdom, during which time we crossed into Roxbury and were about to part for the evening, him to his home and me to mine, when he slowed his bewailments to catch his breath, giving me time to inject, "Keep it in mind. Some Saturday I'll take over for you."

A free Saturday was a rare and glittering prospect, so I knew the torment my offer would cause Tim Conner. He succumbed two days later, then gave me a slew of instructions such as, "Mr. Balfour likes to be saluted in the morning when he enters the carriage," and "If anyone notices you aren't me, tell them I got the mumps and that you're my brother Curran." He lectured me on the peculiarities of the gray and its tackle, which was the first time I ever listened to anything he said because the collar, tugs, reins and crupper were a mysterious jumble to me. The horse's name was Graybar. Conner rigged the gray and cabriolet in a demonstration. I pretended to be insulted—me, an *experienced* driver—and at the same time memorized as much as I could.

Then Conner offered the magical words, "Saturday morning your first job will be to deliver Miss Amy to her piano lesson. It's over on Warren Street."

He continued with other journeys I'd be making, carrying members of the Balfour family to and fro, but the vision of my Amy materialized again, sweetly capturing me as if in an embrace. Tim Conner's voice drifted away, leaving me alone with her.

RAIN WAS FALLING steadily that Saturday. I arrived at the Balfour carriage house an hour early, giving myself extra time to wrestle with Graybar and his tackle. I needed it. A horse is as dumb as a stump, but Graybar possessed just enough cunning to know Woodrow Lowe was at its mercy.

I grappled with that spiteful hayburner for an hour. He kicked my shin, bit my shoulder, stomped my foot, and flung an enormous globule of horse snot onto my shoulder. Horse snot, by the way, is not something you want to spend a lot of time gazing at if you can avoid it.

Graybar bucked, snorted, pranced, and spun. Finally I managed to ensnare him in something resembling a harness, and tenuously con-nected him to the carriage, leaving me just enough time to change into Conner's silly uniform, including black knee-high boots and a cap.

I climbed nervously up to the dickey, then clicked my tongue and gently flicked the reins. Graybar stepped forward, pulling the cabriolet from the carriage house. A moment later I slowly brought back the reins, and the horse stopped right in front of the mansion's side door. This was going to be easier than I had feared. What's to driving a buggy? Flick to go, pull to stop.

Staring anxiously at the door, I waited, rain dripping from the bill of my cap. Ahead, the canopy of sycamore limbs had grown damp and gloomy and menacing with the rain.

My plan was irresistible in its simplicity. At the first possible mo-ment—perhaps at an intersection, perhaps at the door to her piano lesson—I would hop off the seat, throw open the cabriolet door and profess my respect and admiration—nay, my love—for her. She would surely remember her knight gallant who had rescued Graybar from a beating by John L. Sullivan. I would tender myself to her, trusting her compassion and her certain faculty for recognizing the love of her life when he at last found her.

Remember, I weren't but fifteen years old.

The door opened and my heart welled. A servant stepped out holding an umbrella. He stood in the rain, the umbrella to one side over the door until Amy emerged. At least, I assumed she came out, because the door-man moved the umbrella to the cabriolet's step, then held it over the hansom's half-door while he opened it. When the buggy's door closed, the servant lowered the umbrella and returned to the house.

A glimpse of Amy's lustrous strawberry hair would have restored my nerves, but I had not espied her hair or her shoulders or an ankle, nothing. Just the top of an umbrella.

Nevertheless, as my heart had been her captive for weeks, she was now safely mine, secure in the cab below. I fancied that with the special sympathy the fairer sex has for romance and with a woman's profound wisdom in such matters, Amy Balfour intuitively knew her day of days had come. No longer would she be alone.

I snapped the reins. Graybar clopped forward at a quick pace. Too late the thought occurred that the horse might need some direction as to which way to proceed, and I did not know how to give it. I experimented by holding the reins out to my left and whipping them, a mite vigorously as it turns out. That idiot beast sidled to the left, almost off the driveway, pulling the cabriolet under the sycamore boughs.

The gray surged ahead. Limbs from the trees lining the drive rushed at me, aimed for my face. By abruptly bending low so my chin touched my knee, I ducked the first bough as it whistled overhead.

When I glanced behind me to see how close it had come, a second branch that must have had the girth of my leg sailed into my head.

My memory of what happened next stops just then because the bough slammed me into blackness. I presume I eventually toppled off the carriage seat and lay on the street until I came around. When I did, I was lying face down on a brick avenue, tucked against the curb, half-submerged in a puddle of rainwater.

My head ringing with pain, I levered myself to my knees, then rolled to a sitting position on the curb. The back of my head hurt so much I was afraid to touch it, lest some of it be missing.

After a moment I was able to uncross my eyes. The cabriolet, the demon horse, and Amy Balfour weren't nowhere in sight. I picked myself up and reeled home, a long, chilled, stumbling, rueful walk.

No trumpeter had blown the retreat for Woodrow Lowe yet, though.

Tim Conner was surprised to see me catching up to him again on a Saturday several weeks later. After a skein of grousing about my teamstering, he told me Graybar had stopped that day of his own accord half a mile later, and Amy had driven the buggy on to her piano lesson, apparently unconcerned about the fate of the coachman. Lewis Balfour believed Conner had been swatted from the driver's seat and had instructed him to be more careful because the horse and buggy were valuable property.

Conner's bellyaching always produced information. Overwork was his favorite theme. This time he complained of having to drive the Balfours to their boat the following Sunday. "If God wanted us to work seven days in a row, He would have taken seven days to make the world."

"Yeah," I sympathized as we walked along, "the Madisons have a boat, too."

"Not like this one, they don't. The *Empire Princess* is the finest at the Harbor Yacht Club. The whole family is going, so I'll have to take the big carriage. I heard that . . ."

A plan instantly sprang to life, manifest in its brilliance and certain in its conclusion.

At daybreak Sunday I walked along the yacht club's pier. I was as out of place as a boil on the queen's butt, but had no fear of discovery because I figured rich folks didn't get up at dawn. I confirmed this as a fact the day I became wealthy, when I slept until nine in the morning, which I've been doing ever since. I presume the sun still rises in the east but I haven't seen it do so in half a century.

I knew as much about boats as I did horses, but what's to a boat?

Stowaways loom large in Boston Irish legend. During the Great Hunger, ships sailing from Dublin and Belfast might have as many as twenty hidden passengers who would be discovered too late to be deprived of free passage. Finally ship owners began sending stowaways back to the old country. Daniel "Sailor" Bonnet crossed the Atlantic twelve times, six each way, inspiring the drinking song, "For if your ship's on the wide blue sea/ Say hello to Sailor Bonnet/ You won't see him for a while/ But he'll be surely on it."

So although I was as informed about a yacht as a cow is about a holiday, I knew there were places aboard to hide. I aimed to find such a cranny and crawl into it.

My plan? Same as heretofore mentioned. Find Amy alone and press my case.

On the pier I trod carefully around bitts and coiled line, passing several yachts I thought enormous until I came to the *Empire Princess*, identified by the name emblazoned in scarlet across the stern. The Balfours' yacht made the others moored at the pier resemble tenders.

The *Empire Princess* was a seventy-foot yawl, that is, its mainmast was forward while a smaller mast was abaft the rudder post. (Once again, I knew none of this snappy nautical jargon at the time. Later in life I owned a pleasure boat, a schooner.) The yacht was fore-and-aft rigged, and the stays and shrouds formed an intricate web in the sky.

Abovedecks the *Empire Princess* glittered with brass-and-steel fittings: funnels, winches, cleats, portlights, boot tops, stanchions and a windlass. The taffrail was mahogany carved to resemble grape leaves entwined together. At the bow was a carved figurehead. No, it weren't a mermaid thrusting her bare breasts to sea, her gold mane flowing behind her and her green-scaled tail wrapped sinuously across the bow. The *Empire Princess'* figurehead was a black-frocked Puritan woman, her hair under a peaked bonnet, holding a Bible to her chest. The thought occurred that Lewis Balfour would be about as much fun as a catechism class.

I looked left and right along the pier, again saw no one, then grabbed the rail and swung on board. I walked aft in an infantryman's crouch, passing several wood reclining chairs and the cabin's brass-framed portals. The main boom was the size of a telegraph pole. The mainsheet held the boom in place on a fore-aft line.

After stepping down into the cockpit and around the spoked wheel, I tried the companionway hatch. It was locked, so I moved forward again, this time to a glass-and-brass skylight hatch above the cabin. It was also secure. Next was a wood hatch on the foredeck, looking more utilitarian. No lock this time. I lifted it and bent low out of the morning sunlight to peer through the hatch. My eyes adjusted after a moment. Canvas bags filled the hold. I first took them for laundry and laughed aloud—Protestants soil their clothes!—then realized the bags contained sails. I grabbed the hatch frame and dropped into the sail locker.

I closed the hatch above me, then burrowed deep to wedge myself between bags and the hull. There I waited.

An hour elapsed before I heard sounds above—voices calling orders, footsteps on the deck, the rasp of chains—all muffled by the sail bags around me. The crew had arrived. Shafts of light suddenly penetrated the locker. A deckhand lowered himself through the hatch and onto the bags over me, squeezing me against the hull. Another hand helped from above. They were laughing about Lewis Balfour's purse-proud mannerisms—the rake of his cigar and disdainful lift of his eyebrows—and mimicking his crabbed, arrogant voice.

The weight on me lessened as bags were lifted out. Discovery was certain. Lord only knew what these salts did to stowaways, probably keelhauled them. But the *Empire Princess* carried more sail than was being rigged out. The crewman climbed out into daylight, leaving several bags behind, under which I still hid. The locker fell dark. I heard the scrape of bags dragged toward the masts.

The crew laughed and chattered while they prepared the boat. The yacht gently rolled and the mooring lines creaked. A cook arrived—the crew called her "Cookie"—and I smelled chicken, lemon and biscuits wafting from the chest the deckhands helped lift on board. Then I heard the clop and rattle of a coach and four. The crew abruptly fell silent. The sound of footsteps came from the pier.

A bronzed, mirthless voice asked, "Are we ready, captain?"

"We'll slip the lines on your orders, Mr. Balfour."

"Dickie, give your mother your hand."

"Father, can't I join my friends today?" This was apparently Dickie. His voice was both supercilious and sniveling. "They're having a get-together . . ."

"Today the entire family sails," Lewis Balfour replied coldly.

My hopes soared. The whole family. That meant Amy was indeed boarding, just outside my sail locker, inches away.

"And those so-called friends of yours, Dickie." This from a new voice. Mature and precise and exasperated. Mother Balfour. "Honestly. They're nothing but hoodlums. And that Blackstock boy, all he does is push you around."

"It's nothing, mother. Don't worry about me."

Father said, "Up we go, Amy."

Deep in my lightless hideaway, I exulted. Our meeting was now inevitable. The yacht would be our own little world, insulated from the bothers of everyday life, where I could declare myself Amy's paramour and vassal and champion.

The captain's commands came from above. No horseplay or laughing with the Balfours on board. I heard quick steps above and felt the *Empire Princess'* new pitch as it drifted away from the pier. The sails flapped loudly as they were raised. The rigging sang in protest as the canvas filled with air. When the yacht heeled with the wind, I braced myself against the hull. Water surged outside.

I waited. My memory of that time in the sail locker is of my urgent need to urinate.

When I guessed the *Empire Princess* was far enough from land that Lewis Balfour would not dare toss me overboard, I crawled up to the hatch and pushed it open, flooding the locker with sunlight. The hatch fell back onto the deck with a loud crack. I pulled myself out and stepped to the starboard rail, then started walking slowly aft.

Three mountains of gleaming white cloth rose above me—the main, mizzen and jib—taut with wind and shimmering in the morning light, and hiding the Balfours from me, though I could hear them chatting. The main boom was played out over the port rail, on the other side of the boat from me. Boston harbor was hidden behind the sail. To windward were a score of vessels, mostly crabbers and seiners, but also pleasure boats, all coursing to sea, their prows splitting white water. A deckhand was working near the bow pulpit but he weren't looking my way.

The wind roared in my ears, or it might have been the rush of anticipation. I stepped aft along the starboard rail, anticipating my first sight of my love in two months. I could taste her in my mouth, feel her in my bones.

Then the damndest thing happened.

From the cockpit, the skipper called, "Prepare to come about. Mind the booms."

I didn't know what that meant, but I was too close to my dream to be distracted by stupid sailor talk. I stepped lively along the windward rail. Another few feet and I'd see Amy again.

"Come about."

The *Empire Princess* suddenly turned into the wind, its bow sweeping to the right in a grand arch along the blue horizon. Acres of sails luffed for an instant as the yacht came about. Then the sails again swelled with air, this time on the starboard side—my side—of the boat.

A mammoth cloud of sail rushed at me, and instantly surrounded me in a white world. The mainsail boom swung across the deck, coming for me like the wrath of God. The starboard deck sank toward the sea as the boat heeled with the wind.

Propelled by the billowing sail, the tree-trunk boom swept into me, catching me just under the arms, and smacking me into the air. My feet caught on the safety rail, spinning me topsy-turvy as I plummeted into the sea.

I fought the swirling white-and-blue currents, not knowing which way was up and paralyzed by the pain in my chest. After what seemed like a month, I surfaced in the eddies and foam churned by the passing yacht. I spit and gagged. My ribs felt like a cable had been wrapped around them, and breathing was an agonizing business. I wiped the saltwater from my eyes and dogpaddled to stay afloat.

The *Empire Princess* was already fifty yards away and swiftly increasing the distance. The Balfours and the crew were hidden by the mizzen sail. I tried to call out, but my lungs wouldn't work. A whitecap spilled over my head. I bobbed like a buoy, chilled and hurting.

My destiny had overtaken me, so I did not panic. A martyr for love, taken by the cruel sea at his moment of triumph. I was sanguine about my end. I deserved it.

"You there, catch the line." The voice was made uneven by the sea breeze.

I kicked around. A fishing boat was bearing down on me, its skipper leaning over a rail with a coil in his hand. I caught the line and was quickly pulled aboard. I would martyr myself for love sometime later, I happily concluded.

Jack of All Trades was the boat's name, putting to sea for three days of mackerel fishing. The captain, a kindly man but one who brooked no freeloading, weren't about to put back to port just because he had plucked a boy from the Atlantic. I spent the next three days in the *Jack*'s dank, dark, cramped, pitching and yawing hold, perched atop a hillock of salt, packing mackerel and salt into barrels, sitting next to a Portagee who never said a word. Every once in a while I'd climb on deck to lean over the rail to vomit. I've been in merrier situations in this life.

When its barrels were full, *Jack of All Trades* returned to Boston. The captain said if I ever needed work, look him up. I would've shaken my rescuer's hand, but my fingers were cracked, blistered, and bleeding from handling the salt.

Now, as I look back, I speculate there might have been a lesson to be learned from these episodes. If so, it sped right by me because by the time I was again on dry land I had another plan.

And unlike my two prior schemes, this one was positively in-candescent with its author's intelligence and shrewdness. Amy Balfour would have to endure her wait no longer.

From Tim Conner—ever the grumbling informant—I learned that Dickie Balfour was indeed associating with a rough crowd, just as I had overheard his mother complain as the family boarded the yacht. A rough crowd in the Balfour neighborhood was probably some boys who didn't polish their shoes every week and used cusswords like "Jumpin' Jimminy." In my part of town, a rough crowd was one that owned more pistols than there were members of the crowd.

Dickie, it seemed, suffered a curious but recurrent ailment of the wealthy: a fascination with lowlife. He was eighteen years old and on his way to Harvard but spending too much time at Furrow's Night Club on Turnout Road where he was viewed as a rich rattlebrain and dismissed out of hand by the sports unless he happened to be posting a round of drinks, which Dickie did frequently as the price of admission.

Conner reported that one fellow, the tavern bully named Tom Blackstock, had taken a serious disliking to Dickie—perhaps he thought Dickie's money might someday challenge his muscle—and regularly cuffed Dickie around. Like a puppy, Dickie always returned, spotting the tipplers to another round and hoping for an invitation to play billiards.

Conner had described Dickie to me. "Slicked-back hair, mustache looks like it's been plucked with tweezers, big rolling wet eyes, always looks like he's about ready to cry."

I might have felt sorry for the Balfour boy, had Dickie never opened his mouth.

On a Friday night in August of that year—it was still 1879—I waited outside Furrow's until Dickie Balfour came through the door to the street. He was rubbing his chin and indeed looked on the verge of bawling.

I stepped along with him. "Get your chops busted again?"

He sniffed, "Who *are* you?"

I cannot parrot the dripping contempt Dickie Balfour could put into just three words, but it was something to hear, a science, really. He might have been speaking to a pile of dog dung. His crow-black hair was glued to his skull. His bobbed nose had a disdainful lift that invited a poke, and I sorely wanted to accommodate it. He wore worsted pants and a white-and-gray checkered vest.

"I've got a deal for you," I said.

"You just make yourself off to your hovel and let me alone. I've had enough of you contemptible oafs for one night."

"Tom Blackstock slap you around again?" I asked mockingly.

"Get away from me or I'll call the police." He waved a hand at me like he was shooing away a fly.

"Sure would be nice to bust Blackstock on his biscuit, wouldn't it? Show the fellows at Furrow's that you can dish it out, not just take it?"

He hurried along, trying to outpace me. I set the bait. "John L. Sullivan is a good friend of mine."

That slowed him. Even Boston Brahmins knew of John L. Dickie surveyed me skeptically.

"That's right," I went on. "The Boston Strong Boy."

"What are you proposing?"

"I can get John L. to give you a few lessons. Show you the ropes, a few moves Tom Blackstock never even dreamed of."

We stopped in front of a barber shop with its red-and-white pole. Nearby was a posterboard advertising P.T. Barnum's latest discovery, Mahurabi the Magnificent Moroccan Midget.

Dickie narrowed his eyes at me like I might be a pervert. "And what do you want in return?"

"Introduce me to your sister Amy."

He threw his head back and roared. On and on he went. Quite a performance, enough to make someone less poised than myself feel insecure.

Finally he calmed enough to say, "She'd knock the chocks from under an Irish boghopper like you."

"I know where John L. is right now. You can begin tonight."

He glanced back at Furrow's Night Club. We could hear the laughs and snorts of enthusiastic stewies. He palpated his chin for a long moment. "It's a deal."

Now, I had made no such arrangement with John L. But when he was in a generous mood he was known to give out pointers and dance around the ring a while with a pretender. And John L. owed me, I figured, because I had held his wagers while he was massacring a few ill-fated saps.

I said, "He's at Joe Lowe's Museum and Sporting Palace over in Roxbury. Let's go."

Dickie had borrowed the Balfour cabriolet, and I winked with half my face at Tim Conner up on the driver's seat as I followed Dickie into the cab. I inhaled deeply of Amy's lingering scent, or it might have been the seat's rolled and pleated leather or Dickie's hair pomade. Conner called, "Hidap," and we jolted away.

Probably plotting his fistic revenge on Tom Blackstock, Dickie was silent the thirty minutes to my pa's saloon. When we arrived I ran inside and asked pa behind the bar if he'd seen John L. around.

Pa looked up from the stein he was filling. "His kid brother ran in and hollered that their mother had swallowed a chicken bone and was having a choking fit, so John L. went home. But he said he'd be back, one way or the other."

Just then John L. himself pushed his way through the doors. Dickie followed in his wake, signaling me to make the introduction.

John L. announced, "Ma lived, the saints be praised."

The patrons gave him a round of applause.

"I told her she'd best chew them chicken bones before she swallows them."

Chuckles from the group.

Pa was about to hand John L. a stein of beer when I stepped forward. "John L., you got a moment?"

He brought himself up. He filled the sky in front of me like the *Empire Princess*'s sails had. "Sure, Woodrow. Speak fast, though, because I've got a powerful thirst."

"This is Dickie Balfour." I put a begging tremor in my voice. "I'm hoping maybe you'd give him a boxing lesson or two."

Then Dickie had to chirp, "I'm pretty good with my fists already, John L." He brought up his delicate little hands, good for flower arranging or flicking a cigarette holder, the only hands in Boston that made mine look like a fighter's.

Pa held up a glass. "Here's your beer, John L."

Dickie crouched and danced, moving his pretty hands in tiny orbits. "There must be *something* you can show me."

Sensing an outlander, the patrons turned to look. Some smiled, knowing more about the world in general and John L. in particular than did Dickie Balfour.

Along with all other Boston Sons of Erin, John L. Sullivan detested inherited advantage. With his lordly manner and haughty tone, Dickie Balfour exuded privilege, and it stunk up Joe Lowe's Museum and Sporting Palace. Even I, smitten with love and hope, could smell it.

But then John L. said, "Why sure, fella. I'll give you your first lesson right now, and it's the most important one in all of prizefighting."

John L. leaned forward confidentially, glancing left and right, guarding against others hearing his boxing secret.

Dickie's grin announced he had expected no less. This instant and total attention from the Boston Strong Boy was his right as a Balfour. He leaned forward expectantly, his head only inches from John L.'s.

"Now, the first lesson is . . ." John L. paused with a vaudevillian's timing, then his massive head whipped forward and cracked loudly into Dickie's forehead. The sound was like a pool cue snapped over a knee. Dickie dropped to the floor, out and cold.

John L. lectured the patrons, "The first lesson is: never stand between John L. Sullivan and a beer."

This brought a huge laugh from the drinkers. John L. stepped over Dickie and reached for his stein, laughing at his own wit.

You have to agree that under other circumstances, this would have been hilarious. But faced again with dashed dreams, I could only lift Dickie off the floor, carry his inert form through the double doors, and toss him into the cabriolet. I was sick with love and disappointment.

"What happened?" Tim Conner asked from above.

"Ask him when he wakes up," I replied miserably.

BASEBALL WAS IN its infancy at the time, and the term "Three strikes and you're out" weren't in common usage. I didn't know the phrase, but I should have. My three plots to meet Amy Balfour had been whiffs. I took one more swing, and ended up in the ball-breaking cavalry.

I'll make the story short because I'm not fond of looking back on it. From Tim Conner I weaseled the location of Amy's bedroom window. One night in September I climbed over the Balfour gate, found a ladder in the garden house, and propped it against the house. I was going to rap on her window and declare my feelings for her.

The Balfour residence was guarded every night by the Pinkertons, something that moron Tim Conner failed to mention. A guard discovered me on the ladder and turned me over to the police. A jury convicted me of trespass, theft (the ladder), and attempted kidnapping. Back then judges didn't fool around with such sentimental legal niceties as extenuating circumstances or probation. Dickie Balfour, the lying son of a bitch, testified that this was my second attempt to spirit away a Balfour, accusing me of trying to kidnap him the night he met John L. That doomed me. I was sentenced to twelve years in prison or twelve years in the United States Cavalry. I chose the latter.

That's how on July 4, 1886, I found myself in Dickinson, Dakota Territory, as a cook in the goddamn bullocks-bouncing cavalry, about to face John L. Sullivan in a ring. I can rightly blame it all on Amy Balfour, don't you think?

FOUR

Bear Grease

INDEPENDENCE DAY IN Dickinson began with a parade. I watched from the boardwalk in front of a sundry store. Wearing a silver star and riding a pinto, Dickinson's sheriff led the procession as grand marshal. The volunteer fire company came next, the men pulling their hose reel with rope traces and breastbands. The reel was a mechanical pumper mounted on two wheels seven feet high. The firemen wore peaked helmets, belt buckles with large number "1"s on them, and broad-collared shirts. Spectators cheered and waved small American flags. The firemen returned salutes from the children.

Behind the fire engine marched the town band. Twenty musicians carried cornets, French horns, and snare and bass drums. Their uniforms consisted of red arm bands and large feathers tucked into assorted hats. A minstrel troupe was in town for a show that night and had agreed to participate in the parade. The actors and actresses were dressed in a peculiar mix of harlequin costumes, red and purple robes of Shakespearean royalty, and blackface. They marched haphazardly.

Trooper after trooper patted me on the back or briefly rubbed my shoulders, giving words of encouragement. I was so nervous that I had to keep my jaw clamped shut so my teeth wouldn't rattle.

Next in the parade came a mounted cavalry troop down from Fort Buford. At the end of its column was a mule team pulling a ten-barrel, crank-revolved Gatling gun mounted on wheels that had red crepe paper entwined in the spokes, as cheery as I'd ever seen a Gatling gun. Then in line were two buggy floats, one of a bald eagle made with crepe paper and another of Lady Liberty. That was it. A parade as heartfelt as it was short.

My time had come. The soldiers whooped when I walked out into

Villard Street and climbed into the ring. I lifted a blue and gold length of cloth from a pocket and tied it around my corner post, to more huzzahs from the troopers. I took off my uniform shirt, leaving my undershirt and trousers on. The grandstands were overflowing. Other folks were on roofs and in windows. Several boys had climbed telegraph poles and were perched on the crossbars.

Sergeant Rose was my ringman, and he spread bear grease on my face to help my opponent's gloves slip off. I had not shaved in three days, another attempt to keep my face intact.

The sergeant laced my six-ounce gloves. John L. and I would be fighting under Queensberry rules because Queensberry allowed for a more sporting fight than did a bareknuckle contest under London Prize rules. Two reasons accounted for this. Under bareknuckle rules, rounds didn't have a set time such as three minutes. Any time a fighter fell to a knee or his hand touched the mat, the round ended and the fighter was allowed thirty seconds to recover. So a boxer could drop a knee whenever he needed a breather. This was called slogging. Second, with no gloves, both fisticuffers' hands would swell to soft melons after a few minutes. A bareknuckle fight of any length came to resemble a children's bedtime pillow fight for all the effect the blows were having. A lot of folks think the Marquis of Queensberry was interested in the safety of boxers. Not so. He wanted a more savage spectacle.

Sergeant Rose rubbed my shoulders as we waited for John L. My bowels were loose. I surveyed the crowd. A fellow in a white coat, with ruddy hair and a walrus mustache, and smoking a slender cigar was at ringside. I was told later it was Mark Twain. I don't know why he didn't write about this fight like he did every other damned thing he found in front of his eyeballs for more than two seconds. My gaze also found General Sheridan, sitting next to Dickinson's mayor on the land office's banner-bedecked balcony. His frigid countenance told me that if I couldn't last four rounds, he'd find a reason to keep me twenty more years in the cavalry.

While I'm thinking about it: if you don't like parasites, don't join the cavalry. Ringworm, hookworm, scabies, chiggers, crabs, and cooties, I suffered them all. And one time I swallowed a leech that had swum into my canteen when I was filling it at a pond. It grabbed onto my tonsils with its tiny teeth. I'll spare you the description of my ten minutes of gagging and doing the jig until I finally managed to hawk that critter out of my throat. Sergeant Rose witnessed this production with some amusement and commented that the leech probably tasted better than the grub I served.

A referee in a yellow shirt entered the ring. It was the town sheriff, just back from his parade. A shout went up from the crowd, undoubtedly their first glimpse that day of John L. I couldn't see him yet, but a group of fellows were purposely making their way through the crowd to the ring. He must be among them.

Suddenly Sergeant Rose crowed, "We did it. Take a look."

Six men were carrying John L. Sullivan to the ring. The Boston Strong Boy's arms were draped over two men's shoulders. Two others had webbed together their hands in a fireman's carry where John L. sat. Two men each carried a leg. This formation reached the ring. John L. managed to stand at ringside, but three of his aides had to ascend into the ring to help him up.

Rose punched me in the shoulder and exclaimed, "The 7th Cavalry drank him under the table. Look at him. He's blacked out on his feet."

I found General Sheridan again. He nodded. I grinned back, confidence soaring. God and John L.'s thirst had granted me a chance.

One of John L.'s attendants attached a green-and-white silk cloth to a post, then his ringmen climbed out. Fancies yelled and clapped. In his corner, holding the top ropes with both hands, John L. swayed and groaned. His mouth fished open. He blinked blindly against the noonday sun. His feet shifted in tiny steps as he tried to remain upright. Spectators who had wagered on John L. booed and hissed.

Hallelujah. This was going to make me a religious man, after all. The Lord had answered the 7th Cavalry's prayers, and mine.

Then the bell rang.

I learned later that this was not the first time John L. had arrived ringside virtually comatose from drink, nor would it be the last. And I was to learn right then why John L. could let this happen to himself: *it made absolutely no difference in his ring performance.* When he heard that bell, he became electrified and murderous and utterly focused on his enemy: one pathetic, sacrificial soldier named Woodrow C. Lowe, yours truly.

The "C" stands for Carol, if you must know. How I ended up with a girl's name in the middle of two fine ones is something my parents never told me, but I suspect it was the result of a beerhall wager my father lost. When Teddy Roosevelt became president I asked him how I might go about changing it but he said it would require an act of Congress, and he didn't want to spend his precious political capital on such a small issue, so I was stuck with it.

John L. charged from his corner like a bull that had just lost its oysters. Straight for me he came, one hand out front to ward off any impudent folly I might consider, and his business hand—his right one— loaded and cocked next to his ear.

My confidence vanished. I took two tentative steps toward the center of the ring. John L.'s fist was launched from the center of the earth, tore through layers of magma, granite and soil, and ripped into the air to land right between my eyes.

In my career I've been clobbered by a lead-filled garden hose, a Dervish war club, a lead-lined glove, a crowbar, a set of brass knuckles, the stocks of several rifles, a white athletic sock with a stone in it, and a barrel slat, which would have hurt less had there not been a sixpenny nail in it. But I've never felt anything like John L. Sullivan's knuckles ramming into my nose.

My head instantly was transformed into a universe of pain. I pitched to the canvas, landing, of all places, on my already mashed smeller.

When I say mashed, I don't mean metaphorically. I mean, my nose ceased to exist as a protuberance. It lay across my face with the tip almost poking my eye.

I don't know how I remained conscious. I was splayed out, my arms and legs in every possible direction, my neck twisted, as undignified a pose as a man should ever have to assume in front of witnesses. But I was content to lie on that canvas until the next rain.

Then I heard a piping bray of a voice calling me from somewhere beyond the agony of my face. "You, Private Lowe. You get up now."

I could not hear the whistling and catcalls of the Dickinson audience. Only this voice penetrated the pain.

"Private Lowe, remember me? You did that to me once. Remember?"

That chirping voice was vaguely familiar. It demanded attention. Lying there, tasting dust on the canvas, I also became aware of the referee counting. He had pushed John L. back to his corner and was now at three and climbing.

I fervently hoped that strident, high-pitched voice would go away and leave me to my eternal sleep, but it said, "You did it to me at the Harvard gym. You can do it to John L. Sullivan. Get up now, son."

With a sapping effort, I opened my eyes. Standing at the ropes next to Sergeant Rose was that four-eyed pipsqueak I had laid out seven years before in Cambridge. He grinned at me and motioned me to rise from the mat. His teeth had grown, it seemed. So had his head. A peculiar-looking fellow.

And so damned insistent. "Get up now, Private Lowe. Find your strength."

Theodore Roosevelt's voice was itself a bludgeon, but a velvet one. In years to come, I would hear it do miracles. It performed one then.

My knees scraped along the canvas until they were under me, then ratcheted themselves open. I found myself just upright enough for the referee to stop his count.

That Teddy fellow called out, "Keep away from him. Backstep as fast as you can."

What did that little gadfly know about boxing? I asked myself indignantly, backstepping as fast as I could. It seemed the wise course, because John L., his nose flaring at my temerity in rising from the canvas, rushed me again.

Over the years I've spoken with a number of John L.'s opponents. They don't remember much of their matches against him because they were beaten senseless. But they all agreed that John L. whistled wind and grunted when he attacked, the frightening sound of a locomotive.

This noise suddenly stopped, as did John L., right in the middle of the ring. He peered at me through red-rimmed eyes. "Woodrow, is that you?"

"It is, John L."

"Well, how about that?" He lunged again, setting me up by smacking my head twice with his left—much like being inside a bell when it is rung—and ripping open the skin near my right eye, then smashing his right fist into my ribcage. I landed on the canvas again, my insides feeling as if a stick of miner's dynamite had went off. I learned later that two ribs were broken. I lay there in a pool of suffering.

"Now is not the time for failure, but for endurance. Rise, Private Lowe." That same jarring, chopped-off voice. That same curious Teddy chap.

Why wouldn't he leave me to die in peace?

"Get up, Private Lowe. For your mates, for you, and for me."

For him? Not only was he rude in shouting at a semiconscious, broken man, but he was talking nonsense. I wouldn't shout a warning to save this Teddy from falling into a manhole, much less rise again to face John L. Sullivan at his urging.

The referee called four, then five.

"Private Lowe, listen to me. Gather your courage, gather your reserves, face this challenge."

I will tell you this as honestly as I remember it. I was going to lie on that mat until Christ's second coming. I was shut with the cavalry, with boxing and with life. My body ached from toenail to temple. That mat represented safety.

"Private Lowe, bring yourself to do this. Get off that mat."

That voice lifted me off the canvas. I fought it. I cursed the man. But I rose. The throng cheered.

Teddy called, "Keep away from him. Backstep, backstep."

I wobbled backward. I commanded my arms to rise in surrender, but— for the love of God—they came only up to my chest as if I wanted to continue boxing.

The Boston Strong Boy stalked me again. He asked as he came, "How's your pa, Woodrow? I ain't seen him in a couple months."

"He's fine, John L.," I sputtered. "I got a letter from him last week."

I hobbled backward in a circle as fast as my rubbery legs would carry me. He followed. He wound up again, about to blast me to the next century, when the bell rang, ending the first round.

I staggered to my corner. Rose pulled me to his knees and held a ladle of water to my mouth.

That damned Teddy somehow thought he was my new trainer. "Keep your hands up. You'll make it if he can't hit you. Keep out of his range. Backstep."

"Shut the hell up," I replied. I reached for Sergeant Rose's hat to throw it into the ring. Teddy grabbed the hat and we wrestled for it, but it slipped out of my gloves. I wanted to sob.

"Listen to him, Wood," Sergeant Rose advised, reapplying grease to my chin. "I'm out a gold eagle if you don't get off my legs. I was going to send for my ma back in County Cork with that money."

The bell sounded, but I stayed on Rose's knees, reasonably comfortable and certainly happier than I'd be anywhere else in that ring, until Teddy said, "Get up, go out there, and cover the 7th Cavalry in glory."

I stood and once again faced the Strong Boy. The crowd roared. John L. came out of his corner and circled left, maybe as a courtesy. He usually just bulled ahead.

I said, "John L., why don't you beat up that four-eyed idiot in my corner and leave me alone."

John L. glanced at Teddy Roosevelt. "I will, Woodrow, promise. But you got to get out of this ring first."

"I wish I could."

A cannon must have shot John L.'s fist at me. It landed on my chin and caused me to bite my tongue almost in half. I bounced against the ropes and on the rebound John L. shot his fist into my scarred ear. That blow felt like an anvil had been dropped on my head from a three-story building. I once again had no trouble finding the canvas.

I prayed for unconsciousness, but that demented Teddy's voice kept blessed darkness at bay.

"Do this for America, for her Independence Day," he shouted. "Rise again, Private Lowe. Rise, I tell you. Rise once more, and I'll leave you alone."

I muttered through the blood in my mouth, "You'll leave me alone? You promise?"

"Yes, that's a promise. Just find your legs once more."

Like a puppet on a string, I was lifted to my feet by the imperative of his voice. I spat blood. My lips had swollen to the size of beerhall pickles. A gash had opened on my eyebrow so blood cascaded down my face obscuring my view, not that being able to see would have made any difference.

"Turn to him, Private Lowe," Teddy shouted. "Put your dukes up. Backstep. Churn those legs."

As he closed in, John L. said, "Your mum's going to be mad as hell at me already, Woodrow. You'd better stay down this time."

"I'll try, John L." My words were pulpy.

His next shot—a miss, actually, because he was aiming at my face— broke my collarbone. I spun with the force of the blow, and took another hammer to my ear. This time the inky void took me, and I don't remember greeting my old friend the canvas again.

* * *

FOLKS WHO HAVE never been in a serious fray think the soreness lasts a few hours, then you are ready again for the dance. Three weeks passed before I could get out of the bunk, and another two months before I stopped hurting.

I did all this recuperating at Theodore Roosevelt's Elkhorn Ranch fifty miles northwest of Dickinson in the fork where Beaver Creek joins the Little Missouri, where he had went after two years in the New York legislature to be a dilettante cattle rancher. He carted me there, still unconscious, on a wagon he rented. He looked after me all them weeks.

I suppose I should have been grateful, but when I first woke up from my blackout and saw that bespectacled crackpot staring down at me, I admit to shouting out in fear.

Then, when I was sensate enough to understand him, he claimed that I owed him for all that nursing, and he so let on for the next thirty-three years until he died.

John L. Sullivan and Theodore Roosevelt became fans of each other and improbable friends in their later years. John L. told me once that he and Roosevelt laughed long and hard when they discovered both had broken promises made to me that day in Dickinson. John L. never did chase down and flatten Teddy. And Teddy Roosevelt never did leave me alone.

FIVE

Tick Mash

AMY BALFOUR'S WEDDING should have been the triumphant pinnacle of the East Coast social season. She was to marry John Malcolm, eldest son of Randolph Malcolm, the New York department store magnate. I ruined her wedding day for her and four hundred guests. I would have tried to apologize had I not feared her bludgeoning me to death with a silver punch bowl.

I recall her wedding day—Saturday, June 7, 1889—with heartless accuracy. Debacles don't easily fade from the mind.

By then I had been in New York with Teddy Roosevelt three years. General Sheridan's vengeance for my losing the Army of the Missouri's payroll was immediate. The army trumped up a desertion charge against me, when in fact Lieutenant Smythe had allowed his friend Teddy Roosevelt to lug me to the Elkhorn Ranch to recover from the battering. My punishment was a compulsory five-year reenlistment. And as further penalty, I was assigned to Theodore Roosevelt.

How could the army detach me from the cavalry and handcuff me to a private citizen? The answer lay in Roosevelt's ubiquitous contacts and universal influence. I never met a man who had more powerful friends and more people wanting to be in his debt than Roosevelt. He had an uncanny ability to turn heads, to leave an advantageous impression, and to generate loyalty. In 1889, Roosevelt was only a thirty-one-year-old New York City civil service commissioner, yet even then many folks told me he was destined to be president.

It looked like I was destined to be his indentured servant. My assignment to Roosevelt came about this way: Roosevelt asked the mayor of Manhattan, Otis Lenhart, who asked his friend Treasury Secretary Daniel Manning, who asked Secretary of War William Endicott, who requested Gen. Phil Sheridan, who ordered Brig. Thomas Townsend to hand me over to Roosevelt.

That's how it happened, but why it happened has always been a mystery to me. Roosevelt could hold a grudge like a camel, so I have long suspected he snared me, then sent me on my life's wild course as retribution for humiliating him in the Harvard gym. In later years my wife offered that perhaps Teddy appreciated my company. That don't seem likely.

That Saturday morning I rose at five-thirty to make Roosevelt's breakfast like I always did. He was the only person I ever met who enjoyed my eggs-over-easy, which were so greasy they'd slip down your gullet before your teeth had the chance to work on them.

Roosevelt favored living at Sagamore Hill, where his wife Edith and his daughter by his first marriage, Alice, were that summer. When he was in New York, Teddy stayed at his sister Bamie's residence at 689 Madison Avenue. I had a cot in a third-floor garret. I was his bodyguard.

Bodyguarding was a promotion because I had begun my service for him as a butler, valet, and general factotum. During some of this time in New York, he was writing his *Winning of the West,* often sitting in a small office in his publisher's building to get away from the noisy distractions of home. He'd say, "Woodrow, hand me that bottle of India blue, will you?" Or, "It's a little close in here, would you mind, Woodrow?" So I'd open a window. That sort of trifling thing.

Although he had placed third—dead last—in the 1886 mayoral race, Teddy was known as an up-and-coming politician and a firebrand speaker, so he was regularly invited to fill audiences' ears about elk hunting out west, about why Manhattan needed a new water reservoir, about Royal Navy tactics during the War of 1812, anything.

One day on the sidewalk outside Delmonico's, where Teddy was scheduled to give a speech to a contractors' association, he was confronted by a drunk fishmonger who tossed a bucket of eel heads at him. I had been holding Teddy's jacket, and had the regrettable quick-mindedness to jump forward, catching the eel heads and bloody brine full in my face and chest. Teddy ignored the fishmonger. Dry and sweet smelling—the precise opposite of my situation—Teddy walked into the restaurant without a sideways glance at me. I wiped eel parts from my eyes while the drunk mumbled something about Roosevelt's support of a scale tax. The drunk tottered away, still carrying his bucket.

From then on in New York I was Roosevelt's bodyguard more than anything else, although he'd still rattle off lists of picayune household tasks for me to do, like water the Boston ferns or walk his dog Bottsie.

Bottsie was some sort of terrier, a thirty-pound, short-haired, slit-eyed, bowlegged dynamo whose passions in life were Roosevelt and chasing rats. I'd come back from walking that dog sore from wrist to shoulder because Bottsie time and again would abruptly light out after a rat, usually an imaginary one. The yank on the leash would almost dislocate my shoulder. And although I walked him and thus afforded him all this grand entertainment, he reserved his adoration for Teddy, viewing me as nothing but an unwanted anchor.

Despite my earnest wishes, Bottsie lived to be fourteen years old, and near the end of his life his rear hips became displaced. Roosevelt had a cobbler make a little cart with wheels and straps, so the dog could rest his butt and hind legs on this rolling platform while his front legs propelled him along. I suppose I have in my life looked more ridiculous than when I'd walk this dog-on-a-cart up and down Fifth Avenue—Bottsie still rushing after fanciful rats, the cart clacking and swaying behind him—but I can't recall when. More punishment for pelting Teddy at Hemenway Gym, I suspect.

Turns out Teddy needed my protection. As a city commissioner he viewed it as his duty to walk the streets, all neighborhoods, all hours, his pace brisk and his walking stick swinging. He toured the docks, the Gashouse District, and Hell's Kitchen. Once he even walked into the infamous McGurk's Saloon in the Bowery, known as Suicide Hall. Teddy received unending press, and even the city's scoundrels recognized him. He was approached by sharpers, roughs, barrelhouse bums, and frowzy women, sometimes to pick his pocket, sometimes to pick fights, and other times just to bait him.

On such occasions, Teddy would make a half-turn in my direction, and say, "Please take up your business with my associate, Mr. Lowe."

My scarred face, thick neck, and knotty hands told the plug-uglies exactly what kind of business they could expect from me. They always scattered. It's an unkind world when you make your living frightening folks with your face.

But I have wandered from my story.

That morning Roosevelt strolled into the kitchen wearing dapper low-cut shoes, black pants with narrow white stripes, and carrying a straw hat and walking stick. His first words were, "You have a match last night?"

I nodded my head, shaking the eggs in the pan so they wouldn't stick.

He brassily grabbed my chin and turned my face toward him. He laughed in his singular trill as he studied my bruises. "Woodrow, did you try to win the fight by hitting your opponents' fists with your eyebrows and ear? You look like Pearl tenderized you with her meat mallet."

Pearl was Bamie's cook. I was wearing a cut on my left eyebrow and my right eye was swollen almost shut.

I pulled my head away and said with satisfaction, "I went twenty-eight rounds, over an hour and ten minutes."

He chirruped, "But who took the prize?"

I twisted the flue on the wood stove to lower the fire. "I'm poorer now than when I entered the ring." I dumped the eggs onto his plate. The home had a formal dining room, but he preferred breakfast in the kitchen.

He sat at the white, turned-iron table and lifted a fork. I raised the grate, then held bread in a wire basket over the fire. My hands were swollen from the bareknuckle bout, nothing I weren't used to. "There's only fifteen people in this country who are tougher than me, and it's just my luck they're all trying to make a living boxing at Hill's."

Roosevelt chuckled, turned to his eggs, and opened a newspaper. Harry Hill's was a saloon on Houston Street, several doors west of Mulberry, incongruously near police headquarters. Giant blue-and-red lanterns marked the main entrance, and nearby was the private door for women. Harry Hill welcomed everyone: judges, lawyers, bankers, off-duty policemen, soldiers, stevedores, river thieves, fences, damper sneaks, safebreakers, bull-traps, and cutpurses. And of course, he welcomed pugilists because they were the draw in the back room.

There I tried, with only mixed success, to supplement my income. Teddy never paid me a cent, thinking my army draw sufficient for a bodyguard. During my three years in New York, I won forty-two bouts and lost eight. At the time I weighed two-twelve, and I figured ten pounds of it was scar tissue, knuckle calluses, and cauliflower ear.

Once in a while I would return to Roxbury on the train for a two-day visit. My ma would weep at the first sight of me and then follow me around the apartment for most of my stay trying to hold a mirror up to my face as if that might reform me.

I opened the cage and flipped the toast onto Teddy's plate. I never called him Teddy to his face, by the way, only Mr. Roosevelt. A few intimates from his Harvard days used the nickname, and even then he loathed it.

He read a copy of the New York *Journal,* and issues of the *Herald* and *Times* were also on the table. Teddy could read like Diamond Jim Brady could eat. He sped through at least one book a day, sometimes two or three. I never saw his lips move, either, like mine did when plodding through printed matter. It was probably just as well, too, because at the rate of a book a day, anybody who moved his lips probably would have burned them off from friction with the air. Sometimes I think I should have been a scientist.

Bruce Twig-Smathers walked into the kitchen, plucked an orange from the counter basket, then sat opposite Teddy in an iron chair. He said with his Oxford accent, "I put a ten on you last night, through a rather seedy bookmaker, Woodrow. Looks like I can say farewell to the money, what say?"

"If I had known, sir, I would have put up more of a fight."

Twig-Smathers laughed and started peeling his orange, always in one long peel. If the rind broke before he had removed it, he would put that orange aside and begin a new one. Sir Bruce Twig-Smathers, called Twiggy by Roosevelt, was secretary of the British legation in Washington. He had met Roosevelt during one of Roosevelt's journeys to England, and the two had become fast friends. Roosevelt had arranged for Twig-Smathers to become an honorary member of Roosevelt's club, the Century, which to Twig-Smathers's satisfaction was as exclusive as his own London club, the Saville. Twig-Smathers had been staying at Bamie's for a week, and was sailing for England that afternoon. He wore a goatee, and a monocle always hung by a ribbon from his lapel, though I never saw him use it. He was a notorious bachelor, and most evenings during his New York stay he could be seen with one of the city's beauties on his arm. I had never been inside the Century Club, if you're wondering.

Without looking up from his paper, Roosevelt said, "Woodrow, I don't need you following me around today, so you're off until two o'clock, when I've got an unusual assignment for you."

Roosevelt was a compilation of odd habits. He performed one just then, tearing off the first page of the *Journal* and dropping it to the kitchen floor. He did so with magazines and newspapers, ripping off the pages as he churned through them. If he sat in a chair reading periodicals for any length of time, the pile of pages would be up to his ankles.

I scoured the frying pan with a stiff brush, waiting for my day's assignment, undoubtedly a menial task. Teddy should have been a cavalry sergeant, the way he could dream up fussy, bootless chores. I weren't disappointed.

He finally said, "Bertha Malcolm, in one of her usual tizzies, telephoned last evening. Her son is getting married this afternoon at Fifth Avenue Presbyterian. Edith and I received our invitation weeks ago. Old line Boston family joining a New York Shoddyite family. You're invited too, Twiggy."

Back then, the new rich were called Shoddyites, whereas Roosevelt and his ilk were the Old Knickerbockers, descendants of original Dutch settlers. The Knickerbockers claimed social precedence. Later in his career, though, Roosevelt was called "Fifty-Seven Varieties" because of his knack for finding common heritage with any voter who he might be talking to.

He tore off another a page of the *Journal* and let it float to the black-and-white tile. "Apparently the Boston mother couldn't bear to have her daughter's wedding to a sundry-store family take place in Boston, so it's up here."

Twig-Smathers said, "Malcolm's is hardly a sundry store."

It was called a department store, where a shopper could purchase almost every conceivable item on six floors under one roof. Malcolm's was on Printing House Square, near the old post office and the *Times* building. Over ten thousand people spent their money there every day, Randolph Malcolm claimed when puffing the store in the press.

Teddy finished a piece of toast before going on. "Mrs. Malcolm asked if she could borrow you and a few others from this household."

He kept me waiting while he spread strawberry preserves on his second slice of toast. I hoped the Malcolms needed a bodyguard for one of their guests. At the mayor's request, Teddy had frequently loaned me out to New Yorkers or visiting swells who for some reason or another feared walking the streets alone.

That's how I got to know Oscar Wilde. The mayor figured him for a walking target, with his peculiar talk and limpid walk. Wilde usually wore purple pants and a chartreuse cape, so I had to walk ten feet behind him lest I become a laughingstock by association. That's why you don't see me in any newspaper photos of him taken during his New York stay. When I met him at the steamship arriving from Portsmouth, we didn't start off too well because his first words to me were, "Did you use your face to plow a stony field?"

I glanced at his patent leather pumps with the gaudy gold buckles, something Bluebeard would wear, and asked, "How long you got to wear them shoes before you win the bet?"

He came back with, "You and I are going to get along famously, sweetie."

We did, too, although it turns out Oscar didn't need a bodyguard, being a hard customer himself under the garish clothes and swaying manner. I was with him outside Rector's, where he was staying, when a rough—a collier judging from the black dust cloud around him—made a rude comment about Oscar's hair, which was down to his shoulders. Oscar instantly shot his own hand deep into the collier's mouth, almost up to Oscar's wrist. The collier, wild-eyed and helpless, gagged and gurgled, his mouth forced open as wide as a sea bass'. Fingers still wrapped around the man's tongue, Oscar turned to me and said, "I leave them speechless, do I not, Woodrow?" I still laugh, looking back on it.

I also guarded Enrico Caruso, the two of us shoulder-to-shoulder in a hansom, him practicing a few bars, warming up for his recital at Grace Church, where he would be accompanied by the remarkable organ that took four fellows to pump. When the driver opened the trap and told him he was frightening the horse, Caruso desisted. None too soon, too, because he sang right into my cauliflower ear, maybe testing it, his mouth four inches away. I can hear just fine, and his voice had the volume of a six o'clock whistle. Gave me a headache that lasted two days.

I guarded Nellie Melba, who had a thrush's voice. I arrived early at her room at the Hoffman House, and was surprised to find myself invited to breakfast. Coffee and slices of toast dry enough to choke a goat. She later became famous for that toast.

The international beauty and actress Lillian Russell was also one of my charges. In later years I teased my wife, saying Lillian had invited me up to her room at the Lafayette. My wife finally got out of me that Miss Russell only wanted me to muscle open a window that had been painted shut, for which she tipped me a quarter.

Walt Whitman was in my care for a day. In a fit of social conscience inspired by the Pullman Company out in Chicago, the Delta Brick and Stone Company sponsored a reading by Whitman at its brickyard in Newark. The mayor thought Whitman would probably be killed straightaway if he read his sing-song poetry to a gang of brickmakers. I picked up the poet at his Greenwich Village residence. He wore an anarchist's beard and coarse shirt and pants, no collar or necktie. We ferried to the brickyard and he mounted a podium made of two-by-tens laid over sawhorses. I stood right next to him. Getting itchier by the moment, a hundred workers stared at him for two or three poems.

The mayor was right. Suddenly a brickmaker yelled, "Can't you rhyme nothing, for Christ sake?" and launched a shard of brick at him. I saw it coming, tried to catch it, but missed. The fragment hit me in the fore-head, dazing me and opening a gash. Whitman ended his reading right then, to applause from the audience once they were sure he was leaving. The poet helped me back to the carriage.

He was hugely grateful, and when I dropped him off that evening in the Village at Pfaff's—a cellar cafe where he reigned among the Bohemi-ans—he said, "Woodrow, thank you. If there's anything I can ever do, let me know."

I must have still been concussed, because instead of asking for five dollars to pay a doctor to stitch up my head, I said, "You can write me a poem someday."

Well, come to it, later I received by post to Bamie's home an enve-lope. Inside was a poem, written in Whitman's longhand, entitled, "The Canoe Birch." Under the title was a dedication, TO WOODROW LOWE. The poem was of four stanzas, about twenty lines. I didn't know poetry from pottery so I showed it to Teddy. He actually teared over reading it, and went through it four times before giving it back, saying, " 'The Canoe Birch' is a wondrous working of the English language, the finest poem I've ever read." Those are Teddy's exact words. But damn my luck if I didn't leave my poem in my pocket when I threw my trousers into the laundry bin that night.

The pants and poem came back from the laundress, but the ink had bled, and the poem was nothing but a blue stain. I rushed over to Pfaff's to tell Whitman, but he said he didn't keep a copy because the poem was meant for me, to do with what I wanted. I suppose I owe the literary world a debt, and if I could figure out how to pay it, I would.

Getting back to Teddy's kitchen that day, I asked, "Some bodyguarding at the Malcolms'? At the wedding or reception?"

He shook his head. "The caterer got into a titanic quarrel with Mrs. Malcolm, and stomped off the job yesterday. She wants you and the others from many households to stick toothpicks into chunks of melon, set out the place settings, serve champagne, that sort of thing. She's going to put you in tails. Jones and Mary and Pearl will be there, too."

Jones was his butler, Mary the maid, and Pearl the cook.

I lowered myself into a third chair, between Twig-Smathers and Roosevelt. "I don't suppose you can think of anything more lowly for me to do? Me, a full corporal in the United States Army."

He looked up from his paper. "Not today I can't. Maybe Twiggy here can. The British are good at that sort of thing. But cheer up. You've got the morning off. Show up at the Malcolms' at two."

He focused again on his newspaper. Theodore Roosevelt brought to the presidency more intelligence than any president before or since. He once told me that genius was but concentration. He frequently concentrated me right out of his presence, which he did then with his newspaper. Twig-Smathers and I were instantly forgotten.

Through my life, I attempted to imitate Teddy in many ways for my betterment. I'm happy to say that I learned to concentrate—to increase my innate mental powers through focusing on a subject—from Teddy. It has served me well. Exclude distractions. Bring light to bear on the subject.

Now where was I? Something about hors d'oeuvres.

Yes. That was Teddy's idea of a joke, saying I had the morning free. He well knew that any time, six days a week, that he didn't use my services I had to report to the Twenty-third Cavalry Regiment (called Lincoln's Blues) of the First Division of the National Guard of the State of New York, to the Blues' armory on Ninth Avenue, three blocks from Washington Square.

That morning I left Teddy and Twig-Smathers at the front steps of Bamie's brownstone, Teddy turning toward Morton Hall, headquarters of the Twenty-first District Republican Association, Twig-Smathers going uptown for a breakfast engagement, me heading for a horse car to take me downtown.

I was regular army, posted to the Blues, ostensibly to train them in cavalry tactics, but in truth to be loaned out to Roosevelt. Nearly all

First Division troops had fought in the late war, and each regiment cherished its bullet-riddled, cannonsmoke-blackened flag. Since the war, the regiments had been called upon to put down a few riots, most notably in the summer of 1871 when the Orange Lodges wanted to march back and forth in front of a few Catholic churches, and the Catholics took offense. Mostly, though, the First Division put on majestic parades through the streets of Manhattan. The federal government provided uniforms, but the guardsmen didn't view them as sufficiently elegant for a city parade, so the soldiers outfitted themselves, some with red piping, some with soave hats, that sort of folderol. Crowds lined the streets for these processions, and applauded mightily, especially for the more popular units, the Seventh, Ninth, and Twenty-ninth. And the Ninth had the best marching band in the city, and always received an especially rousing cheer. I was allowed to participate in none of this, being regular army.

I arrived at the armory about nine that morning, passing through its narrow door from the street, narrow so that the guardsmen inside would have to fight only one invading attacker at a time. Instead of windows at the street level, the red brick building had two-inch rifle slits. On the third-story roof were more rifle ports, resembling an English castle's battlements. All this on Ninth Avenue in the middle of Manhattan. Would've made Sergeant Rose laugh.

Anyway, I approached the sergeant's desk with some trepidation because he was endlessly inventive in the tasks he assigned me, and they were harsh on yours truly. The sergeant despised me because I was regular army, had been in the glamorous cavalry (for Pete's sake) out west, was enjoying a soft job uptown with Roosevelt, and was a hard-looking lad. Sergeant Purdy was a hitching rail of a man who gained all his authority from his stripes and none from his appearance. Add to his peabrain the temperament of one whose drawers were always hitched up, and you can see I never looked forward to reporting to the armory.

I walked past the circular rifle racks to his desk. He looked up from his roster. Sergeant Purdy had lost his left hand at Gettysburg and wore a shiny hook, but otherwise was an ugly fellow. Missing lower teeth, and wall-eyed, so I never knew whether he was looking at me or over my shoulder.

He asked, "Lose another one?" His voice echoed in the dark hall.

I remained silent.

"Must have. Your face looks like you laid it on the Long Island Line rail and let the trains roll over it for an hour or two."

Sergeant Purdy was hilarious, if I've failed to mention it.

I said smugly, "I've been told to be back uptown at two o'clock."

He snarled, "This won't take that long, corporal. You are to report to the Aldrich Laboratory. Dismissed."

Lord almighty, the worst. "Sergeant, that's two weeks in a row you've sent me over there."

"I can make it every other day, if you like." He smiled sweetly up at me. "Corporal, I said you are dismissed."

The Aldrich Laboratory was also on Ninth, three doors away. I left the gloom of the armory and walked along Ninth toward the gloom of the lab, passing a pushcart of flowers and an organ grinder whose monkey, dressed in a gypsy vest, was perched on his hat eating an apple. The lab was in a townhouse, and still appeared to be an innocent residence, judging from the ivy planters on the porch and the absence of a sign over the cut-glass door. No sense frightening the populace.

I pushed through the door, which rang several horse bells hanging on the knob. A rotund clerk with Ben Franklin spectacles balanced on the tip of his nose said cheerily, "I thought that last batch would probably put you into potter's field, Woodrow."

"Nothing to it, Clement. I sat on the donnicker for a couple hours, is all."

He nodded at the door to the clinic. "You can join the line."

A swinging door brought me to the lab. Four other regular army soldiers were waiting near a table in the center of the room. All were assigned to the Blues, sent here by Sergeant Purdy. The room was painted in butcher-shop white. Glass beakers, retorts, and specimen bottles lined shelves on the walls. On the table were glass jars filled with sponges, swabs, and tongue depressors. Three black microscopes were mounted on a side table near gas lamps hung from the wall on a steel arm and swivel. Open mahogany cases near each microscope contained glass slides, filed in perfect, glittering rows. On yet another table were mortars, pestles, crockery canisters and a balance scale. In one corner was an open armoire fitted with narrow racks, holding at least two hundred small bottles, most topped with droppers. In another corner was a wood cooler with sawdust insulation, the middle cabinet for specimens and the top and bottom cabinets for block ice. A thermometer on the middle door indicated the temperature within. Next to the cooler was a copper tub in which was a centrifuge, motionless at the moment, but often powered by a bicycle on a stand, connected to gearing under the tub by a chain. On a few fortunate occasions, Dr. Aldrich ordered me to pedal the bicycle and make the centrifuge spin. This weren't one of them occasions.

The doctor stood across the table from the volunteers. He waved me into line. I nodded at the soldiers, recognizing these unfortunates from prior sessions. They were dressed in street clothes, same as me. I hadn't worn an army uniform since arriving in New York.

Aldrich's face appeared hewn out of a log with an ax, at odds with his highbrow profession. Knobby cheekbones, a nose with a thirty-degree bend, and an unnaturally square jaw. I'd never seen him without a pencil stuck behind an ear. The skin on the right side of his neck was a purple crepe. Several years before, one of his experiments had blown up on him. Served him right.

He brought his gaze up to find me. "Shut eye, gashes above your brows, fingers like blood sausages. Corporal Lowe, how am I supposed to quantify my experiments when you always come to the lab looking like a terminal case."

The others laughed nervously.

I didn't reply.

Dr. Aldrich weren't a bad sort, except that he was intent on poisoning us to death. He said, "Gentlemen, you'll be happy to hear there'll be no stickers today."

That's what hypodermic needles were called back then. He reached into a drawer to produce five petri plates. Each contained several table-spoons of paste resembling mashed potatoes. Would God they were potatoes. One at a time he slid a petri dish in front of us, placing each one exactly six inches from our belt buckle, as if that distance had something to do with his test. From another drawer he pulled five spoons.

He glanced at an August Junghans clock on the wall. "Let's wait two minutes until the top of the hour. Easier bookkeeping for me."

I stared dolefully at the paste in my dish. Ever since Louis Pasteur had administered the first successful rabies vaccine five years before, scientists and physicians around the world had been racing for their own fame and fortune with petri dishes. A Russian named Melchinikoff had been first to describe phagocytosis, a part of the body's defense system. The

Japanese doctor Shibasaburo Kitasato had just a few months before become the first to isolate the tetanus bug. Word had it that an Englishman named Ross was trying to find the agent that spread malaria. And over in Brooklyn, the Hoagland Laboratory had opened the prior year to study bacteria. Dr. Aldrich viewed Hoagland as a mortal enemy, to be defeated in discovery at all costs. My lab mates and I were part of that cost. The doctor had convinced the New York National Guard that by providing human cultures for his experiments, a portion of his imminent glory would be reflected onto the guard. I, regular army, was swept up in it.

This was perhaps my fortieth visit to the Aldrich Laboratory. I had been stuck by needles, had the skin on my arm scraped open and then rubbed with a stinging swab of something, swallowed scores of pills, had drops put into my eyes, peed into dozens of beakers, sniffed some green speckles up my nose, and had a suppository shoved up where the light of day had never before shined.

What were the purposes of all these experiments? Dr. Aldrich never told us, before or after. I only know that they periodically made me vomit, urinate blue water, cough until my ribcage ached, scratch my head until clumps of hair fell out, and bleed from my gums. At times the experiments clogged my nose with mucus, left an orange sheen on my tongue, turned the whites of my eyes red, and left gin-roses all over my face. And try facing Junior Puloski in a bareknuckle match when your scrotum itches so bad you want to straddle a fence post. I was so distracted it took Junior just twelve minutes to send me down for good.

Clement at the front desk told me once that Dr. Aldrich had spent a year trying to solve the mystery of cattle fever, a disease that decimates cattle herds in the south. Aldrich had us eating a tick mash every week for a month, the little critters crushed by Clement himself in the mortar. I never asked why soldiers were fed pulped ticks when it was cows he was trying to cure. Maybe I should have.

Tick mash tastes exactly like goose liver pate, by the way. Maybe a bit more grainy.

Dr. Aldrich said, "All right, gentlemen, it's time to eat your samples."

"What is it?" asked one of the soldiers, futilely, we all knew.

"Now, now, my troops. Let's just pretend it's plum pudding, and we'll all be happy."

I stirred my mash with my fingers, hoping to make it look more appetizing. It didn't work. So I ladled up the mash with my spoon and swallowed it, my gag reflex working against me.

"Tastes like chicken," one of us said.

"It is indeed chicken broth," Aldrich replied. Then he added with a wily grin, "At least, ninety-nine percent of it is. These are precisely measured doses, gentlemen. So please lick your dishes clean."

A revelation as to your place in this world occurs when you are forced to clean out a petri dish with your tongue.

We scooted our empty dishes across the table to the doctor. As he always did, Aldrich passed us sheets of paper, on which were listed about a hundred different symptoms we were to watch for. Things like, "Pustules under armpits," and "Skin flaking off." We were supposed to check off anything that happened to us, and give the date and time. The bottom one was, "Death," although I don't know how we were expected to check off that one.

"Now remember," the doctor advised in his eternally optimistic voice, "no alcohol of any sort for two days. No wine, whiskey, or beer."

I mouthed it along with him, I'd heard it so often. The troops and I left Clement at the desk and went directly across the street to Rudy's Saloon for several short beers to get the taste out of our mouths.

My mind was quite active after these sessions at the laboratory, searching for discolorations, boils, bleeding, dizziness, and anything else Dr. Aldrich might have inflicted on me. This time, I couldn't even dream up anything. I felt fine, and I appeared at the Malcolms' at two o'clock that afternoon as ordered.

SIX

Salad Puffs

THE MALCOLMS' HOME was on the northwest corner of Fifth Avenue and Thirty-fourth Street, across the street from John Jacob Astor's, and was known by those who didn't live in it as the Mausoleum. Malcolm had arrived in New York in 1860 from Belfast with a Trinity College degree and one hundred dollars, and had transformed them dollars into a vast merchandising and real estate fortune. His home was a palazzo of white marble, with white columns, octagonal windows, and green marble on the stairway from the avenue to the brass-fronted doors.

Fifth Avenue society had ignored the Malcolms until the Malcolms' eldest son married one of the Astors, and from then on the merchandizer was accepted, but only reluctantly. So Teddy—to whom even Mrs. Astor would return a wave when their carriages passed in Grand Army Plaza— had been inside the mausoleum before, and with much amusement had described to me the three drawing rooms hung with Vermeers and Rembrandts, the pillared library filled floor to ceiling with the rarest of Moroccan leatherbound editions, and the gold faucets in the bathrooms. I don't know why Teddy found all this humorous, but he did.

I knew better than to ring at the Fifth Avenue entrance. I walked along the carriage concourse to the kitchen entry. The door was open. I spit into my hands to slick back my short hair, then stepped inside.

The Malcolms' kitchen, pantry, wine room, silver and china rooms, and ice room were in an uproar, with butlers, cooks, and maids running about, and with the loaned servants adding to the confusion. I stood to one side for a moment, watching domestics rushing here and there with wine goblets and coffee cups, cleaning lettuce at the sinks, chipping ice from blocks, inserting pimentos into olives, stirring sauce at the bank of stoves, and a host of other activities, all accompanied by orders shouted above the din.

The caterer's defection seemed to have left the place in turmoil. But after a moment, a chain of command became apparent. The head cook, a woman in a tomato-stained white apron and a blue bandanna, should have been a cavalry quartermaster. She stood in the center of the kitchen, near a rack of ladles and pans, and issued a stream of orders with rhythm and speed, pointing at cooks and servants as she did so. Her orders were obeyed with alacrity. Through the swinging doors to the vast dining room, I glimpsed a fellow in a black coat, who I would learn was the main floor butler. He, too, was quickly giving out orders regarding the place settings and champagne stations. When he had a moment, he turned to the five men next to him—loaners, I guessed—and instructed them on their roles as valets, where to take the carriages, and the signals for bringing them back. I wondered for a moment why Mrs. Malcolm was not directing this production, until I realized she would be at the wedding, undoubtedly faint with worry as to how her domestics were faring at home preparing the reception. I concluded she needn't have worried. Things would be ready.

Bamie's cook, Pearl, was at a side table, hunched over a tray. She waved me over. She was Irish, like me, but with black hair and eyebrows that grew together over her nose.

"Woodrow, you can help me."

"I don't know anything about cooking."

"You were a cook in the cavalry for six years."

"Just like I said."

"All you have to do is stuff pastries."

She pointed at the even rows of puff pastries, hundreds of golden flaky shells. In front of her was a glass mixing bowl two feet across. "I'll cut them in half, then you put a teaspoon of mix into them."

"What is it?"

"Chunks of chicken, mayonnaise, halved grapes, pine nuts, bits of pineapple, some spices. Molly, the Malcolms' cook, calls them chicken salad puffs."

I did as told, standing over the bowl and daubing chicken salad into the shells until my back hurt. I ate a few of them salad puffs and they weren't bad. Then I sliced carrots for a while. Just before the reception was to begin, the butler helped me find a coat with tails, a white shirt, trousers, and black brogans from a horse cart at the side entrance. The cart had CENTRAL RENTALS painted on its canvas flaps.

By three-thirty, when the guests began appearing, the Malcolm residence was in remarkable order. Flowers on every horizontal surface, champagne chilled, Burgundy opened and aired, tables glimmering with silver and crystal, a sixteen-piece orchestra on a dais in the ballroom. The Vanderbilts arrived, then the Harrimans, the Dodges, the Iselins, Mrs. Stuyvesant Fish, the Whitneys and Rockefellers, Gov. Levi Morton and his wife, and the two feuding branches of the Astor family. Teddy came with Edith. Even then, Teddy had the habit of pausing just inside any door so all eyes in the room could find him. Bruce Twig-Smathers almost bumped into him from behind. Teddy immediately began pumping hands, working the room as if it were Tammany Hall. He greeted Ohio congressman William McKinley, and they leaned together, foreheads almost touching, to do some plotting, I presumed. Most everybody carried a glass. There was a lot of liquor in the room, like snuff at a wake.

The Boston contingent included the Wallaces, Marchands, and MacMillans. I don't have to tell you I had prayed since early that morning that the Balfours would be guests. I strolled from room to room, carrying champagne flutes on a silver platter at ear level, frequently glancing out the windows at the arriving carriages, looking for Amy Balfour.

Let me pause in all this excitement to mention my state of mind. You would think that seven years in Indian country wearing blue would have leached away my ardor for that girl. Or that my visits to the army and New York's rings to be beat about the head and shoulders by some of the country's best prizefighters would have knocked some sense into me. You'd be wrong on both counts. I admitted to myself then, and I'll confess to you now, that my mind had seized on her in an unhealthy manner. A normal heart does not love a girl having seen her once, then not again for ten years. I do not have a normal heart. The only thing that had prevented me from trying to see her during my trips to Boston was the sure knowledge that I'd be arrested and sent to prison should I be found anywhere in her vicinity.

Now, I can tell, with you over there playing pocket pool for two hours straight, that you've been waiting for me to graphically describe my first introduction to the pleasures of the opposite sex, in the current fashion of tell-all memoirs. You've been hoping for some lurid account of me using my considerable powers of persuasion to seduce some sweet young lady. Too bad for you. Today, when morals are looser than cow lips, it'll be hard for you to believe that at age twenty-five, I had never made love to a woman. This sorry state of affairs was because I refused to separate romance from taking my clothes off in a woman's presence. This pleasure lay in the future, and when I get there, don't worry, I'll set it out in such detail that it'll make you bleed, just like it did me.

When I say I'd never made love, I'm not counting whores, of course. I'd had plenty of honey on my stinger from them. What cavalry trooper hasn't? I'm talking about making love. That was still in the days ahead.

The butler ordered me to switch from champagne service to passing out hors d'oeuvres. I was offering Pearl's chicken salad puffs to Mrs. Reed Sumpter when the Balfours did arrive, Dickie walking through the Malcolms' door like he owned the place, same smirk I remembered at my trial. He was followed by his parents. Lewis Balfour wore the disagreeable expression of one wearing tight shoes. They were greeted warmly at the door by Mrs. Malcolm. I arched my neck, looking for Amy. In the process, I jerked the tray, jamming a chicken puff into Mr. Sumpter's hand. He grunted, and loudly licked the paste off his finger, earning a sharp look from his wife.

I served more of the pastries, staying near the main door, until the bride made her entrance, to a hearty round of applause.

It was Amy Balfour.

That she would be the bride from Boston just hadn't occurred to me until that moment, though it may have to you, when she paused at the door to gather her tribute, her bridal train trailing after her, attended by two girls. The door's beveled glass caught the sun and scattered it in a glittering array. The diamonds of her bridal tiara also sparked light, and the hundreds of pearls sewn into the organdy and lace of her dress flickered and opalesced. She was caught in this flashing wash of radiance, throwing off shafts of light, illuminating the room and blinding me. I have no recollection of her groom, the Malcolm lad named John who arrived with her.

At that instant, I would have expected my heart to miss a stroke. Instead, my bowels lurched left and right, then rolled over with a gurgle that should have been heard throughout the Malcolm residence were not Amy at that moment receiving her applause. I put the tray of chicken pastries onto an end table and glanced around for the bathroom, knowing an emergency when I felt one. I double-timed through the crowd into the hall and found the main-floor powder room, just in time.

My insides felt as if someone was using a plumber's helper to evacuate me. I was on the pot—actually, one of the new toilets invented by Thomas Crapper, with a pull-chain—for ten full minutes before I could stand aright, and by then I had figured out that Dr. Aldrich had struck again. Whatever he had me eat out of the petri plate had turned my insides into a burbling swamp. I'm glad God made assholes elastic, or I might've broke myself in two on that toilet, such was the volume.

When I left the powder room I was wan and sweating. I picked up my tray again, but swayed so much the Malcolms' butler took me aside and accused me of drinking. He stuck his nose in my face but couldn't smell no alcohol so he let me return to my duties, but he continued to eye me.

During the next hour, Amy was hidden from my view by the reception line. Just as well, because I lurched into the toilet three times, my bowels knotting in pneumatic spasms. When she started to mingle, I sidled near her for a look, got close enough so that she took a pastry from my tray.

In my ten-year absence from her, she had left her girlhood behind and had matured into a woman of startling beauty, the haughty, elegant lines of her face contrasting with her wild red-and-blue coloring. Back then, a woman's beauty was measured in part by the shock-white of her skin, parasols and hats and powder keeping it that way. Not so with Amy. She did nothing to mute her furious coloring. Her skin was still a pink and red palette, a gaudy mix of colors, with half a pound of darker freckles cast onto her. Her teeth dazzled as if carved of white ice. Her face fit perfectly into my memory of her, elegant but not severe, displaying her wisdom and humor. Her mouth had twin peaks and a full lower lip. Her cornflower blue eyes granted all whom they fell upon a moment of treasured familiarity. Under the gems and lace of her tiara and veil, her red-and-gold hair seemed ablaze.

I might have said something to her then, but from my left came a rumble, as if a gold miner had opened his sluice. Dickie Balfour stood next to a fern stand, his eyes wide, and his hands trembling. That cave-chested weasel had not recognized me, and as yet he had been spared me dragging him outside and stuffing him down a storm drain as I had promised myself years before to do the first time I saw him again.

Dickie's bowels again flopped over, and he sprinted toward the powder room, brushing Mrs. Astor's arm and spilling champagne on her dove-colored satin dress. Probably drank too much, I thought. Serves him right, making a spectacle of himself. Dickie almost collided with Mr. Malcolm, who was also rushing toward the toilet. Teddy Roosevelt whispered a few words to Mrs. Malcolm, and she pointed up the spiral staircase, and Teddy ran up it, moving as quickly as I'd ever seen him.

Mrs. Malcolm wore a mauve silk dress, braided and bugled with sleeves to match. She hesitated only a moment before following Teddy up the stairs, the sound of her roiling innards trailing after her. Bruce Twig-Smathers lowered himself into a Louix XVI chair, his hand between his knees, and began to moan. Almost doubled over in distress, Lewis Balfour could not wait in the powder room line, so he loudly demanded of the butler the location of the servants' water closet. He reeled away in that direction, through the kitchen. Dickie Balfour reappeared, weaving and blank-eyed, took a few steps toward the bar, but his eyes widened and he spun around and took off again for the powder room. I heard scuffling in the line, harsh words just short of a fistfight, and a melee was prevented only by the participants being unable to stand upright.

One by one, the guests sped away in search of toilets. Amy Balfour watched in horror as her grand reception disintegrated before her eyes. Mrs. Malcolm reappeared, and Amy shouted something unladylike at her. Amy turned to her new husband. I couldn't hear the conversation, but it appeared to be one-sided. The groom seemed to grow smaller with her scolding. He shrugged his shoulders, as puzzled and frightened as everyone else.

Suddenly Amy's face opened. She grabbed at her stomach, then swayed into her husband. "Oh my God, I'm going to be sick. John, help me."

The groom replied, "Tell me what to do, darling."

Amy's face blanched. She hobbled toward the hall, toward the line of knee-locked, reverberant guests anxiously waiting their turns, a few angrily pounding on the powder room door. I put down my tray and followed her, still weak myself.

"Get out of my way," she demanded. "I can't wait."

One of the men in line groaned, "I got here first. I'm going to die if I don't get in there."

The others in line shook their heads miserably, not about to give up their spots, some jumping up and down trying to contain themselves.

"This is my wedding day," she snapped through clenched teeth. "Get out of my way."

They refused to move. The first man in line kicked the powder room door. "Come on out of there."

Amy leaned into the wall, tilting a framed hunting club painting.

I came to her rescue, not for the first time in my life. I grabbed her arm and dragged her to the head of the whimpering line. I balled my hand, drew back, and shot my fist through the door just above the knob. Wood cracked and burst. I shoved my hand into the powder room through the hole in the door. A shout of outrage came from within. I twisted my hand around and undid the lock from inside, then yanked open the door.

Dickie Balfour sat there with pin-striped pants down around his ankles. His eyes were crazed with fear and humiliation. I yanked him by the collar, swung him around and threw him at the waiting line, toppling two of the guests. Dickie hit the floor cursing.

I shoved the bride into the powder room, stuffed her train in behind her, and slammed the door shut. I stood in front of the door, my arms crossed menacingly in front of me. The guests, heretofore too polite or indifferent to mention the bruises and cuts on my face, now knew what they meant. They didn't protest, only staggered away to find other commodes.

For five minutes I listened through the door to my love making earthy sounds I would never have dreamed her capable of. Finally she emerged, weaving, mouth hanging open. She brushed by me, muttering imprecations about her new mother-in-law, who had arranged the food. She didn't even see me. Her hair brushed my nose. She smelled of lilacs.

It was only then that I made the connection. The mad doctor Aldrich had made me take in hand and lap up some paste filled with gut-blasting hidden bugs, and I had passed them along when I stuffed the pastry shells with chicken salad, then served the tasty treats to the guests. No doubt had the stuff under my fingernails. And I had spit into my hands to brush back my hair. Years later I ran into Clement, Dr. Aldrich's assistant, who told me the doctor had been searching for the secrets of salmonella, the bacteria that lurks in mayonnaise.

I figured I had done enough, so I changed into my street clothes in a third-floor maid's quarters set aside for that purpose, then headed for the door, passing Teddy Roosevelt's elegant wife, Edith, bent over a planter, losing her hors d'oeuvres. Near the bar, Amy and Mrs. Malcolm were craned toward each other, gesturing wildly. Most of the guests had vanished.

Now if you doubt my account of Amy Balfour Malcolm's calamitous wedding reception, all you need do is check the society and business pages of the *New York Times* for the week following the wedding, like I did many years later at the New York Public Library. The Malcolms' were able to keep an account of the disaster out of the paper, but you will find a brief notice that Mrs. Astor's garden party the following Tuesday for the visiting French ambassador has been rescheduled. Other small articles state that the boards of directors of the New York Union Bank, the Chesapeake Railway, the Morgan Bank and numerous other corporations were postponed. Most of them directors had attended the reception. Mrs. Whitney's gala dinner auction to benefit the public library's building fund, scheduled for that Wednesday, was also postponed, to be rescheduled at a later date. Josephine Wanamaker's coming-out party for her daughter was put off for a week. And on and on. New York's social swirl and board-room business shuddered to a stop for much of a week.

My hand was on the front door's brass handle when Teddy called out, "Woodrow, we've got something of an emergency here."

I turned to see Teddy with his arms supporting Twig-Smathers, helping him get to the door. The Englishman's face was a mottled yellow and white. His dress shirt was stained. His hand was at his stomach and his eyes were rolling in his head.

Teddy passed him to me. "Take him to the Trans-Atlantic dock, two slips this side of the Camden and Amboy dock, near the Battery. Put him on the *India Courser*. His trunks are already on board. Use my carriage."

I braced Twig-Smathers, trying to get his feet under him, but his legs were weak so I hefted him like a bride.

Teddy held open the door, an effort, because he was still hobbling from the effects of the chicken salad. He said, "So long, Twiggy. Delighted with your stay."

Twig-Smathers made some whimpered lamentation. The Roosevelt carriage was already in the drive. Hurst, the chauffeur, made a motion to climb down to help, but I waved him away, pulled open the door and gently placed Twig-Smathers on the seat. I climbed in next to him.

We had to stop briefly at the Albemarle and the Brevoort Hotels so Twig-Smathers could use their lobby privies, me rushing in and out, dragging him along. We rattled by the Hay Scales and oyster boats and the ferry terminal to Brooklyn, Long Island City, and Hunter's Point, and finally reached the Trans-Atlantic dock.

As I pulled Twig-Smathers from the carriage, the *India Courser*'s steam whistle sent forth one long and two short blasts. The ship was of British registry, and had two smokestacks and a frost-white hull. Near the bow was painted the company's logo, a blue "I" inside a blue circle. Hundreds of travelers lined the ship's safety rail, waving to friends and relatives on the dock.

I lugged Twig-Smathers to the gangway and gave the steward his name. The steward told me his cabin number, and when I started the climb up the gangway with the Englishman, the steward said, "Sir, the gangway is about to be taken away and the lines slipped."

"I'll drop him in his berth and come straight back."

"Sir, wait . . ." the steward called after me.

Twig-Smathers was recovering, taking more of his weight on his own legs. I guided him up the steep gangway and asked the deck officer at the top the location of cabin twenty-one.

He glanced nervously at the deck below and said, "There's no time—"

"Just tell me," I ordered.

"This side, just aft of the lifeboat."

As I brought him along, the Englishman gulped, "I can't thank you enough, Woodrow. Christ, my bloody bowels feel like—"

The ship's steam whistle cut him off with a shrill scream that must have been heard in Jersey. We passed a life-jacket locker and a brass funnel. On our left were the offices and warehouses of the Battery. I knew I had to hurry.

Twig-Smathers abruptly bent over and groaned, "It's back. Christ, don't bounce me around."

He lowered himself to the deck and leaned against the stanchions supporting the safety rail. His mouth wagged open. Off the seaward quarter, a tugboat whistled, ready to assist the *India Courser* away from the pier.

I said, "You can get to your cabin on your own, sir. I've got to get off this boat."

Twig-Smathers rolled onto his stomach, pushed his head through the stanchions—a tight fit, as they creased his ears back—and let loose with more of my chicken surprise. On and on he went, gripping a post on either side of him like a jailbird, his supine body wracked with convulsions as he stained the gleaming white hull below.

"Oh, God," he moaned, finally empty.

"So long, sir."

Twig-Smathers pulled his head from between the posts. That is, he tried to. The stanchions bumped against the back of his ears.

"Woodrow?" he asked, as if I were pinning him there.

I glanced over the rail. Below, deckhands were on both sides of the gangway, about to roll it away from the ship. "I'm off, sir."

The Englishman tried again, banging his head against the wood posts. He bunched up his face, gripped the stanchions until his knuckles were white, and banged his head against them again. No luck.

"Woodrow, help me."

I kneeled to the deck, grabbed his shoulders, and yanked him back. He yelled with pain, still stuck.

"I've got to get off this boat, sir."

"Woodrow, you cannot leave me like this," he said from between the posts. "I absolutely forbid it."

Looking back, I wish I would have replied, "I don't take orders from the folks who hung Nathan Hale. So long." Instead, with the servile instincts of one who had obeyed stern voices all his life, I rushed into a hatchway and down a ladder, roughly, I guessed, toward the engine room. Somewhere in one of the companionways passengers don't normally visit I found an oiler, who, when I explained the difficulty, quickly located a tin of grease, and followed me topside.

The oiler and I lathered Twig-Smathers' neck and ears and head with grease, Twig-Smathers muttering about having never been so humiliated, and the oiler adding to his abasement by chuckling all the while. We finally nudged Twig-Smathers's head through the posts, and he was none too grateful.

But when I finally had the chance to look up, the *India Courser* was several hundred yards to sea, leaving its tugs behind, its engines gaining the deep throb of three-quarter throttle. Above, black coal smoke poured from the stacks. On the Trans-Atlantic dock, people waved the ship goodbye.

Without a word, Twig-Smathers left for his cabin to wash away the grease. The oiler returned to work.

I stayed at that rail another two hours as the ship passed Ellis Island and the new Statue of Liberty. The buildings of New York became smaller and smaller, and the *India Courser* steamed through the narrows to sea.

Almost ten years would pass before I saw America again.

SEVEN

Four Nines

I GOT BEAT up by an Englishwoman on that ship. By that time my face didn't have much space left for scars but it received some fresh ones anyway.

We were four days out of New York, sailing east at a steady fifteen knots. The *India Courser* was a new ship, one of the first steamers with twin screws, which meant that the chance of a shaft breakdown was eliminated, and so the vessel didn't need masts for back-up propulsion. Earlier liners had the profile of an upside-down bathtub, all hull and no superstructure, but without masts and sails the *India Courser* weren't limited to one deck. It had three above the main deck, so the amount of public rooms was enormous compared to earlier ships. The liner was 600 feet long, and its two stacks were the largest ever seen at sea, twenty feet in diameter, with the tops 130 feet above the waterline. The vessel accommodated 600 first-class passengers, 400 second, and 1,000 in steerage. I slept in steerage but worked in first class.

And first class it was. That night I was standing against a tapestry that depicted three rosy, corpulent women who had somehow lost most of their clothing while dancing around a fig tree. My station was behind Bruce Twig-Smathers as he sat at a poker table. He had made me his butler for the journey, a two-bit job I took because I had found myself on the ship without a single frogskin in my pocket. I stood more or less at attention, waiting to be summoned to fire Twig-Smathers's cigar, replenish his brandy and such like. He had told me he needed a butler for appearances in the *India Courser*'s grand saloon and gentleman's smoking room, but he said I wouldn't be called on to do much. What claptrap that turned out to be.

I wouldn't have minded butler duty so much if Twig-Smathers didn't insist that my uniform each day match his cravat. Today's tie was green, so I stood there in a monkey suit made of bottle green broadcloth. I don't know where the rich get these ideas. Twenty or twenty-five other butlers stood around, holding up the walls.

"And I'll raise you fifty," Twig-Smathers said in his club accent, pushing two orange chips to the center of the round table.

"I'll be damned if I can let that pass," replied the big man opposite Twig-Smathers, meeting the wager with two chips.

The big man was Diamond Jim Brady, and let me say something about Diamond Jim. To all appearances, I was a serf on that boat, yet Diamond Jim had taken the time to befriend me, and would remain a friend until he died almost thirty years later. He was the only man I ever met who didn't have an enemy, not one soul on this earth who wished him harm, and I can't think of anything better to say about a person. He made pals like Carter made liver pills, a lot of them.

Teddy Roosevelt and John L. Sullivan and Diamond Jim Brady all knew each other, by the way. When John L. was visiting town and drunk and tearing up a saloon, and Teddy as police commissioner didn't want to risk the eight cops who would have been required to subdue John L., Teddy would call on Diamond Jim, who was the only man in the city who could handle John L. in his cups. Jim would quickly travel to the saloon and persuade the staggering, dangerous boxer to follow him home to bed. Folks purely liked Diamond Jim.

Diamond Jim threw in more chips. "And I'll raise you another fifty." These were dollars they were talking about, not cents. He reached into a box of Huyler's chocolate-covered nuts he always kept at his elbow and threw eight or ten of them into his mouth. Every waking moment he kept a box of Huyler's near his elbow. Or there'd be Maillard's coconut creams or Allegrettie's chocolates. He ate ten pounds of candy a day.

"Do not think you can frighten me away, gentlemen," said the lady at the table, delicately adding her chips to the pile. She had an accent like Twig-Smathers's.

Despite the dazzle of Jim Brady's jewelry, I could scarcely take my cheaters off the English lady. First, of course, was her effrontery in being in the men's smoking room. This was still a time when men and women separated into different rooms after dinner, the men to smoke cigars and chew doodoges and drink brandy, the women to do whatever they did, me never having been in a women's sitting room. But here she was, an elbow on the table, fingering a pile of chips, looking down her thin nose at Diamond Jim and Twig-Smathers and the other player, a fellow named Bertrum McCook, president of the Glasgow-Northern Rail Line who Diamond Jim was doing business with while they played poker, though McCook didn't know it yet. Later that evening Jim would sell the Scot—who would by then view Jim as one of his closest friends— fifteen thousand dollars' worth of leather palace-car chairs.

Lady Elizabeth Coleridge had spent three months in the colonies, visiting the Astors in New York, the Cabots and Lowells in Boston, and the Palmers in Savannah. Her beauty and wealth and lineage were such that no doors were closed to her, despite the pool of scandal that always swirled around her. The skin of Lady Elizabeth's face was milk white, a color I had never seen before, so pale that tiny blue blood vessels were visible underneath. Her skin would have suggested frailty were it not for her other colors. Framing her face were fierce curls, so black they shone like obsidian and reflected light from the chandelier's gas lamps. Her eyes were ice blue and always amused. Her painted mouth was deep red, and often pursed with humor. Her cheekbones were so high they threw pale shadows on the skin below. Her chin was delicately notched. When she smiled she revealed teeth of such brilliant white they must have been lit from within, as if Mr. Edison had illuminated them like he was lighting up everything else. She had a swan's neck, and her head was always perched on it coquettishly, an angle that suggested both an invitation and innocence, a bit at odds with the faint lines around her eyes that showed she had lived some. Lived a lot, I was soon to learn. Lady Elizabeth's fingernails were raptorial, each an inch long and painted blood red. She wore a pearl dog collar around her neck and a diamond the size of a chestnut on her right hand.

And she was frilled out. Her gown was vibrant red silk, the color of her mouth and nails. The fabric was a lacy ribbon knit, and the skirt had ten gores, each with silk braids anchoring red silk taffeta squares to the lower flare. Shirred chiffon, also red, made up the vest front. The bodice was trimmed with silk scroll braiding and latticed knots. Silk appliqués decorated the sleeves. All was red except a black ruffled taffeta petticoat that could be glimpsed when she moved her legs, her black beaded reticule that was on her lap, and a black plume fan that lay on the table next to her brandy snifter. She was black and red and white, shimmering with allure and intrigue.

I thought I saw her glance at me above her diamond ring. I looked over my shoulder. She might have been trying to see the chubby ladies do their jig around the fig tree.

The Scot met the wager, and Diamond Jim was the first to lay down his cards. He smiled modestly and raked in the chips. Lady Elizabeth dealt the next hand, five cards to each player. She said, "Shall we raise the ante? Say, double it? My mind strays with these small sums."

"I'm just along for the ride," Diamond Jim said, dropping a hundred dollars into the pot.

Bertrum McCook's hand hesitated. He glanced at his dwindling reserve, then slowly pushed four chips forward with his fingertips.

After Twig-Smathers threw in his ante, Lady Elizabeth took the cards from Diamond Jim, declined her turn to deal with a lovely curwhibble and slid them along the felt table cloth to Twig-Smathers. A curwhibble? That's old Irish for a little gesture. Twig-Smathers shuffled diligently and dealt the cards. Judging from Lady Elizabeth's face, every hand she received was a delight. The players began the round of wagering.

I rocked back on my heels and surveyed the saloon. Back then it was fashionable for a home to have a Turkish corner, sometimes called a cozy corner, and the *India Courser*'s smoking room was decorated like a cozy corner, bursting with burnt-leather pillows and cushions, silver and pearl inlaid taborets and gilded rolling pins. Katzatz rugs covered the deck and much of the walls. Gold-plated hookahs were near the spittoons. The ceiling and trim were American walnut and satinwood, and were imbedded with faceted red, green and orange glass resembling fist-sized jewels. Four Bengal tiger skins lay on top of the rugs and another two tigers— these upright, stuffed and snarling—guarded the room's main entrance. Leather on the chairs was dyed scarlet and the armrests were inlaid with fire opals. Fern stands were made of Santo Domingo mahogany and encrusted with tiny chips of glass made to look like emeralds, or maybe they *were* emeralds. The ferns' fronds swung idly with the ship's roll. Umbrella stands were made of elephant feet. Waiters wore turbans and billowy pants. Stuffed cobras were coiled around champagne buckets. Tassels hung from everything. If this was Turkey I was going to avoid the place.

The smoking room accommodated 130 first-class passengers, and almost every chair was occupied by a smoker working away on a six- or eight-inch Havana, producing fumes like a smelter. Cigar smoke hid the far walls, and was so thick that passers-by materialized then vanished again in the haze. A gleaming black Bösendorfer piano was in a corner, played quite loudly to override the bass rumble of the triple-expansion steam engines. Overhead a crystal dome glittered yellow with moon-light. Ordinarily the gentlemen sitting around in their rolled and pleated leather chairs would be reading magazines or idly chatting or playing cards. But Lady Elizabeth occupied all their attention this night. They rested their eyes on her, nodding approvingly, using her as a restorative, their daydreams abetted by the haze of silver smoke that lingered in the room, isolating and softening her.

Twig-Smathers's stack of chips had been dwindling steadily. "I'm in," he said, meeting Lady Elizabeth's raise.

The Scot was also in, and so was Diamond Jim. I detected a slight shift in the amiable chatter at the table. Diamond Jim's favorite games were faro and pinochle, and he never claimed an expertise at poker. In fact, he didn't like gambling much, despite spending many an evening at the 818, the gambling parlor at that address on Broadway. He liked the joint not for its cards or dice but for the free food. So Jim's poker face and poker voice might not have been as steady as he would have liked. Nor were Twig-Smathers's. Two people at the table had exceptional hands, or maybe three. I casually stepped forward to glance over Twig-Smathers's shoulder. Three aces, a king and a three. They bet around again, bumping each other's raises, then took another draw. There were already four hundred dollars in the pot. And remember, this was when a dollar was a dollar, not something you might paper your washroom with, like today.

When the betting came around to Twig-Smathers no chips remained in front of him. He cleared his throat in the phlegmy British way. "I'm afraid you find me a bit embarrassed."

"You can fold," McCook said.

Twig-Smathers knew better than to look at his cards. "I would like to play this hand."

The Scot clinked his chips together. "I'd like you to play your cards, too. Reach for your wallet."

Again Twig-Smathers made an appropriate sound in his throat. "My wallet seems to be thinner than I would like."

Diamond Jim said loudly, "I'll be damned if a friend of mine goes begging at the card table." He started to gather up a fistful of chips to push to Twig-Smathers, but discovered his pile was smaller than he thought. He raised an arm to summon the purser's representative but Lady Elizabeth gently touched Jim's wrist.

She said sweetly, "I'll take care of it, Mr. Brady." She passed a stack to Twig-Smathers.

"Well, no lady is going to be more generous than Jim Brady," said Jim Brady, again attempting to cast chips in Twig-Smathers's direction.

She was polite but insistent. "Twiggy is a countryman, after all, Mr. Brady. If he must prostrate himself before someone for a loan it should be me." She turned to Twig-Smathers. "Your credit is good with me, Twiggy."

Again, I swear, that English noblewoman's eyes found mine. This time she took her time, running her orbs up and down. I began to feel like a bug under one of Dr. Aldrich's microscopes.

"You are as gracious as the reputation that precedes you suggests, milady." Twig-Smathers dropped chips into the pile. "I'm in."

"I'll be damned if I'm going to let someone operating on credit run me out of the play." Diamond Jim's reserve of chips was getting smaller at about the same pace as Twig-Smathers's.

Jim's mahogany hair was parted in the middle and swept to both sides. His mustache covered narrow lips. His pinprick eyes were both shrewd and avuncular. He always had his hand out, ready to shake a hand or take the dinner bill or open the champagne to pour for you. Over the years I have heard his weight guessed at 350 pounds, 420 pounds, even 510 pounds. I saw him get on a scale at his Manhattan club once, and he weighed in at 240, which was his tonnage all his adult life.

Diamond Jim was no industrialist, no robber baron or land tycoon, and he didn't inherit a dime from his folks. But Diamond Jim was the greatest salesman this country ever produced. He began by selling railroad gear—everything from gandy dancers' shovels to replacement wheel bearings—and he sold successfully because he made everybody like him and remember him. He made most of his fortune selling the Fox Truck, a rail-car undercarriage made of pressed steel and manufactured by the Leeds Forge Company. Its English inventor, Sampson Fox, couldn't sell a one of them when he visited the United States, but then he gave Jim Brady a thirty-three percent commission on the trucks. Diamond Jim soon convinced the Pennsylvania Railroad that the Fox Truck allowed a rail car to carry twice its previous load. He then sold the trucks to the Pennsy and every other railroad in the country, and was soon worth twelve million dollars. That's when a dollar was a dollar, not something you'd use to wipe the oil off your automobile's dipstick, like today. Did I say that already?

Diamond Jim was known more for his jewelry than his girth. Back then all traveling salesmen wore a few loud jewels, most particularly a diamond pinkie ring, the mark of a successful drummer. Diamond Jim was no dandy, nothing like Berry Wall or Bob Hilliard, two New Yorkers who spent their lives feuding over the title "King of the Dudes." For Diamond Jim, clothes were mostly to hang his jewelry on. That night Diamond Jim had tossed onto a neighboring chair his high silk hat and Inverness cape, revealing his glittering, shimmering self beneath. He threw reflected light around like a crystal ball twirling from a dance-hall ceiling.

I gazed in stupefaction at his assemblage: a six-carat pinkie, a three-carat stone mounted in the ferrule of his cane, a belt buckle containing 546 diamonds (I was to learn later), a tie clip with thirty diamonds, a watch chain with that same number, two three-carat shirt studs, five two-carat shirt buttons, five two-carat vest buttons, two two-carat collar buttons, an eyeglass case covered with forty diamonds, a pocketbook clasp with two dozen diamonds, a pencil with ten mounted gems, a button on his coat formed of diamonds that spelled out the letter B, a scarf pin in diamonds also spelling out B, and an Audemars Piguet watch with stones on all surfaces. Diamond Jim usually changed his clothes six times a day, and he had a similar set of diamond accessories for every change. Diamond Jim's favorite phrase was, "I'll take a dozen of them," and it applied to everything from oysters to neckties to diamonds.

Sitting there in his Mark Herald shirt, Prince Albert cutaway, Budd necktie, and Canal Street shoes, Bruce Twig-Smathers fancied himself a dandy, but he faded to insignificance next to Diamond Jim. All Twig-Smathers could do was act as a surface for the endless stabs of light coming from Jim's jewelry.

And Diamond Jim faded next to Lady Elizabeth. I do believe Jim was uncomfortable that night in the *India Courser*'s smoking room, not being the object of wonder and envy as he usually was, as all eyes were on the English lady. Diamond Jim only reflected light while she radiated it. The splendor of her face and figure overwhelmed Diamond Jim's jewelry, made them seem small and tawdry.

Was it Goethe who said, "Large breasts are the great puzzle"? We Irish believe as an article of our faith that English women are built like bed slats because God is punishing Englishmen for occupying some of our country. Lady Elizabeth appeared to counter this wisdom, pushing as she did against the silk of her dress. With her narrow waist—I believe I could have circled her waist with my hands, touching fingers and thumbs—she had a voluptuous hourglass body, and she wore the imperious, mischievous expression of one who knew precisely her effect on the men in the room.

Bertrum McCook wore no ornaments except for a pocket watch connected to a button by a black ribbon fob. He was a small man, hardly up to my chin, and thin, probably from a lifetime of eating moss and lichen, the only crops that grow in Scotland, I've heard. There isn't a Scot alive who doesn't have a *skean dhub*—a black knife—tucked inside his hosiery. It's a secret they've kept pretty well, but now I've told it. They'd as soon stick us Irish as look at us. We Irish gave the Scots the bagpipes four hundred years ago, and they never figured out it was a joke. Can you imagine, marching into battle with an inflated goat skin stuck to your mouth? But I wander.

McCook's porcine eyes settled on Diamond Jim as he pushed forward two more chips. "You don't have the cards, sir."

Diamond Jim smiled. "Trying to get a free look at my hand, Mr. McCook? That ain't going to work on this Yankee. Even if it mostly taps me out, here's your fifty, and fifty more. It's a hundred to you, Lady Elizabeth."

"I can count, Mr. Brady." Without hesitation she met the bet and bumped it another fifty. "It's up to you, Twiggy."

"Yes." He stared at the mound of chips in the center of the table. "Yes, indeed." He glanced morosely at the lady. "But once again, milady . . ."

She passed him more chips, another loan. He accepted without a nod, and met the wager, and added another two chips. "To you, Mr. McCook."

The Scot clicked his teeth, looked sternly at Diamond Jim, then abruptly tossed in his cards. "I'm out."

Some of the smokers' eyes had ratcheted themselves from Lady Elizabeth, surely with difficulty, and were now on the pot. This was a rare pile, a power of money.

Diamond Jim grinned broadly. "Two to me, and two more." His chips clattered onto the pot. "Milady?"

She met the wager but did not raise it. With an audible sigh Twig-Smathers also met the raise.

With a flourish, Diamond Jim lay out his cards. A full house, queens followed by tens. He asked, "Shall I reach for my pot?"

"No, if you please." Twig-Smathers put down his cards. He had picked up a king on the draw, and his aces-kings full house nudged out Diamond Jim.

Jim harumphed pleasantly at his defeat.

Twig-Smathers licked his lips. "Milady?"

"Sorry, Twiggy." She spread her cards on the table. Four nines. The winner.

Twig-Smathers slumped in his chair. He wouldn't have enough cash for a quid of tobacco the rest of the voyage. He blinked at her cards, then shook his head.

Diamond Jim gallantly helped her gather and stack her winnings, but then she said, "Gentlemen, poker chips bore me terribly." She pronounced it "teddibly."

"They're as good as cash," Diamond Jim exclaimed. "And that's what the world is all about, cash."

"Tut, tut, tut," she said. The English actually say that. Anybody uttering those consonants at Joe Lowe's Museum and Sporting Palace would be killed on the spot and never mourned. "I know what I want but it isn't these clay poker chips." She moved stacks toward Diamond Jim and Twig-Smathers and the Scot, all the money they had lost to her four of a kind. But she didn't quite push the stacks up all the way to them. They were still hers. She was tempting them with the chips.

In an oddly compelling yet silky voice, she said, "But, Mr. Brady and Twiggy, you can do me a bit of a favor." With a haughty wag of her finger, she drew Diamond Jim and Twig-Smathers close for a whispered conference. I leaned forward as subtly as I could but couldn't make out nothing over the piano music and the *India Courser*'s engines. Then Lady Elizabeth, Diamond Jim, and Twig-Smathers turned in unison to stare at me, and I was pushed back against the tapestry by the force of their gazes. Lady Elizabeth's crested and lush red mouth turned up. She had the look of a bidder at a horse auction, judging musculature and gait.

Twig-Smathers and Diamond Jim rose from the game table and stepped toward me.

The Englishman said, "You are my butler, Woodrow, an employee not a serf, so I know I can't order you to do this thing."

"What thing?"

Twig-Smathers went on, "But I find I must ask a service of you."

"You're an American," Diamond Jim said. "You must carry the Stars and Stripes aloft, held firmly and proudly, among the foreigners."

"A service to me, Woodrow," Twig-Smathers said. "I'd be enormously in your debt if you'd do me this favor."

"You'll be able to carry the regal banner," Diamond Jim intoned. "The majestic eagle of freedom, held high by Woodrow. The shackles of colonialism will finally fall away due to your efforts. No more will our English cousins sniff their noses at us Americans."

Diamond Jim could talk the teeth out of a saw but I didn't have a clue as to his point. His jewels scattered light all across me. I blame them for my befuddlement.

"It turns out," Twig-Smathers said, "that I just lost you in a poker game, Woodrow."

"Lost me? You never had me."

The Englishman said, "Lady Elizabeth will return our wagers on that last hand if you consent to spend the night in her suite."

Well, this certainly picked up my interest. I looked past Twig-Smathers to the lady. She was resting her exquisite, marble-white chin on the point of a fingernail, watching me steadily, a slight pucker to her mouth. She was a fulsome sight, and my mouth went dry as a lime-burner's wig from either desire or fright, I couldn't tell which.

And an alarm sounded within me, as loud as the *India Courser's* abandon ship bell I had heard during drills. The loser—the loser?—in a poker game had to pony up his butler to spend the night with a beautiful woman? Something was wrong here. Still gazing at Lady Elizabeth, I tried to bring my innate intelligence to the puzzle, and so naturally the answer eluded me.

I said, "Something is fishy."

Twig-Smathers exclaimed, "So you'll do it. Grand, just grand, Woodrow." He pumped my hand. "Eleven o'clock this evening. Suite six."

Diamond Jim gripped my arm. "Banner high, Woodrow. Do us Yankees proud."

They collected their chips and made their way to the bar where Bertrum McCook was waiting for them. Lady Elizabeth turned away and smiled at an acquaintance, a Frenchman, judging from his twirled mustache, mincing walk, and air of surrender. He walked over to converse with her, kissing her hand. I was forgotten, standing there at my post.

After a while I began to think that Diamond Jim and Twig-Smathers might be up to some magnificent joke on yours truly, something we'd all be able to slap our knees about later. But then Lady Elizabeth shot one more glance at me, fusing my eyeballs to the backs of their sockets, and I resolved to knock on the door to suite six at eleven o'clock.

KNOCK I DID. Her rooms could be entered from the outside deck. I stood there, hand upraised, ash from the smoke stacks swirling around me, not sure I had rapped loud enough, so I did so again. To my right was a small three-panel window, the center was of leaded and stained glass showing a scene that I took for a wolf playing a squeezebox, maybe from the Bible. I was about to knock again when the door drifted open slightly, a few inches, no more. It was dark inside. I waited a moment, then pushed the door open and stepped inside.

The room was lit by a single gas lamp, turned down low and casting a dim nimbus of light. I had never been in a suite, and in fact they were a new idea at sea, first brought to the Atlantic by the Cunard Line. The *India Courser* had ten *suites de luxe*, and they sold for six hundred dollars a crossing, twelve times more than was charged for my steerage berth. The suite consisted of a sitting room, bed chamber, and lavatory and bath. The sitting room smelled of lilac, her scent, I suppose. A chintz-covered love seat was against one wall, near a small bookstand containing a dozen leatherbound volumes with gold lettering on the spines. The rug was plush and red, and I sank to my ankles in it. Brocaded red drapes hung to my left and right, covering the windows. The gas lamp's bracket was a mermaid made of iron and inlaid with mother-of-pearl, holding the flame in her upraised hand. In a corner was a bird's-eye maple display case containing several tiny Dresden and Tanagra figurines. In another corner was a bronze statue of a dog being gored by a bull. The top of a coffee table was imbedded with lapis lazuli and onyx in fleur-de-lis patterns. The small room was cluttered.

I looked left and right but saw no one. I glanced over my shoulder at the open door to make sure a six was on the center panel. It was. I pulled out my pocket watch. Eleven o'clock. Well, maybe the prank was on me. Send a butler to a noblewoman's boudoir. I already thought it was a gutbuster, the cavalry having refined my sense of humor. I started a turn toward the door. Then a shadow moved in the boudoir. Another lamp was in there, and a black phantom had moved across the pale light.

Lady Elizabeth stepped to the door. "You don't have the look of a butler, Mr. Lowe."

"No, ma'am. I'm not too sure what I'm doing here at your door but if it's my mistake, I'll say my apologies and go."

She put her hands behind her back and leaned against the wall, eyeing me all the while. Her teeth were white and glowing. "You are here at my invitation, Mr. Lowe."

Her voice had gained a peculiar purring quality, the sound coming from deep within her. She had pushed more of that lilac scent into the room with her, and its tendrils reached for me. She was wearing the same red silk gown, and it shimmered with iridescence in the gaslight, making her seem hesitant and fleeting, like a dragonfly. Her blue eyes were sparkling like Diamond Jim's jewelry.

"Twiggy said you are a soldier."

"A cavalry trooper, ma'am. A corporal."

"Is the cavalry where you got the scars on your face, and your ear?"

"Some." I ran my tongue across my upper lip. "But mostly it was in the ring."

"Are you nervous?" she asked, stepping away from the wall toward me, more of a glide, as if she were floating across the rug.

I cleared my throat. "I've faced the Sioux in the field, ma'am. When you've done that, not much makes you nervous thereafter." I didn't explain that the Sioux had soup bowls in their hands while I held a ladle. I was determined to carry the banner high, like Diamond Jim had enjoined me.

She drifted closer and lowered her chin demurely. I had never been this close to this fine a woman in my life. She touched my hand, just the tip of the fingers, then slid her hand into mine.

"You've got calluses on your hands," she said, holding one up to examine it, turning it slowly and caressing the fleshy bumps with a long fingernail. "Do you know anything about me, corporal?"

"No, ma'am."

"I've been married three times. Not one of my husbands had a callus anywhere on his body. Their skins were soft like girls'. And perfumed."

I tilted my head to look over her shoulder into the bedroom. "You aren't married now, are you, ma'am?"

She caught her fingernail on a particularly large callus on the palm of my hand below the trigger finger. "I've been widowed three times."

"Sorry, ma'am."

"It has been a life of grief." She didn't sound too grieved. She tugged at my callus with her fingernail, which I thought odd. The scent of her hair surrounded me, lilac, but also something else, maybe musk. When there was nothing else for the 7th Cavalry's pot, I'd occasionally trap muskrats. They had this same odor after they lay dead in the sun a while.

"Is there something dead in here, ma'am?" I can sweet-talk them, can't I?

"It's my perfume," she said softly. "I'm wearing it for you."

Never, not once in my life, had a woman put on a perfume for me, even a dead smell. I was taking a shine to this lady, even though I remained afraid of her, and even though she continued to pick at the callus on my hand. Maybe it was some English courtship ritual, another reason the Pilgrims got on the boat. It was my potato peeler callus, and I had maintained it helping Bamie's cook, Pearl, peel spuds, and I had grown fond of it over the years.

"Come with me, corporal." She took my hand in both of hers and led me into the bedroom. "My first husband was Earl Blythe. Have you heard of him?"

"No, ma'am. But I've always liked the name 'Earl.'"

"That was his rank. His first name was Chauncey, though I seldom heard it. He even demanded I call him Earl Blythe, except in bed, and then it was 'My Bengal Lancer.'"

"I'm not following you, ma'am."

"Chauncey was killed on the Prince of Wales' birthday, during a ball we were giving. He was down in the wine cellar making a last-minute selection of wine, and was killed by an errant champagne cork. It hit him on the temple and he collapsed. I found him there a few minutes later. Later the doctor said he had a condition called a paper skull. The slightest of knocks can kill someone with a paper skull." She turned her back to me. "Will you help me with this?"

Like a dancer she raised her long arms above her neck, then lowered them to the clasp at the back of her neck to show me where it was. I fumbled with the tiny mechanism. Saddle cinches and horse hobbles and meat grinders were more my line. It took me a moment and she talked all the while.

"My second husband was Viscount Barr. He was an old man when I married him, walking with a cane. He fell down the entryway stairs of our Mayfair home, all thirty steps, and was nothing but a pile of broken bones when I found him a few minutes later."

Her bed was covered with a flower print spread. On the nightstand were three photographs, two framed in crystal frames and one in black wood. On a dresser were a silver-framed hand mirror and a hairbrush with a filigreed silver handle and a dozen crystal perfume bottles. I finally convinced the clasp to open. She turned to face me.

"And lastly there was Jerome Brandon, the owner of the *Daily Telegraph*. He committed suicide with his pistol behind the Cupid fountain in our garden. Most of his head ended up in the water."

"Did you find him, too?"

"Yes. A few minutes later." She sighed up at me. Her breath was of cinnamon. "It has all been rather trying. And now you know the grief of a widow who has no one to take the chill from the long nights." She reached up and drew her fingernail along the abnormal ridge of skin on my eyebrow. "How did you acquire this scar?"

"From being beaten on the face by fistic scientists."

"It's quite attractive, you know, corporal. And how about this one?" She drew her fingernail along the side of my eye, where a berm of skin radiated from the corner of my eye like an inverted wrinkle. She dug her nail in, a bit painfully.

"The great John L. Sullivan gave me that," I replied proudly. "He opened up that skin real deep one time out in the Badlands."

"And this?" She tapped the knot that was the bridge of my nose.

"The same John L."

"It looks like this John L. was having quite a frolic."

"He is known for his sense of humor, ma'am."

She came even closer, then went up on her toes as she turned my head. "And this exquisite ear."

"That ear has been the hobby of quite a few boxers."

Her lips found the ear. I thought she was going to whisper some endearment but instead her teeth sank into it. I started with pain. "Ma'am?"

"Did that hurt, corporal?"

Hell, yes. "I've been hurt worse," I managed, "but not by a woman, I don't suppose."

She pressed her hands into my chest, gently pushing me back until my legs caught on the bedframe and I stumbled onto the bed. I touched my ear. It was damp and stinging. She had drawn blood with those shining teeth.

Lady Elizabeth's long fingers began on the buttons of her gown but she must have been practiced at it because her eyes never left me. Up the side her hands went, and the silk slowly fell away from her like the opening petals of a flower. I stared with some interest.

"Do you appreciate nicely shaped breasts, corporal?" She worked away on buttons and clasps.

"I . . . I don't know," I rasped. And I didn't. A frontier whore wants you in and out of her crib in five minutes and isn't going to remove her shirt if she can help it. My knowledge of breasts was sadly lacking.

"I've been told mine are the finest in England." The gown finally released its grip on her. She wiggled her hips back and forth as her hands drew down all those yards of fabric, over her belly, over her hips, making a soft soughing sound, down her thighs and onto the floor. She stepped out of the mountain of silk. Her black slip was as formidable as the red gown but again her hands were busy, popping buttons. Ornamental black lace played across the front of the slip, and her hands disappeared beneath the lace, working expertly. Her hands pushed the fabric back, emphasizing the heavy swells there.

Then she stopped, her slip still in place but with a few corners hanging down, revealing bone white skin. "Corporal, you have me at a disadvantage."

I couldn't figure out how.

She dropped her eyes to the floor, her long black lashes falling and rising like fans. "I am a shy lass, corporal."

"I don't doubt it, ma'am." I grabbed fistfuls of bedspread to keep my hands from trembling.

"Would you do a little something for me?" She floated over to the bed and pressed her fingernails onto my chest, forcing me back onto the bed. "My confidence in these matters has been shattered by my husbands' deaths." She loomed above me, stray bits of black lace crossing my face like a breeze. She gripped my wrist and pulled it to one side, smiling, her mouth curved and damp. I felt something tug at my wrist.

"This will help me so," she said huskily.

"Anything, ma'am."

She sat on the bed to reach across for my other wrist. She leaned across me, the lengths of ribbon lowering to my face again, then the soft pressure of her breasts pushed my head down into the pillow. She fiddled with my wrist but I was lost in the expanse of feathery fabric and the supple insistence of her breasts against my nose and cheeks. I inhaled but the fabric filled my mouth, blocking the air. I drew my head back, pressing it further into the pillow to try to find air, but her chest followed me down, and my mouth was covered by those hillocks and I couldn't get a breath. I was drowning in black lace and perfume. She worked on my wrist, tugging and fiddling. Finally she rose, lifting herself from across me. I gulped cool air.

Only then did I realize she had tied my hands to the bedposts. I was spread-eagled, held in place by black ribbons that bit into my wrists. I'd heard the Apaches did this sort of thing but this was news to me about the English nobility.

"You'll forgive me, corporal," she said, extinguishing the gas lamp, then arching her back to find yet more clasps on her slip.

The room was cast in shadows, lit only by weak moonlight coming through two circular brass portals. The ship rolled slowly, and she rose above me then sank again. Vibrations from the engines shivered the bed.

"But be critical, corporal. Tell me what you think. You need not be slathering with your praise in hopes of having me. You already have me. Are my breasts what you'd hoped?"

The slip fell away and her breasts sprang forth, full and heavy and eerily white in the faint light. They seemed to take up all the remaining space in the room. She cupped them in both hands. "Are they what you wanted, corporal?"

Now I don't mind admitting to being confused at this point in the evening. I was either going to have more joy than I had ever before known, or I was going to be killed dead, and I was not able to discern which. Bewilderment crimped my ardor. Maybe it showed on my face. I jerked my right wrist. I was held tight.

"Are my nipples the right color for you, corporal? Shall I bring them closer?"

"Lord, yes." I yanked my wrist again. "But maybe not."

She sat on the edge of the bed and leaned toward me, unbuttoning my shirt, then running her hand over my chest, kneading the muscles there. Again she brought her breasts up, to within inches of my face, then closer, and closer. My mouth opened involuntarily.

Then she let one breast fall as she reached for a framed photograph. "This is a photograph of Earl Blythe."

I couldn't see well in the darkness. The man in the picture frame wore elegant Galway whiskers and a frown.

"I loathed him." She pressed the frame against my forehead, pushing my head into the pillow again. She rubbed the frame against my skull.

"He was detestable, with the breath of a garbage box and soft, limp fingers and greasy hair. I hated him and his mother."

She cracked the frame against my head and the glass shattered. Shards slid down my face and over my ears to land on my neck. She picked up a triangle of glass.

"The earl was utterly uninterested in my breasts." Her voice had gained a dreamy breathlessness. She pushed those hillocks forward until a pink nipple pushed against my cheekbone. She brought the shard of glass against my temple. It painfully sank into my skin. I tried to cry out but suddenly her breast was covering my mouth, a vast expanse of warm skin. With that piece of glass she carved a line below my temple. Blood seeped down my head. It smarted like hell.

I mumbled a protest into her breast but the fullness muffled me. She moved left and right so that my face settled into her deep cleavage. I was surrounded by mounds of flesh. From the corner of my eye I saw her lift another framed photograph. She held it up to the meager light coming through the porthole.

"And Viscount Barr," she panted. "The man was intimidated by my breasts. And he was so old he couldn't even lift them."

She smashed the frame against my head. Glass fractured and slid off me. I felt a shard dig into my cauliflower ear. Other pieces gathered about my shoulders.

"You aren't intimidated, are you, corporal?"

To tell you the truth, I was beginning to be.

She rose above me, her breasts enormous moons, her face distant beyond them, and plucked at my belt, then the buttons on my broad-cloth trousers. She yanked my shoes off, then my pants down my legs. She dropped them at the foot of the bed. She drew down my drawers and tossed them on the pile of clothing. She gazed out the porthole.

I tried to touch my wound, but my hand was brought up by the ribbon that bound me. She reached for the last framed photograph.

Her voice was strangely remote. "And Mr. Brandon, the Fleet Street magnate. He cared more for newspaper ink than my breasts. Where do men get these ideas, corporal? But Jerome is dead and there's nothing I can do but grieve."

She smashed Jerome's framed photograph against my cheek. I yelped. The glass splintered and rained down, bits of it catching here and there, a glass needle lodging at the corner of my mouth and drawing blood.

Lady Elizabeth finished with the buttons on my shirt, then ran her hand down my sternum. She pushed the shirt back around my shoulders. Blood ran down my neck. I was naked, save for my bunched-up shirt.

"Ma'am, I'd best go."

"My husbands were weak, corporal. They didn't have one backbone between them."

"Maybe if you'd release my wrists." I tried to keep a desperate tenor out of my voice but failed.

She settled over me, her hips across my pelvis. She leaned forward. The white globes hung over me, swaying gently, then lowering, filling my horizon.

"You aren't a coward, are you, corporal?"

My voice wavered. "I hadn't thought so, ma'am, but now I'm not so sure."

"I despise cowards." She lifted a shard of glass from my chest. "All three of my husbands were cowards. But how could you be, with all your scars?" Her other hand disappeared and she did something with my privates, but that shard of glass glittered above me and I was dulled by fear so I couldn't tell what.

Her breasts came down, about to envelop my head again. My nose entered the canyon of her cleavage. "You soldiers aren't cowards, are you?"

"Cavalryman, ma'am," I said around all that flesh. "We cavalrymen take umbrage at being called soldiers."

"These scars," she hissed with what I took to be pleasure. "I adore them. Bring them to me. Bring me your scars. Let me take care of them."

At that moment she stabbed that piece of glass at my cheek, cutting me from cheek bone to lower mandible, clean through my skin to dig into my tongue. My mouth instantly filled with blood. The glass grated against my teeth and slit my gums. With a groan she sat on me. I believe I had just begun my first sexual act with someone I hadn't paid, but I couldn't be sure because of the pain rocketing around in my head.

She bounced and bounced and I bled and bled. I shook my head and the glass fragment slid out of the hole in my cheek. I bled down my face and chin, quarts of it, it seemed, soaking the bedspread. Moaning, she pulled my head into her breasts, smearing blood over her chest and cutting off my breath. I fought for air, but found only her soft flesh. I was drowning in her. Each time I tried to suck in life-giving air, I got more of her breast in my mouth. Both her hands gripped my head, holding it fast to those suffocating folds of flesh. My strength was ebbing. I searched for air, but only succeeded in drawing her nipple into my mouth as far as my tonsils. Wind whistled through the gash in my cheek. I choked on blood. I fought for air, twisting fiercely left and right, trying to free my throat of her breast, but she pinned me to her, jumping up and down on my hips all the while and making these appreciative animal noises, yipping and caterwauling.

I don't know whether it was lack of air or loss of blood or fright or some combination of them all, but my consciousness fled me. I can only hope Lady Elizabeth completed her fun but I don't know if she did because I sank into darkness, so my merriment was over for the evening, that was for sure.

I woke up some time later in my steerage bunk, my head on a bloody pillow, my face afire with pain. I stuck my tongue through my cheek and could almost touch my earlobe with it, which would have provided me some amusement had it not hurt so much. I stood unsteadily, the ship rolling under me, and my wobbly legs only exaggerating the motion. When westbound, the *India Courser*'s steerage was packed with immigrants, but heading east only a few adventurous students occupied the lowest deck. They snored and tossed all around me. My cheek hung out like a flap, like a bloodhound's dewlap. I staggered to the companionway ladder, on my way to first class. I was going to have a few words with Twig-Smathers.

EIGHT

A Duel

THE SOUND OF a shot reached me, muffled and faint, but unmistakable. A pistol, probably, a heavy one. I had heard enough gunfire in the cavalry so that a shot didn't bother me much because they usually weren't any of my concern, being a cavalry cook. At Blechfield Hall I was a scullery boy, a job considerably lower than the cook. So I figured this shot was none of my business, and I went right on eating.

I was sitting in the Blechfield servants' hall, where the butler and his footmen, the coachman and his grooms, and the housekeeper and her maids all ate. Baron and Baroness Twig-Smathers employed a passel of folks, and while the male servants slept in one servants' wing and the female servants in another, they all ate in the servants' hall, which connected the two wings. My task as a scullery boy was to wash dishes and pots and silverware. The baron and baroness had entertained forty-five guests that evening, serving each of them nine courses, not counting dessert, coffee and walnuts. It was one o'clock in the morning. Yours truly, Woodrow Lowe, had just cleaned a Pike's Peak of kitchen and dinnerware using scalding water and lye, a combination harder on the hands than a prizefight. Servants in an English manor house have a more rigid hierarchy than the British peerage, and I—a scullery boy—was at the bottom.

How I came to this sorry state is easy to say. When I had arrived in England with Twig-Smathers two weeks before, I was penniless. Back then in order to eat, you worked, plain and simple, and this was the only job offered me.

Twig-Smathers was not one for gratitude, by the way. I had yanked his head out of ship's railing, and then I had saved him from a gambling debt by subjecting myself to Lady Elizabeth, and I was scarcely given a nod of recognition for either service. In fact, that night aboard ship when I had approached Twig-Smathers, my face hanging open and bleeding from my just-completed assignation with Lady Elizabeth, Twig-Smathers was astonished that I felt I had been put upon. "Every duke and earl and count in the kingdom would have traded places with you, Woodrow," he had exclaimed. "You should count yourself fortunate."

I can't say he changed my mind that night, but his argument did prevent me from throwing him into the sea. I have always been susceptible to smooth talkers, and that's the hell of it.

The noise of a second shot reached me, closer and more insistent. Someone was in trouble, that was for sure. I didn't give a damn who. I sliced off more of the roast saddle of mutton, which I was eating with beetroot and asparagus, and plovers' eggs in aspic jelly, leftovers from that evening's gala. We cavalry cooks always have a weakness for plover eggs in aspic jelly.

Blechfield Manor was in Kent, north of Ashford. The building was in the center of twenty acres of rose gardens, fountains, and shrubs, all within a three-thousand-acre estate. I had never seen anything like those shrubs, by the way. They were clipped to resemble elephants and camels and bears. And we wonder why the English lost their empire.

The three-story manor house was constructed of gray stone, with spires, cupolas and sixteen chimneys. The estate's outbuildings included a dairy, stables, kennels, a brewery, and a washhouse. More than once I had become lost inside the manor house, wandering hopelessly within the billiard and smoking rooms, a library, three conservatories, and even a long hallway to nowhere, which I was told was for promenades on rainy evenings.

The servants' hall had one long table down the center, and I sat at the head of the table in a straight-back cane chair. Linen cupboards were along one side of the room. The hall was lit with hissing gas lamps. Scullery boys always were the last to be done with the day's work, and I was alone in the hall.

Just as I popped another plover egg into my mouth, wondering whether a plover was a bird or a reptile, Bruce Twig-Smathers rushed down the servants' stairs and into the hall. He was red-faced and gasping, and he fearfully glanced over his shoulder to the stairs, then sprinted toward the kitchen, a small cry of fear coming from him. At that moment he saw me and he fixed on me like a drowning man would a life ring. He changed directions.

He dashed to me and grabbed both my arms, almost lifting me from my chair. I chewed my egg.

"Woodrow, my God, you've got to help me." Again he looked with wild and rolling eyes at the servants' stairs. "Woodrow, please."

"I'm eating dinner."

He shook my arms. "I beg you, Woodrow. That madman is going to kill me. He's coming for me and he's got a pistol."

"I'm too tired from washing your dishes." I can be petulant on occasion.

I heard footsteps on the stairs. A bass voice yelled, "Twig-Smathers, you are finished, do you hear me, you scoundrel."

Twig-Smathers spewed out his words. "Woodrow, please, save my life. For old times' sake."

That must have been his idea of humor, old times' sake. But someone with a handgun was after him and although I didn't feel I owed Twig-Smathers a damned thing I couldn't let him be shot down. I grabbed him by the elbow, took ten steps across the hall and into the kitchen, opened the produce pantry and threw him in. I closed the door and returned to the table just as the gunman entered the room from the stairs.

"You," he hollered, jabbing the gun in my direction. "Where did he go?"

I shrugged, sat down, and lifted my knife. The man ran over, waving his pistol. "I demand you tell me where that lecher went."

I said calmly, "You point that pistol at me again, I'm going to stick my thumb in your eye."

That brought him up. My abused face—with its new scars courtesy of Lady Elizabeth—suggested I did that sort of thing for a living.

"Sir, were I you I would be more circumspect," he said in his plumb-stone accent. "You are speaking to a gentleman carrying a loaded pistol."

"And I'll poke that pistol in your other eye."

He stared at me a long moment, then looked meanly around the hall and stretched his backbone for some height. He spoke loudly, probably suspecting Twig-Smathers was within earshot. "That scoundrel has dishonored me, has cuckolded me. I demand satisfaction."

His face was a mash of rage and anger. He had shallow blue eyes and a pencil mustache. He had tried to hide his baldness with a few carefully placed strands that made his head look wet. He was wearing a cutaway coat and a white shirt with pearl buttons. The pistol looked comfortable in his hand.

"You are hiding him, sir." His scowl was black and his words chopped. "You tell him that I will meet him at dawn on Saturday at Pheasant's Field by the gazebo. Tell him to bring a matching set."

He turned on his heel and clicked out of the hall, disappearing up the stairs. I rose and returned to the pantry.

I pulled open the door. Surrounded by bags of beets and carrots and sacks of flour, Twig-Smathers was cringing in the corner.

"You must feel silly in there," I said.

"Is he gone?"

I nodded.

He pushed himself upright. He warily peered around the door into the hall. Trying to restore a modicum of dignity, he brushed his lapels. He stepped grandly from the pantry, clearing his throat at the slight inconvenience.

"He wants to meet you Saturday at dawn at Pheasant's Field," I said. "He says to bring a matched set."

Twig-Smathers whirled to me, his eyes white all around. "Oh my Lord. He has challenged me to a duel."

Returning to my chair, I replied, "That's what I figured. What'd you do to get him so riled up?"

"That fellow is Sir Charles Priestly." Twig-Smathers intoned this like I might know the man.

I shrugged and reached for another plover egg.

Twig-Smathers rushed over to me, leaning over the table, almost putting his elbow into my mutton so he could catch my eye. He stuttered apoplectically, "Sir . . . Sir Charles has already killed two men in duels."

I chewed the egg.

"Woodrow," he cried, "Sir Charles is going to kill me."

"What'd you do to get his dander up, Bruce?" I had never before called him Bruce, usually using "sir." I hadn't met any male in England yet who I didn't have to call "sir" and I was tired of it. And I somehow felt that I had suddenly gotten the upper hand with Twig-Smathers.

He stood upright and shook his head. "He caught me tapping on the door to his wife's room. She and I had agreed to a little assignation, and we thought Sir Charles would spend much of the evening playing cards like he always does." His voice rose. "And he shows up in the hallway just as his wife is opening the door to me and saying 'It's about time, Brucey.' Oh my God, Sir Charles is going to kill me."

"I didn't think you English allowed dueling."

"We don't. We now travel to the Continent for duels. But Sir Charles has never let things like the law stand in his way." He wrung his hands and paced back and forth in the hall. "My God, my God, what am I going to do? I scarcely know one end of a pistol from the other."

"I thought you were an officer in a county regiment."

He waved his hand.

"Looks like you're going to die come Saturday," I said mildly, cutting off a strip of mutton, "Bruce."

Twig-Smathers croaked piteously, "Sir Charles is going to shoot me down."

I chewed loudly, enjoying the moment. Then I said, "I'll save your life."

He stopped dead, then leaped at me, grabbing both of my arms again and shaking them. "You can? You'll do it? You can save me?"

I shook free to wipe my mouth with a linen napkin. "Yep."

"How? What can you do?" Gleaming hope charged his words.

"It'll cost you a hundred pounds." That'd get me back to the United States in fine style. First-class stateroom, some Cuban cigars, enough money to leave a tip here and there, get my shoes shined professionally.

But judging from Twig-Smathers's reaction, I might as well have said a million pounds. He gasped, "A hundred pounds? I haven't got a hundred pounds."

"You're the son of a baron," I scoffed. "A hundred pounds is pocket money for you."

He held up a hand, showing four fingers. "I am the fourth son of a baron."

"So?"

"I am penniless, Woodrow. I survive on a tiny sum—a pittance—that my mother and father grudgingly allow me. My older brother stands to inherit everything."

"But you live so grandly." I waved my hand, encompassing the entire manor house.

Twig-Smathers shook his head. "I live in my parents' home. I belong to my father's club and he pays the dues. My position at the foreign office is unpaid except for a pound-a-year honorarium. I had to beg my mother to buy me a captain's commission, and that pays nothing."

"Then I'll take that handsome black stallion you hunt foxes with every day."

"That horse belongs to my father."

I pointed. "Then I'll take that diamond stickpin in your tie." Hell, that should be worth a second-class passage.

He laughed mirthlessly and snatched the stickpin from his tie. He dropped it onto the floor and ground it under his heel. He lifted his shoe to show it pulverized. "Glass. A fraud."

I turned back to my meal. "Looks like you're going to die come Saturday."

He glanced anxiously at the stairs as if afraid Sir Charles would return. Once again he gripped my arm. "Teddy Roosevelt would order you to save my life."

"Teddy Roosevelt is an ocean away."

He breathed raggedly. I lifted a fork to go after some asparagus tips. Twig-Smathers calmed some. He licked his lips and looked left and right. He was calculating.

"Woodrow, you know violence. You understand violence. Just look at your face. And you've been in the American cavalry. Only you can help me." He slid into the chair at my left. "Woodrow, if you save my life I'll give you the only valuable thing I have."

"What is it?"

"I'll get it." He jumped up from the seat and took off toward the stairs.

I rose to follow him but he called over his shoulder, "Scullery boys aren't allowed in the main house, Woodrow."

"It's one in the morning, for Pete's sake."

"Even then. Mother would know somehow that a kitchen servant had been in her house. She has an infallible sense for infractions by her inferiors."

Any wonder why Bruce Twig-Smathers could put me off? He was gone five minutes, during which time I finished off the mutton. Could have used more salt.

He returned carrying a piece of paper, maybe three inches by four inches. He held it delicately in both hands. As he neared I could see it was yellowed with age, and was quartered by creases.

"Here." He pushed my plate and cutlery away, then put the paper in front of me tenderly as if it were an offering on an altar.

"It's a piece of paper," I said with my usual insight.

"Read it."

When I reached to square the paper in front of me, he started, as if I were about to erase the words or tear the document up. He was nervous about the paper so I left it alone. I bent down nearer the table top and read aloud, " 'One mile due south of the island's highest peak is a pool. One hundred thirty yards further south is a two-man stone with an hourglass mark. Under the stone.' "

I looked up at him. "What's under the stone?"

"I don't know. My grandfather never told me. I'm not sure he knew."

"What island?"

He smiled grimly. "Two minutes ago I clipped off the top of that piece of paper. The island's name is on it. You save me from being killed Saturday morning, I'll give you that piece of paper."

I stared at him, looking for some sign that this was a grand joke. Then I burst out laughing. I reached for the paper, about to wad it up, but he fairly jumped on me, and I let him snatch it up.

But I still laughed.

"Woodrow, please . . ."

Finally I could manage, "A buried treasure? Is that it?"

"I told you," he said stiffly. "I don't know what is under that stone."

"Pirates must have left a buried treasure. Doubloons and pieces of eight and ruby necklaces, maybe an old skull lying nearby. And it's all mine."

"It was the secret of my grandfather's life. He told me many times that if he were younger, he'd go find it and dig it up and have a glorious time. He cared for me more than anyone else in the family. And it's the only thing he left me."

I laughed anew.

"Woodrow, my dear man, I beg you."

I said, "You must think Joe and Annie Lowe of Boston, Massachusetts, raised a dunce for a son." I held up my hand before he could answer that. No sense tempting truth. "You go to your duel, and good luck. I'll see you in hell, but some years in the future, I hope."

"It's the only thing of value I own." He lifted the fragile paper and thrust it at me. "For the love of God, at least think about it."

Something about abject groveling always touches me. I stared at him a moment, his face contorted to look like a begging hound. Finally I pinched the bridge of my nose in a nice histrionic gesture. "All right. I'll think about it."

And maybe I would.

That apparently was enough. "Thank God." Twig-Smathers raced off. He called back, "And remember, Woodrow, servants aren't allowed in the main house."

But, then, maybe I wouldn't.

DIAMOND JIM BRADY was a guest at the baron's summer home for that week. The cook had taken a liking to him, and was making sure Diamond Jim always had enough to eat, which kept the kitchen staff busy. The next day I approached Diamond Jim, intent on asking his advice. He was having dinner by himself in a sunroom. I approached by way of the garden, not wanting to risk walking through the house. I tapped on the window and he waved me in.

"Woodrow," he exclaimed, tucking his napkin into his collar. "What brings you around?"

"I need to ask your advice, Mr. Brady. On a business matter."

"Only too happy to oblige, Woodrow." He lifted a fork slowly with two fingers, weighing it, as if testing whether it was suitable for the arduous task at hand. "But I don't like to talk business at a meal. Will you wait a while?"

He motioned me to a seat opposite him at the iron table. The servants began arriving with his food. They were surprised to see me, the scullery boy, sitting across from one of Baron Twig-Smathers's guests, but they limited themselves to raising eyebrows.

I sat there an hour while Diamond Jim ate. Several times he offered to share his repast, but I was happy just to sit there and watch that mouth work. And I'm here to tell you Diamond Jim's mouth knew what it was doing. I memorized his fare back then because I wanted to keep the memory with me. It served me well, too. During the times in my life when I was starving I would repeat it again and again like a litany, and a benevolent calm would come over me and my hunger would abate. That day I saw Diamond Jim Brady throw the following down his gullet, and in this order: three dozen raw oysters, four bowls of mock turtle soup, a plate of timbales, mousselines and croustades, one open-mouth bass, six lobsters, eight servings of lamb, a small bowl of orange sherbert, three wild ducks, an English hare, aspic of goose, two dozen apple fritters, four servings of pudding, a plate of candied fruits and mottoes, and finally Turkish coffee. Amidst all this were assorted side dishes: carrots cut to look like roses, camellias carved from turnips, potato patties pressed to resemble Queen Victoria's profile. I took it that Diamond Jim never ate vegetables unless they looked like something else. He kept four servants running to and fro between the sunroom and the kitchen.

Finally Diamond Jim whipped his napkin from his collar, wiped his mouth with a broad pass, leaned back in the chair, and asked, "Now, Woodrow, what can I do for you?"

"I've been offered a business proposition, and I was hoping you would direct your judgment to it."

He nodded sagely, his double chin bulging out like a frog's. His jewelry today was limited to several rings and a lapel pin of perhaps ten pea-size diamonds. His suit was of navy blue wool with narrow white stripes. His dark hair was combed straight back, making him look like he was on a galloping horse, face to the wind.

"It involves a treasure on an island," I began, not without some embarrassment.

Diamond Jim's eyes narrowed. I told him the entire story, finally producing the tattered piece of paper. Jim studied it.

"Are you sure you can save Bruce's life?" he asked after a moment.

"Nothing to it."

He pulled a wrapper of bon bons from his pocket, and after I shook my head at them he tossed a few down his throat. He said, "An Englishman's honor is a fragile thing."

I replied, "An Englishman's honor and a nickel will only buy me a cup of coffee."

"What I mean, Woodrow, is that Sir Charles has obviously taken this affront to his honor seriously. He isn't going to be assuaged by some foolishness on your part. And Bruce must appear at the duel. To avoid it will brand him as a coward, and ruin him socially and politically. He will have to flee to Australia or somewhere even farther."

"I know how to save Bruce's skin, honor intact, don't worry."

He drew a finger along his upper lip. "What will saving Bruce's life cost you, Woodrow?"

"Couple hours of my time."

He pronounced, "This piece of paper, with the directions to this boulder and its mystery beneath, is almost surely a fraud. I mean, who could believe in such a thing?"

"That's what I thought, too." I half rose from my chair and reached for the paper, thinking the discussion over. "Looks like Bruce is going to meet his Maker tomorrow at dawn."

Diamond Jim held his hand up. "But I say 'almost surely.' Let us suppose there is a one percent chance something of great value lies beneath this stone. So your bargain is: a few hours of your time for a one-in-a-hundred chance at riches."

I nodded.

"That's a very good deal, Woodrow. Your investment is tiny. The chance of a reward is also tiny. But that reward could be huge."

I nodded again, believing I was following his logic.

He added, "That's the reason I believe in God. The chance God exists is small but the reward of eternal life for the devout is so grand that it pays to believe."

I braved, "That's a poor reason to believe in the Almighty, Mr. Brady."

The corners of Diamond Jim's mouth turned up. "Do you believe in God, Woodrow?"

"I'm Irish. I have to." I hurried on, "If this piece of paper isn't a fraud, what do you think might be under that stone?"

Diamond Jim took his left thumb in his right hand and cracked a knuckle, a resounding report not unlike a champagne bottle being opened. "If, and only if, that paper is not a fraud, here are the things we can reasonably presume. First, someone went to considerable trouble to hide whatever it is. Second, that person intended to return to it. And we know that Bruce Twig-Smathers's family has a long military tradition, both in the English army and Royal Navy. As I recall his stories, his grandfather was the captain of a privateer with a letter of marque from His Majesty's government to capture French and Spanish vessels and keep their cargoes as prizes. So perhaps there is gold below the rock, vast quantities."

"Gold," I repeated. Unaccountably, Amy Balfour's lovely visage rose in front of me. "You think so? Gold?"

"No, I don't think so." He popped another knuckle. "More probably there are documents beneath that rock, probably worthless. Maybe a sailor's diary. Or it could be some weapons, rifles and cutlasses and the like, with only a small worth. Maybe a body, though I don't know why anybody would want to return to a skeleton. Or there could be nothing below the rock, just an empty hole. And if I were a wagering man, which I certainly am, I would wager on the empty hole."

"But there could be gold or jewels?"

"Woodrow, if the boulder covers something of value, it is probably a gold ring or a few coins or a locket with strands of hair in it, and while they would have a certain value they wouldn't warrant traipsing across the world to claim, if indeed that's where your island is."

"Gold," I said, more to myself. Then I surfaced and asked, "So if Bruce had offered you this deal you'd accept it?"

He shook his head, exploding another knuckle. "I would not be able to accept the deal because I don't have the slightest idea how to save Bruce from Sir Charles' vengeance. Unless you are smarter than your outward appearance suggests, Bruce will indeed meet his Maker tomorrow."

I reclaimed the paper and rose from the table. "Thank you, Mr. Brady."

"Woodrow, I make my money on commissions." He smiled. "I do not work for free."

"Sir?"

"Five percent of whatever is beneath that stone."

I grinned back at him. "I'll make sure you get it."

DAWN WAS GRAY and weeping, the mist drifting from the trees onto the duelers' field and washing over us, softening the field and its trees, making this business seem anything but deadly. Six of us stood on the long and wet grass; two duelers, two seconds (I was Twig-Smathers's second), a surgeon, and an umpire. Four carriages were parked at the end of the field, the horses low in their traces to eat the grass.

"Gentlemen," the umpire called, "the rules will be declared."

I shoved a bullet into Twig-Smathers's revolver, a new Webley. He had brought a set, borrowed from somebody, but instead had chosen Sir Charles' revolvers.

Twig-Smathers's entire body was shaking, and he looked beseechingly at me again and again. "Woodrow, what is your plan? Woodrow, are you listening to me? I'm sixty seconds from dying and you don't look concerned at all."

Sir Charles stood forty feet away, wearing loose clothing in an attempt to hide the precise location of his vital organs, not that he thought, in all likelihood, that Twig-Smathers would get off a shot. His blue ballbearing eyes on his opponent, Sir Charles seemed utterly calm as his second loaded his pistol. Sir Charles's mustache hid his mouth, but I was sure there was a wicked grin below the hair.

The umpire stood midway between the two duelers, but off to one side. He called, "On the ready, you will raise your pistols to the sky. When my handkerchief hits the ground you will lower the pistols and each fire one shot."

I filled the Webley's chambers with its stubby bullets. They clicked into place. I snapped closed the cylinder and handed the weapon to Twig-Smathers. The weight of the pistol pulled him off balance. His fingers shook as if with the palsy.

Twig-Smathers whispered hoarsely, "Woodrow, we have a deal. What is your plan? Tell me what to do."

"You don't have to do anything. Don't worry."

He shrieked, but in a whisper. "Don't worry? My God, man, it's not you Sir Charles is going to be aiming at. Help me, Woodrow."

The umpire was dressed like an undertaker, with a black cutaway coat, top hat, and white gloves. He had a beak of a nose, a real air-slicer. He intoned, "Seconds, please step away."

I asked, "You got the top half of that old piece of paper with you, with the island's name on it?"

"Yes, bloody yes. It's in my shirt pocket."

"Then don't worry," I said, walking a dozen steps away from Twig-Smathers toward the surgeon, who had a mournful countenance and who worked as a barber when there weren't wounds to heal.

"Woodrow," almost a screech, Twig-Smathers's eyes round and wild, jerking between his persecutor and me. "Woodrow, help me."

A flock of starlings worked the grass to my west, rattling and squeaking. A horse snorted. A tuft of wind swayed tree boughs.

"Gentlemen," the umpire called, "raise your weapons to an upright position."

His eyes riveted on me, Twig-Smathers struggled to raise the Webley. His legs swayed as if made of rope. He was breathing like a quarterhorse.

Staring down at his opponent, Sir Charles moved as smoothly as if he was made of gears and ratchets. Up the pistol came.

"Gentlemen, here is the handkerchief." The umpire held it aloft. He looked to his left at Sir Charles. "Sir, are you ready?"

Sir Charles dropped his chin a fraction. His backbone must have been made of iron. His gaze cut across the grass and into his opponent.

The umpire's head swiveled right to Twig-Smathers. "Sir, are you ready?"

Bruce yelped some reply.

The umpire's hand was steady, about to release the handkerchief.

Then yours truly, Woodrow C. Lowe, sprang into action. I quickly stepped toward Twig-Smathers. The handkerchief began its fluttering descent, but I reached Twig-Smathers before it hit the grass. I stepped into Sir Charles's line of fire. I don't know whether Twig-Smathers was more terrified or puzzled when I grabbed his shirtfront just below his neck and fairly lifted him off the ground.

My right fist smashed into Twig-Smathers's nose, snapping it. I hit it again, a second blow, pushing it sideways so that it rested against his cheek, grotesque and bleeding. His eyes rolled skyward in fear and pain.

"Sir, sir, these actions are not sanctioned by the rules," the umpire called out, a parliamentarian to his soul.

Again my fist lit into Twig-Smathers's face, opening up a one-inch slash on his cheekbone. Then I shifted him a little and sent my fist into his other cheek. Another gash appeared, spilling blood. Then I popped him in the forehead. I was bringing away blood with each hit, spreading and splashing it. Twig-Smathers howled, and his face was beginning to resemble a peach left too long in the sun. He sagged but I held him up.

Now let me say that if I know anything it's how to punch someone, and while Twig-Smathers was undoubtedly hurting—in fact by that time I had beaten him to unconsciousness—I was being more artful than damaging. I know how to pop a man so it sounds worse than it feels, and I know how to break skin but not the bone underneath. The latter, by the way, was accomplished by suddenly twisting my fist as it landed on his face, wrenching the skin and splitting it open. Every person has a talent, and mine happens to be smacking someone upside the head.

I sent a right cross into Twig-Smathers's temple, and it produced a resounding crack, then I released his shirt and he fell to the ground and landed like a sack of grain, senseless and bleeding.

I turned to Sir Charles and called over the grass between us, "Sir, I am going to beat Twig-Smathers until your honor has been restored."

His pistol still in the air near his ear, Sir Charles stared at me, his eyes sunken and unreadable.

"And I will beat him to death if necessary." I reached down to Twig-Smathers and once again gathered his shirtfront in my left hand. "Sir Charles, you tell me when your honor has been satisfied."

I brought Twig-Smathers up. He hung there like an empty coat. My fist rocketed into his jaw, then into his cheek, then into his forehead. Blood seeped and fell. All I could see of Twig-Smathers's eyes were the whites. The sounds of the blows were too much even for the starlings, and they took off, circling and squawking and then disappearing in the trees.

The umpire called, "Sir, this is highly irregular and you should . . ."

I smacked Twig-Smathers yet again. His head swung as if on a swivel. His face resembled a cheap cut of meat, bloating and purpling. Triangular flaps of skin hung and swayed. I could see glimpses of bone. I hit him again.

"That will just about do, sir." Sir Charles's voice sounded like carriage wheels rolling across gravel.

My fist hesitated.

"I said 'just about,' " he added.

My knuckles bounced off Twig-Smathers's ear, where they tore away his ear lobe so that it dangled like a pendant. I busted him once more on what was left of his nose.

"Now that will do," Sir Charles finally allowed. His voice contained undisguised glee. This humbling had surely been more satisfying than a mere shooting. And what a story this would make at his Pall Mall club.

I released Twig-Smathers and once again he landed on the grass, a shapeless, undignified lump. I turned to Sir Charles to face him squarely.

Let me inject that my visage—with its scars and bumps and its turned-down mouth, its low brows and spiky haircut—could send a powerful message. I asked loudly so the umpire and the surgeon and Sir Charles's second could all hear, "Then your honor has been fully restored, Sir Charles?"

The message—doubtless understood by Sir Charles—was that any further discussions on the topic of Sir Charles's honor would have to be taken up with me.

"Yes, fully," he called.

"And you and Twig-Smathers are quits?"

"We are quits, sir."

The surgeon clucked his tongue at the spectacle. I bent over Twig-Smathers and searched through his shirt pockets until I found the piece of paper. It was mustard-colored with age. The bottom was a ragged tear. I held it up to my eyes. It said only, ON THE ISLE OF ANGUILLA. I had never heard of the place. I hoped it was nearby.

I stuffed the paper in my pants pocket, then lifted Twig-Smathers's limp form and hauled him to his carriage.

Now I never did understand why Bruce Twig-Smathers didn't never thank me for this service I performed. By pummeling him I saved his life, pure and simple. A moron could have understood that equation. Were it not for my good work Twig-Smathers would have left the duelers' field a corpse. But he was an ingrate, as you will shortly see again.

NINE

Spears and Chains

A DERVISH WAR formation is a terrible and frightening sight especially when coming right at you. Five thousand of the frothing buggers lined up in a long row, ten or twelve deep, all waving their javelins and spears and hatchets and knobkerries and rifles. They howl and stomp and bang their blades against their shields, and surge forward accompanied by pounding war drums and roaring *ombeyehs*, which are elephant tusk war trumpets.

The Sudan desert sun was an evil yellow orb that sent out rays that had a weight, pressing a man down and crushing his spirit, and making the enemy line appear as a shimmering mirage. Red dust rolled away from the dervishes' stamping feet, forming a red cloud, making the warriors seem gauzy, and offering the hope that these ferocious tribesmen were indeed the product of the sun's tinkering with the mind. But overhead, carrion kites—black slashes against a sulfurous yellow sky—circled and circled, and we desert men know these devil birds never appear in a mirage and so the dervish warriors must be real, too.

Dervish weapons bobbed up and down, filling the sky. The sun glinted off spears and axes. I'd heard that a dervish never washes his weapons, happy to have blood and hair cling to them, and as I squinted at the approaching mob I could see tufts of hair and bits of dried scalp on those blades and points. Bright, flapping flags, some inscribed with the Mahdi's name, were attached to long spears. The enemy line flowed forward relentlessly, thousands of heathens shrieking for blood, closing in on me across the baked and cracked desert.

And the racket. I don't mind saying I was about ready to pee my pants, the noise was such. Some of the dervishes were shrieking "God is

125

great" in their impenetrable language and others were doing this ear-busting falsetto yodel that sounded like dozens of cat organs.

You've never heard of a cat organ? You take six or eight cats, put them in a cage with their tails hanging down through holes. Their tails are tied so they can't lift them. Each cat's shriek has a different pitch, and so you can play simple songs by yanking the cats' tails in the proper order. They were quite common in London back then. A cat organ isn't as melodic as I've made it sound. But back to the dervishes.

Most of them wore *jibbahs*, which are long white shirts, patched and filthy, some with yellow-and-blue cloth streamers hanging from them. The warriors also wore loose drawers and cotton skull caps called *takias*. A few horsemen rode behind the dervish line, and I guessed these were officers. And the damndest thing: two of the mounted officers were wearing ancient chainmail and helmets. I later learned that armor from the Crusades was commonly seen among dervish officers, the breast-plates and helmets and chainmail having been handed down through many generations.

The heaving line drew closer, and spears and razor-sharp boomerangs called *safarofs*—yes, they had boomerangs, too, just like in Australia—started landing around me. The few with Remingtons started firing in my direction—a dervish almost always shoots high, thank the Lord for this small favor—and bullets hissed and whistled overhead.

A dervish war formation moves four times as quickly as an advancing British infantry line, so these savages were coming on and I mean quickly. The air was soon filled with their projectiles, and I could make out faces, brown and tan and snarling, and growing bigger, all of them peering at me. I was about to die, I knew that much, my innards pierced, my head bludgeoned, my throat slit, or some combination of these, Annie and Joe Lowe's boy lying dead on the Sudan desert, his bones soon to be picked apart by carrion kites.

You might be wondering how I got into this fix.

Well, a week after I saved Bruce Twig-Smathers's life by putting my fist to his conk a number of times, his mother, Lady Twig-Smathers—the same one who didn't want a scullery boy walking through her house—called me into her office at Blechfield. She was a handsome woman in her early fifties, wearing a dove-gray dress with a maroon belt and cuffs, and an emerald on her finger the size of a .38 slug. Her mahogany hair was tied loosely behind her head. Her eyes were jackdaw blue and all business. She surveyed me up and down, then said, "I have heard several accounts of your actions on Pheasant's Field."

"Yes, ma'am."

She lifted a bone china tea cup, and put it almost to her mouth before continuing. "I had earlier found out about this absurd duel, I knew of Sir Charles Priestly's prowess with dueling pistols, and I frankly believed I had seen the last of my son. I have concluded you saved my son's life, Mr. Lowe. Your ingenuity on Pheasant's Field is to be commended. Bruce may not have had occasion to thank you, and he very well may, once the swelling around his mouth goes down sufficiently so that he can speak."

This woman was smarter than her boy, that was plain. I gripped my cap in front of me, wondering what she wanted.

"I understand you were in the American cavalry and are also a boxer."

"A fistic scientist, yes, ma'am."

Her lips pursed, she looked at me again, slowly, up and down.

She said, "Bruce's regiment has been called to Africa. He is to put aboard a steamer at Dover two weeks hence. He is going to assist putting down the Mahdi's rebellion."

I had no idea what she was talking about. Who was the Mahdi?

"Africa is a hard place and the dervishes are treacherous enemies. The fate of Chinese Gordon will testify to that." She finally sipped her tea. "My son is a naïf, Mr. Lowe. He will surely be killed in Africa."

"Doubtless, ma'am."

"That is why I want you to accompany him. Go to Africa as his batman and bodyguard."

Her suggestion was so outlandish it took me a moment to grasp it. Then I blurted, "Why in the world would I do that?"

"Because I will pay you one hundred pounds now and another hundred when Bruce returns to England alive."

A hundred pounds was a satchel full of money, three years' wages for a workingman. A hundred now, a hundred later. Six years' salary just to bring her lad back from Africa? This was like finding money lying in the street.

"You got yourself a batman and bodyguard, ma'am." I paused. "What's a batman, by the way?"

"A servant to an army officer." She turned to her desk and brought out a bank draft. She handed me the check and that's the last I ever saw of her.

Let me also mention a curious note I received from the War Department two days before I boarded that steamer. It was hand-delivered to me by John Laramie, the second man at the United States embassy, who had traveled from London to Dover to give it to me. He had decoded the telegram himself. He told me to read it. It said in its entirety, YOU ARE TO MAKE CAREFUL NOTATIONS OF BRITISH DEPLOYMENTS IN EGYPT AND THE SUDAN. PHIL SHERIDAN, GENERAL, UNITED STATES ARMY.

I asked Laramie, "Why does the United States want to spy on the British army?"

He replied, "You forget that the British army burned our White House. Do you understand your orders, corporal?"

"As much as I ever understand anything." I handed the note back to him and he destroyed it in front of me. So that's how I came to the spying profession.

I became Bruce Twig-Smathers's batman and bodyguard, and went with him to Africa, and that's how I found myself facing a dervish war formation.

That day in the Sudan desert, my situation was not as hopeless as I have heretofore painted it. I was standing in the middle of a British square, the most formidable military invention of the age. Napoleon never did figure it out, and it chased him from Europe. This was the Anglo-Egyptian Army, and our field was commanded by Grenfell Pasha, Sirdar of the Army. The walls of my square were comprised of Coldstream Guards, 5th Lancers, Scots Grays, Marines, Grenadiers, 16th Lancers, and the 1st and 2nd Life Guards Blues. Hard men and good soldiers, the lot of them. These troops stood behind a *zareba*, a hastily constructed but still vicious wall of stakes and thorns. Thousands of caltrops—four-pointed spikes, the medieval invention that cripples cavalry and ill-shod infantry—had been strewn in front of the *zareba*. We had four Krupp guns, two brass howitzers, and one Gatling gun. The soldiers were armed mostly with Martini-Henry rifles which had a tendency to clog, which is what an Englishman calls jamming, and bayonets that bent too easily.

In the center of the square with me were our camels and horses and mules, doctors, artillery, a few officers such as Bruce Twig-Smathers, and other batmen. I was holding the reins of Twig-Smathers's horse, an ornery animal named Sakr ed Dijaj, the Chickenhawk, a suitable appellation, at least the first part of it. The horse whinnied and tried to bolt but I held him there, the reins tight in my fist. Swatting his quirt against his high boots, Twig-Smathers paced back and forth, his back held as rigidly as if he had a board down his uniform. I give the man credit. I thought he'd turn tail and trot at the first sign of the enemy, but he stood there, under the eye of Sirdar Grenfell, keeping his lip stiff and his pace brisk.

In they came, this phalanx of murderous heathens, howling and marching, waving their blades and bludgeons and rifles. A few English soldiers fell, pitching forward or sinking to their knees, blood spouting, but the square immediately closed in. My two-hundred-pound reward for looking after Bruce was looking like less of a bargain, frankly.

When the dervishes were forty yards away, Sirdar Grenfell announced quietly, "Fire, if you please."

Captain Twig-Smathers and the other officers instantly barked the order. The thunder of rifles and the Gatling gun and howitzers filled the universe, and the dervishes were instantly hidden behind a haze of gray gunsmoke.

"Fire at will," Grenfell ordered.

The peal of gunfire was continuous. The camels growled and spit. Horses and mules danced. Regimental colors fluttered, held proudly aloft by their bearers. Wounded British soldiers were passed back to the square's center, and the square filled in, filled in, filled in. The surgeons brought out their tourniquets and compresses.

The wind abruptly lifted the smoke and dust. The dervish line was devastated, a gap-toothed, staggering wall of shattered bone and flapping skin, of gushing blood and flying limbs.

But they still came, singing their song of praise.

And the British fired. Methodically, efficiently, ruthlessly.

Years later Rudyard Kipling would write a poem about these dervish warriors. One line was, "You're a pore benighted 'eathen but a first-class fighting man;" I can so testify. Not one dervish soldier hesitated. Not one ran. Gut-shot warriors kept coming. Men whose legs had been shot off kept coming on their bellies. Their *jibbahs* awash in blood, the dervishes kept coming.

Their shattered line climbed through the *zareba* to the tips of the British bayonets. The first row of English soldiers hacked and hewed at the dervishes with their bayonets and rifle butts while the second, third and fourth rows kept pouring fire into the heathen mass over the shoulders of the first British line. The wind carried the sickening scents of blood and fear and cordite.

A spear ripped my shirt sleeve, gashing my ribcage, and buried itself in the Chickenhawk's flank. The horse rose and kicked and shrieked but I pulled him down, dodging his hoofs. Twenty yards away, Twig-Smathers was calmly firing and loading his Webley pistol. The barrel glowed red. The British army had taught him something about pistols since his meeting with Sir Charles. And Bruce's mother had underestimated him.

Before I recount what happened to me—and I was but a footnote in this matter—let me summarize the Battle of Toski, as this event came to be known. The date was August 3, 1889, and on that day in this field over five thousand dervish warriors were released from this life. These utterly fearless soldiers paraded right into the British rifles and right onto their bayonets, and the British obliged. It was a massacre. British losses were light.

Now, back to me. The dervish line finally staggered and collapsed, not for lack of will or courage but for lack of bodies. The British found their voices, and began whooping and hollering, still in their lines and still firing mercilessly. The dervish flags had all fallen. The desert was covered with their bodies, so many it appeared I could have walked to the horizon on corpses. The desert sand was red.

And then one of those boomerangs, perhaps thrown from the last standing dervish, clipped the Chickenhawk's brow. That accursed animal jerked its head sideways, and my arm suddenly slipped between the horse's cheek and the bridle. My arm was caught, tied to the Chickenhawk's head by leather straps, my thumb in that dumb animal's eye.

Off that wretched creature went, helter-skelter, bruising through the British line, tearing through the spikes and thorns, lunging over hillocks of fallen dervish warriors and skidding in their gore. I was dragged alongside, Chickenhawk's front knees bashing my legs, caltrops sticking me again and again. I twisted and pulled but I couldn't free my arm, and the panicked horse was traveling too fast for me to find my feet. And Lord, after a few moments we dashed by several dervish warriors who had seen the inevitable and had begun an orderly retreat. I was among the enemy.

They don't like to be called dervish, I was to learn. That word means "poor men," a term first used by the Mahdi. Later he called his soldiers "ansars," which means either "helpers" or "those consecrated by God," I never figured out which. In any event, the word "ansars" was used by the Prophet, and became the preferred word for themselves.

The dervish warrior is usually too poor to own a horse but oftentimes his enemy is not, so among the dervishes' many fighting skills is hamstringing. The Chickenhawk buckled. His leg cut cruelly by a dervish hatchet, the horse toppled, pulling me down with it. A hatchet next took off most of the Chickenhawk's head, and then went up into the air to come down for mine.

But the dervish's arm stopped. To this day I think it was my green eyes. The warrior had been told that Anglos have the red eyes of Satan. Instead of using the hatchet's sharp edge, he used the blunt side, and that found my forehead. Out I went.

So that's how I came to be a captive of the dervish.

I REGAINED CONSCIOUSNESS after most of the skin on my backside was scraped away from being dragged across the desert, and I suppose the pain is what brought me around, and there was a world of pain back there, I'll guarantee you that, being hauled across yellow halfa grass and through spiky mimosa shrubs and across sharp stones.

I was tied by my feet to a jackass, my ankles bound together with strands of palm fiber, my arms sliding along above my head. When my captors saw my eyes open, they halted the procession and prodded me to my feet with their spears. When I stumbled and sagged, I was kicked to standing. My blouse was gone, and my pants were missing a leg. Someone had taken my boots and socks. I was bleeding from scores of cuts and scrapes but I couldn't see any of them because of the flies—thousands of them—that covered my torso like a knobby shirt the moment I was still.

Then, probably for sport, two trumpeters, one on each side of me, placed the mouths of their *ombeyehs* against my ears and let loose with a blare so loud and deep that I blacked out and fell to my knees.

I was being kicked in the head by several fellows when I came to again. They grabbed my hair and yanked me to my feet. The same rope that had been tied to my feet was now wrapped around my neck, and this rope was still attached to the donkey. My hands were tied with palm fiber, which was tightened with a wood tourniquet, and then water was poured over the fiber, which shrank as it dried, drawing the fiber into my skin.

About fifteen dervish warriors surrounded me, and this group was growing by twos and threes as survivors straggled in. Only one dervish officer had lived through the charge, and he was a big fellow, about my size. His shaved head was covered with a straw cap and he wore symbolic badges on his fine cotton shirt. He smiled malevolently at me and spoke in their garbled language. His shoulder was gashed, exposing his collarbone. Blood ran down his right sleeve and dripped onto the ground. He seemed oblivious to his wound.

I shrugged my ignorance of what he was saying so he brought up a finger and ran it across his throat. I did understand that, all right. They were going to chop Woodrow Lowe's head off. Perspiration dripped into my eyes. He did it again lest I missed it the first time. Then he slapped the donkey's flanks. I was yanked forward.

I walked somewhere between seven days and ten days, I have never been sure, all the while tugged along by the donkey. Once in a while I was given water from a gourd. The only thing I had to eat were several handfuls of *kamar-el-din*—which was dried apricots mixed with water, which was always covered with flies, which I ate flies and all because I weren't in a position to be too particular—and Sodom apples, so called because they cause endless flatulence. I walked the skin off my feet. The cord around my wrists cut to the bones and I still wear those scars. I was delirious much of the time so I had Teddy Roosevelt and John L. and Amy Balfour and Lady Elizabeth as company. We marched along the river, and the desert eventually gave way to fields of cotton, sugar cane and melons.

The journey ended in Khartoum. I was taken to the gate of the Saier prison where an anvil had been sunk into the yellow ground so that it was almost level with the roadway. The rope was removed from my neck. My wrists had swollen over the palm fiber. A guard cut away the rope and some of my skin, freeing my hands.

I was made to put one foot then the other on the anvil. Fetters were hammered onto my legs with a short chain between. An iron ring was fitted around my neck. Two more rings were locked around my wrists and were connected to each other by an eight-inch iron bar. More iron links connected my wrist cuffs to the ring around my neck.

Then I was marched through Khartoum, passing beehive huts, along winding mud-walled streets, along fetid sewage ditches. I was boxed in by guards. A growing crowd of the curious followed us. We passed the slave market, the Mahdi's tomb and the great mosque, then finally reached the Khalif's compound.

The residence was walled with red brick. We passed through a gate into a small court. I was to learn later the compound's layout. Nearest the mosque were the Khalif's private apartments and reception rooms. Ranging east of his chambers were the apartments for his wives and the harem for his concubines. Next east were food and munitions warehouses, stables, and the eunuchs' and guards' quarters.

When I was shoved into a reception room only four of the guards accompanied me. I rattled as I walked, and my gait was shortened by the shackles. Near the north wall was an *angareb*, a bench eight inches off the ground and covered with a palm mat. Silk-covered cushions lay on much of the floor. Curtains of all colors hung over the walls, even where there weren't windows. A brass chandelier was centered on the ceiling.

Let me describe my condition, and it was piteous. I was by then suffering from dysentery so my ribs and hips were protruding. I was dagger-thin, except for those parts of me that were swollen. My wrists had bloated, and were swelling over the cuffs. The anklets had debarked my legs, and the iron clanked against bone. My feet were so puffed they looked like round knobs. The ring around my neck had rubbed off the skin, and the iron lay on white bone. I was a mass of infections. My back and buttocks had not healed from the scraping across the desert, courtesy of that donkey. My tongue was swollen, and I could not fully close my mouth. I was so weak that I staggered. Each time I was about to fall, a spear point jabbed my ribs.

When the Khalif entered I was clubbed on the back of the head so that I fell to my knees. An Anglo dressed in a *jibbah* also came into the room. The Khalif sat on the *angareb*, crossed his legs, and stared at me a full minute without speaking. Then he leaned back on a large bundle of cotton cloth that formed a pillow. Expressionless, the Anglo took a position behind him. The Khalif was wearing a white *jibbah* with a red border. A narrow strip of cloth five yards long called a *wassan* was wrapped around his waist and he also wore a shawl fastened at his left shoulder. He was the first dervish I'd seen wear shoes and socks. The Khalif had sharp features: black eyes like a kite, a hooked nose that hung over his lips, and a pointed chin.

Also in the room were six adolescent boys, children of Abyssinian Christian slaves, whose duty was to follow the Khalif morning to night to act as his message runners. Along the walls were his household body-guards, mostly from Mahmud Ahmed and Zeki Tummal's armies, but also free Arabs from the Tama, Beni Hussein and Gimr tribes. No fire-arms were present but the guards stood at attention, spears at their sides. Their uniforms were unadorned long shirts. The room was crowded.

Who were these people? In Islam, the Mahdi (which is Arabic for one who is divinely guided) is to appear at the end of time to restore faith and justice on earth. Muhammad Ahmad, a riveting itinerant religious teacher in the Sudan, declared himself to be the Mahdi in 1881, and had gathered an enormous following of men at arms with the purpose of driving the infidel English from the desert. He came close, capturing Khartoum in 1885, killing General Gordon and most of his troops. When the Mahdi died later that year his ardent follower, the Khalif, assumed military command of the ansars. Khalif means successor. His full name was Abdullah Ibn Muhammad. The dervishes were a move-ment, not a people or a tribe. In fact, the dervishes included almost six hundred tribes speaking over a hundred different languages, none of them the queen's English.

The Khalif finally spoke, an action that didn't seem to affect his lips, more a hissing through clenched teeth.

The Anglo interpreted, rendering in English with a strong German accent. "The Khalif prays for Allah's mercy upon you."

I stood there.

More from the Khalif, then more translation. "You are to be crucified, as was Jesus the Prophet."

"Crucified?" I croaked. "You mean, on a cross with nails? Like in the Bible?"

The German dipped his chin.

That was grim news, indeed. As I recalled, Jesus hung there six hours before the spirit fled his body.

My throat was chalk-dry, my words raspy. "I don't suppose I have a choice."

More translation. The Khalif's eyes were locked on mine.

The German had dark patches under his eyes and ears that stuck out like bat wings. He interpreted. "Your life will be spared if you convert to the true faith."

"Sure," I said quickly. "What is the true faith?"

The German didn't translate that question, probably saving my life.

"Islam," he said dryly.

"Well, I'm your man. Islam it is."

Does my conversion sound a trifle opportune? Let me point out, with all due respect, that you weren't there.

The German spoke to the Khalif, who lowered his chin fractionally. A slave, dressed only in baggy drawers, stepped forward to hand me a rolled *farwa*, a prayer rug.

"We are now going to the mosque to pray," the German said. "You will join us."

"I don't mind a little prayer now and then," I said, trying to sound friendly.

"We pray five times a day and we pray fervently."

"Five times a day? Every day? That's a passel of praying, isn't it?"

"You will learn to hold your tongue." The German's voice dropped, and I detected a note of sympathy. "Believe me, you will learn."

The Khalif rose from the bench and exited a side door, followed by the German, then six senior guards, the messenger boys, two dozen more guards, and several eunuchs. At the point of a spear I was herded after them, my shackles rattling and clanging, headed in this procession to the mosque.

I prayed that day, and I prayed every day. My shackles—legs, arms, and neck, about forty pounds of iron—were not removed once in the next eight years. Not for any reason, not for any amount of time. My life, from age twenty-five to age thirty-three, was spent in chains.

And I prayed. I have not told you this as yet but you have been listening all this while to a Moslem. Beginning that day in the Khalif's mosque I learned the way of the true faith and I practiced the way of the true faith, and Allah, in his infinite and undeserved mercy, succored me and guided me, and let me survive those years.

TEN

A Shovel and Chains

YOU MAY HAVE thought that yours truly, Woodrow C. Lowe, had reached the nadir of his existence as a scullery boy, scraping leftover food from the plates of English nobility then plunging my arms into lye suds. You'd be right, if you didn't count the eight years I cleaned the johnny houses for eight thousand heathen tribesmen.

That's right, that was my job all them years in captivity. The Khalif's household staff and guards numbered eight thousand, all living in his compound or nearby barracks. Dervishes produce poop just like the rest of us, and when you have eight thousand of them it's a mountain of poop.

I was in charge of it. My tools were a shovel and a mule and a cart. My rounds included the barracks privies, private apartment privies, the harem privy, the eunuch dormitory privies, the privies of the homes of the Khalif's brothers and uncles and cousins, and the stables. If it stunk, I shoveled it. I would load the cart, then sit on the back of the wagon while a donkey pulled it the short distance to the River Nile, where I would shovel all that poop in. The Khalif's residence was in Omdurman, across the river from Khartoum, at the confluence of the White Nile and the Blue Nile. White or Blue, downstream from me and my shovel the river was mostly brown.

And lest you think any of this was fun, remember I was in chains the entire time. My steps were constricted, my wrists held firmly eight inches apart by the iron rod between the cuffs, my neck encircled by iron and connected by iron links to all the rest. All the while I was guarded by an ax-carrying slave named Abu Anga—that jackal's whelp—a surly, agate-eyed mute who every minute or so would swat my butt with the flat of his blade to encourage me to work harder. So I moved the poop, and

136

Abu Anga—that engorged tapeworm—guarded me while I moved the poop.

I had a partner in poop removal, a fellow named Ahmed Siwah, who must have been viewed as less a threat to the dervish empire because he wore only shackles around his feet and no other chains. He worked with me two or three days a week. The other days he wandered among Omdurman's alleys removing bloated horse and mule carcasses.

I was not a prisoner of war, with the attendant rights of such prisoners. In combat the dervishes expect no quarter and give no quarter. They don't take prisoners. Those not killed on the battlefield are taken as slaves, and that's what I was, a slave. I had no rights whatsoever. I was *ghanima*, captured war plunder. Abu Anga—that quivering pile of green phlegm—pointed, and I did whatever task he was pointing at, which was cleaning privies. I complained once, my third day on the job, and Abu Anga—that pussed-out sore—broke my cheekbone with the butt of his sword, and he never heard me say another word again.

I was always hungry. Once or twice a week I'd be tossed a bit of unrecognizable meat, but I subsisted mostly on a yellow vegetable I never did learn the name of. And, oddly, almonds. Almonds were plentiful, and I was given a bowl of them every day. I grew to detest the taste of almonds, but they kept me from starving.

I am not going to talk about them eight years of moving poop. With the exception of my encounter with the concubine, nothing—absolutely nothing—happened to me other than the privy patrol and getting swatted by Abu Anga, that infected tooth of a man. Eight years of it. And my praying, of course.

My guess is that the Khalif had ninety women in his harem. They were organized into groups of fifteen or twenty, and each of them groups was presided over by a free woman, usually a senior concubine, but not a slave like most of them. The Khalif issued money and grain each month to these forewomen, and they provisioned their respective houses. It seemed to me the funds were used mostly for cosmetics, all the oils and scents of the harem. The Khalif liked his women gamy with smells; clove, sandalwood, and lilac. The chief eunuch issued the clothing, with the finest silks and jewelry going to the most beautiful women. The concubines lived in four houses, collectively called the harem, all within the compound. Every month or so the Khalif would tour his harem, and with a gesture of a finger cull out them concubines that no longer met his standards, and who would then be given to his cousins and generals, to be replaced by even more winsome women recently purchased or captured. The concubines had utterly no contact with the outside world except once a year when female relations could visit. Each night the Khalif would send one of his boy messengers to the harem with his choice of a concubine for the evening.

My contact with these women was limited to removing their night soil. The privy for all four concubine houses was north of their buildings, near the compound's north wall. I'd trod back and forth between the harem's privy and my cart, watched closely by Abu Anga—that ulcerating carbuncle—and by the eunuchs who guarded the gate in the wall.

These beardless sopranos were tough customers. They'd watch me, their arms folded, swords hanging from waist bands, hoping I'd make one misstep so they could carve me up. When near the harem I did my work with my eyes carefully on the ground. Gazing upon a concubine was punishable by a flailing.

One November day in my sixth year of captivity I was moving the harem's poop, Abu Anga—that odious hemorrhoid—patting my rear with his sword, when I heard a shout, followed by another from a different direction, then a scream of fear and pain. The eunuchs and Abu Anga and I turned to the nearest harem house in time to see a man rush out the door, blood pouring from a slash across his cheek.

He was a trespasser—one of the Khalif's second cousins, it turned out—who was crazed with love and lust for one of the Successor's favorite concubines, an auburn-haired Abyssinian. The interloper was wearing a white *jibbah* and a wild expression.

With one whirling movement, a eunuch drew his sword and slashed at the trespasser, whose severed left arm fell to the ground. The cousin shrieked in agony, wildly spun around and dashed back into the harem, squirting the eunuch and the harem wall with blood. The eunuch, then three other eunuchs, rushed in after him. Women screamed. I heard the hiss of a blade sailing through the air.

One more shout came from the harem, and it ended in a terrible gurgle and sigh. Then a eunuch emerged, pointed his blade at me and gestured me into the harem. I had some cleaning up to do, it appeared.

I may be the only testicled Anglo in history to enter a harem and survive to tell the tale, by the way. Quite a distinction. I rattled and clacked toward the door, Abu Anga hammering on my butt with his ax to show the eunuchs he was in control of the situation. I carried my shovel under the doorway arch. A eunuch held open a silk curtain and I slipped under it.

The room was disorienting. It had no hard edges, nothing firm. Carpets and pillows covered the floor. The walls were hidden behind billowing fabric. Two boys worked palm fans, pushing air around the room. The one large room was divided by bead curtains into several areas, one of which had eight Western-style brass beds with mosquito nets hung over them. Another area was filled with mirrors and tall cupboards that resembled armoires. The place smelled of rose petals and sandalwood, an almost overpowering scent that curled under my nose like a temptress' finger.

And the women. There were eight concubines in the room, all standing, their eyes wide, some with their hands at their mouths. None had had time to don their veils so their faces were cruelly exposed to my view. These women were the finest Africa and the East could produce, voluptuous and curving and scented and fine-boned. Their skin was of all colors of Africa, from ebony to honey. The Khalif liked them with large eyes and long limbs and high necks and mountainous bosoms. Silver jewelry was forbidden, but around their necks and arms and ankles were mother-of-pearl buttons and necklaces and bracelets made of copper strands decorated with onyx and lapis lazuli and pink and red coral. They wore silk and woven cotton cloth with brightly colored borders.

In horror, the women stepped back, away from me. I was an ogre in chains, my legs dappled with poop, my six-year beard matted and filthy, my clothes tattered and stained.

Or perhaps it was the trespasser's body they recoiled from. It was in five parts: head, trunk, and three limbs. All surgically severed. Blood was puddling beneath the pieces. The dead man wore an odd smile, and his black eyes stared reproachfully at me. I used my shovel to lift the head—they're heavier than you'd think—and I turned back to the door.

That's when she caught my attention. I hadn't seen her until that instant, a concubine in a white robe trimmed with gold and red. A shawl hid her hair. The eunuch at the doorway was looking with satisfaction at the bloody head on my shovel blade, then turned to chatter over his shoulder to one of his mates so I braved a second quick glance at her, slowing my gait a little.

Except for the German, who would cross my path once in a while, and who was a slave like me, I had not seen a pair of blue eyes in six years. Yet this woman's eyes were blue, and pale like milk glass. Her full lips were painted rose red like the others. Her cheekbones were wide and her nose a slender chip. She hadn't really stepped to intercept me but rather shifted her weight on her hip, just enough so that I would risk one more glance at her. And when I did, she lifted the corner of her shawl, a small, seemingly cavalier gesture that revealed blond hair, tresses the color of the sun.

My breath caught. This concubine was a European, maybe English or French or German or Italian. And she was deliberately telling me so.

Confused, I took several more steps to the door. I let the severed head drop off my shovel blade, and it hit the floor face first with a squish. As I scooped it up, I glanced again at the woman. Her eyes were still fast on mine. She did not smile or nod or anything else. Her shawl was back in place. I shuffled through the door, where a crowd of fifteen or twenty eunuchs had gathered. The sword-wielding eunuch was showing off his strokes to the smiling appreciation of the others.

I was to learn later that the eunuch who had cut down the trespasser was named Hamed Ibn Belal, and the cousin weren't the first man deranged with lust he had slashed apart. This eunuch wore fat like I wore poop. It was all over him, hanging from his arms and thighs and chin. His fingers resembled sausages and he had a roll of fat at the back of his neck that ballooned in and out whenever he nodded his head. He was missing all his front teeth except his canines, and when he breathed heavily with exertion his lips blew in and out. His flat nose was as wide as his mouth.

Hamed Ibn Belal again flashed his blade through the air, recreating the event. I kept my eyes low as I passed him and the other eunuchs, carrying the head to my cart. Abu Anga mercilessly whacked my butt with the flat of his ax, showing the eunuchs he was in charge of me. The eunuchs had considerably more status in the compound than did a slave-guard like Abu Anga—though I don't know if he'd trade places with one of them, given the surgery involved.

I made four more trips back into the harem for body parts but the blond concubine and the other women had retreated to another building. I had her fixed in my mind, though, so I would have someone to think about during my rounds. I tapped the mule's flank and Abu Anga tapped my flank, and we made our way to the Nile to dispose of the body.

Turns out I didn't need that blond woman in my memory. An eerie thing began to happen, as spooky as a desert mirage. That European concubine began regularly appearing in my line of sight. Magically, it seemed. I would be short-stepping along, clinking my chains, my shovel over my shoulder, Abu Anga following along, and suddenly there she would be. In a window. At the end of a walkway. Under an arbor. Just around a corner. On a balcony. Always just a glimpse of her. She never smiled or nodded or signaled or said a word. For an instant her eyes would burn into mine. And then she would disappear.

This happened about once a week for two years. At first I thought her appearances were coincidental but later knew differently because they continued and she always was gazing right into my eyes. Abu Anga never caught on.

Talk of the harem, or indeed of any of the Khalif's business or pleasure, was forbidden. One day, about six months after the blond concubine began inserting herself into my line of sight, when Abu Anga was out of earshot, I summoned the courage to whisper a question to my partner in poop, Ahmed Siwah. Did he know the blond concubine's name? By then I was fluent in Arabic. He blanched at the question, and moved his head with a sudden jerk as if suffering a nervous tic, then plunged his shovel back into the brown pile. He refused to meet my gaze the rest of the day.

Apparently the compound's walls had ears. The next day the eunuch Hamed Ibn Belal walked up to me, grabbed me by the back of the neck, lifted me off the ground, chains and all, and marched me to the whipping posts near the front gate. These were two poles, each with the girth of a man's thigh, imbedded in the ground five feet apart. He and another eunuch strung me up, securing me with rawhide strips.

Hamed Ibn Belal announced to the gathering crowd of guards and eunuchs that I had been sentenced to five hundred stripes for "an indiscretion." From the folds of his sleeve he brought a rhinoceros-hide whip called a *kourbash*, a villianous instrument with a one-foot-long handle and three feet of hide.

The Khalif watched from his balcony.

Now, you may have never been flailed by a eunuch but let me confide that the experience is unpleasant. He said in a low voice, "*Malish kullu shai bi iradet Illahi.*" It doesn't matter because all happens as God ordains.

Then he lit into me.

A lash with a *kourbash* does not do the damage a Royal Navy cat-o'-nine-tails does, where a hundred strokes will kill the sailor. Nevertheless, the rhinoceros-hide whip still slices and skins. He followed the required procedure. Two hundred stripes on my lower back. The air was filled with bits of my skin brought away by the hide. Then two hundred on my shoulders at which point I passed out. The final hundred strokes were to my breast, but I was out and cold and didn't feel them until I woke up an hour later, lying in my straw hut, shackles still on but much of my skin off.

My partner Ahmed Siwah was there, and he helped me sip water from a wood cup. I never determined if he had ratted on me to the eunuch but because he gave me that water and tried to clean my wounds, I forgave him. I needed that water.

I was a mass of open sores. I was unable to stand for a week, but as soon as I could I was back on the poop patrol. With the flies and infections, I didn't heal for five weeks. And to this day the skin over much of my body is nothing but purple, papery scars.

And then, damn my eyes, if about a month after I was mended the blond concubine didn't again begin appearing in front of me. A veiled and shawled chimera but as real as my shackles. I wouldn't survive another flailing so I diverted my gaze. But she kept appearing, suddenly, always gazing at me. So after a fashion I returned her stare. Two or three seconds of escape, once or twice a week, whenever she magically appeared.

I never spoke with this woman, never touched her, knew nothing of her, yet she gave me hope. And maybe I gave her hope.

ON A MOONLESS night eight years and four months into my captivity I lay on my straw mat trying to recall Boston and my mother and father and Joe Lowe's Museum and Sporting Palace and John L. and Amy Balfour, anything and anyone from my life in Boston, but was having trouble conjuring up the images. That town and them folks were so far away and so long ago that they had begun to recede from my mind. Soon I would have nothing left of my free life, not even memories, and I was frightened. I rolled onto my side, my chains slithering after me. In such times I turned to thoughts of the blond concubine. Unconsummated dreams of a mysterious women.

My partner Ahmed Siwah was asleep on his mat six feet away, tossing and gassifying like he always did. The air in the hut was stifling. A red-tail scorpion walked into my hut like he owned the place, its poisonous tail high and ready. I shuddered. I hated them crawly things but I knew after innumerable encounters with them that my finger was faster than their stingers. I flicked it back out the door. A cloud of flies hovered above my head, waiting for me to drift off so they could drink the moisture at the corners of my eyes.

A hand came out of the night and clamped over my mouth, choking off my cry of alarm. Another hand gripped my hair and lifted me several inches from the ground. I ratcheted my eyes around.

Oh Lord, it was the eunuch, Hamed Ibn Belal, come to flail me again. What had I done? Looked at the concubine one second too long? Had I been caught? I would not live through another five hundred stripes, I knew that.

The big eunuch brought my ear to his lips and whispered in Arabic, "Take this box. It has a false bottom."

He released my head and pressed into my hand a wood box, not a large container, just the size of my palm. Then he disappeared.

In the dim light I made out a few letters of a language I didn't know printed on the box, and the picture of an eyeball. Maybe the box had once contained eye ointment. I glanced at Ahmed Siwah. Still asleep. My fingers trembled as I opened the container.

The interior was lined in cloth, but nothing else was inside. I picked at the cloth until a corner came away. I peeled it back and inserted a fingernail and levered out the false bottom.

The space of the hidden compartment was small, no more than half an inch deep. Inside was a folded piece of paper.

As if it might turn to dust in my hands, I opened it carefully. My breathing was stilled. I placed the paper in front of my eyes to read it. Not enough light. I moved carefully to the open door of my hut, trying not to ring my chains. Again I held up the note.

By starlight I read, YOU CAN TRUST HAMED IBN BELAL. TR.

Trust the eunuch? Why would I want to trust the eunuch? And who would know of him and me and my plight? TR. I scratched my chin. Then it came to me.

Teddy Roosevelt.

The spirit of hope filled me so quickly I felt giddy. Theodore Roosevelt. Allah bless him and his children. Tears filled my eyes. Somehow that four-eyed nut had reached across the ocean and desert, had reached back in time to the primitive heathens, and was trying to rescue me. Teddy could do anything.

I leaned back against the wall, clasping the note to my scarred chest, my eyes closed, offering my thanks to the one God.

Teddy Roosevelt would end my years of captivity. Somehow, some way. I didn't need to ask Allah to assist Teddy Roosevelt because TR was sufficiently formidable. But I did ask the Merciful Creator to grant me patience. Grant me the composure and stamina to wait until Teddy Roosevelt could do his work. Then I destroyed the box and the note.

I didn't wait long. Two nights later, my partner Ahmed Siwah was missing from his mat next to me. By some prearrangement, I figured, and I was right. I lay awake until Hamed Ibn Belal appeared. The eunuch could move quietly, I'll grant him that. He weren't there, then he was, filling my small hut, smiling toothlessly, his big sword on his belt. He smelled of lavender. He carried a cloth bag.

He said in his sweet, high voice, "Let us go. To the Goat Well near the north gate. Bring everything. You won't be coming back."

"I have nothing to bring."

He smiled, revealing his black maw of a mouth. "Then just bring your chains."

I had told a small lie. I had more than my chains. I had carried my piece of paper with directions to the treasure with me all them years of captivity, folded into a tiny square and hidden in my blouse. I had tossed away the upper part of the page, the part with the island's name on it. I figured I could remember Anguilla.

The eunuch produced strips of cotton cloth from his bag and wrapped them around the chain between my ankles to silence the clanking links. "Follow me."

He was about to disappear but I seized his meaty arm. "Go get the blond woman. Bring her to the Goat Well."

"The one who stares at you?"

"You see everything, don't you, Hamed Ibn Belal?"

"I am missing my testicles, not my eyes." Another smile. "You are asking the impossible, me procuring the woman."

"I'm not going anywhere without her," I insisted. "You're a harem eunuch. You can enter the harem at will. Go to her bed, put your hand over her mouth, and carry her to the Goat Well. I'll meet you there."

The eunuch chewed toothlessly on that a moment. He nodded, then vanished.

I left the hut. My chains were almost silent, and for the first time in eight years my walk weren't accompanied by their cheery chiming. I can't say as I missed the noise. I moved in a good infantryman's crouch, hugging the walls of the guards' barrack, then the apartment of one of the Khalif's brothers, then I passed the brothers' privy I had visited thousands of times. Around me rose the walls and buildings of the compound. Not a sound from anywhere. A few oil lamps burned here and there, but I stayed away from their light, and I walked in darkness.

Moving slowly so my restricted gait would be less noticeable to the chance observer, I walked into the central courtyard, passed a trickling fountain, then under a rose arbor. I passed the stone vault where *El Mansura*—the Victorious—the Khalif's great war drum, was stored, then came to the Goat Well, a brick building with an interior well. I stepped into the recess of the door to wait.

The eunuch appeared almost immediately, carrying the woman in both arms, one hand firmly over her mouth. She struggled, kicking at his legs. She was wearing a cotton nightdress. No shawl or veil. Hamed Ibn Belal planted her in front of me and gave her time to see me before he removed his hand from her mouth.

Her gold hair was loose to her arms. Her eyes were wide and blue and alluring. Her chest rose and fell under her robe. She stood silently.

I held out my shackled hands. "It's time to go."

She gazed into my eyes like she always did, then brought up her hands to grip mine, and we moved from the well toward the north wall. I was accustomed to the feel of my shovel handle, and her hand was soft and exotic.

We followed the eunuch toward the gatehouse. I knew there were always two guards at the gate. Had Hamed Ibn Belal taken care of them? We turned a corner. The woman gasped. Or maybe it was me. The guards were at their post, their Remingtons across their chests. How could we pass them?

But the damndest thing. Each guard then put one hand across his eyes, pantomiming blindness.

The fix was in.

The eunuch escorted us through the gate. A horse was waiting, a good one, an Anafi stallion. Without ceremony, Hamed Ibn Belal lifted me onto the horse—side-saddle because of my leg irons—then put the woman behind me. He handed me the reins.

"Go north along the river," he said, "past the quarters of the Wad el Besier and Hellawin tribes. Among the date trees behind the Hejra Mosque will be four camels and a guide. Trust the guide. He will take you north into the desert."

The eunuch stepped back to the guardhouse, then brought forth a hide bag. He said, "Your guide at the mosque will have provisions, including an ax for your chains. But in this bag is a token of esteem. And it is for good luck. From me and Teddy. Go with Allah and may He protect you."

I took the bag and placed it against my stomach. The woman's arms slipped around my waist. I leaned down to grip the eunuch's shoulder in thanks, then I nudged the horse's flank with my heel. The animal shot forward. The concubine squeezed me.

I was not familiar with Omdurman, not having been outside the gates in all them years except to walk directly to the Nile to unload the cart, but the woman pointed, and we passed through the silent streets of the town. The sound of my horse's hooves seemed to fill the streets. At any moment I expected to hear mounted guards behind us, chasing us down, closing in, but only silence and darkness were behind us. We passed a gallows, nothing more than a horizontal pole mounted on two supports where the *Mehekemet es Suk*—the market police who maintain order in the town—brought those they arrested.

We rode by the mosque, then into a glade of trees. The hidden camels were snorting and smacking, easy to find. A slip of a man—so thin his legs resembled shovel handles—stood alongside the beasts. He was wearing a white *farda*, a cotton wrap, against the cold. He smiled hugely at us, then helped us dismount. I put the eunuch's hide bag on the ground. If the man was alarmed by the unexpected presence of the woman, he didn't show it. He pointed to a flat stone in the ground, then lifted an ax and waved it merrily.

I knelt in a reverential position to place my wrist fetters on the stone. "May Allah guide your blade."

The ax came down and cleanly split the rod between my wrists. Then I lay on my side, and he slashed down again with the blade. Links that had held my neck ring to my wrists sprang apart.

I stood to spread my arms like the wings of a bird. So long out of use, my muscles cried out but I stretched anyway, pushing my hands as far apart as they would go. I smiled maniacally, suffused with the joy of liberation. The woman watched from under a fig tree.

Next the guide placed my ankle chains on the stone. Down came the ax. My legs were free. I took a huge step, then another and another. I marched up and down, regaining the knowledge of walking like a human being. Sensations that were both old and new flooded me as my legs relearned their full work. The guide smiled and nodded. The iron rings would have to wait for a saw, but without the chains the rings were only nuisances.

Unable to prevent myself from grinning, I approached the concubine. She gazed at me like she always did, unknowable and steadfast.

"I'm no longer a slave," I said in Arabic. "I'm free. And so are you."

She still said nothing.

I switched languages. "Do you speak English?"

Her voice was hushed. "I'm from London."

"Friends, we must go," the guide called. "We only have a few hours before you will be reported missing. The Khalif will send his soldiers."

Her face glowed in the starlight. The Khalif indeed had his choice of the fair. Her yellow hair seemed alive, a river flowing around her neck and shoulders, splashing down her chest. Even in the dim light I could see that her hair was of many colors subtly woven together: amber and straw and apricot and gold. Her eyes were high-sky blue with tiny gray flecks in the irises. Her lips were full and peaked, and when she smiled as she did just then she revealed a keyboard of teeth the color of fine ivory. Her nose was as thin as a scimitar. Her skin was frost white. She stepped to me, moving with a cat's grace, gliding over the ground, her nightgown drifting behind her. Her breasts rose and fell as she breathed, sending long starlight shadows across the fabric of her nightgown.

The guide called urgently, "Friends, let us go." Using a quirt and rope, he brought a camel to its knees to allow her to mount it. The animal bellowed a protest. Then the guide lowered a camel for me. I climbed on. Our camels rose to their feet.

A trace of humor touched her voice. "I knew if I stared at you long enough you would save me."

"Please, let us do our talking later," the guide said. "After we are deep in the desert."

I suddenly remembered the eunuch's gift. "Let's see what Hamed gave us." I smiled at the irony of the eunuch who had striped me five hundred times giving me a present. Our guide tossed up the hide bag.

"He said it was for luck," I said.

I dug into the bag. And brought out the severed head of my guard for eight years, Abu Anga.

ELEVEN

More Scorpions

WE TRAVELED NORTH, reaching Wadi Bishara at sunrise, and passing the hills of Habegi that evening. Tracing the route of the Nile about a day's ride west of the river, we were on the high ground northwest of Metemma for the next sunrise. Our camels were working without sleep and so were we. Each time we paused vultures appeared over our heads. We spotted dervish soldiers three times but always at long distances, and we got our camels down on the ground before they saw us.

Our guide belonged to the Kababish tribe from the Gilf Mountains. His name was Ali Wad Abdalla, and he had brought with him a hundred Maria Theresa dollars, inflatable water skins, a dagger, dates, dhurra flour, a wood bowl, and a flint, all of which he said were already paid for and were mine. When we reached the Gilf Range, two of his brothers were waiting for us with four Anafi mares, which they exchanged for our camels. Ali Wad Abdalla said he had done all he could for us, and was leaving us to return to his mountains. His risk had been huge, and I gave him all my dollars and my thanks. He and his kin turned toward the hills, and the woman and I continued north on the horses.

We reached the Kerraba Plateau. We were still in Mahdist territory but had not seen other humans for an entire day. The plateau was sandy soil spotted with shiny head-size black stones. The horses had to pick their way through the rocks. As the sun set, the Nile was a silver streak miles away on the eastern horizon. The woman had been seasick on her camel, eating and drinking nothing, but recovered when we switched to horses.

That night I helped her from her horse, then removed the saddles and bridles. Night or day, the desert is a bitter place, always threatening, always testing. I gathered stones and placed them in a circle, building a wall the shape of a horseshoe two feet high that would keep the night wind from cutting into us, a trick our guide had taught us. As the woman collected dried mimosa branches I made a bed of fist-size stones, then mixed dhurra with water in the bowl. Next I lit the mimosa with flint and tinder. The fire worked rapidly on the dry wood. She sat on the stone wall and watched the yellow licks of fire. For the first time we had the time and the inclination to talk.

"My name is Victoria Littlewood." She smiled with her entire face, and it changed the mood of the desert. Her voice was honeyed and full. "I would not have lasted much longer in the Khalif's harem. You saved my life."

"How long were you in the harem?" I separated the burning branches, letting the fire die down.

"Four years ago last May I was on my way from London to visit my father in the East Africa Protectorate. He was there to open a coffee and cotton plantation. I crossed the Channel at Dover, and took trains to Paris then south to Marseilles, where I boarded a steamer."

I was gazing at her, nodding occasionally to disguise my stare. Her loveliness was confusing me, because I have no idea how long that scorpion was on my foot. It moved suddenly up my ankle, and the thrill of cold fear soared up my backbone. I frantically kicked my leg, looking like a dervish whirling, and managed to loosen the thing from my skin. The scorpion landed between Victoria and me, and immediately scurried to the backend of our horseshoe wall. It disappeared in the ground near one of the rocks.

"Them little things make my skin clammy." I walked over to that stone and carefully nudged it aside with my foot. As a kid I could never resist looking under the rock for crawly, ghastly bugs, usually regretting it.

I regretted it this time. A scorpion nest lay below. Skittering and crawling, waving their legs and tails. The hole was filled with the critters, a hundred or more, a writhing mass. Yours truly had seen a lot of disgusting things in his life but nothing like this. They were hissing and roaring, a hackle-raising sound. I'm sure now, looking back, that this fearsome noise was in my head and nowhere else. They were all looking up at me with their little ruby eyes, daring me to have anything to do with them. I declined. Shivering, I inched the rock back over their hole, then jammed a wad of cloth into the entrance.

I returned to the fire. I kneaded the dhurra dough. After a moment the hair on the back of my neck lay down again.

Victoria went on with her story hesitatingly, as though reentering an old life. "A storm rose as we approached Alexandria. The ship ran aground. I survived the surf only to be taken prisoner by the Adandafi tribe. They took me south to sell me to the Khalif. He bought me for seventy-five camels, the highest price he had ever paid for a concubine, I heard."

"And you were forced to enter his harem?"

"After two months of schooling."

"Schooling?" I asked, patting the dough flat. "In what?"

She blushed and looked into the dying fire. "You must know."

Sometimes the obvious needs to beat me about the face and shoulders for a while. Finally I exclaimed, "A school for that? For doing the . . . for that?"

"My life depended on pleasing the Khalif. I learned everything I could from the harem master. It was an explicit education."

With a stick I removed the embers from the glowing stones, then poured the dough over the hot rocks. "It's a wonder you survived."

"I had two lives. Alone in the harem, I was a proper English maiden, never allowing my thoughts to stray from my parents and my church and my school. When I was called to the Khalif's chamber, I transformed myself into a harlot, a wanton woman who lived only to satisfy my master's most carnal needs."

"Lordy."

I rearranged the embers on top of the dough, bringing my eyes up occasionally to look at her. Victoria's eyes were hooded and sultry and immense. Her mouth was arched and its natural resting position was in a bit of a pout. In the red setting sun and in the gentle tossing wind her gold hair seemed tendrils of flame framing her face. Each time she moved, the cotton fabric stretched across her bosom, outlining it, showing off its bounty.

"He told me I was the most passionate and learned concubine in his harem," she said softly, fighting the memory, "and he called for me at least once every week. I left him exhausted each time."

"Lordy." I swatted the embers from the top of the bread, then pulled it from the stones. I beat it with the stick to rid it of most of the ashes then lay the blackened loaf on a stone to cool. I sat on the ground, my legs out, and pulled out a handful of dates from a bag.

This woman was beyond the imagination, beyond anyone I had constructed in my mind during them lonely years on the Dakota plains or in my dervish hut. She gestured as she talked, and smiled and frowned, and pulled her wrap tight against the cold, and shifted on the stones, and each motion was an unconscious but vast display of sensuality. The Khalif had his choice of half a continent of women, and here was the one he beckoned once a week. I certainly understood why.

"I cannot catalogue the things I did to pleasure the Khalif."

"That's just as well, ma'am, because after eight years of captivity I don't think my constitution could endure such a list."

Her eyes canted merrily but then they opened fully and abruptly. She rose from the stone and stared over my shoulder. I turned to follow her gaze.

And knew instantly we had been caught. Six horsemen galloped toward us, black silhouettes against the purple sky, dervish soldiers, whooping and carrying on, their legs raking their horses' flanks in the warriors' eagerness to get to us. Dust billowed behind them and drifted east in the wind.

Her voice was twisted by disappointment and fear. "I cannot go back. I cannot return to the harem."

I added, "And if they take me back, I'll be dangled from a gallows."

So I had nothing to lose, which explains what happened next, maybe.

The horsemen closed, grinning widely, the lot of them, and waving their spears in the air. Hooves pounded, and the dervishes called their shrill war cry. They flowed around us, then pulled to a stop in a loose circle ten yards from the woman and me. The horses had been ridden hard, and were blowing and heaving.

The one closest to me carried a Remington rifle, sawed off for easier handling on a horse. Still grinning wickedly, the warrior said, "The peace of Allah be upon you."

I replied in Arabic, "And upon you."

He pointed at me with his rifle. "You are the Successor's slave." The rifle moved fractionally to her. "And you are his concubine. We have been sent to bring you back to Omdurman."

"We are not going back," I stated calmly.

The dervishes laughed.

"You are dressed like us ansars," the leader said with satisfaction, looking at his men to make sure they were nodding and smiling at his prowess, "and your camp looks like an ansars' camp, but I saw the white bottoms of your feet as you sat there. They gave you away."

The leader was a *Ras Miya*, a rank equivalent to a captain. He wore a towel on his head and a white *jibbah* covered with dust. "We must bring the woman back alive but the Successor has required only your skull."

He aimed the rifle at my heart and said, "You will be easier to take back dead. Make your peace with the Forgiving God."

The Remington's muzzle seemed the size of an eight pounder.

Victoria gasped, "No."

Was everything she said or did, under every possible circumstance, voluptuous? I was about to take a bullet in the chest and her voice still had the power to stir me.

I held up my hand. "I cannot be killed."

More laughter from the troops. Wearing a smirk, the leader looked up from the rifle barrel.

I hurried on, "Allah has willed that I leave the land of the Mahdists. And he has willed that I live."

The leader again lowered his eyeball to the rifle barrel, sighting me in. I could see his trigger finger pull back.

"Many people have tried to kill me and none have succeeded." Hopelessness calmed my voice. "And each has paid a terrible price."

The dervish cavalrymen laughed yet again.

"Look at me." I pointed to my cheek, where Lady Elizabeth in her ardor had cut me open. I lied, "This came from a knifeman. He died horribly."

Then I pointed at my scarred eyebrows and my cauliflower ear. "Men have tried to beat me to death. They died in agony." Then I lifted my shirt. "And you may have witnessed my flailing. You know it would have killed most men. Yet here I am."

The warriors had stopped their guffawing and were now silently staring at me. Just like me, they believed in the grace and mercy of Allah. Perhaps the God of the Faithful had truly meant for me to be spared. I certainly spoke with confidence about it, and no one tempted the Merciful One.

But their leader was not convinced. "Perhaps you live only because no one has tried to kill you with a rifle."

And, so saying, he shot me.

The bullet soared into my shoulder below the collarbone and out the other side. I blew off my feet backward, and landed hard against a boulder. Like I said before, the dervish always aim high. He had been aiming for my heart.

You have gathered by now that what Woodrow Lowe lacks in brain power he makes up for in doggedness and toughness. I simply willed myself off the ground, once again to stand before the dervish captain, whose face registered astonishment that, had I not been about ready to expire, I would have found gratifying.

"And every one who has tried to kill me has suffered horribly." My words were still level and forceful, spoken in the tone of a prophet.

Fighting spreading pain and a blackness that was reaching for me from the ground, I stepped quickly to the leader, swatted aside his rifle, grabbed him by the shirtfront, and yanked him off his horse. He cried out as I dragged him across the ground.

Blood squirted from my shoulder and I could feel it spilling down my back below the exit wound. My shoulder and arm were a vast pit of pain but I shook it off. The white cotton of shock began dabbing at my mind. The captain kicked at me and howled orders at his men but they were transfixed by the spectacle of the dead man risen.

I carried the dervish captain over our wind wall and across the coals of our fire. I kicked aside the rock that covered the scorpion pit. There they still were, dreadful and poisonous and wriggling, their spikes up.

I crammed the man's head into the hole, face down, and I held him there. His scream was muffled by the dirt and the mass of scorpions attacking his face. The captain kicked and bucked, his hands flailing the air, but I held him down.

After fifteen seconds, I brought him back up. A dozen scorpions were attached to his face by their stingers, and they moved their little feet through the air, looking for purchase. The captain shrieked and shrieked, a pitiful wail that was being closed off by his swelling lips. A few scorpions dropped off. One had its stinger planted in the captain's eyeball. Below my feet, others scurried away.

The captain moaned and grabbed at his head as I dragged him back to his horse. A few more scorpions fell away from him. His face began an awful swelling, bloating so quickly that his humanness seemed to be fleeing him. I dropped him at the foot of a cavalryman.

I breathed quickly against the pain. My head was light. I did not have long. I managed to inquire grandly, "Who will be next to try to kill me, against the will of Allah?"

Nobody, and that was for damned sure. I don't believe a one of them was drawing a breath. A trooper scooped up his captain and they all took off, back the way they had come, their horses kicking up another cloud.

I turned to Victoria and smiled weakly.

Then the blackness came over me. Victoria Littlewood winked out, and in front of me were all the stars in their heaven, and then they too were gone.

"I SUPPOSE I owe you my thanks." Sir Fitzhugh Littlewood raised his wine glass. "And here they are. Thank you, Mr. Lowe, for rescuing my daughter from her captivity."

"Yes, Mr. Lowe," Victoria's mother said. "You are certainly the gallant. We thought she had died in the shipwreck."

I lifted my glass and nodded at Sir Fitzhugh and his wife Lady Gwendolyn. "She and I are even, I figure. I got her the first two hundred and fifty miles, and she got me the rest of the way."

And that was true. Victoria had stopped the bleeding from the hole in my shoulder and the other out my back, and had spent three more days at that campsite nursing me until she thought I could be moved. I was in and out of consciousness, with a burning fever, but I was able to tell her how to rig a travois like I'd seen in the Badlands. It's my guess that word got out that I couldn't be killed because although we saw five bands of dervish warriors on our journey north through the Nubian Desert and passed Wadi Halfa, none of them patrols approached. We followed the Nile, but always a day's ride west of the river to avoid civilization. I could do little but encourage Victoria. We traveled by night, eating dhurra bread and occasionally approaching the river to steal oranges and dates from orchards. We were hungry much of the time, and had to make a coarse bread from the pith of palm trees, and we also consumed gum tree pith. She took care of me, looking for signs of infection and changing the dressing on my shoulder, insisting we rest when she determined I could go no further. My fever finally broke and for the last several days I could ride a horse. By the time we entered the British-held town of Aswan, at the Nile's First Cataract, we had traveled over five hundred miles from Omdurman.

The British garrison commander in Aswan wired the Cairo legation of our arrival, and Victoria's parents were found at their home in Tuscany, where they were wintering. They boarded a steamer and were in Cairo by the time we arrived on the slow train from Aswan.

This dinner at the Continental Hotel in Cairo was their thanks to me, I suppose. Victoria and I had been in the city four days by then. I had used most of that time delousing and washing and clipping and shaving. Getting eight years of dervish poop and dirt and vermin off me was a chore. An English Army doctor checked out my shoulder and announced that I'd live, which I knew well enough by then. The doctor said he'd never seen so many scars on one body, which I took as a compliment. That night I was wearing clothes loaned me by the doctor. Even though Sir Fitzhugh and Lady Gwendolyn looked put-upon to be hosting a beat-up, dog-thin Irish-American Moslem, I was glad for the meal. I was penniless. The dervishes had long ago taken my hundred pounds I'd received for agreeing to protect Bruce Twig-Smathers. Just as well, given the job I did. I didn't have a Mahdi dollar, a Makbul dollar, a crossed-spear dollar, an Ibrahim Adlan dollar, or a British pound to my name.

"To think," Lady Gwendolyn said in her windy voice, "a daughter of Sir Fitzhugh Littlewood spending four years cooking for a tribe of savages."

I glanced across the table at Victoria. She raised an eyebrow and smiled. So that's how her parents would deal with their precious daughter having been a concubine? They would never learn of it.

Lady Gwendolyn was a mirror image of her daughter but a generation older. Small lines had formed around her eyes, and her neck had loosened a bit but was still a few years from looking like a gobbler's. Her blond hair had begun to silver, and she wore it pinned up behind her head, but loose and alluring. On one finger was an emerald the size of a cockroach and on another a diamond I'd have trouble lifting.

She said, "We'll take you back to the city right away, Victoria, and you can begin the rounds again. You are only twenty-eight years old. It's still not too late for you. Lord Whitan has not as yet married, have I said? He always was rather forward around you, and you'll still be able to turn his head. I'll begin working on a meeting the minute we arrive home."

Victoria said, "I'm sure, mother." She lifted a slice of mutton with her fork and stared at it. Her mouth turned down. She was wearing a lime-green silk dress with a forest-green waistband and cuffs. Her hair was tied behind her neck with green ribbon. She looked entirely Western and subdued.

Time had played harder with Sir Fitzhugh than with his wife. It had taken most of his hair and had reddened his nose and yellowed his teeth. He carried himself, even when sitting, with starched dignity. His pin-prick eyes were far back in his head, and they were restless, always searching for something to disapprove. They tended to land on me during that dinner.

"And where do you go from here, Mr. Lowe?" Sir Fitzhugh's tone suggested that the farther I went—the more distance between me and his daughter—the better.

"Back to the United States, then on to Anguilla. I've got some business on that island." Calling it business made my fool's errand sound worthwhile. My voice hopeful, I added, "As soon as I can come by the funds for my Atlantic passage, I'm on my way."

He cleared his throat in the proper English manner. "A man of your energy doubtless will earn the money quickly."

So there went any thought I had of financial largesse from Victoria's parents. Damn, all I needed was one second-class fare.

I asked, "Do you know anything of Bruce Twig-Smathers, who was at Toski with me?"

Lady Gwendolyn said, "Now, Victoria, that's someone else we must invite over. I saw Bruce just three months ago. He is of a marriageable age."

So Twig-Smathers had made it out of the desert. I can't recall whether I was relieved or disappointed.

"He's the fourth son," I said petulantly. "He inherits nothing."

Lady Gwendolyn looked at me. "Quite. I had forgotten."

The dinner passed by in a blur of chit-chat. Lady Gwendolyn held forth mostly, scheming on how to reintroduce Victoria to London society. Largely forgotten, I ate my meal, but slowly, so the richness of the food would not come back on me later. I caught Victoria glancing at me a few times but she only smiled sadly and looked away. She nodded or said, "Yes, mum," for each new angle her mother invented to get Victoria back into the rounds and to get her married before she reached the age—about thirty, I gathered—where Victoria would be doomed to spend her life as a spinster. Sir Fitzhugh and his wife asked their daughter only a few questions about her captivity, and she answered them evasively. They asked me nothing.

The waiters whisked away plates to be replaced by more plates. They filled our glasses. They lit Sir Fitzhugh's cigar. Candlelight played across Victoria's face, coloring it in reds and oranges and blues. I had never possessed her, of course, but I was losing her, just the same. The sight of her—those eyes above the veil—had kept me going in Omdurman when I was at the end of my resources. Tomorrow she and her parents were boarding a boat and heading home to England.

At ten sharp, Fitzhugh Littlewood rose, announced the dinner had been grand and shook my hand goodbye. His wife smiled at my departure.

Victoria came around the table to meet me at the dining room door. She held out her hand. I shook it. I wanted to weep at the prospect of never seeing her again, but I held back. I had never entertained any realistic hope along them lines, just idle dreams fanned by my captivity and hardships.

"Someday maybe we'll see each other again," she said, and I was startled when she stealthily and secretly pressed a note into my hand. A piece of paper carefully folded.

Her eyes were unreadable. I turned to go.

I was on the grand staircase exiting the Continental Hotel before I dared open the note. In small, precise handwriting, it said, MY ROOM NUMBER IS 22. COME TO ME AT MIDNIGHT.

I SPENT THEM two hours in the hotel bar, my foot up on the brass railing. I didn't have any money but the bartender was kind enough to keep filling a water glass and once he put an orange slice in it. I could scarcely breathe. I didn't dare form any hopes as to what Victoria had in mind. And as the lobby grandfather clock struck the last note of midnight, I knocked gently on the door, just below the brass numbers two and two. It opened immediately.

Wild scents rushed out at me, gathering around my head like long arms and pulling me into her room. Rose and jasmine and sandalwood, which after eight years of poop almost overcame me. I gasped against the fragrances but let them lift me into the room.

For one desperate moment I thought time had played a cruel trick, had transported me back to Omdurman and had returned the shackles to my neck and feet and wrists. I had been here before. The harem, a shovel in my hand, and a sliced-up body in front of me.

But there were no chains and no dead body. Only the soft contours of the harem, with the silk and cotton, the pillows and rugs. Scented wood was burning on a small brass brazier. The bed had a silk coverlet over it. Muslin drapes wafted in the slow air coming in the window. Light from a brass lamp flickered on the bedstand.

She stood by the bed. I valiantly tried not to swoon at the sight of her. My ears started ringing. I tried to breathe but my chest wouldn't cooperate.

"Oh Lordy," I muttered raggedly.

One of her hands was on the bed, the other on her hip. Across her shoulder was a silk transparent netting that fell to her feet. Her bosom was hidden behind a strip of silk that seemed to be struggling not to burst. Around her neck was a messaline cord from which hung a small silk bag, nestled in the canyon between her breasts. I can't really call what she was wearing on her bottom "underwear," because there was too little cloth, and it was silk, and where it circled her hips it was only a string, and the rest of it in front was just a triangle. A red shiny silk triangle. I'm sure somebody, probably the French, have a word for this kind of underwear. I wobbled but saved myself by leaning back against the door.

Her gold hair covered her shoulders to the top of her bosom. She smiled at me, then her lips puckered. Her eyes did not leave mine for a moment.

"Woodrow, I thought you would want to know how I kept the Khalif happy."

I couldn't get any air into my chest, as if my nose and mouth were stoppered. I dropped my eyes to her breasts but brought them quickly back up, not wanting to be rude.

She lifted a hand to indicate the room. "So I visited the market today and purchased a few things. I've made this your harem."

"My harem?" I croaked.

"Close the door, Woodrow. And lock it."

My hand fumbled with the latch.

She moved toward me, gliding slowly across the rug, the netting sliding across her skin, caressing her.

"You should know how I suffered, shouldn't you, Woodrow?" Her tongue ran along her lower lip, moistening it. "You should know what I learned in the harem school, and what I had to endure those four years, don't you think?"

I pressed back against the closed door. I was frightened out of my wits. Scorpions were nothing compared to this. "You aren't going to tie me to a bed, are you? I haven't had much luck with that."

"You risked your escape for me. You risked your life for me. Now I am your reward." She slowly removed the pouch from around her neck to put it on the bedside table.

My shirtback was suddenly wet. "Ma'am, I mean, Victoria. I was so many years in chains that if I ever knew anything about this type of thing, I've forgotten. It's been eight years."

She drifted closer. Her hand languidly reached for my chin and she drew a finger along my jawbone. Her breasts filled the space between us.

She said softly, "Eight years is a long time without a woman, Woodrow."

"And the last one hurt me pretty bad." I was squeaking.

She smiled slowly. Everything she did she was doing slowly. She even spoke slowly. "She broke your heart?"

"She cut my face with a piece of glass. Cut clean through my cheek into my tongue. Hurt like hell, I don't mind saying."

"Is this the scar?" She lifted herself on her toes and ran her tongue along the scar. Her breath was hot on my cheek. "She sounds like quite a woman."

"I was lucky to get out of her room alive." I found strength in talk but my voice was frogged.

She pulled back just a little and stared deeply into my eyes. "Woodrow, you don't know much about these affairs, do you?"

"I overheard my pa cry out to Ma, 'Brace yourself, Annie,' in their bedroom a couple times, but that's about all I know."

"Then I had best take special care of you." She lifted one of my hands in hers. "Have you ever loved anyone, Woodrow?"

"Yes."

"Did she spurn you?"

"She didn't know me well enough to spurn me." This was Amy Balfour, of course. "I've never even been introduced to her. And lately I've been having trouble bringing her face to mind."

She drew her fingernails along the back of my hand then brought my hand to her chest. "There must be a draft in the room, Woodrow." She was whispering. "Do you feel it?"

"No, ma'am. Victoria."

"Sure there is. It must be the chill that is making my nipples so tight."

It was a hundred and twenty degrees in that room, I can attest to that.

"Just look at them. Maybe they are reaching for you."

My hand trembled. She held my finger a quarter-inch from the fabric covering her breast.

"Would you like to touch my nipple, Woodrow? It's so taut it's aching. Maybe your touch would help? Do you think?"

I weren't thinking. I weren't breathing.

She moved my hand, just a fraction, and moved it more until the tip of my finger reached her nipple, pressing it in.

"That certainly is soothing, Woodrow. I feel better. But it just doesn't seem enough."

She formed a cup of my hand.

"Maybe you should hold it," she whispered. "Do you think you can? It would be such a tonic."

She placed my palm gently over her breast, then molded my fingers around it, pressing my hand firmly. Mounds of her flesh spilled around my hand. A little gasp escaped her. A big one escaped me.

"Goodness, Woodrow," she breathed. "My breast is too large for your hand. What should we do? Do you have any ideas? It's such a bother."

My mouth was as dry as the country we had crossed together.

"Maybe if you sat on the bed we could discuss this problem, do you think?"

She kept my hand on her breast as she guided me those few steps to the bed, her eyes never leaving mine. Her breast was a furnace, warming my hand and arm up to my shoulder. I was lost.

Victoria pushed me back onto the bed so that I was sitting in front of her. She brought up my other hand and cupped it and filled it with herself. Her neck arced back and her lips parted. My breath was blowing patterns in the silk netting across her breasts.

"My clothes, Woodrow. All this silk. It's suddenly so heavy. I can't bear up under the weight another moment. What should we do?" She untied a bow at her shoulder. The silk drifted off her to collect around my full hands.

Her hands moved to my head. Her nails slowly raked my scalp, then she brought my head forward into the deep valley between her breasts. Silk and flesh filled my horizon. She firmly gripped my head, holding it in that lovely depth, as she gracefully climbed onto the bed, pushing me back into the soft folds of the coverlet.

She hovered above me, her hanging breasts filling the world between us. "Woodrow, do you know what to do?"

I mumbled, "Not hardly, no."

I don't think she really wanted an answer to any of her questions, by the way. And you may have noticed a pattern here. Something about my abused face, with its scars and bumps and swollen ear, made women want to cradle it between their breasts, to cuddle and heal it, to press their breasts in on me, to smother me. I can't say this made all the trauma to my face over the years worthwhile, but it was close.

Victoria directed my hand to her thigh and pressed it onto the satin skin there, sliding my hand up and down, then urging it around to the firm globes of her posterior.

"Press me there, Woodrow. How do I feel?"

Lordy.

My head was still firmly gripped between her breasts, and she started doing things with my hand behind her.

"My breasts are so dry, Woodrow. It's this desert air. Can you help me? I'm so helpless. With your tongue, maybe?"

I cannot utter another word of this encounter with Victoria Little-wood. Even after all these decades, the memory of what happened next will rush back with such force that it might break something in this hundred-eight-year-old body. Let me say, though, that I was with her until morning, and I swam in her again and again and again. She showed me things that perhaps only she has known in history, techniques she invented.

During a brief interlude—I had begged her for a moment to regain my strength—she picked up the pouch that had been around her neck. She spilled out rubies and emeralds and diamonds, about two dozen in all. Occasionally the Khalif had rewarded her with a bauble. She said she knew I had no money, and said I could have all of her gems. I took only three to get me back to the United States and then on to Anguilla.

When I finally sighed a good-bye at her door, she kissed me on the cheek as if she were my sister. I was just a husk of my former self. My legs were so wobbly the doorman at the hotel entrance had to assist me down the steps.

I had intended to see her and her family off at the Empire dock but I slept through it, more a coma. When I awoke I ran to the pier but only in time to see her steamer round a bend and disappear from sight. I watched that piece of river for another half hour, tears rolling down my face.

TWELVE

A Gunboat

You'd think shoveling poop for eight years would have prepared me fairly well to return to Teddy Roosevelt's service, but it didn't, and I didn't do much of a job. As we ran up San Juan Hill, Teddy on his little horse Texas, me following along on foot, my main view was of that cursed animal's rump because carbine and pistol smoke hid most everything else. Texas repeatedly kicked back to try to shake me but I stuck to her despite the beating my legs took from her hoofs.

Overhead, Mauser bullets soared through tree leaves and palm fronds, a ceaseless piping. The slugs' thin screams dropped to low buzzes as they passed and raced away to the rear. And they made flit, flit, flit sounds punching through leaves, and all too often hollow plops when they found flesh. The Spanish fired down at us from the heights of San Juan Hill, sending so many bullets the sky rippled and flashed like the surface of a pond, a power of lead.

The Roughriders were cavalry but on this day they were fighting as infantry because most of their horses hadn't yet arrived from Florida. An infantryman's first instinct under fire is to look for cover. Men dropped behind rotted stumps and dived into guava thickets. The advance up the hill was stalling before murderous fire.

Roosevelt yelled back over his shoulder, "Afraid to stand up, men? Hell, I'm on horseback. Stand and charge."

He waved his pistol and pointed it up the incline. A bullet shrieked past my ear, sounding like a silk dress tearing. I was carrying a Winchester rifle, and hoping I had the correct end forward. I knew ladles and pots and shovels, not firearms, and I wouldn't have been able to hit a hole in a ladder with that rifle. I couldn't see anything to fire at even if I'd had the inclination, what with all the gray smoke and leaves.

The temperature on that jungle hill was over a hundred degrees, and it was so humid that Teddy had to pause in his haranguing his troops to wipe mist from his glasses. I was awash in my own sweat, and enough of it had rolled down my legs that my boots squished as I ran. I kept that horse tail right in front of my eyes. We old Indian fighters know that a horse's most noble calling is to put itself between you and incoming projectiles.

Teddy waved his gun arm again, urging us on. He was wearing a sombrero with a Roughrider blue and yellow polka-dot kerchief hanging from the rear brim, a blue shirt and yellow suspenders, all of it bouncing along on that horse. I don't think he had a sense of the ridiculous. And he was grinning with those huge snappers. His teeth must have constituted 40 percent of his body weight.

Tripping, flailing at underbrush, scrambling over embankments and barbed-wire defenses, searching for targets, Roughriders followed him and me up the hill. When he was forming up the regiment, Teddy had rejected twenty volunteers for every one he accepted. The Roughriders were crack shots, the lot of them, but San Juan Hill offered few targets. The Spanish snipers were dressed in green, and many of them were hidden high in the fronds of royal palms. Spaniards may all lisp in that language of theirs, but they're hellish fighters, you give them some rifles and rile them up about invading Yankees. A bullet slapped into the heel of my left boot, knocking the heel off. Now I limped after Teddy, keeping him and Texas between the snipers and me as best I could.

A mortar shell exploded behind me and I turned my head to see three Roughriders tossed into the air and land and not get back up. Another Roughrider—this one off to my left in the trees—cried out as his leg was whipped out from under him and he was dragged by a snare across the ground that had been planted with sharpened bamboo stakes. He didn't get up either. Another soldier fell into a tiger pit that had been covered with palm fronds and a smattering of dirt, and he was run through by pointed staves at the bottom of the hole. The Spaniards had expected us to rush up this slope, and had set these nasty surprises, and now we were obliging them.

My main memory of the charge up San Juan Hill, other than my desperate attempt to keep my nose right at Texas' tail, was of the utter confusion of the event. I suppose it was mostly the jungle. Man was never meant to enter a jungle, and when you do you will become disoriented and listless and afraid. The rotting bogs emit sulfurous, inescapable vapor. The vines and branches incessantly reach for you. The ground gives way under your feet, sucking at you, not allowing you to get your bearings. The parrots and insects maintain a constant hair-standing racket. Things slither and slide at the edge of your vision. Nothing can be seen but a wall of vegetation in all directions, trees glistening like oilskin, and if you try to escape by slogging across the loose earth, that green wall seems to move with you. It is close and hot, with the jungle's sour breath all around you, corrosive and sticky.

Now add bullets to the mix. And a strange pigeonlike cooing from many sides, which we learned later were spotters setting us up for Spanish snipers. We were all tromping up through this. Texas suddenly struggled, catching a hoof on an exposed root, so Teddy dismounted and freed her and led her by the reins, still encouraging his men by yelling and slashing his pistol over his head.

A shell whistled in and exploded near Teddy, instantly coppering the left side of his face and raising a shrapnel bump on his cheek. Texas reared, but Teddy pulled the horse down and continued his charge. The air was alive with streaking slugs.

The Roughrider on my right took a bullet through his nose, and it blasted out the back of his head, leaving nothing but a flap of a face that trailed blood and gore as he rolled back down the hill. As we neared the crest, trees gave way to coarse grass and more open ground. A blockhouse was to our left and a revetment to our right, and both bristled with Spanish rifles. Men fell all around, and still we came on.

Over the years, Teddy's charge up San Juan Hill has gained a comic overtone, enlivened by historians who have focused on the barrel-chested, nearsighted New Yorker in his yellow suspenders who made his men sing "Fair Harvard" while they trained, and who later called it "the great day of my life." But I'm here to tell you this was a close-fought, bloody, terrifying encounter.

As we neared the top, some Spaniards scattered like poultry, fleeing their positions for the safety of the trees on the backside of the hill. But many kept firing, and I suddenly realized that I was their main target, out front of all the Roughriders, at the very front of the charge, not counting the bespectacled nutcake on his horse directly in front of me.

You may be wondering how I went from shoveling dervish poop to charging up San Juan Hill. Well, it happened about as quickly as it takes to tell it. I arrived in New York to learn Teddy had been assistant secretary of the Navy for one year, and it had taken him just that amount of time to get the United States into a war. I was told I was still attached to Teddy, and was to report immediately to Tampa, where he was forming up his regiment.

Why had I agreed to rejoin Teddy, to immediately travel to his camp in Florida and then go on to Cuba with him? First, I was still a soldier, and Teddy had left orders in the event I returned to New York that I was to follow him south. But there was more to it than that. For many years I had been carrying Bruce Twig-Smathers's piece of paper. By then it was frayed and limp, but it still had those magical words on it. The import of those few words had grown in my mind over the years. Surely the Compassionate One offered a balancing scale in this life. The more you suffered, the greater the reward at the end of the suffering. The scale would inevitably balance itself. As I endured moving those mountains of dervish poop, I became convinced that my slip of paper was my reward. All I needed to do was to get to Anguilla and find that hole in the ground. I had walked those paces from the pool to the stone with the hourglass mark ten thousand times in my mind. In Omdurman the buried treasure went from being a preposterous notion to a life-saving certainty. By the time I reached New York I had learned Anguilla was in the Caribbean, and so I was nothing loathe to take the train south to find Teddy. I'd get me closer to my treasure.

You also may be wondering about Teddy's and my first encounter, about what heartfelt, joyous thing he would say to me when he first saw me after more than eight years. That day I arrived in Tampa, I bent low to enter his tent near the parade ground, and found him at a desk busily filling out a roster. He was magnificent in his high boots and stiff collar, his spectacles reflecting lamp light.

I stood there, silently at attention, as he was now a lieutenant colonel. After a moment he looked up and said rather absently, "Woodrow, hand me that ledger, will you? The one over there on the trunk."

That was it, after eight years. When I told this story to my wife many years later she offered that Teddy was known for his powers of concentration, and perhaps he was working so hard it didn't cross his mind I'd been absent all those years. My explanation is far better: Teddy could be a horse's patoot.

But to be fair to the man: he found me the next day washing myself with a towel, dipping it again and again into a barrel of water. I had no clothes on whatsoever. This was still in Tampa before we shipped to Cuba. He came up and pointed at my back and said, "Looks like you upset someone over there in Africa."

The skin on my back, shoulders, and buttocks was ridged and purpled. Those scars from the eunuch Hamen Ibn Belal never did go away, and I still wear them as I speak to you. And they are pronounced, giving me the look of a zebra. When I turned to him, Teddy added, "And that slash on your cheek. Woodrow, I thought you had deserted the army to go on a European holiday, but it looks like you did some difficult service."

I suppose that passed as his welcome home. At least, he was smiling when he said it. That night he told me with great relish how he had sprung me from slavery. Turns out it had cost him a box car of money and a lot of his time. I can't tell you how he determined I was in Omdurman, because it was vastly complicated and I don't remember all of it. But this is how he got me out of my shackles once he knew where I was: he sent ten thousand dollars—most mansions cost less in them days—to Lady Twig-Smathers—an old friend of the Roosevelt family, it turns out—who converted it to gold coin and sent it on a packet to Cairo. Sir Harold Simpson of the British legation in Cairo gave the gold to the emir of Beni Jerar, who took a cut of it for his troubles before passing along the balance to Birabi Sun Tali of the Takruri tribe, who also subtracted some as a commission. Birabi knew a Bedouin chief who had a cousin who had joined the dervishes and was one of the Khalif's palace guards. The cousin propositioned the eunuch Hamen Ibn Belal. Teddy speculated that only about five thousand dollars of gold remained when it finally reached Hamen, having been bled off by intermediaries. Still and all, that was enough for the eunuch to buy off several gate guards and to hire the guide and buy the camels, probably leaving Hamen with four thousand dollars for his troubles.

When I asked Teddy how the eunuch Hamen Ibn Belal could possibly get away with freeing me and Victoria Littlewood, the Khalif's favorite concubine, Teddy laughed and said he had learned in a cable from Sir Harold that Hamen fled Omdurman that very night, his fortune in gold strapped to his belly with a cloth. The eunuch was now in Cairo, enjoying a home with a walled courtyard and three servants. I was glad to hear it, even if Hamen had striped me almost to death.

Before I return to San Juan Hill, let me tell you of one of the very few times in my long relationship with him where I actually shut Theodore Roosevelt up, where I actually had the last word. During my third day at the Roughrider camp in Tampa, he found me on my knees on a prayer rug, bowing toward Mecca. He said, "Woodrow, I've noticed you pray a lot, even for a papist, and what's that funny little rug?" Without opening my eyes I replied, "I am a follower of the prophet Mohammed, and those disrespectful of the prophet are punished as surely as night follows day." My eyes were closed in reverence so I didn't see his formidable choppers snap together, but I heard them, and they sounded like the shot of a small caliber rifle, say a .22 rimfire. Without another word, he walked away, and Allah will surely forgive my surge of satisfaction.

Back to San Juan Hill, Teddy released his horse and scrambled up the last ledge. A surprised Spaniard tried to bring his Mauser around but when Teddy gut-shot him, the Spaniard folded up as neatly as a jack-knife and died. Teddy rushed toward the top of the hill, and the enemy fled, most of them anyway. Teddy was bound for the very summit. I was still following Texas, who had slowed, then stopped to eat at a bunch of grass. Gunfire didn't bother that animal any. Maybe I should've stayed there, tucked behind that horse, but Texas turned to stare balefully at me, shaming me, so I ran toward Teddy. We had outpaced the other Roughriders. He was firing his pistol again and again, but smoke obscured his targets. His back was to a copse of small palm trees, and he was still grinning crazily. He cracked the pistol to reload. Bullets cut the air all around.

Now, I am about to rewrite history, and I don't do so lightly. History has it that Theodore Roosevelt was the first to the top of San Juan Hill. But history should be a servant to the truth. And here is the truth: Woodrow C. Lowe was the first to the top.

Teddy was still twenty yards from the top. He had just reloaded, and quickly resumed his charge. Five paces away from a glade of palms, his feet were rocketed out from under him. He did a quick somersault, losing his pistol and spectacles, and a snare lifted him into the air, where he hung like a dressed-out goose. He was held up by the suddenly righted palm tree. The rope snare had him by an ankle.

Three Spaniards emerged from behind the blockhouse. With a dervish war cry—that piercing, falsetto "ulululu"—I sprinted toward them, up and over the crest. I entirely forgot my Winchester, left it on the grass. But I brought up my weapon of choice, my scarred fists. One Spaniard turned tail. Maybe it was my face. The other pulled his trigger, but did so before his rifle barrel was fully up. The bullet kicked up sod next to my feet. I lit into the rifleman, cracking his temple with a left hook that lifted him off the ground. I could still throw a punch, I learned then. I spun to the third man, but his face opened in fright and he about-faced and ran away.

I turned back to Teddy. He was hanging there, just over the crest of the hill, upside down, churning his arms, trying to bounce himself up and down. With each bounce he got nearer and nearer to the ground. He was trying to snatch his spectacles, which were lying on a mat of wild grass, just out of his reach, glistening tantalizingly in the sun. Up and down he went, higher and higher, lower and lower, with each descent bringing his outstretched fingers nearer to his specs.

I wished then that I had the luxury of watching this performance a while longer. Up and down, up and down bobbed Theodore Roosevelt, the old Knickerbocker, the colonel, the assistant secretary of the Navy, everybody's pick for president some day. But the Spaniards had only fallen back down the hill a hundred yards into a plantain grove, and were still throwing slugs our way as fast as they could work the Mauser bolts. A bullet nipped my shirt sleeve and another tapped my left pointer finger, just a touch. The slugs stirred the air around my head, and their whup whup whup was constant. Pulling my service knife, I ran toward Teddy. That is, I ran up and over the summit again, then down twenty paces to the tree that held him aloft. So, you see, I reached the crest of San Juan Hill twice before Teddy ever did.

"Don't step on my spectacles, Woodrow," he called, upside down.

I stopped his bouncing by clutching his legs, then I cut the rope above his foot. When I lowered him to the ground, he grabbed his specs and wrapped them around his head. His soldiers called him "Storm Windows," by the way, but never to his face.

He reached for his pistol. "Let's take the summit, Woodrow."

"I already did, sir."

"To the summit," he ordered. "Follow me."

He churned his little bow legs up the hill, firing once at the wood blockhouse, cutting through the clouds of gunsmoke and leaving a wake of it trailing behind him. I stayed close to him, using him as a shield.

I have always suspected Teddy Roosevelt was a lunatic, but there was no question he was brave. As he topped the hill he seemed to be daring the Spaniards to kill him, and they tried mightily but couldn't. Bullets framed him. Bullets plowed the earth at his feet. Bullets split the air above him. None touched him. He reloaded and yelled a challenge—it was in Latin, so I don't know what he said—and sped down the hill, firing at muzzle flashes in the tree grove. Other Roughriders at last reached the summit and provided cover by firing into the plantains on both sides of Teddy and me. I had no weapon in my hands except the knife, so I didn't know exactly what I was doing, not for the first time. Following Teddy, just as I'd been ordered, I suppose. Teddy rushed into the trees, firing at the retreating Spanish.

Then I got shot. A bullet hit me, but it was in the head so it didn't hurt me much. Just spilled me to the ground where I rolled and rolled downhill, blood from the crease in my head marking my path. I tumbled and tossed and spun down that slope, then bounced to a stop against a tree trunk. A moment passed before I could gather my senses—what little there was to gather—and I heard Spanish voices in all directions, and close-by Mauser fire. I had somehow rolled down through the Spanish line. I was in enemy territory.

When I dabbed at my head, I could feel the gritty bone of my skull. Blood cascaded down the front of my face. I collected my legs and was about to climb the hill to rejoin Teddy, who was up there somewhere, but then I heard a Spaniard yell out from a guava thicket uphill, and I heard "Yankee," so I figured they had seen my wild roll. The brush uphill wiggled, and a rifle barrel pushed through the leaves. Above it was a mustache and eyes bright with anticipation of a kill. A Spanish soldier was about to shoot me again.

I took off downhill through the brush. That bastard's slug came close enough to my earlobe to redden it. I dove through a wall of marabu, its thorns tugging at my uniform. I tried to wipe my eyes but blood kept me blind. I stumbled and fell. Another bullet rushed by me.

I ran for twenty minutes before stopping. I leaned against a mango tree, my chest caving in and out, and finally could clear my eyes. Banana and soursop trees surrounded me. Frangipani scented the still air. I breathed hugely, my mouth was straw-dry. Then I heard more Spanish, and the swish of machetes and dogs barking. They were searching for me. Off I went again, slapping through the brush.

I ran for two days. Whether I ran in a straight line or took a wandering route I'll never know. The Spanish were on my heels that entire time. They wanted a Yankee prisoner, that was for sure. Maybe to make an example of me. They never seemed more than a hundred yards to the rear.

I finally found the sea. I emerged from the jungle near the tiny fishing village of Sebella on Cuba's southeast coast (I determined later), and with enemy soldiers rattling the bougainvillea and jacaranda behind me, I pushed a fishing boat across the sand and into the Caribbean.

The boat was about fourteen feet long and although it had a mast there was no sail on board, not that I'd have had time to rig a sail. When the water was up to my chest I climbed on board, the boat tipping so that the rail almost reached the water. As I was fitting the oarlocks, a bullet smashed into the stern, and another flickered by my nose.

Spanish soldiers streamed out of the jungle. They lined up on the beach like a firing squad, maybe eight of them, and loosed bullet after bullet at me. Spouts of water surrounded the boat, but water is notoriously difficult to find the range over, and after a few moments of my frantic rowing the water squirts fell away behind my boat. I left those soldiers on the beach. Their captain—I could tell because he carried only a pistol—was so angry he danced a jig and cuffed several of his riflemen.

I was already parched when I got into that boat, and during the forty-two days I was adrift I got thirstier. Some days brought rain, which collected in the bottom of the boat, and which I'd lap up like a dog. But never enough, not nearly enough. The boat had no fishing gear on board but a dozen times or so I snatched a flying fish right out of the air as it whisked by. I ate every bit of those fish, even crunching up the skulls. My face and neck and hands burned red, and I swear I had blisters on top of blisters. Even today, after all these years, the backs of my hands still resemble a burned field.

The current carried me east. East was the direction of my treasure so in that there was some solace. I was delirious much of the time, but in a lucid moment I christened my little craft, *Theodore Roosevelt, You'd Better Pray Woodrow C. Lowe Never Gets His Hands on You*. The boat's stern probably weren't big enough to paint all this on it, had I any paint, but you have to admit my predicament was entirely Teddy's fault. Or maybe Amy Balfour's.

On the forty-second day of my journey I spotted a gunboat sailing toward me. Half an hour elapsed before I was convinced it actually was a ship, because my mind had produced Bo Latts, John L. Sullivan, my bedroom at home in Boston, and most often Joe Lowe's Museum and Sporting Palace, its swinging doors open invitingly, just forty yards across the water.

But this vessel got closer and closer, and I couldn't make it vanish by blinking my eyes or shaking my head, so it was a gunboat, all right.

Now, most ships are things of beauty, and they always have been down through history, I believe. This particular ship, though, had been constructed during that brief time when sail was giving way to power. So it had both engines and sails, and it was uglier than a scab. The fore and aft masts were separated by a funnel that billowed black smoke. No sail was up. As it drew near I saw it was iron-clad, and had fore and aft turrets, both with small guns, maybe three-inchers. The prow had no rake, but rather dropped straight into the water from the bowsprit. And damned my blurry eyes, if it weren't carrying the standard of the Royal Spanish Navy. She made straight for me.

The boat—the *Marqués Antelo*, I was to learn later—had been at sea for months. Rust streaked the hull, and brown stains colored the hull where the galley crew threw slops overboard after every meal.

A marine on the bowsprit pointed a rifle at me as the *Marqués Antelo* came alongside. A rope ladder was lowered and I was ordered to board. I could barely lift my head, much less climb a ladder. So a sailor came down in a bo's'n's chair and tied a line around my waist. I was hoisted to the gunboat's deck, none too carefully.

The vessel's compliment of marines surrounded me. When I tottered, they prompted me aright with the tips of their bayonets. The sailor's uniforms were haphazard, some blue, some white, all in need of repairs. Some wore no shoes. The deck was streaked with dried salt spray. Buckets and chains and shell boxes lay about. Everything needed paint.

Through cracked lips I pleaded, "Water."

The captain appeared beside me. His eyes had a mirthless shine. His hair was so greasy he might've washed it last at puberty. His face was red, as if all his capillaries were surfacing. His khaki uniform was soiled and creaseless. He spat Spanish words. I didn't answer, so he tried English. "Are you a North American?"

My tired and bleached clothing had lost any semblance to a uniform. I croaked, "United States, sir. May I have some water?"

He signaled with a finger and three Spanish sailors roughly pulled off my pants and shirt and boots, leaving me in my underwear. Then they tied my hands behind my back with a rawhide thong. I was thin as a blade of grass, and covered with scars and burns, and wearing a filthy, matted beard. I shook like a man with the ague. The *Marqués Antelo* and I were in the same condition.

Sailors searched through my clothing and tried things on, one holding up the heel of my boot to his feet to see if he could wear my boots.

Before I knew what they were about, a marine behind me slipped a noose over my head, then yanked it tight, the knot just at my left ear. Above me was a derrick from which hung the rope that ended around my neck. I turned around, more a stagger, to see five sailors holding the other end of the rope, ready to pull me off the deck.

I coughed out, "I'm a United States Army soldier. I'm your prisoner of war. You can't hang me."

The captain smiled villainously. "I bet we can, Yankee pig."

The noose jerked skyward, lifting me to my toes. I gagged but managed to gargle, "You can't . . ."

That rope squeezed my neck, and the deck slipped away. The sailors pulled me high. I stretched out. I gasped for breath. My tongue pushed through my teeth. The derrick and masts overhead swirled around and around. Then the sun and sky began to fade. Tiny speckles of color blinked in front of my sightless eyes, and then all was black.

Then, after an age, and only at the far edge of an almost-stilled consciousness was I aware of my feet hitting the boat's deck, and then of being slapped repeatedly across the face. Finally water was thrown on me.

The wretched day formed again in front of me. I was lying on the deck, the noose still around my neck, cutting into the skin all around. The Spanish captain bent over me, holding my beloved piece of paper in both hands. A sailor must have found it in my pants pocket.

"What does this mean? 'One mile due south of the island's highest peak is a pool. One hundred thirty yards further south is a two-man stone with an hourglass mark. Under the stone.' What does that mean, Yankee?"

I tried to speak, but could only gurgle. He yanked the noose so that it loosened its grip on my neck.

"Gaaack." I couldn't get my tongue back into my mouth. "Gaaackk."

When the captain snapped his fingers, a tin of water was produced. He let me sip it while he fanned my face with his cap.

"What is this paper?" he demanded again.

"You go piss blood." It was the dumbest thing I could possibly say, so naturally I said it.

"All right, then," he replied equably.

The captain stood away from me. The sailors on the rope once again did their work, and skyward I went, up toward the rigging. This time the blackness came more quickly, stealing over me like an executioner's hood. I don't know how long I dangled, twitching and frothing, providing sprightly entertainment for the *Marqués Antelo*'s crew.

Then I was on the deck again, with more water splashed in my face.

"Yankee, this piece of paper." The tone of the captain's voice was avuncular. "We should discuss it."

"I . . . I don't know what's buried there."

The captain dipped his chin. "No? Then tell me the name of the island."

The noose was still pinching my neck. I fought to form the words. "Why in hell would I do that?"

"We can be partners," he suggested with a placatory smile. His English was good. Droplets of sweat clung to the hairs of his mustache.

"My pa once told me—" I gagged and my words were chopped off.

Once again the captain held the water tin to my lips. He nodded encouragement, leaning closer, putting his ear to my mouth.

"My pa once told me," I said in a strangled voice, "never to do business with someone who smells like a privy."

His face contorted with anger. He leaped away and instantly my new friend the noose got serious again. The deck and the captain and his crew fell away. The sailors pulled and up I went toward the derrick's pulley. And once again that black cloud came for me.

A blast of heat and small bits of metal flew into me. The rope was released and I fell to the deck. I fought for breath, wiggling my head back and forth to loosen the noose. The rope lay all about. Sailors and marines were scrambling over the deck to battle stations. I lay in a heap. A horn above the bridge blew its single strident note.

A shell had exploded in the forward quarter, knocking down a mast, streaking the turret with black, and starting a fire in the lockers. Just then another shell hit the aft hull at the waterline, and the *Marqués Antelo* bucked like a horse.

I pushed myself to my knees and looked over the rail. Her bow splitting white water and her two funnels pouring black smoke, a man-of-war was closing on the Spanish vessel. The man-of-war's forward gun flashed, and I could make out the path of the incoming shell, which harmlessly sailed over the bridge. Stars and stripes flew from the warship's rigging.

Such had been the spectacle of the Yankee going up and down, up and down, that the Spanish sailors standing watch had watched me rather than the sea. The American ship had snuck up on the *Marqués Antelo*. And now only one Spanish marine had been left to guard me. He nervously pointed his rifle at me, the bayonet six inches from my belly. My piece of paper, forgotten, had blown against a rail stanchion.

The *Marqués Antelo* came about. Her forward gun fired, sending up a shaft of water two hundred yards ahead of the American vessel. The Spanish captain's voice came from the bridge. He was yelling orders into the tube to the engine room, then into the tubes to the gun turrets, and out the open bridge portal to the fire team setting up a hose to fight the forward fire.

Another shell shot through the funnel, punching a hole in one side and out the other, but not exploding. Thick coal smoke rushed out the new holes.

I looked at the marine guarding me. "That buried treasure . . ."

The guard screwed up his eyes suspiciously.

I let myself stagger and lowered my voice. "It's on the island of . . ."

The marine leaned forward. Maybe he spoke English, maybe he didn't. But he was interested.

I whispered brokenly. "The island of . . ."

When he put his bayonet to one side to step closer to hear, I shot my head forward, just like I'd seen John L. do to Dickie Balfour. My forehead slammed into his, and he dropped to the deck as surely as cow crap hits the pasture.

I fell with him and lay there as if injured. But I worked his rifle around to my back, and after a moment of scraping the bayonet cut through the leather thong around my wrists.

It occurred to me much later that Teddy Roosevelt's and my life had at least one similarity: we both went up and down, up and down at the end of a Spanish rope, not to either of our liking.

I grabbed my piece of paper, stuffed it into my mouth, then without another look at that Spanish ship, I stepped over the rail and dropped into the sea.

I dog-paddled for five minutes until the U.S. warship drew near. Then I waved and splashed but that ship was splitting the sea in chase, its forward gun blazing. The crew saw me, all right, because one of them threw a life ring in my direction. I swam to it, and there I rested fairly comfortably. Both ships quickly disappeared over my short horizon, but after a while I saw a roiling black cloud of smoke fairly leap into the air, and I suspected an American shell had found the *Marqués Antelo*'s magazine.

That's precisely what had happened. Then the U.S. warship, the *John Jay*, returned for me, and I was plucked from the water.

A canvas bag of water was produced. I drank until my belly was about to give way. The captain, a white-haired gentleman with an agreeable stoop, was in fine humor, and invited me to dine with him to celebrate his victory. He assured me the Spanish navy in the Caribbean was being rapidly destroyed, and so it was.

And he wanted to show me new additions to his butterfly collection, of which he was quite proud. "I'm a member of the American Lepidoptera Society, you know."

I stealthily removed the paper from my mouth, and asked if the *John Jay* was going to sail near Anguilla any time soon.

The captain pointed at a distant green ridge of land, a slight warp on the sea's horizon. "That's Anguilla. We stopped for six hours at the coaling station there. And I found three new specimens during that time. But as you can see, we are steaming away from it."

I had to be forcibly prevented from jumping overboard to make a swim of it.

The captain patted me on the shoulder. "You don't look fit for a swim, and I'm having fresh flank steak and an apple pie for dinner. And I have a grand *Caligo memmon* I'll show you. Just caught it. Come join me."

I did join him, eventually, after miserably watching Anguilla get smaller and smaller and finally disappear off the stern.

I still wear a scar from my hanging on the *Marqués Antelo*, by the way. That's why I'm partial to turtle-neck sweaters.

THIRTEEN

The Amazon

COLLECTING BUTTERFLIES ISN'T one of them pastimes I ever thought I'd take a shine to, me being a fistic scientist and all, but for thirty days, every day but Sunday, Capt. Horace Hohner would have a tender lowered into the river, and he and I would row away to the butterfly grounds. That is, I'd do the rowing and he would stand in the bow, butterfly net in hand, swishing it at any bit of color that flickered by, and then he would put his catch into a jar. The captain could fill a boat with butterflies in an afternoon.

This was easy work, as close to a holiday as I'd ever experienced. We'd find a narrow tributary and I would row us upstream, deep into the jungle, with vines and leaves hanging out over the water, usually with a canopy of vegetation overhead. The captain wanted me to row slowly, lest he miss a single butterfly, and I was happy to oblige, dipping the oars into the black water, then resting a while. The heat would have bothered any other two men, but I was fresh out of the Sudan, and the captain was something of a lunatic, and heat doesn't slow lunatics much, I've noticed over the years.

I don't mean to say he belonged in a bin with a straitjacket, but anybody who would traipse around after butterflies day after day is suspect, you have to admit. And all the while keeping up a monologue about one thing or another. Over those thirty days I heard all there was to hear about a secret society called the Lamplighters, the history of coal-fired naval vessels, Admiral Nelson at Trafalgar, and bee farming. I didn't pay any attention, of course, because if you let a useless fact enter your brain through an ear, some fact you might need some day will be pushed out the other ear and fall to the deck.

So I sat there day after day in a pleasant haze, the captain droning

178

away, interrupting himself now and again to tell me to row closer to the bank or to avoid a half-sunken log or to pass him a water jug. Our fourteen-foot lapstrake boat pushed aside water lilies. The captain used an arm to part the ficus and rubber leaves. Pau-rosa blossoms left their cloying scent. Occasionally I used an oar to pole us along. We would wind our way deep into the foliage, our boat swallowed by vegetation, the captain steady, his narrow eyes on prey that fluttered out in front of him.

On the last day of his life, he said over his shoulder, "I've had six butterflies named after me. Have I told you that before, Woodrow?"

Not more than once a day for a month.

"I had a signet ring made with the words 'Lepidoptera hohnerus' engraved on top." He held up his hand so the ring could flash in the light. Captain Hohner's eyes were deeply lined. His smile always carried a mild cynicism, unless he was discoursing on his beloved butterflies. The skin of his face was pink, always burned and never tanned by the tropical sun. The sharp angles of his face had not been softened at all by age. He was in his sixties. He was wearing white trousers, a singlet, a vest made of canvas to ward off branches, and a straw hat. Jugs of water, chicken breasts wrapped in brown paper, and a .30–06 deer rifle were in the aft end of the boat. I had been eating steadily on the Navy's chit, and had put back on those thirty pounds I had lost adrift in the Caribbean.

"My old friend Lawrence Outland has had eleven species named after him, though he claims a new species every time a moth comes to his lamp. Doubtless I'll catch him on this trip."

"Doubtless." My mind was on Victoria Littlewood. Once in a while I would repeat one of the captain's finer words, and that was sufficient for him.

"I would rather be chasing Spaniards, as you know, Woodrow." He brought his net over his head in a high arc, but missed. "But if I had to break down, I'm happy to be on the Amazon."

So was I. Now when I say Captain Hohner was a kook, I don't mean to detract from his warrior's disposition. That man had been ordered to sink Spanish tonnage, and he was good at it. The Marqués Antelo was his fourth victim of the voyage, and he found another sailing south from Anguilla, somewhere in the Leeward Islands, and he and his crew destroyed the vessel in quick fashion, rescuing thirteen Spaniards who were put into the brig until they gave their parole, and who now scraped

and painted along with everybody else on the *John Jay*. The Spanish
fleet was in disarray, and trying to return to Spain from Cuba, but Captain Hohner was determined to send as many to the bottom as he could
find. He was a skilled officer and a hardhearted pursuer, and his crew
would have done anything for him.

Then in the Windwards, we came upon the *Abrillo*, a thousand-ton-
ner that Captain Hohner wanted as a prize more than he wanted most
butterflies. We chased the *Abrillo* out of the Windwards, and coaled in
Trinidad and then at Georgetown in Guyana. The Spanish vessel would
occasionally sink below the horizon, but Captain Hohner had the instincts of a predator, and soon we'd again see the *Abrillo*'s black smoke.

In full flight and trying to shake us, the Spanish warship entered the
Amazon's Canal do Norte with us only an hour behind. The *Abrillo* fled
past the town of Almeirim, about two hundred miles up the river, and
then passed Prainha, another seventy miles. Then two more days' journey upstream the *John Jay*'s pistons seized up due to an oil leak. Four
rowboats, each with eight men on eight oars, towed the ship to the tiny
village of Manhana on the Amazon's southern shore. The second mate
and a crew were sent downstream in one of the tenders to find a telegraph station—the captain thought there might be one in Belem—so
parts could be shipped to us from Florida. We could do nothing but wait,
and Captain Hohner said the earliest we could expect to see a rescue
vessel would be in eight weeks. So he and I began butterfly collecting,
him in exceptional humor, even though the *Abrillo* slipped by the dis-
abled *John Jay* and returned downriver and then on to Spain.

That day he flicked the net at another butterfly, missed again, then
began a complicated explanation about how the Masons started the
Franco-Prussian War. I was doing my usual idling over the oars. We had
been out six hours, perhaps two miles from the *John Jay*, up a foliage-
clotted stream that fed into the Amazon. An azure blue sky was overhead but I could only see silver-dollar–size dots of it as the trees had
closed in over us. Some of them trees were two hundred feet high, called
Bombacacene, with trunks twenty-five feet around. I thought I'd seen
jungle in Cuba but that was a Fifth Avenue parlor compared to the
Amazon jungle. The cedars and castor trees, the kapoks and mahoganies
formed a green prison where at any given time an avenue of escape was
undetectable. The vegetation always seemed to be moving, usually
toward me. Curling, oozing, green tendrils.

The noise was stifling. Macaws and toucans and ibis let their agitation at our presence be known by their constant grinding-wheel shrieks. Add to that the low buzz of the fist-sized flying cockroaches that had taken a liking to me. One time two of those buggers landed exactly at the same instant, one on each of my eyes. Suddenly I was blinded by cockroaches that covered half my skull. They gripped my skin with their bony legs. I suppose they would have been delighted to sit on my face until the sun went down but I was not so accommodating. I swatted them away and for the rest of the day felt a tad ill from the experience.

That weren't the worst treatment I received from an Amazon critter, and I'll get to that in a bit.

Anyway, that day in the boat, closeted all around by jungle foliage, I interrupted his discourse on the Masons. "Captain Hohner, have you ever heard of a British captain named Twig-Smathers?"

He looked around, perhaps startled I had asked anything. "I have, Woodrow. Why do you ask?"

"It's the only topic you haven't touched upon. I was hoping you'd get to it, just to complete my education."

I don't say enough snappy things for one to be wasted but this one was.

He nodded sagely. "Captain Twig-Smathers lived in the middle of the last century. He was drummed out of the Royal Navy."

"Why?"

"Whitehall never disclosed the reason. Twig-Smathers then purchased a vessel of his own, the *Golden Ram*, with sixteen ten-inchers, hired a crew, and sailed as a privateer under English letters of marque. Some say he was more pirate than privateer, but either way he was a real fighting man."

"What happened to him?" I held my breath.

"No one is quite sure. It is believed that he took three, maybe four vessels that were transporting gems and gold back from South America, headed to Spain. Every Spanish vessel lost in the Caribbean over a three-year time was credited to Twig-Smathers."

"Is it just a legend?" I pulled a few times on the oars. "Did he really take those vessels?"

"He claimed that a hurricane ran his vessel aground in the Caribbean. He would never say precisely where. He and the others—only three men didn't drown—waited months for a rescue that never came. The English were at war with the United States, and he saw no point in sailing to the States. So they set off across the Atlantic in a longboat that had survived the wreck."

"Did they make it to England?"

On the stream bank an alligator the size of our boat appeared to be grinning at me. It slid off the shore and into the water. Its nostrils and eyes were visible for a moment, then the monster disappeared below the surface. Its tail bumped our boat. I shivered in the heat.

"Twig-Smathers and two of his men began the voyage in the longboat. Only Twig-Smathers and one man arrived in Falmouth in the spring of 1775." Captain Hohner flicked the net at a passing bit of blue, but missed. "They killed and ate the third man, some said, though Twig-Smathers denied it."

A jaguar roared from the east. Or it might have been west. A whooping crane croaked, its sound seeming to come from all directions at once. I batted at a fly on my forehead. A hundred tree frogs were adding their clicks to the crushing noise.

"Twig-Smathers was suffering from malaria when he arrived at Falmouth," Captain Hohner went on. "The other survivor died in the Cheapside, knifed."

"So what happened to the booty he took from the Spanish vessels?"

Again the net shot out.

"Hah," he exclaimed. "Got you."

He carefully pulled a gold and green butterfly from the net. "A Placidus. I already have a couple." He released the insect and it fluttered up into the trees.

I tried again. "So what happened to the Spanish gold and gems?"

"The Admiralty called Twig-Smathers to Whitehall several times for interrogations. Even the first lord interviewed him, trying to discover if any of the Spanish gold survived the shipwreck. Did it go down with the ship? Or was Twig-Smathers able to save it? You see, Admiralty was owed a large portion of any prize. Twig-Smathers swore it all sank with the ship, and he never changed his story. He died of malaria a few months after he arrived at Falmouth."

"What do you think happened to the gold, captain?"

"Gold is precious to folks unless they are about to die." He lifted his hat to draw a sleeve across his brow. The air was so wet I seemed to be breathing a damp towel.

I asked, "What do you mean, sir?"

"None of the sailors aboard the sinking *Golden Ram* would have let Twig-Smathers put gold and gems aboard a tender in a storm, abandoning ship, if it meant leaving sailors behind. It is improbable the Spanish gold got off the *Golden Ram.*"

I nodded in agreement, but I trusted the Twig-Smathers's luck (Bruce had somehow survived Africa) and cunning (his mother, Lady Twig-Smathers, was a sharpie, I knew that on first sight of her) so I weren't discouraged in the least. All I needed to do was get out of the reeking jungle and find my way back to Anguilla. Under my breath I repeated my mantra, "One mile due south of the island's highest peak is a pool. One hundred thirty yards further south is a two-man stone with an hourglass mark."

Captain Hohner's voice had gained the sonorous tones of professorial importance. He was about to impart some special dab of wisdom. "Woodrow, there's only one thing in this world I know more about than butterflies."

I twisted on the bench to look at him, my hands still on the oars.

Captain Hohner half turned. "It is more than improbable that Twig-Smathers got the treasure off his boat. It is impossible. I know sailors and . . ."

One instant he was standing there talking, and the next he was standing there with an arrow through his head. And I mean squarely through his head, the sharp point sticking out his right ear and the feathers out his left ear.

He stopped his lecture with a startled look, as if someone had had the temerity to interrupt him. His face twitched twice, and he collapsed as if he had been deboned. His body scattered his collecting bottles. His little net landed in the dark water.

I dropped my oars and scrambled for the rifle. My feet slipped on the bottles and shattered a few. Suddenly free, butterflies winged skyward. Kneeling on the bottom of the boat, I brought up the rifle, clicked off the safety, and swung the barrel around.

There was nothing to shoot at. Just the close wall of jungle, with the vines and trunks and leaves, and the boggy shore, and the blackened deadheads bumping the hull. I turned and turned, my boots squishing in the blood leaking from the captain's ears. Only then did I notice that the jungle was utterly silent. The insects and frogs and birds had been stilled, and the leaves no longer rustled, out of respect for the captain's killer.

I saw nothing and heard nothing. Yet behind the first layer of jungle lay a vast peril. I was being viewed down the shaft of an arrow, I was certain. Maybe the shooter was waiting until my ears were properly aligned. With one hand around the rifle's grip and my finger at the ready, I reached for an oar. I awkwardly pushed at the bank, trying to send the boat back downstream, holding the rifle and trying to look like I meant business.

Every breath might've been my last. I pushed again, the oar sinking into the mud. The tender started sliding back the way we had come, but the jungle conspired to slow me. I ducked below an overhanging bough, then felt the boat catch on a deadhead. I reached over the stern to push the boat away from the rotted log. I kept the rifle up. Slowly the jungle moved past me, unchanging and dangerous.

I had retreated perhaps fifty yards downstream when I was toppled by a sack of cement. Or a falling tree. Or a human body. No, it was heavier than a body. Whatever it was slammed me to the tender's deck, where I lay right on top of the captain's body in a state of some intimacy. And then this thing began squirming and sliding, moving all of itself all at once. Some part of it reached across my chest and shot under my arm and then began crushing me.

I struggled to my knees with the weight of the jungle pressing down on me, so much weight wrapped around my shoulders and chest I thought I'd break through the boat's decking. My tormentor glided all around me, getting tighter and tighter. My vision was filled with shades of green and yellow and brown, moving all around, giving me less and less room. I tried to inhale but the thing squeezed. I gasped, and when I attempted to refill my lungs, it had constricted further. It was suffocating me.

I slipped sideways on a bottle, and bounced off the boat's rail, then back down to the captain's corpse. The boat wobbled. A head appeared above me. A snake's head the size of a medicine ball. A blunt nose, slanted nostrils, devil's eyes, and, everything considered, a pleasant smile. It had dinner on its mind.

I had the insane notion I had shrunk to the size of a whiskey bottle, and a garter snake was wrestling with me. I had never heard of a snake this size. Or a tenth this size. I later guessed it was thirty feet long, with a girth the size of my girth. An anaconda. I was learning that they kill by squeezing the air out of you and not letting any back in. The snake breaks bones and generally makes you thinner so it can get its mouth around you, and swallow you whole. Then it lies in the fork of a tree for a month while you are digested.

A coil opened and looped outward, aiming for my arm. If I had any chance against the demon, I had to keep my hands free. I jerked my arm away from the coil. The anaconda's body slid up another notch, tightening its embrace. I heard one of my ribs crack, then another. The snake cinched even tighter. A coil found my foot and doubled my leg back so that it pressed against my rump. The snake tightened yet again, sliding all around, wringing me out.

But I am not helpless in matters involving the physical. My first instinct in such situations is to do damage. So when that snake's head drew near I jammed my thumb at its eye, and my thumb sank into moisture. The anaconda recoiled, at least its head did, and then it paid me back by constricting even more.

Maybe the damned thing could be drowned. I used my free leg to push myself up the side of the tender, then I toppled over, splashing into the black water, the reptile all around me. I had no breath to hold, it had been squeezed out of me.

I was under the black current but had the suspicion the snake's head was happily above the surface. Everywhere was snake, muscled and sleek and cinching up at every chance. I kicked with my free leg, and my boot found the stream's soft bottom. When I ratcheted my leg straight, my head rose above the surface. A coil tried again for an arm but I dodged it. The water was up to my chest. The snake's head was above me. Layers and layers of its body surrounded me. My lungs were paralyzed, and my thoughts began to drift, a euphoric disassociation with my dire predicament.

The snake was winning. I was suffocating. I vaguely wondered how the reptile would digest my belt buckle.

Then the anaconda made its mistake. The massive head dipped low— maybe to measure its jaw span against my head—and I snatched the snake by the neck with my left hand, my thumb pressed into the soft scales below its jaw, my fingers around the back of its neck. And with my right hand I hit its big snout. I mean I rocketed my balled hand into its head. John L. Sullivan could put his entire being into his fist and lash it out, and I did the same, savagely pounding the snake's head. Then again and again. My right arm worked like a steam piston. Out and back, out and back. I held the anaconda's head in front of me as I pummeled it. I cracked into it again and again, fighting against the giant snake and against the unconsciousness that wanted to swarm over me. The skin on my knuckles split open, and drops of my blood sprayed around.

And I know my fist was having effect. Against John L., I fought only for a prize and for pride. Against the snake I was fighting for my life. I beat that snake terribly. Few species—and no human—could have survived the punishment.

But, looking back, I don't think I did anything but surprise that snake. It usually ate tapirs and antelopes and rats, nothing that fought back with any success.

The startled anaconda tried to twist its head away but I desperately held it and lashed into it again and again. I was weakening. I had only seconds before eternal night came over me. I whipped my fist into that head.

The snake released the pressure, just a fraction, maybe from indecision. I sucked in air, and it fueled my fist. I slammed my balled hand into its snout.

The reptile abruptly began to uncurl. All of those coils loosened. The scaly yoke fell away from me, dropping into the water. The snake twisted over and over as it tried to flee. I released its head. The anaconda sank under the surface, then a few seconds later crawled up the stream bank and disappeared in the vegetation.

I gasped for breath. The sticky jungle air was sweet and life-giving. I staggered in the water. The tender had drifted downstream thirty yards. I would rest on the bank a few minutes then wade to it. Only when I fully regained my wind did I notice that each inhale hurt badly. The snake had broken some ribs. I didn't care. As I waded toward the bank I cackled victoriously. Woodrow C. Lowe, lord of the jungle. If that's the worst the Amazon could throw at me, I'd be all right.

It weren't the worst, I was about to learn. Grabbing branches, I scrambled up the embankment, mud sucking at my boots. I made my way onto solid ground, or sort of solid, as I sank up to my ankles. Limbs and vines and leaves hid everything more than a yard away. I looked for a fallen log to sit on so I could recover for a few minutes. I took a few steps across the spongy ground.

Then the memory of Captain Hohner's fate returned, and with it the certain knowledge I was in mortal danger. I had to flee, to get back to the tender, and then to the *John Jay*.

Too late. A spearhead appeared out of the foliage, and came to rest gently on my nose between my eyes. I instinctively stepped back but the point stayed right with me, right between my peepers.

Then the owner of that weapon stepped out of the leaves. A woman. Black hair. Caramel skin. Wearing a bark-cloth skirt but nothing on her chest. A tiny waist. Muscular arms and legs. Large breasts at which I would have stared longer under most any other circumstance. A turtle carved of a lime-green stone hung from her neck on a cord. On her wrists were beaded bracelets. She smiled at me with teeth unnaturally white in the jungle's gloom.

I backstepped once again. A second spearpoint found me. Then a third. Two more women stepped into view. Both wore carved stones and bracelets and bark-cloth skirts and nothing more.

The spearhead was removed from my nose. One of the women nodded upstream. When I hesitated, a spear cut into me from behind, just under a short rib. My blood spurted out and down my leg. Another woman appeared, then yet another. These two carried bows and quivers. I stumbled off in the direction indicated.

I had been captured by the Women Who Live Alone. I walked for five days. I would learn they went to considerable trouble to take me. They had plans for me. Big plans.

FOURTEEN

A Slave Again

OCCASIONALLY WE WALKED on what might be considered, if you had a good imagination, footpaths, but for most of those five days we traveled through theretofore untrammeled jungle. The women did not bother with binding my hands or guarding me closely. I had nowhere to run. With the broadleaf and evergreen canopy overhead and with green-and-brown foliage in every direction, I was thoroughly lost, and they knew it.

Their gait was economical and fluid, their feet falling on just the right piece of firmament. I slogged along, high-stepping, falling, branches grabbing at me, usually soaked to the waist, mud caked on me. About every hour I'd be bitten by a matuca, a black fly that grabbed my skin with horned lancets, and left a gash.

During daylight hours we stopped only for midday meals, usually eels and berries and rice, one time a peccary, a sort of wild pig, which I didn't eat, of course. Once the women had to halt when a hand-sized spider called a caranguajeira leaped onto my shoulder and bit me, and I suffered from drunken movements for most of an afternoon. Another time we stopped when we came to a river of forager ants ten feet across and moving steadily. We apparently had no way across the ants so we waited four hours until the last of them passed by.

Over the course of the march I noticed a few odd things. Though I was their captive, I was treated courteously and with some deference. I did not understand a word they spoke, but it was clear they were doing their best to insure I arrived at our destination in good health. They plugged up my spear wound—it was only an inch deep, and I've been hurt worse just thinking about that bout with John L. Sullivan out in the Badlands—with a medicinal leaf ball. They gave me the greasiest, most plump parts of anything we ate. I ate my fill and they didn't eat until I

188

was done. I prayed to the One Maker that they weren't cannibals, fattening me up for a pagan feast. They carefully rigged a hemp hammock for me every night, and one of them would tenderly search me for ticks. When she found one she would apply a lotion of crushed leaves on it, and the tick would back out of my skin.

We passed through several Indian villages. They were in clearings on higher ground. The huts were made of stones and thatch. Chickens ran about, or some species resembling a chicken except they had long head feathers that drooped down, looking like umbrellas that almost hid their heads. The inhabitants bowed as we walked by, not daring to make eye contact with the Women Who Live Alone. My escorts took from these villages whatever they needed: manioc, sassafras, cocoa. I suppose the villagers viewed it as taxation, for none of them objected when the women entered huts and carried away the foodstuffs. These villagers were scrawny, with a perpetually underfed look to them.

In these villages almost every waking moment is spent finding food, because the jungle gives it up only grudgingly. But the Women Who Live Alone were filled out. Their bodies were lush, with rounded hips and heavy breasts. And they were all tall, at least five feet ten. Their legs were finely turned, and their arms muscled. They ate well, apparently. Their hair was worn in long braids. They had full lips, and their noses were straight but with lovely flares at the nostrils. All wore green stones hung on leather strips. When one of the women walked in front of me, leading me along, I would watch the muscles of her legs and back, fairly hypnotized by the undulations rippling across her skin.

We reached their village on the fifth day, entering between two stone pillars topped with carved wood birds with wings and talons outstretched. An open cobblestone square was in the center of the village. An obelisk rose forty feet in the square, carved in the shapes of frogs and deer and snakes, in the same designs of the green stones the women wore. The buildings were made of stone. All doors faced the courtyard. I guessed the village contained two hundred structures. Cobblestone lanes radiated away from the square in a spiderweb pattern. The village was as clean as Captain Hohner's deck, and I couldn't even see a stray leaf.

Or a man. Dozens of natives emerged from their homes to watch me as I was escorted along the lanes, and not one of them was male. No men, no boys. Only these tall women and their girls. Every one wore a green stone talisman. Some of the women smiled at me, while the girls pointed and asked questions.

I was led by my hunting party to a rock building on the edge of the square opposite the totem pole. A wood door on leather hinges was pushed aside, and I was waved inside.

The hut had one room, with a stone floor, and a window opening in each wall except the front. A fire pit was in the middle of the room, and the ceiling contained an opening to allow smoke to escape. A bed dominated the room, a Western-style bed, not a hammock, with a wood frame and a thick feather mattress. A foot-long lizard on a tether was near the bed, flicking its tongue out at me. I learned later most homes kept lizards to gather up errant insects.

I turned back to the door and stepped outside. The hunting party had disappeared, but two other women had taken up positions outside my door. They each carried a *borduna*, a flat club with a sharp edge. They smiled at me and made no attempt to stop me as I returned to the village square. Both followed a few paces behind me. Everywhere I looked, a woman looked back. I strolled the square, my guards right behind. Then I walked out one of the lanes to the edge of the village. Where the huts ended, one of the guards tapped me nicely on the shoulder and pointed back to the center of town. So I knew the limits of the town were the limits of my freedom.

I started back to the square along another lane, passing between neat rows of stone huts, and you can imagine my stupefaction when I came upon Captain Hohner.

He was wearing a small smile, his eyes alert, and he seemed none the worse for wear. Until I realized it was only his head, right at my eye level, mounted on a pole. Nearby a woman—the oldest I'd seen, perhaps sixty, but still bounteous and lovely—was preparing her tools on a mat. She gestured that I was welcome to sit down. She had made a mound of sand about knee high. A fire of wood chips and dried leaves burned next to the sand. The woman lifted the captain's head off the pole, and knelt on her haunches to place the head between her knees. Then with a sharpened shell she quickly sliced open the back of the head, the two cuts running up over the ears to the temples. With a practiced motion, she then cut lengthwise down the back of the head to the neck. She pulled the skin apart, peeling it off the skull.

The captain's expression remained steadfast throughout this indignity, but I'm afraid I let a touch of disgust cross my face. The lady clucked at me, and continued her work. With a fishbone needle and a waxed fiber thread she sewed the captain's eyelids and mouth closed. Then, holding the captain by the chin with his hair and flaps of his skin hanging down around her hand, she used a smooth stone to chip away at the skull. She occasionally tended the fire, which heated the pile of sand next to it.

I watched for an hour as she methodically reduced the captain's skull to chips and removed scoops of his brain. She chatted all the while. I suppose she was dispensing knowledge of her craft but I didn't understand a word. Bone and brain and teeth were discarded. Finally only skin and hair remained. She sewed the scalp back together using great concentration and tiny stitches.

Next she packed the skin with hot sand. When it was full, she tapped and prodded the face back into a natural appearance, reforming the captain out of the skin bag. She poked several sticks into the ground downwind of the fire, and suspended the head on them. She tossed green leaves on the fire. The smoke became blacker. She used a straw fan to help the smoke along toward the captain's head. She halted her narration, so I assumed she had accomplished her last ghastly act. I made my way back to my hut, my guards behind me.

My surprises that day were not done. When I reentered the hut, four women were waiting for me. They were youths, actually, maybe fifteen or sixteen. All wore braids and the green stones and bark skirts. They had brought skins of water and a wood pot containing a salve. They surrounded me to remove my soiled shirt. When one of the girls went for my belt buckle, I backstepped to the door, but was stopped by the blunt side of a *borduna*, held by a guard.

So I let them take off my boots and socks and pants. I stood there naked as a piglet, all my scars visible for their inspection. They wet their hands from the waterskins, took up dollops of the salve, and began rubbing me all over. My ribs didn't hurt too badly.

They bathed me with their hands, over and over every inch until the salve was gone. This substance might have been a soap, but it also contained an abrasive, maybe sand, and it had a mint scent. They turned me around and spread me out and raised and lowered assorted parts of me until I was cleaned to their satisfaction.

Then a second wood pot was delivered through the door, and I was anointed with its contents. They rubbed it on and rubbed it in until it disappeared of its own. This substance caused my skin to warm, and then warm some more, until it became uncomfortable. But just as I was about to complain, yet another pot came in through the door. This salve was green, and the young women applied it all over, and my skin cooled immediately. This lotion smelled of frangipani. It seemed to tighten my skin. I could not remember ever being more refreshed. My skin tingled, even the scars, and my skin was mostly scars. And I appeared to be glowing a cool green.

A crowd of women had gathered to watch my bath. They peered in through the windows, nodding knowingly and commenting to each other about various aspects of the operation.

A leather contraption was sent in. One of the young women handed it to me. I held it up, stumped. She lifted one of my legs, then the other, putting this thing on. It was a loin cloth, covering my privates and nothing else. It was all the clothes they would ever give me. Clothes would only have been a nuisance, it turned out.

My strengthening began that evening, with my meal of broiled monkey paws and jaguar livers. The monkey paws were reserved for honored guests, and the jaguar livers gave one courage. Well, I was indeed beginning to feel welcome, despite the *bordunas* that were never far away. And I would indeed need an inordinate amount of courage.

Monkey paws taste like chicken wings, by the way, only you have to remember to spit out the nails.

I ate until I was full, and slept the sleep of the happily unknowing.

Next day I visited the old lady again. The captain's skin had darkened. She carefully removed the head from the rack of sticks, and poured out the sand. She then refilled the head with more hot sand, but less of it, because the skin case was smaller. She molded the captain's features back into place with her fingers, and rehung the head near the fire. I learned she emptied and refilled the head every two hours, day and night. For a week my routine was pleasant and predictable. In the morning I would walk to the old woman's house to watch her work on the captain's head. She occasionally looked at my noggin with professional interest, I thought. It occurred to me that the Women Who Live Alone had shot Captain Hohner through the ears so as not to disfigure his face. In the afternoon Winter, Spring, Summer and Autumn, as I had named those young ladies, entered my hut to give me a bath, which lasted about two hours, dry to dry.

Then there was the eating, three full meals a day. I ate armadillos and deer, a fish called cachama, alligators, and such fruit as bacuni, cucuacu, macarandha and graviola. The food was seasoned with pepper, nutmeg, cinnamon, and cloves, and these were only the flavors I recognized. I ate heartily. The Women Who Live Alone visited in turns during my meals to encourage me to eat, nodding their approval and pantomiming the act of eating.

They didn't care what I ate, or how much, except for the first dish they served every evening. It was a brown soup with lumps in it, and its fish taste led me to believe it was a bouillabaisse. I didn't much care for it but when I set the bowl aside, a guard stepped through the crowd of female onlookers and gave it back to me, and the first night the guard did this four times until I at last understood. I could turn aside any other dish, but I was to eat the bouillabaisse. So I did, all the women smiling at my efforts.

Later in that week I stumbled across their butchery. Meat hung about on thorn hooks, and fresh and dried blood covered the stones below. I watched for several hours. Two hunters came in—I recognized them as two of the women who had captured me—and dropped a dead jaguar in front of the butchers. The jaguar had four arrow punctures in its side. The first thing the butcher did was to slice off the jaguar's testicles, then drop them into a wood bowl. I walked over to look at the bowl's contents. A pile of brown and red gonads from a number of different species, judging from the different sizes of the round little balls. As I watched, the butcher cut off the testicles of an anteater, and added them to the bowl. They smiled at me as they worked. My *borduna*-wielding guards smiled at me. All the women smiled at me. I didn't feel safe.

Only that night when I was handed my bouillabaisse did I realize it weren't fish soup after all. It was testicle soup. I had no idea what the brown sauce was, that fishy taste. Probably fish testicles. I've never bothered to find out if fish have testicles, but if they did, they were in the soup. I'd have preferred a plum pudding.

That night I flatly refused to eat the soup, so one of the guards leveled me with the flat of her *borduna*. When I crawled to a sitting position— the world chasing itself around and around—she put the bowl of testicles back in my hand. And I ate.

Now I want to give you a warning, you sitting over there as frail as tissue, with your legs crossed and your hand jiggling away in your pocket, and to anyone who might ever read a transcript of my story. I am about to describe my next two weeks, and unless I do so in some detail, you won't understand my ordeal. You'll think being a sex slave was fun. I am going to disabuse you of that notion but if you are sensitive to detail, you can excuse yourself and I'll talk into the tape recorder on my own for a while. You still here? You have hardly recovered from my description of my night with Victoria. Well, here goes.

At dusk on my seventh day in the village of the Women Who Live Alone, Winter, Spring, Summer and Autumn entered my hut. I was surprised to see the girls because until then they had only appeared for my afternoon baths. This time they carried palm fronds, and they laid them along the short route from the door to the bed. Tucked among the fronds were white lilies. Autumn then brought a burning taper into the hut, and lit a fire in the pit. She put what appeared to be herbs across the fire. Then the girls left the hut.

Next into my room came three women I had not seen in my walks through the village. All three were six feet tall, and if I had to pick out a difference between them, as they had the similarity of triplets, it would be the hues of their skin. One was the color of a chestnut, another burnt cream, and another honey. Their black hair was loose and flowing, the first time I'd seen a Woman Who Lives Alone without braids. In their hair were sprinklings of glass beads. Their lips were livid red from urucum tree paint, and their eyebrows had been limned black with root dye. They were scented with wild roses. Their skin glistened with oil.

These three women were exaggerations of the beauty of the Women Who Live Alone. Everything about them was more curved, larger and grander. Their waists were tiny, and rumps were as curved and full as a mare's, and their breasts reminded me of high season cantaloupes at Dewy O'Brien's Market in my old Roxbury neighborhood, except larger. Their legs were long and tight. These women loomed over me.

My first instinct was to get out of their way. But that proved not what they wanted. They were on business and their business was with me. In concert, the three pushed me back toward the bed. When I resisted, a club-carrying guard came into the hut to remind me with a quick gesture that she would lay her *borduna* alongside my head if I didn't cooperate.

So back onto the bed I went. These women began immodestly rubbing my body. My memory has named these three Dawn, Day and Dusk. All evidence indicated they had agreed on their procedure before it began because Dawn massaged my head and neck and shoulders only, Day my chest and back and rump, and Dusk my legs and feet. Their attention was infinite and their skill vast. They periodically dipped their hands into a bowl of oil.

Now, the Four Seasons' baths had been utterly clinical, with the girls intent only on cleaning me until I shone. Any impudence on my part—unintended, I assure you, because of their tender ages—was met with a smart slap on the offending part, which sank immediately. But after a few minutes of this massage by Dawn, Day and Dusk, it became apparent that cleanliness was not their purpose. They probed and caressed, their fingers leaving almost nothing unattended. I feared a slap, but I responded, rising to the occasion, which brought smiles from the three ladies. Though they carefully avoided touching my privates, their hands quickened the pace—over my chest, along my legs, inside my thighs, deep into my stomach muscles, on my temples—and I began to strain against their hands, looking for some release. They kept me pinned to the bed.

The pit fire was filling my hut with a green-gray pungent smoke that had an herbal taste, not unpleasant. After a few moments of breathing it I began to feel lightheaded. The breasts above me began to float free and rotate, as if in a kaleidoscope. All the world was made of those breasts.

Then Day pinched my left nipple, and before I knew what was occurring, shot a sharpened fish bone through it. Clean through it, and left it there. She squeezed my other nipple, and pierced it through, too. Beads of blood seeped from my nipples onto my chest. But, peculiarly, the fierce stinging gave way to an exquisite pleasure. I shuddered on the bed, increasingly desperate with desire.

Then the three produced blue-and-green feathers, each three feet long and iridescent, resembling a peacock's, though I never saw a peacock in the jungle. Dawn, Day and Dusk each dipped a feather into the bowl of oil, then drew the oiled feather tips along my body, up and down, in and out, the feathers' touch so slight it was mostly in my imagination. Each time I tried to rise—entreaties for satisfaction on my lips—they pushed me back down. My Mr. Happy ached, and I'm telling you, all these decades later, I remember with painful yearning the force of my desire at that moment.

Passed in through the door and appearing as if by sleight of hand in the smoke came a curious leather apparatus. I'd never seen anything like it, and I first thought it was for a horse, a miniature oat bucket maybe. It consisted of a leather pouch filled with a thick buttery unguent. A small circular leather loop was above the pouch, and long leather belts were also attached to the pouch. Day attached this mechanism to my privates. That is, she pushed my testicles into the pouch where they soaked in a cool solution. She tightened the pouch, closing it so none of this paste could splash out. Then she ringed my Johnson with the short thong, cinching it up a bit painfully. And then she pulled belts through my legs and around my waist and tied them behind me.

The batter in this leather codpiece had a decidedly calming effect on me for a few seconds but then it began to warm me, a luxurious and provocative heat spreading from my loins up my stomach and down my legs. But most of the unguent's energy was sent into my priapus, a coursing wave of strength that extended me and filled me to a point where I feared an explosion like an overstuffed sausage, the skin on my maypole not strong enough to contain the new energy. I shook and shifted and gasped and still those heavy breasts spun above me, and no relief was offered.

Then the Queen Bee entered the hut. That is what my memory has named her for that is what she was. She filled the door frame. She was at least six and a half feet tall, and her skin was an oiled and shimmering bronze. Her hair was the color of a raven's wing, and it fanned out from her head as if blown by a breeze. She wore nothing but braided twine around her waist and a green jaguar head around her neck.

She stepped along the palm fronds through the clouds of smoke to the foot of the bed where I lay pierced and prodded and soaking. I have no doubt I was hallucinating by the time the Queen Bee arrived, for it seemed my Oscar grew in front of me, rising and rising, an enormous and stately pole, its grand head pointed right at the Queen Bee.

Dusk and Day slipped a piece of leather the size and shape of a barber's sharpening strop beneath my buttocks. The strop had handholds at the ends. While Dawn gripped my head, Dusk and Day seized the strap's handholds. Thus they could raise and lower my center.

The Queen Bee climbed onto the bed, and hesitated for a moment, a leg on each side of me. She was a giantess, and all of her aspects were proportionately large. She settled into position, her breasts orbiting above me like two harvest moons, so large they crowded the hut, their areolas like saucers and nipples the size of my little fingers. They were rigid, sticking right out in front of her.

She either grimaced or grinned—I couldn't tell which—as she straddled me. Her teeth were so white they shone like beacons in the smoke. Her lips were voluptuous and painted red. Her brown eyes were the shape of almonds, and her cheekbones were wide and high. She possessed an elemental sexual power, and she was about to use it on me.

From above my head, Dawn reached down along my body to grip my member. I was astonished her fingers could fit around it, the way it had risen, the way it competed with the Queen Bee's breasts for room in the hut.

Dawn aimed it, and down came the Queen Bee. She slid down and down and down on me. Day and Dusk began yanking the straps up and down, up and down, a mechanical pumping.

The smoke, the oil, the breasts, the pouch, Dusk and Day's rhythmic exertions, the needles through my nipples; I was amazed I lasted as long as I did, about a minute, and then I exploded with such force that the velocity and mass of my fluid propelled the Queen Bee entirely off the bed. I'm sure a physicist could explain it with a formula, and maybe also my howl of indecent pleasure that came with it.

She landed lightly, and without another look at me, exited the hut.

She was replaced by Dusk, who was spitted on me before the Queen Bee was out of sight. Day and Dawn worked the straps. This time I lasted maybe two minutes.

Then Day had a turn, then Dawn. The combined effects of all the stimuli meant that I never shriveled from the tasks, and that I performed all four times in an exemplary and manly fashion.

My sexual servitude lasted two weeks. Each day would see the repeating of the same ritual, from the fishbone needles, to the mystery balm in the leather pocket, to the medicinal smoke. Every day the Queen Bee mounted me, and when she was done, the others did the same in turn.

I faced this ordeal with courage and stamina, but at the end of those fourteen days I had lost those thirty pounds again, and was having difficulty walking.

But I did walk. The hunters came for me one morning and led me back along the route I had come. Five days later we arrived at the same tributary. The boat was on the shore. One of the women pushed it into the water and helped me get on board.

As a gift of appreciation, I suppose, they handed me Captain Hohner's head, as small as an apple and as brown as a raisin.

They waved goodbye and disappeared in the foliage. It was the work of an entire day to row back to the *John Jay*, still moored at Almeirim and still waiting for parts, which arrived two days later. The vessel sailed downstream with me in the officers' wardroom, so weak I was unable to go on deck for almost four days. The *John Jay* motored out of the Amazon and into the sea, and left the Women Who Live Alone far behind.

Let me tell you now that it was no accident that anaconda dropped on me. Through pantomime, the Four Seasons had let me know that the snake was a test. The hunters had held it on a bough above me, and dropped it when the boat passed under. I had survived, so I was sturdy enough for their queen.

I warned you a while back about my narration, now I issue another warning. You may have been able to listen with some dispassion about the Women Who Live Alone and their treatment of me, but you will not be so complacent about the worm I somehow picked up in the Amazon jungle. Turn away now. Listen no further.

Five days out into the Pacific, me lying on a cot in an officer's stateroom, I abruptly felt a bizarre combination of stinging and tickling in my right side. I looked down to find the head of a white worm poking out of my skin just below my ribs. Mouthless and eyeless, the translucent color of weak milk, it wiggled and rolled, four inches of it extending from my side.

I hollered and leaped off the cot. Fortunately, the ship's surgeon was in the ward, and he rushed over. He stopped my hand just as I was about to try to rip that crawler out of me. Good thing, too. The surgeon explained it was a Guyana worm, that it was three or four feet long, twisted all about my innards, and that had I yanked it, the worm's head would have snapped off, and the rest of its body would have been left to rot inside me, causing massive infections and probably death.

The surgeon wrapped the four inches of worm around a wood spoon, and tied the head in place so it couldn't unwrap itself and disappear back inside me. Then every day for a month he smoothly pulled another inch or two or three out, wrapping it around the spoon, which at other times I wore inside my shirt, reluctantly displaying it to the sailors when they so requested, which was often, but never near meal times. They dubbed him Walter, and they'd say things like, "Why, here come Woodrow and

Walter." The worm was alive during the long procedure, and at night it squirmed beside me.

At the end of a month the tail finally slid out, and the entire worm was twisted around the spoon like kite string. I tossed Walter into the ocean.

Even after all these years, the thought of that worm can still activate my gag reflex. So I don't look back too affectionately on the Amazon, despite the Queen Bee and her attendants, who treated me kindly, all things considered. And I've often wondered if I sired any children by these women, which of course was their purpose.

I still have the captain's shrunken head, by the way. I toyed with sending it to his widow but finally thought better of that idea. I keep it in a jar in the kitchen, and when one of my cooks asks about it I say it's a Christmas tree ornament. I've never been asked twice about it by the same cook.

FIFTEEN

My Love, Again

THE *JOHN JAY* coaled in Montevideo without giving the crew any leave, then pushed diagonally up and across the Rio de la Plata. Two lines of buoys marked the channel. The river was shallow and brown. Little of Buenos Aires was visible as we approached because the city is flat. La Plata is so wide that I could no longer see the Uruguayan shore behind us. The *John Jay* sailed for Buenos Aires' north harbor, opposite Santa Fé Street. The harbor had been dredged out behind a wall of masonry. The ship entered a wide basin, the Dársena Norte, then turned left to the docks.

Few United States men-o'-war visited Buenos Aires, and a gathering of notables waited on the dock. Our vessel was nudged into place by a tug. Red, white and blue bunting hung from poles, and a twelve-piece brass band played a march. Umbrellas up against the sun hid most of the crowd from my view as I leaned against the port rail, sailors in white on both sides of me, their pay heavy in their pockets and their throats parched as only the throats of sailors long at sea can be parched. A few sailors rocked back and forth against the safety rail to propel the *John Jay* more quickly into its berth. After lines were secured, a derrick lowered the gangplank.

The bo's'n's piercing whistle sounded. The United States ambassador and his wife and several Argentine officials came up the ramp. The wife lowered her parasol so the *John Jay*'s officers could be presented to her.

There have been times when I felt as if a sledgehammer hovers above me, always following me around, looming and dangerous, until for some reason or another, usually when I am being mindful of my own business, it decides I need a powerful whack. So the hammer started down at that moment, when the ambassador's wife emerged from her umbrella.

Oh Lordy. It was Amy Balfour. The sledgehammer landed right between my eyes.

I had not seen that woman—for that was what she had truly become—for almost ten years, the last time being on her wedding day. Now here she was again, standing on the *John Jay*'s deck in Buenos Aires, nodding vaguely at one officer after another, looking supremely bored and put upon, while her husband, Ambassador John Malcolm, shook each officer's hand.

"The heart has its reasons which reason knows nothing of," said Pascal. Amy had the same effect on me then as she had all those years ago—almost two decades ago—when I saved her in front of my pa's saloon. As she drew near, my hands began to shake, and I could feel all reason flee me. Her hair was a flame of glorious red and gold, casting shadows all around. Some of her hair was held up by a turtle-shell comb and some fell to her shoulders, daring for the time. New and fine lines were at the corners of her eyes, and their effect was to frame her crystal blue eyes and give her the authority of wisdom and experience. And she still had all those freckles, handfuls of them tossed across her cheeks and nose and chin. Her nose was a lovely sharp blade. Her mouth was curved and lush, with a full lower lip that was both inviting and insolent.

Amy was wearing a cotton dress the same riveting blue as her eyes. Her abundant figure flowed to and fro in that dress because she obviously weren't wearing a whalebone corset underneath, also provocative for the day. She wet her lips with her tongue, and looked away once in a while as if she had something better to do.

In a black-and-white morning coat, her husband dutifully chatted with the officers. The sun beat down with heat. Lines of sweat grew across the ambassador's forehead and upper lip. I learned later that Amy's husband had been a long-time supporter of the new president, William McKinley, who had appointed him to the post in Argentina. McKinley had been at Amy's wedding, you'll remember.

Malcolm and Amy continued down the line of officers and sailors, their pace quickening as the ranks became lower. She passed me without a glance, but her jasmine scent lingered. She disappeared behind the superstructure aft, and that's the last I saw of her until she and her husband descended the gangplank thirty minutes later, having taken libations in the officers' mess.

John L. Sullivan once told me, "Woodrow, women are like trolleys.

Never run after one because another will be along in ten minutes." But after I met Amy Balfour that first time, I realized John L. knew boxing but not much else, and certainly not women. Another Amy Balfour would never come along. I resolved then and there, on the deck of the gunboat, to try again with her.

Now, I can hear the clank and groan of your brain being engaged, rusty from disuse and protesting all the while, and you are thinking, "Woodrow, every time you light out after that lady, a cartload of bricks drops on your head, so why in the world don't you avert your eyes and cut her out of your memory and be the healthier for it?" And my response to you is, "Would that I could." Against the gas lamp, the moth is powerless.

Besides, I hadn't been beaten or hung or dragged or crushed or stabbed to within an inch of my life in—what?—weeks, so I had some stamina stored up. I was ready for Amy. As I saw her and the ambassador and their entourage disappear behind a building on the wharf, I already had a plan.

I would simply present myself to her and tell my story, and describe to her all the travail I had endured on her account, and settle for whatever sentiment she would bestow on me. I had shoveled eight years of dervish dung on account of her. Was that not worth some sort of regard? Or a thank you? I was determined to get my due.

Today Buenos Aires claims to have the widest avenue in the world, the Avenida 9 de Julio, which became wide when it was bulldozed by the military government thirty-five or so years later. Back then, though, it was a grand and not-too-wide boulevard full of pink blossoming trees called drunken trees, with two long rows of French-inspired mansions with mansard roofs and more chimneys than required by the climate. The ambassador and his wife lived in one of those big houses, so that's where I appeared later that same day.

The *John Jay*'s gunner had loaned me some civvies, and I was brushed up and turned out, my nails clean and my hair combed, when I pulled the cord next to the front door. I waited a moment. I heard the crash of breaking glass somewhere in the house above me. I pulled the bell cord again, and after a fashion a butler opened the door.

The sound of another crash came from within. The butler, a gloomy fellow with a turned-down mouth and doleful eyes, glanced disconcertedly over his shoulder up the stairway toward the noise. Then he turned back and asked in a tone that made my borrowed suit feel cheap, "May I help you?"

"I'm here to see Mrs. Malcolm."

Another piece of glass shattered, again upstairs.

From up the stairs: "How could you, you oaf?"

I recognized the caustic tone Amy had used on John L.

The butler cleared his throat imperiously. "Is she expecting you?"

You'll recall that in my prior attempts to see Amy, some roadblock always appeared in my way at the last instant, and I would be diverted before I got to her.

So I rose on my toes and announced, "She'll be glad to see me, I'm sure."

I put a finger on his breastbone and pushed him aside like a gate. He sputtered and huffed and chased after me as I crossed the marble foyer toward the stairs.

From upstairs came her voice, "You'll ruin the whole family, you contemptible lout."

The stairs were covered with a Persian runner held in place by brass fixtures at the base of the risers. I climbed quickly, passed a stand with a marble bust of George Washington on the landing, up to the second floor.

"You don't have that kind of money," she yelled. "How could you be such a dullard? Where did you get the money?"

I turned left toward her voice, the butler puffing behind me. A man's voice—at once cringing and challenging—came from down the hall. I couldn't make out his words.

Then Amy cried, "You *what*? Oh my God, he'll kill you. And me."

I reached the open door from which came the sounds of this argument. Or, more accurately, this dressing down. The door was open to a bedroom suite. I knocked loudly.

"Leave me alone, Edgar," she snapped, out of my sight behind the door.

Edgar must have been the butler's name. I knocked again.

I heard quick footsteps, and she appeared in front of me. "Edgar, didn't I make myself clear? Leave—"

"Hello again," I said pleasantly.

She inhaled sharply. "Who are you? How did you get into this house?" She was as cross as a bag of cats.

Edgar appeared behind me, his nostrils flaring. "Madam, he bolted his way past me. A criminal, no doubt. He touched me and I may have been injured in your service. I shall call the police."

"Don't you remember me?" I asked.

"Edgar," she said, "Captain Pérez owes me a favor. Tell him I want six of his policemen over here instantly to deal with this trespasser." She could have chopped ice with that voice.

I do believe now that her colors had a chemical effect on me. The blue of her eyes and red and gold of her hair, the white of her skin and brown of her freckles. The colors intoxicated me, and I don't mean in a poet's sense. They actually made me loopy and vapid. My wife once suggested I ask a psychologist about this odd effect. A psychologist? Might as well interview a tarot-card reader. A chemist would have more likely produced an answer. So I stood in Amy's bedroom doorway, her colors a rainbow in front of me, and my intelligence began its rapid descent to stupid, not that it had far to fall.

"I helped you into the water closet at your wedding. Remember?"

She cocked her head at me, one eyebrow raised a fraction. Then she held up a finger, indicating Edgar should wait a moment.

I pressed on. "Your stomach sounded like a sump pump, and you were pounding on the toilet door and—"

"I remember." She assayed me with her eyes, a serious inventory of my physical assets. "That was you?"

"Yes, ma'am."

I saw no profit in telling her I was also the boy who kept John L. from beating her horse, or that I was the boy who had been arrested trying to climb a ladder to her room. She apparently had never made the connection. My appearance had changed drastically over the years. She didn't recognize me as that Boston boy from so long ago.

She abruptly reached for my chin and turned my head sideways so she could examine my cheek. "What happened to your face?"

I replied honestly, if not completely, "I got cut in sort of a fight." This was Lady Elizabeth's passionate gash.

She moved my head back and forth, eyeing me. I let her hold my chin. I was made even dumber by the softness of her fingers and their flowery fragrance.

I caught a movement at the corner of my eye. A man stepped into view, walking behind her on bits of broken glass. A beanpole-thin chap with greased-back hair, a damp mouth and weak chin. The skin on his face was shiny and pale, the color of a fried egg white. I knew that face, that simpering countenance that demanded to be punched. It was her brother, Dickie.

I had promised myself the next time I ran into Dickie Balfour I would stick my hand down his throat and rip out his stomach. But such was his sister's power over me that I stood there content, with her wagging my chin back and forth as she examined me.

"Come into the room," she demanded, pulling me by the arm.

The room was dominated by a poster bed with a sky-blue spread and three matching pillows each the size of a steer. Blue swags hung at the windows. A mahogany writing desk with a red leather inlay was in front of a window. Ink bottles and a signature blotter were on the desk. The house was built before clothing closets became common, so three armoires lined the walls, each with a beveled mirror in the center. The only item on the walls was a beach scene—the people looked French, I can spot the French—drawn using only tiny points of paint, something a child might try.

She led me to her brother. He didn't recognize me either, or maybe he weren't looking closely. He kept his eyes on his sister, afraid of her, hoping to dodge the next vase or picture frame she threw at him. One had hit its mark. A thin line of blood dribbled down from under his hair onto his forehead. He dabbed at it with a finger, and shuddered at the sight of it.

"What happened to your ear?" She grabbed my cauliflower ear and spread the folds of flesh with her fingers.

"I was a prizefighter, ma'am."

Still holding my ear, she turned to her brother, freezing him with a glare of contempt. "My brother Dickie fancies himself an athlete, an airy bit of dreaming he has engaged in since childhood. Now his delusion about his athletic prowess is about to ruin me."

I had not the slightest idea what she was talking about, but my cauliflower ear had never been treated so kindly. She stroked it lightly as she upbraided her brother.

"I should have Dickie imprisoned for theft." She turned to me. "And what about these—what are they? Scars—on your eyebrows? From your prizefighting? And this knob on your nose?"

I pushed out my chest. "I've fought John L. Sullivan, Tobias Brown, and Bruiser Turner." I didn't add that I'd lost to all three.

Up came her other hand. She softly touched my neck, then slid her fingers down, pushing away my shirt collar. "And what are these marks on your neck?"

"Some fellows tried to hang me. They underestimated me."

She inhaled hugely so that her breasts almost touched my shirt. She again looked at her brother, who was standing near a dresser on which was a washbasin. The water pitcher had already been thrown at him, and its shards lay on the floor near an armoire. Amy dipped her chin at him but his face refused to register comprehension.

Back to me. "What else do you have?"

"Pardon?"

"Scars."

"Plenty, but the others are not in places appropriate to show a lady." Dickie snorted, "A lady?"

"Show me," she ordered, sounding much like a cavalry sergeant.

"Ma'am?"

"Take your shirt off." She began with my shirt buttons.

I modestly stepped back, but she yanked me to her with surprising strength. She undid one button after another and then peeled the shirt off my arms.

"What are these?" She traced a finger across my chest and onto my shoulder.

"More scars, ma'am."

"Yes?" Her voice had gained a strange huskiness.

"Some fellow whipped me pretty bad one time in the Sudan." I was referring to Hamed Ibn Belal. "Like to kill most anybody else, I reckon."

"And this purple pucker?"

"A bullet." From the dervish captain whose aim was high.

She turned me by the shoulders. A small gasp escaped her. I felt her fingers run along the scar on my back, the big one that stood out from all the whip scars.

"And this?" she breathed.

"A spear stuck me." I didn't add that a woman had been at the other end of the weapon.

She said, "That looks like it could have killed most anybody else, too."

"Why, I believe you're right, ma'am."

"And this?" she probed with a finger.

"That's where the bullet came out."

"And what's this purple color and this dappled skin among all the scars?"

"I was adrift in the ocean for a month. Those're sunburn scars. Almost killed me dead."

"Take your pants off," she commanded.

I hesitated. "Ma'am, under any other circumstances . . ." I nodded at Dickie. "It'd be a pleasure, a lifelong dream, actually, and—"

"Be silent and do as I tell you."

That woman had a mouth at odds with her voluptuous appearance, didn't she? She didn't wait for me. She grappled with my belt buckle and the buttons of my fly, then yanked my pants down to my brogans. I was wearing Navy-issue cotton briefs, yellowed by a hundred washings in salt water.

"And these?" She knelt in front of me and ran her hand down my leg. "These are extraordinarily purple, aren't they?"

The raised scar tissue on my legs had never regained a flesh color.

"Same Sudan whipping, ma'am."

She stood up and took both my hands in hers. For an instant I thought she wanted to hold hands, maybe for old times' sake. Instead, she explored my hands with hers, pressing my knobby, callused and scarred knuckles. She brought them up to her eyes, then nodded to herself as if some calculation of hers all added up.

"You were at my wedding, you say?"

She had no memory of me, after all. "Yes, ma'am."

"Then may I call on an old friendship?"

Silence your mouth, Woodrow, you smitten fool. Just press your lips together and don't let any words out. Save yourself.

But . . . no. "Of course, ma'am."

She spun away from me, pressing a hand to her temple in a gesture of despair. "What I'm about to ask of you is extraordinary. But you obviously are an extraordinary gentleman."

"Ma'am?"

"You cannot be killed," she declared, turning and pointing at me like a lawyer in the heat of cross-examination. "Isn't that as plain as the crook in your nose? Many men and all the forces of nature have tried to kill you but have failed. You are invincible."

"I suppose I am."

"I cannot ask this favor of you without telling you that my brother is a simpering fool, and has succeeded at last in almost destroying me. Only you can prevent that."

I was encouraged. "Can I beat him up for you?"

She shook her head, her glorious gold-and-red locks trailing back and forth across her shoulders. "My brother lives off an allowance from our father. He receives this allowance once a month, and it takes him three or four days of strenuous effort each month to gamble and drink it away, all of it, except for those few dollars he spends on women of the street, and they were only a few dollars because Dickie's stamina in that regard only equals his athletic ability, so I've heard."

Dickie blushed the color of her hair. "Amy, you shouldn't—"

"Stop your sniveling. In the presence of a genuine man you should cower behind that curtain."

I didn't want to beat up Dickie, after all. His sister was doing it for me.

"He loses all his money each month, and then has the temerity to come to my house to borrow more from me. I am weak . . ."

He snorted again.

". . . and I give him substantial sums each month to tide him over until his next allowance, but then a few days ago, tired of his wasting all that money, I drew the purse strings on him. He whined and cried like a child."

I suffered from a frightening delusion just then. There Amy was, having captured me with her gaze, her wild and ravishing face in front of me, when for an instant—and only an instant—her freckles and skin and hair vanished to reveal the skull beneath. Hollowed black eyes, long teeth, chalk-white bone, and ferocious. A death's head, something a sailor would have tattooed on his arm. I gasped and blinked. She was instantly back to normal, her loveliness swatting aside reason and caution and suspicion.

"And this morning Dickie took my jewelry—"

He cut in. "It wasn't your jewelry. It was your mother-in-law's."

"It would have been mine shortly," she snapped. "The doctor has given her two months, maybe three. How many more strokes can an eighty-year-old woman have?" She inhaled through her teeth. "Dickie took the jewelry—a diamond bracelet and an emerald pendant and three diamond rings—to make a wager on a fight."

"I could have won five thousand U.S. dollars," Dickie exclaimed. "That's how much the jewelry brought as a wager."

His sister paced back and forth. "My husband is going to throw me out of a window when he discovers it's gone. And I'll land on Dickie's body below."

I shrugged. "Maybe your man will win the fight."

Amy pressed a finger to her temple as if suffering from a sudden headache. "I haven't told you all of it." She thumbed her brother. "Dickie here put the wager on himself, if you can imagine."

"On himself?"

"I was known around Boston for a certain manliness, and I can handle . . ." Dickie's words withered under his sister's gaze.

"Stated bluntly, my brother is going to be killed." She brought both hands up to gather her hair, then let it fall to her shoulders, as appealing a gesture as I had ever seen. "That doesn't trouble me, frankly. But that jewelry. I must get it back."

I asked, "May I pull up my pants?"

She waved her hand absently, and I was disappointed that she apparently didn't care whether my pants were up or down. I hastened back into my clothes, buttoning and buckling.

"But you see," she said, "Dickie didn't put the wager on himself necessarily. He put the money on anyone he produces. He needs to produce somebody—anybody—at the ring."

I finally determined the direction of the conversation. "I'm not going to fight on your brother's behalf, I know that much."

"For five hundred dollars." When speaking of money her face gained something of her father's cast, harder, with veiled and remote eyes.

"Not for five thousand dollars. I don't like your brother."

She looked at Dickie. "You aren't the first to take an immediate dislike to him, believe me. Look at him. Pathetic and weak. And look at you." She stepped close to grab my biceps, digging her fingernails into the muscles. "Just look at you. You are the strongest and hardest man in Argentina."

Modesty does not prevent me from saying that I didn't doubt her.

"Nothing can defeat you." She gazed into my eyes, her face only a foot away from mine. Her eyes deeply probed me. I could not have looked away had my head been prodded with a gun muzzle.

Then she added in a boudoir tone, "And I would be so grateful."

How grateful? I wanted to ask.

She must have been a mentalist. She whispered, "You cannot imagine how grateful I would be."

I still hesitated.

So she added in a voice that could have melted candle wax, "And I would show all my gratitude, all of it."

I peered into her eyes. She would not look away. "Five hundred dollars and your gratitude?"

My mind was certainly playful that day, for just then a klaxon went off right between my ears, sounding like the *John Jay*'s abandon-ship bell I'd heard during drills. I shook my head and silenced it.

"The event is this afternoon at three o'clock."

"Who would be my opponent?"

"I don't know." She arched an eyebrow, a challenge. "Would it matter?"

"Not in the slightest." The only man in the world I would hesitate to get into the ring against was John L. Sullivan, and he was in New York City. I might lose to a few other prize fighters but nobody except John L. terrified me. "Bare knuckles or Marquis of Queensberry?"

She looked at Dickie, who was pouring himself a glass of sherry from a crystal decanter that had been on a side table. "Bare knuckles."

I pursed my lips, then said, "It's a deal."

Dickie threw back the sherry with the exuberance of one just granted a reprieve.

Amy nodded. Her eyes were unknowable and shaded, but they were so alluringly blue, so blue.

That same damn bell in my head went off again, and this time I couldn't silence it. Only when she offered me a glass of sherry did it fade away, but slowly.

I was shortly to wish I had heeded that klaxon and had abandoned ship.

In her carriage we drove through the streets of Buenos Aires, southwest, I thought. The driver above us clicked and whistled, directing the horse.

Dickie sat on the pleated leather cushion to my left and his sister was across from me. She had changed to a crimson dress with gray trim at the neck and cuffs, and with two lines of silver buttons in front, the effect being rather military. She also wore a gray felt hat held in place by a silver pin. On her lap was a matching handbag.

Amy must have thought my courage would ebb and that I would welch on our deal, because she stared at me intently for the entire drive. She knew by then, of course, her power over me, and probably regretted the five-hundred-dollar part of the deal.

We arrived at a small stadium. I could hear the cheers of the crowd behind the walls. The driver jumped down to open the door and place a footstool on the cobblestones. The stadium was only two stories high, and had no windows to the outside. The neighborhood was of cattle-related enterprises. I saw signs for a tannery, a rendering plant, and a butcher.

I was dressed in my same borrowed outfit, except at my insistence Dickie had found a pair of long johns, which would suffice in lieu of tights, and blue-and-gold strips of silk to use as my colors.

When a gate to the stadium opened, a mule team in harnesses emerged. A skinner walked alongside the two mules, a quirt in one hand and reins in the other. At first I couldn't make out what the mule team was dragging. A sizable brown lump. Then I saw horns. A bull carcass, headed for an open shed attached to the stadium where four butchers awaited, all in bloody white aprons and carrying long knives.

I stopped. "This is a ring for bullfights."

"Yes, it is," Amy replied.

"I'm no bullfighter." I had never even seen a bullfight. "I'm not fighting any farm animals."

"Of course not." She patted my arm. "Don't be silly. Our event follows the last bullfight of the afternoon. I'd never ask you to be a matador."

We entered the side of the building, passing a row of those brightly colored bullfight posters. We walked through a short tunnel, and then the plaza de toros opened in front of us. Dickie snickered at something or other.

The circular arena was surrounded by a strong wood parapet about chest-high, resting on a red brick wall. Above the parapet was the first row of spectators' seats, about eight feet off the ground, and below the parapet was the *callejón*, the circular alleyway separated from the ring by a stout wood wall. Several openings were in this wall from which men and bulls had access to the ring. One of the doors was the *toril*, which led directly to the bull pen. I guessed the arena had seating for two thousand aficionados, and every seat was filled. Cigar smoke rose skyward in vast waves, so thick that the far seats were obscured.

Amy led me to a plank seat. She was the only woman in the stadium but none of the spectators' eyes were on her because the matador was preparing for a kill. He was dressed in a red vest with gold trim. He was assisted by lance-carrying picadors on their horses. Six *monosabios* were dressed in red blouses and caps, prepared to rescue a picador who had fallen from a saddle, and to kill a badly wounded horse. Several other peons were also in the ring, whose job I never figured out.

The bull was chestnut brown with red circles around its eyes, called partridge eyes. Three *banderillas*, paper-decorated wood poles with barbed metal points, were stuck into the animal. Its nose was low and blowing sand.

Then it charged, hoofs thundering. The matador performed a *pase de la muerte*, bringing the red cape up and over the bull's horns and letting the cape flow along the animal's back. The crowd roared.

By the time the bull turned, the matador had a sword in his hand. I had no idea where he got it from. The bull pawed the ground twice, and bolted forward. The cape flashed. The matador's hands came up. Too fast for me to follow. The bull collapsed like a dropped puppet. The crowd howled with delight. The matador stepped away from the bull.

The handle of the sword stuck into the air at a forty-five degree angle, just behind the bull's neck. The animal had died instantly. Flowers were thrown into the arena. When a gate in the wall opened, the mule team and skinner entered to drag the carcass away.

"It's your turn." Amy caressed my arm. "Dickie will lead you down to the dressing room."

I asked, "You been here before, ma'am?"

"Once or twice. I love the spectacle. Off you go now."

I followed Dickie out of the stands to a small room under the seats. The room was painted sanitarium green and had a wood bench along one wall. From above came footsteps of the crowd. Many were leaving, it sounded like. I warmed up by jumping in place and shadow boxing.

Dickie sat on the bench, lit a cheroot, and used most of his brainpower by blowing smoke rings.

Four fellows walked into the room, all wearing loose trousers and skivvies. They spoke lowly among themselves in Spanish, and were all agitated, wringing their hands and looking around. Feeling more confident, I wondered which one was my opponent. None looked like a fighter, but they were all young men in good shape. Two wore mustaches.

Then a trainer—at least, that's what I took him for—entered the room. He held a cigar between his yellow teeth, and his belly hung over his belt. He carried five cloth banners, each with a number on it.

He read from a piece of paper. "Ramirez? *Numero uno.*"

One of the young men stepped forward to accept the square banner, which had strings hanging from each corner.

"Gueterez? *Numero dos.*"

A man identified himself as Gueterez, and accepted the banner with the black two on it.

"Lowe? *Numero tres.*"

I took number three, and imitated the others by tying it around my neck and waist so that the black three covered my chest. The trainer handed out numbers four and five to the remaining men. I wondered at the odd number of fighters, five in all. Who would be the odd man? Perhaps I would have to fight twice. I looked at the others again. That prospect didn't bother me. Amy would have the pleasure of seeing her champion perform twice.

I heard trumpets call from the arena, a disturbing tune I later learned was the Dequella, the Spanish march of no quarter, the last music heard on this earth by the defenders of the Alamo.

The trainer signaled that we should follow him by number. We walked out, one through five, into the alleyway, where a peon opened a gate to the ring. The trumpets sounded again. The crowed cheered.

The trainer stepped aside, but we continued on. Twelve men dressed in gaudy gold and red-and-black blouses and trousers had formed a chute, six on each side, that we walked into. They were an escort. They marched along with us to the center of the ring where four more men, each on a gray horse decorated with a hundred pounds of hammered silver on the saddles and stirrups, were waiting for us. The horsemen were also wearing vibrant red and gold. They moved the horses into a square, each horse at a corner, with the five of us and our twelve escorts inside.

As I looked around for Amy, I noticed that the crowd had changed in both quantity and quality. Perhaps only two hundred spectators remained, and these were finely dressed men, wearing black suits and fresh shirts. Some wore hats with leather and silver bands. A few had quirts in their hands. Many of these aficionados were wealthy *caudillos*, cruel and greedy potentates from country fiefdoms who were on holiday in Buenos Aires.

We were after-hours entertainment. They pointed at us and talked back and forth, judging us for endurance and skill. A vast amount of bank notes was changing hands, mostly U.S. dollars. We were the object of heavy gambling. I'd never been to a prizefight where this weren't so. I again scanned the other four fighters, and guessed I'd be the heavy favorite, just from my looks. I didn't see the posts or ropes of a boxing ring anywhere, but that didn't bother me. In the cavalry I'd fought several times inside squares drawn in the dirt.

I shook my arms, keeping them loose. I finally found Amy. Her fists were filled with money, and she was talking animatedly to two gentlemen, both of whom were waving bills and pointing at us fighters.

At another trumpet call—the five trumpeters were on matching gray stallions at one side of the ring—our escorts and the four corner horsemen left us, marching back to disappear through a gate. At yet another trumpet signal, twenty or so men appeared above the ring wall, each carrying a *banderilla*, one of those poles I saw stuck into the bull. These men were standing on a rail behind the wall so that only their chests and arms and heads showed to us. They held the *banderillas* vertically in front of them in the present-arms position.

The trumpeters exited the ring, and that gate closed, leaving the five of us in the middle of the ring. I admit to being a bit puzzled at that point.

Things became much clearer ten seconds later when one trumpet sounded, the bullpen gate opened, and a bull burst through.

Now, you've conjured up a bull you've seen at a dude ranch or in a John Wayne movie. But I'm speaking of something else entirely. The animal that charged through that gate was fourteen hundred pounds of muscle and hooves and horns, a mountain of steaming anger, its evil red eyes glaring right at yours truly. The ground under my feet trembled with that animal's weight as it closed.

I was to learn later this was one of the Miura breed, disfavored among matadors because of its ability to distinguish the man from the cloth. And this particular animal had been bred and trained not for bullfighting but for the bout it had just entered. The bull's horns had been sharpened to needle points, and it had been taught to charge humans.

The event was the Dequella, named after the aforementioned march. The sport was little known outside Buenos Aires' wealthy and fashionable degenerates. Fortunes changed hands at the monthly matches.

The bull rushed at me. I'd like to fib and say that I quickly came up with a strategy but in truth terror froze me. My feet seemed set in cement, and finally when bull eyeballs and horns and wet nose entirely filled my vision I collapsed from fear as if I'd suddenly turned to jelly.

The damn bull ran right over me, a hoof stomping on my knee, which made a sound much like one of Amy's vases hitting a wall.

The young man standing behind me—number four—weren't so lucky. One of the bull's horns shot through his chest, and he died while still impaled. The bull stopped long enough to toss him off, which took three or four bucks of that massive head, further opening up that lad. Gore dappled the bull's head.

I later was told this bull's name was Illustrado. It wore its breeder's colors, called *divisa*, black-and-red ribbons pinned to its shoulders with a dart.

The bull came in again but I just lay there, and number one—Ramirez—tried to dodge but Illustrado anticipated the move and turned at the last instant, lifting Ramirez up on its head between its horns, then slowing to a canter, Ramirez screaming. The bull moseyed up to the wall below Amy and butted the boards, gently, it seemed to me, but with sufficient force to crush Ramirez, who fell to the ground and lay still.

My knee was shattered but I rolled over and climbed to my feet and ran toward the wall. Each step with my right leg sent a bolt of pain through me but I ran anyway and when I reached the wall I grabbed the top and scrambled up.

Until the razorlike point of a *banderilla* came down past my chin and sank into my chest. The crowd hooted and whistled at me. The fellow up there yanked it out and held it above me, my blood dripping down in my face, and barked something in Spanish. I don't speak the language but I knew what he meant well enough. There was no way out of that ring as long as the bull was still doing its work.

And it was. I fell back to the sand ring, squirting blood from my chest. I turned in time to see the bull trampling over number five. The bull spun like a dog chasing its tail, all on top of number five, who was driven into the ground and who would never rise again.

Now there were only two of us left: number two—Gueterez—and me. The bull pranced toward the side of the ring, and the crowd clapped and hollered its approval. Illustrado had a length of human intestine caught on its right horn that trailed along like a flag.

The bull wheeled about, got me in its sights and charged again. Its huffing sounded like the *John Jay*'s steam pistons. I waited until I could see the *rodete*, three dark rings at the base of its horns, which meant—I was informed later—that Illustrado was five years old. I feinted right and dove left. Not far enough. A horn sliced into my leg. My thigh muscle lay open to the daylight. I landed on the sand and rolled in time to see Gueterez flung into the air, must have been fifteen feet, and land. He could not get up.

Now I was alone with the bull. Illustrado lowered its head and blew hard enough to bring up a cloud of sand. The bull bellowed, a hollow roar that brought the crowd to its feet. The animal charged again, throwing up clods of dirt. I ran—limped quickly—toward the wall, to the same spot where I'd been stabbed. The peon was waiting for me, his pole raised high, a mean grin on his face. I started to climb that wall.

The *banderilla* plunged down. But my reflexes are those of a boxer's. I caught that pole and yanked it out of the man's hand. Behind me, Illustrado rushed in, sounding like a train wreck.

I spun around and leaped to one side and brought the pole with its steel point around in a vicious swing, catching the bull behind the ear, sinking the blade into muscle. Illustrado blew in rage and its hot breath enveloped me. The pole's steel point was barbed, and I had to yank it twice to get it out, wheeling alongside the bull as it turned. The spectators cheered but I couldn't tell whether for me or the bull. And all I had done was make that animal mad.

Illustrado came at me again. With the *banderilla* in both hands, I ducked left but the bull turned with me and caught me square. The mammoth head smashed the breath out of me and lifted me, rolling me onto its back, a horn tearing a big chunk out of my shoulder. I spilled off the bull's back to land face down in the dirt. Blood gushed from the new wound. My world started to fade.

A sharp pain in my chin might've been the only thing that kept me from passing out. My face had landed on the pole blade, opening up my chin. I pushed myself up with my arms, then brought my knees under me. My chest was paralyzed. I fought for breath. Gripping the *banderilla*, I struggled to my feet.

A red flare caught my eye. Amy's hair. She was gripping two fistfuls of money. The handbag on her lap—she was the only spectator not standing—was so full of currency she had not been able to close it. She obviously had bet on number three, Woodrow C. Lowe, and he had lasted the longest. She was a big winner.

That damned animal came for me again, storming across the arena, its horns dripping blood, foam at its mouth, its eyes the devil's own.

My thoughts were like drifting clouds, soft and of little import. I couldn't bring my mind to bear on the problem. I staggered but caught myself with the pole. I had seen a bull killed a few moments before, I was sure of it. Bulls can be stopped, I knew dreamily. If only I could pick that memory out of the white void in my head.

Hooves pounding, Illustrado roared in, its head low, its horns stained red. I backstepped, the *banderilla* in both hands. Illustrado's head caught me again, full in the stomach, a horn on each side of me. In an instant it would shake its head, either throwing me off or spiking me with a horn.

With the last of my strength, with an effort that made me scream, I brought the pole down and jammed it into the bull behind its neck.

The animal fell so quickly I was left for an instant in the air above him. Then I toppled onto the carcass and slid to the dirt next to its haunches. The blade had severed the bull's rear aorta.

Gasping and coughing, I rubbed sand out of my eyes. My leg and shoulder pumped pain into me. I found Amy. She was stuffing even more money into her handbag, then trying to close the clasps over the wad of bills. Dickie laughed at something she said. Neither of them looked back at me as they exited the arena through the tunnel. My blood soaking the sand, a comforting blackness drifted over me.

Although I have no memory of it, I was carried from the stadium on a litter. The five hundred dollars Amy had promised was in fact the prize to the last man standing, or to his next of kin, which was the usual case. The trainer was kind enough to put that money in my pocket as he dropped me off at St. Anthony's Hospital, where I remained fully seven months recovering from the deep wounds and the subsequent infections. Then I spent another year in a sanitarium recovering from the tuberculosis I caught at the hospital.

During those first few months I thought maybe Amy would visit me but she never came. The doctor—buzzards the world around—took my five hundred dollars and demanded more. Not knowing Diamond Jim Brady's regular address, I sent a plea to him at the Waldorf Astoria where he hung out. My wire said, I HOPE YOU REMEMBER ME BECAUSE MY LIFE DEPENDS ON YOU SENDING ME $1,000. Three weeks later—as fast as a message and its return could travel in them days—the money arrived at the hospital, no questions asked. Diamond Jim's telegram said only, THAT'S ANOTHER TEN PERCENT OF YOUR ISLAND TREASURE YOU OWE ME. Fair enough.

And I received a letter from Theodore Roosevelt: "Report on Argentine navy readiness and shore defenses at Buenos Aires." I wadded it up and tossed it into a basket.

So it weren't until May 1900 when I could stagger out of the bughouse, cured more or less. I went directly to the ambassador's house, where a caretaker told me the ambassador and his wife had been summoned to Washington, D.C. Little Dickie and the butler Edgar had went with them, so I had nobody to poke.

I was alone in Buenos Aires, which was surely safer than being with Amy in Buenos Aires.

My luck hadn't run entirely out, though. The *John Jay* was long gone but another United States Navy gunboat was at the dock. I was still a serviceman—army, not navy—but I convinced the captain he owed me a ride and he agreed to post me to his complement of marines.

And I had luckily acquired four new scars. One on my chin, another on my leg, another on my chest, and another on my shoulder. I have found over the years that they make fine conversation pieces.

Trouble was, though, that gunboat—*Texas*, same name as Teddy's idiot horse—was headed the wrong way.

SIXTEEN

Boxers

I RULED CHINA for two years. A just and wise ruler, I led half a billion Chinese through a tumultuous time. I profited nothing. China was a better place when I left than when I had arrived. How this came about is worth a comment or two.

The *Texas* had been ordered from Buenos Aires to China to help put down an uprising by the Boxers, who called themselves the Fists of Righteous Harmony. I never did understand all the politics of it, but the Boxers wanted to rid China of foreigners. In particular they detested missionaries, so you can see why the Boxers deserved some sympathy.

Many countries had spheres of influence in China, and *Texas* sailed into the mouth of the Peiho River to join an armada from Great Britain, France, Germany, Italy, Russia, Japan, and maybe some others I've forgotten. Another American vessel was already there, the *Monocacy*, a side-wheeler built during the Civil War that resembled a Staten Island ferry. The Taku forts that guarded the city of Tientsin had already been taken, and *Texas*'s marines and I joined the international force as it began its journey to Peking to relieve the siege of the Legation Quarter, where Western diplomats lived, including one named Herbert Hoover. Boxers had destroyed bridges on the rail line between Tientsin and Peking so we marched along, the temperature about 104 and the Boxers sniping.

Much like the Sioux Ghost Dancers who were slaughtered at Wounded Knee ten years before, the Boxers viewed themselves as invulnerable, and they were prone to attack with only their bare fists for weapons, hence their name. The Marine colonel, Harlan Frawley, thought this rather impudent—fighting with fists rather than properly with carbines and bayonets—and he kept me by his side in case one of

219

the Boxers got near him. He had learned I was a fistic scientist. So I was a bodyguard again.

I didn't do much on the eighty-mile march except hold the reins when the colonel got off his horse to pee. And he made me shine his boots twice a day. And because he thought Orientals to be masters of poison, I had to sample his food before he ate it. I balked when he ordered me to pick nits from his hair but he threatened to flail me, so I picked nits, which weren't as much fun as it sounds.

The Chinese fled in front of our columns. We reached the red walls of the Imperial City, which lay between the Tartar section in the north and the Chinese section to the south. The city was a thousand years older than Paris. The expedition paused at the Yun Ting Gate. Inside was the crowded outer city, with its shops and outdoor markets. And beyond that was the citadel of the Forbidden City, hidden behind high purple walls two miles long, and barred to all but the imperial court.

The air smelled of garlic, sesame oil, beetroot, and night soil. Awaiting the order to dash to the Legation, the marines honed their bayonets with whetstones. I could hear the howls of Boxer mobs behind the walls, waiting for us. Boxers wore red ribbons around their wrists, and yellow sashes around their trunks. Green-and-blue scarves I learned were talismans hung from the sashes. So they were a colorful lot, but not invincible, because once in a while one of them would rush from an alleyway toward us, braying curses, eyes wild with hate, and would end up as dead as anybody I'd ever seen dead, courtesy of a marine sharpshooter.

I looked around for a weapon of some sort, wondering if it would be unseemly to walk directly behind the colonel's horse during the coming charge, my nose planted in its tail, like I had done up San Juan Hill, which had proved fairly safe. I felt ridiculous in the Marine Corps high-crowned campaign hat, me being a cavalry man. The rest of my uniform was khaki.

A messenger—a lime juicer—ran up to Colonel Frawley and spoke into his ear. The colonel chewed on nothing for a moment, his eyes sweeping his men. I was sort of hiding behind his horse, knowing the colonel often looked for volunteers, and my heart sank when he found me anyway. Lime juicers is what Marines called British soldiers, by the way.

"You, Corporal Lowe." He pointed at my nose. "I have a mission for you."

"I'm still in the U.S. Cavalry, sir, not the Marines, really."

The colonel was so unused to any sort of demurral—that's not the Marine Corps way—that I don't think he heard me.

"You were in the cavalry, corporal," he said, putting his hand on my shoulder. "So you know horses."

"I was a cook, sir."

"And we need a horseman right now."

"Not even a good cook, sir."

He didn't hear a word I said. When he volunteered one of his men, he was volunteered, no argument.

"An important potentatess has escaped the city, and I want you and a dozen other Marines and this Chinee volunteer to chase her down and bring her back." He waved his hand, and a Chinese man stepped through the ranks of marines. He wore black pajama bottoms, a Western-style shirt, and a green silk sash around his waist. "This Chinee knows the road, and will be your scout."

"A potentatess, sir?" I ventured.

He gripped the Chinese fellow by the shoulder and said to me, "This one speaks English, though it sounds like he's got a mouthful of ballbearings. He's a dragoman, a professional interpreter, educated in a cornfield seminary. He'll fill you in. You ride like hell and bring back that little lady, you hear, corporal?"

So I was brought a horse—a foul-tempered killer named Spats—and we lit out cross-country in pursuit of the potentatess, Spats trying to buck me off at every opportunity. I clung to its neck like a rube, and the Chinee held onto his horse just like me. I don't think he'd ever been on a horse before.

We followed the potentatess north. We learned she was traveling in a horse-drawn cart, trying to pass as a peasant. China was in chaos. Famine had caused some of the unrest, and the Boxers' inflammatory posters and propaganda leaflets and public square exhortations had added to the lawlessness. We passed hundreds of bodies, ruptured in the heat and covered with maggots. Shops had been plundered by Chinese troops that had deserted in front of the international force. The countryside had been laid to waste, fires everywhere, black smoke rising in all directions resembling columns holding up the sky. Even the opium dens—hundreds of them—had been burned, and the addicts lay alongside the roads, their hands over their eyes to block the sun, or they were slumped against buildings, their heads nodding and bumping against their knees. We evaded mobs of Boxers and remnants of the royal army. We stopped at a well for water and found it filled with human heads. We passed the ruins of an orphanage, the foundation still smoking. Children walked about, dazed, too weary and hungry to weep. Fifteen miles north of Peking we passed the Summer Palace, and twenty miles later came to the ruined temple at Kuanhsi.

There we found her. Because she had been traveling incognito, she had no bodyguards, only a few in her retinue, who stared at the ground and refused to look at us, and probably thought we were going to shoot them on the spot. I don't think Colonel Frawley knew who we were after when he sent us on our mission. He'd just been told to find this important personage.

The lady didn't look any too important. She stared at me defiantly. She looked about forty, but I'd find out later she was sixty-three. A tiny woman dressed in cotton clothes with her hair in a knot on top of her head. That morning she had cut her long fingernails to disguise herself. The dragoman fell off his horse and prostrated himself, his nose in the dirt, kowtowing.

Once in a while my instincts pay off. They did then. I dismounted Spats and lay on the ground in front of her cart right next to the dragoman. The mounted marines behind me snickered and made catcalls. But I lay still.

"*Pu yung hsing li,*" she said. You need not stay there.

The dragoman rose and so did I.

I said to the dragoman, "Tell her that I have been sent to escort her back to the Forbidden City."

She had slanty eyes. Of course, they all had slanty eyes. But them black eyes narrowed even more as she stared at me.

She said something to the dragoman, who interpreted. "She says she cannot go back. The first-class devils will murder her."

She had a low, velvety voice, and I was to learn that much of her allure as a young concubine had come from her sultry voice. First-class devils was the Chinese name for Westerners. Second-class devils were Chinese converts to Christianity. Third-class devils were any Chinese who collaborated with first-class devils.

My instincts came to the fore again, and I said the right thing. "Tell her that I will guarantee her safety."

The dragoman translated. One of her retinue said something but she waved him to silence. She continued to stare at me. Forty yards behind me, three huts were furiously burning. She spoke again. I was oddly attracted to that contralto voice.

The dragoman said, "She asks if you will personally see that she is unharmed."

"Yes," I answered without hesitation. I was assuming authority a corporal didn't have.

"Then she will go back with us," the dragoman interpreted.

Just then I cemented my worth to her. A scream came from behind me, a mad howl of anger, and a Chinee dashed between burning buildings toward her cart. Red ribbons tied to his wrists and ankles trailed behind him, and his hair was tied up in a red ribbon. He wore a white robe with a red girdle around his waist. His legs churned as he closed on us. In his hand was a dagger with a curved blade in the Manchu style, and it was raised over his head. He bulled across the road, and almost got to the old lady's cart.

He screeched, "*Sha, sha, sha.*" Kill, kill, kill.

He probably was aiming for me, an Anglo, but the potentatess was between him and me, and it sure looked like his blade was headed her way. I took two steps and hit him so hard upside the jaw that it lifted him off the ground. He landed in a heap near her cart's wheel, his lower jaw full of new angles.

The old lady barked something to one of her retinue, who guided the horse around so that it was pointed back toward Peking. She didn't say anything more, just dipped her chin at me. I remounted, and the dragoman and I took positions at a respectful distance behind her cart. I looked back to see one of the retinue use a sword to separate the assassin's head from his shoulders. The marines led the way, followed by the cart and the lady's followers. I trailed the cart in a cloud of gritty yellow dust kicked up by the horses.

Her name was Tz'u-hsi, pronounced tsoo-shee. As a young woman, she was known as Orchid. Because of her beauty and her entrancing voice she had been selected among hundreds of eligible girls as a concubine for Emperor Hsing-feng. She bore his only son. When the boy was five years old he became emperor of China, and his mother Tz'u-hsi ruled as regent. When her son died—some said she had poisoned him because he had become too independent—she put her infant nephew on the throne, and continued ruling as dowager empress. Through intrigue and ruthlessness, she had run China for almost forty years, and had become known as Old Buddha. She was also known as the only man in China.

Even though she had supported the Boxers in their efforts to toss out the first-class devils, the Westerners wanted her on the throne for the stability she would provide while they sliced up China. That's why I'd been ordered to fetch her back to Peking.

On the way back I stopped the column long enough to procure my prayer rug from my pack, roll it out on the ground, and ask the dragoman which way was Mecca so I would be pointed the right way. He shook his head. I don't think that heathen had ever heard of Mecca. So I had to guess, and I got down on my knees. This normally would've resulted in hoots from the marines, loitering around on their horses, but they'd seen how I'd dressed out that dagger-wielding assassin and they remained silent.

After my prayer, I climbed aboard Spats, who tried to bite my hand off, as usual. With her finger, the empress beckoned me, then slapped the side of her cart. She wanted me to ride alongside. She'd heard of Muslims, turns out. At least they weren't Christians. And from that moment for the next two years, I was seldom more than a loud holler from the Old Buddha.

A short time later our column was intercepted by a Marine Corps messenger who told me I was to take the empress to the Summer Palace rather than the Forbidden City. She was vastly relieved. She had never favored the Forbidden City, and loved the Summer Palace more than she had ever loved any human being.

I viewed my job as done when I delivered her to the Summer Palace's Rose Gate, and I was about to ride away when the empress motioned me again. She pointed at me, then gestured at the gate.

Well, I weren't really a marine, so Colonel Frawley weren't really my superior. And I was tired of marines, who are always at the end of their leashes, like Teddy's dog Bottsie.

"You marines return to Peking," I ordered.

I clucked at Spats and followed Old Buddha and her retinue through the gate. The marines yelled after me, but I weren't interested in whatever they had to say. I was the first Westerner to enter the Summer Palace.

That term was a misnomer. The Summer Palace was in fact many buildings placed in a vast garden, hundreds of acres, set out in a dazzling Confucian geometry. We passed marble palaces and temples, all surrounded by seas of blooms. Three hundred gardeners—all eunuchs—rotated the plants so all windows from all buildings always looked upon long stretches of flowers. The gardens contained more than a hundred varieties of chrysanthemums, with names such as Purple Phoenix Rejoicing at the Sun, Dragon's Whiskers, and Frost's Descent. I rode by an artificial lake called Kun Ning that contained huge spotted goldfish swimming below expanses of floating lotus, the sacred water lily. Swans idly drifted among the lotus islands. Powered by hidden oarsmen, a dragon forty feet long and fifteen feet high and entirely coated in gold moved around the lake in a wide circle, just for the empress' amusement. An island in the middle of Kun Ning contained a dozen tigers. At least, they looked like tigers, except they were pure white with only a suggestion of gray stripes. They paced listlessly in the heat. On a second island were blue-rumped orangutans, maybe fifty of them, climbing in trees.

We neared a copse of maples that appeared to have been caught in an ice storm, all glittering, sending out shafts of refracted light in all the colors of the rainbow. As I drew near I saw that these trees had thousands of pea-size diamonds hanging by silk cords from their branches. The leaves and branches and trunks and the ground below shimmered in light thrown by the diamonds. I had to squint to look at the trees. Old Buddha nodded at my reaction to her display, for that's all it was, something interesting for her to look at occasionally.

Next were three willows that bowed under the weight of thousands of rubies attached to their boughs. When the soft wind stirred the rubied boughs, the willows cast forth a galaxy of red flashes. Twenty jewelers were assigned to the Summer Palace to keep the willows and maples in repair.

Down one of the broad, pebbled avenues came ten eunuchs carrying a palanquin on their shoulders. Someone had recognized Old Buddha in her horsecart and had sent transportation befitting an empress. The gardeners and jewelers and guards all kowtowed in her presence. With surprising agility, she climbed out of the cart and entered the sedan chair. She pushed the curtain open, I think so that she could continue to watch me. The eunuchs holding the sedan chair did not march in time, but rather walked at ease, so that her ride was smoother.

We circled the lake, headed roughly south, away from the larger palaces. We passed rivulets and pools and small bridges, then a hundred life-size marble statues of Manchu bannermen marching to war, shiny white under the sun. The silk banners were of all colors, wafting in the wind.

Farther along the path, set between two low hills was a village, perhaps fifty structures, everything from pavilions to temples to residences, all in quarter scale, the roofs being about five feet off the ground. Several miniature carts were tied to goats. I counted ten large dolls, but later heard there were about a hundred, all exquisitely detailed, and all at work or play or prayer. On the north side of this doll town was an elevated grandstand from which the empress would direct the doll town's activities, eunuchs moving the dolls about as she ordered, much like moving chess pieces around a board.

A few moments later I reined in Spats so I could stare down at a sundial built into the ground. This instrument was forty feet across, and its surface was a mosaic of jade tiles in a dragon design, the dragon breathing fire. The jade was all shades of green, from lima bean to forest. The hour markers were twenty-pound lumps of silver called sycee. The dragon's jade scales reflected sparks of light like the sea at sunset.

We finally arrived at a pavilion, modest by Summer Palace standards, on a promontory at the south edge of the park. The post-and-lintel structure was made of a red wood I'd never seen before called teak, and the walls were rubbed to a new shine every day. Overhanging eaves were supported by a series of cantilevered brackets, each decorated with tile patterns. Of the dowager empress' eight palaces on the grounds, this was her favorite because it overlooked the road to Peking. She spent hours each day watching oxen and horses and pedestrians on the road. It appealed to me that this woman, with all her marble soldiers and her doll village and her jeweled forests, relaxed most often by doing something that any Chinese peasant could do, watch traffic pass on a road.

The Old Buddha called this home her Road and Rose House. Rose trellises surrounded the structure, and the air was heavy with the scent of the roses. The house had perhaps twenty rooms. She spoke briefly to a eunuch, who then showed me to a room on the eastern end of the house.

I sat in that room on an embroidered stool so short that my chin was on my knees, wondering whether I was a guest or a prisoner, most of that afternoon. The room had two doors that were made of carved rosewood.

On a table were a porcelain and jade jewel tree and a box of pale blue and yellow handkerchiefs. A black lacquer dresser with inlaid gold and silver stood next to a gilt bronze statuette of Shakyamuni Buddha.

Then about the time my belly started to growl, the door opened and another eunuch entered. He bowed low to me, and then introduced himself in English. "My name is Li Su Shi but I am called by my nickname Pi Siao Li, which means Cobbler's Wax Li. I am your factotum."

"I'm delighted, I'm sure," I replied. "What's a factotum?"

"I have been told by the Motherly and Auspicious Ruler of the Celestial Empire that my duty and pleasure will be to serve you."

"Serve me dinner?"

"Serve you in any way you request."

"Let's start with dinner."

Cobbler's Wax smiled as he spoke, not a happy grin, but a smile resembling a half-concealed knife. I would seldom see him without that same smile. The eunuch was wearing red silk pantaloons and a vest of green silk. His skin was darker than I'd seen in China, the color of a peach pit. His eyes were far back in his head, under boxer's brows. His lips were narrow, and his upper one in particular was so narrow it almost weren't there. He was as thin as a whipping post. His black hair was cropped in a Western style, with a part to one side. He wore a ruby ring on his left hand. He smelled of spices.

"May I ask what you desire for dinner?"

I scratched my head. "Whatever the empress is having."

He nodded. "One small thing before dinner." When he opened the door and beckoned down the hall, a eunuch delivered a dog to him. Cobbler's Wax brought the animal into the room, the largest dog I'd ever seen, resembling a mastiff, but bigger, with dewlaps that swung when he walked and a tail as thick as my arm. Its coat was tan and its legs were black. Its head was bigger than mine. The dog eyed me suspiciously.

"The palace is a place of intrigue. This dog will growl if anybody approaches the room except me. Its name is Wi. Now for dinner." He backed out of the room, and a few moments later eunuchs carrying platters began entering the room.

My dinner consisted of 110 courses served over three hours. The empress never ate a meal with less than 100 courses, I learned, and I ate what she ate that evening. Walnuts served eight different ways, sweetmeats, lotus flower seeds cooked with sugar, saffron this and saffron that, spicy watermelon seeds, more kinds of fruit than I knew existed, crunchy black balls that I hoped weren't beetles, hot noodles, cold noodles, greasy noodles, crackly noodles, fish eyeballs in a puree of something green, six different kinds of eggs, a dozen meats (I didn't even want to guess which kinds), plate after plate of unrecognizable vegetables, berries spun in sugar, and I could go on. I drank from a goblet carved from white jade, and my plate was solid gold. The eunuch showed me how to manipulate them two little sticks. I fed my new dog Wi whatever didn't catch my fancy, and he seemed appreciative.

During dinner I asked the eunuch, "How'd you get the nickname Cobbler's Wax?"

"My father was a poor cobbler, and could never provide enough for our family. I don't think I had enough to eat once in my childhood. I was determined to improve my lot, and the only way I could think of was to join the royal court. And to do that you must be a *castrato.*"

I asked around a mouthful of melon, "What sort of a doctor would perform a castration?"

"A family that cannot afford food cannot afford a doctor. I did it myself, using one of my father's knives, and then I plugged the wound with cobbler's wax."

"Must've hurt." I can be profound, can't I?

"So I am now called Cobbler's Wax." He directed several eunuchs to clear away the last of my plates. "You have an audience with the Old Buddha tomorrow at sunrise. You should be prepared."

"Sunrise? One of the main reasons I rode through your Summer Palace gate was to get away from them marines, who do everything at sunrise."

"All imperial audiences are held at sunrise," Cobbler's Wax explained with his usual half smile. "You must bathe tonight. Every knob and every orifice must be scrubbed."

"I washed up yesterday." When he frowned, I added, "A Scotch lick, anyway." That's what we Irish call applying a few drops of water to your face.

"Old Buddha complained of your scent."

"That was my horse."

Cobbler's Wax shook his head. "That was you."

He opened a side door to reveal a bathing room with a wood tub of steaming water. Standing there were two women, one with a brush and the other with a pot of soap. Both of them were squat and muscular, and wore white headdresses much like a nurse's cap, and aprons. On the floor were buckets of warm water for rinsing.

Cobbler's Wax bid me goodnight, and I removed my marine uniform as discreetly as I could, my back turned to them two ladies. The dog watched me carefully. I slid into the tub sideways, trying to hide as much of myself as possible, not that those ladies appeared curious. Her nose curled up, one of them removed my clothes with a tool resembling a pitchfork. I will spare you the details of the next hour, but them two muscular ladies worked me over, and it was more a beating than a bath.

I emerged cleaner than a new penny, all my muscles sore, but entirely refreshed. I lay on the down mattress, alternatively thinking of Amy Balfour, Victoria Littlewood, and the Women Who Live Alone, and after a while had myself fairly worked up. The dog sat near the door, watching me.

The sun was still below the horizon when I was wakened by the sound of a gong. I found new clothes next to the bed. After a moment I figured out how to get into the long robe decorated with a dragon, and which had horse-hoof cuffs. Over the robe went a court-robe collar. The cap had a short feather in it. The shoes were made of pliable leather and silk, and felt like slippers.

Cobbler's Wax appeared at the door to escort me to the throne room. We passed through a hallway that had about fifty Western clocks, all of them ticking, sounding like a field of crickets. All the dowager empress' residences had throne rooms. This one, on the far side of the house from my room, contained a sandalwood and peachwood throne imbedded with intricate jade patterns. Behind the throne was a brocaded yellow silk curtain. Yellow was the royal color, reserved throughout China for the imperial household. The room had many sliding carved wood doors, more space taken up by doors than by walls.

Cobbler's Wax directed me to the back of the room, where he held apart the curtain. There was Old Buddha, sitting on a folding chair. She smiled up at me.

The eunuch instantly kowtowed, and I was on my way down, too, but she waved me aright. She motioned me to a second chair. Cobbler's Wax stood at my shoulder.

Around the empress's neck and gathered on her lap was the necklace she always wore for royal audiences, containing three hundred knuckle-size pearls. She wore matching long earrings. Her yellow robe was heavily brocaded, and cinched with a diamond-and-emerald-encrusted belt. She wore ten ruby-and-diamond-studded nail protectors, even though she had cut off her nails the day before. On her head was a Manchu headdress, held in place by jeweled pins. On her feet were satin booties with pearl tassels and high platform heels.

Despite all the jewels, the brightest thing about her was her smile. She seemed delighted to see me. She patted my wrist, then noticed the hair there, and plucked at it to see if it was genuine or some sort of Western ornament. From that moment I was known as Hairy One.

A fuss of footsteps and throat clearing and whispered words came from the throne room. Old Buddha carefully pulled back an edge of a curtain. Three Western diplomats in morning coats stood before the throne, their top hats under their arms. A Japanese admiral—a mass of shiny buttons and epaulets and scabbards and medals—stood rigidly at attention. A Russian general in dress greens was next to him. And Colonel Frawley stood there, too, underdressed in a campaign uniform. He wrung his hat in his two hands.

After a moment this group was joined by Prince Tuan, one of Old Buddha's nephews, who spoke English. Like the others, Prince Tuan faced the throne as if the dowager empress were sitting there. These foreigners had been granted this audience in the Summer Palace under threat of force. But the empress never allowed a foreigner—except, now, Woodrow C. Lowe—to look upon her. An empty throne at the Forbidden City was the way she always received foreigners.

The tallest of the diplomats spoke first, and in French. He wore a delicately clipped goatee, and his fingernails were shiny. Garnet studs were in his shirtsleeve. He had the look of one who gave unstinting dedication to his morning toilet. The Frenchman spoke at length, and Prince Tuan interpreted. As he talked, the French diplomat indignantly pounded the air with his fist. He was giving an ultimatum, I was sure.

Old Buddha motioned me closer. She whispered something into my ear as if I could understand her. Cobbler's Wax bent close and translated, finishing an instant behind her.

He said, "The Auspicious Mother desires to know about the French."

I thought for a moment. "Their women put perfume on their private parts."

That, indeed, was all I knew about the French. My old cavalry team-ster, Bo Latts, had told me that. The eunuch translated briskly.

She nodded, weighing my words.

Next to speak was a German in a morning coat. He was a small, nippy man who barked his words.

Again Old Buddha asked me a question, and Cobbler's Wax trans-lated. "The Auspicious Mother wishes to know about the Germans."

I scratched my nose. I'd met a few Pennsylvania Germans in the cavalry. "They eat cabbage but only after it has rotted in a barrel for a month."

When she dipped her chin, Cobbler's Wax nodded also, as if her nods needed translating.

Then the English diplomat spoke to the empty throne, and the prince translated. This one I could understand, and he talked of guarantees of safety for the foreign legation and indemnity for the damage done by the Boxers.

Old Buddha asked me, "What about the English?"

I touched the scar on my cheek. "An English woman cut me here with a piece of glass just for fun."

The Japanese admiral and the Russian general and an Italian diplomat also spoke to the curtain, and I offered similarly succinct observations about them people.

Then Colonel Frawley stepped forward. "Your highness, one of my men, Corp. Woodrow Lowe, was last seen riding into the grounds of the Summer Palace. I am not clear as to whether he was kidnapped or went voluntarily but I demand the corporal's return."

Old Buddha whispered to me, and Cobbler's Wax translated, "Do you want to go back?"

"It depends on what I'm getting for dinner."

Her face screwed up in a laugh and she patted my forearm. Then she spoke through the curtain for the first time. Her voice was sweet but throaty, and compelling. It filled the throne room.

On the other side of the curtain, Prince Tuan translated her words, "Corporal Lowe has been made Beneficent Counselor to the Auspicious Mother. He will return when his services are no longer required by the imperial court."

Colonel Frawley gaped at the curtain. "Are we talking about the same person? This fellow is a corporal, a lifer in the army, and is something of a moron."

Prince Tuan translated, and perhaps I should've taken offense but Old Buddha beat me to it. Her voice rose, but only a little. An imperial command, it sounded like. Neither Prince Tuan nor Cobbler's Wax translated.

A sliding door behind the diplomats opened quickly, and in stepped the largest human being I've ever seen, perhaps eight inches taller than myself and weighing twice what I weighed. Much of his heft was in his belly, which entered the room well ahead of him, but he also carried a lot of meat on his arms and chest and legs. He was shaved bald, except for a long braid of black hair as thick as my wrist down his back, and on his pate was a tattooed Men Shen, a god who warded away evil spirits. His tiny eyes were lost in the flesh of his face. His nose was flat and broad, looking as if it had been smashed into its shape. His ears were flat buttons, so small they looked useless. Muscle and fat bulged at the back of his neck. His mouth was open, and his front teeth threw off sparks as if they were made of tiny mirrors. He wore silk pantaloons and a vest open to reveal his amber chest and enormous gut. His feet were bare. His fists were the size of hams, and in one of them he had a leather black-jack.

He slipped soundlessly across the floor, clipped Colonel Frawley's head with the sap, and retreated as quickly as he'd come. I don't think any of the diplomats or military men saw him. They just saw Colonel Frawley collapse to his knees and grab his head. He was about to sag onto the floor when the Japanese admiral and Russian general grabbed him by the arms and forced him to stand. After a moment Frawley could lower his hands. When he stopped teetering, the general and admiral released his arms.

Old Buddha said, and Prince Tuan translated, "A first-class devil should not call a trusted imperial advisor a moron."

"I misspoke, your highness," the colonel said through clenched teeth. "But Corporal Lowe's advice can hardly be said to be worth much . . ."

Faster than I can relate it, Old Buddha gave another sharp command. Colonel Frawley spun toward the screen behind him, but this time the giant came from yet another sliding screen, opening it silently, gliding across the floor, his long queue swinging The giant was smiling, and I saw that his teeth were made of diamonds imbedded in a porcelain bridge. He sparkled when he smiled but I got the impression he didn't smile a lot, only when doing his job, like right then. He brought the sap down across the colonel's temple from behind.

Not a terrible blow. Colonel Frawley's knees buckled, but this time he caught himself, and with the general and admiral's assistance managed to stay aright. By the time he could focus his eyes, the giant was again gone. I don't think the colonel ever saw him.

Prince Tuan translated the empress' words. "You were saying about the imperial advisor?"

"I misspoke again, your highness." Colonel Frawley's voice wavered with pain. "Your new Beneficent Counselor is indeed a wise man."

I was getting smarter all the time.

The Frenchman regained the floor, spouting off again for a few minutes, and then with curt bows, the diplomats and military men walked out of the throne room, Colonel Frawley rubbing his head. Prince Tuan left with them, closing the door.

I was about to rise from my chair, thinking my audience at an end along with them other Westerners, but a screen opened and a young woman entered the throne room. She kowtowed, then stood in front of the throne, her head bowed in submission and her hands clasped in front of her. She chewed her lip nervously, and her eyes flickered between the throne and the yellow curtain.

She was a member of the imperial household rather than a foreigner so Cobbler's Wax pulled back the yellow curtain to reveal Old Buddha to her, but the young woman continued to stare at the floor.

Old Buddha said to me, "This is the Jade Concubine. She belongs to my senior nephew. She was impertinent to me yesterday. She is to be punished."

The Jade Concubine's eyes were perfect ovals. Her nose was a short, straight line. Her mouth was pouty and painted red. The skin of her hands and face seemed to be glowing gold. Her body was hidden entirely behind silk robes and sashes, yet it seemed all that cloth had been arranged to suggest the voluptuousness beneath. Her eyes lifted as far as the foot of the empty throne. She was at once meek and mysterious.

"Punished?" I asked. "What did she do?"

After Cobbler's Wax translated my question, the empress replied, "She suggested that I remain at the Summer Palace rather than try to escape the foreign devils. She therefore contradicted the imperial will."

"What is to be her punishment?"

"She will be wrapped in a rug and thrown down a well where she will drown, but slowly."

I nodded. "Sounds fair."

She turned to call the giant to take her away, but I added, "But she might prove useful to your majesty if she lives."

The dowager empress looked at me closely, as if peering through a misted window. I was being tested.

I went on, "If you could look at the Jade Concubine through the eyes of a man, you would see that she has quite an effect."

"She is beautiful, you are telling me?"

"A person of your august position is often the object of palace conspiracies. Many men have tried and will continue to try to take the throne from you."

She nodded vigorously. "Countless times. Even my son conspired against me, and so he mounted the dragon."

Mounting the dragon means to die.

"Your highness, it is one of the world's great truths," I advised, "that beautiful women make men stupid."

Cobbler's Wax translated.

Old Buddha leaned closer. "Has that happened to you?"

"A few times," I blurted with some feeling.

She chewed on that a moment.

I continued, "If she remains at the palace, she will unwittingly work to your advantage, dazzling and befuddling your enemies."

That decided it. The empress made some remark through the curtain. The Jade Concubine knew better than to jump for joy and click her heels at the pardon, but she did draw in a huge breath, and she finally looked up at the curtain. She said something I took to be a thank you, then turned and left the throne room.

Old Buddha said to me, "You still smell. You are to take another bath, and this time I will have four women scrub you."

I protested, "I just barely survived the two-woman bath, your highness."

"And then you will join me this evening for dinner, at which time you will tell me one wise thing." She rose from her chair. "And every day you will tell me one wise thing, and you may stay here under my protection until you run out of wise things."

"But what if I can't come up with a new wise thing?"

She smiled thinly, swept her dress behind her, and left the anteroom through a carved peachwood door. The bald giant—who I took for a bodyguard—was waiting for her. He glanced at me through the door. He looked like he'd like to get his big hands around my throat.

Cobbler's Wax led me back to my room. I endured another bath, but I was too worried to notice my pummeling. I had made one wise comment in my entire life, and it had been that very day, to the Old Buddha about the Jade Concubine. How in the world would I come up with another wise saying by dinner time?

SEVENTEEN

Pearls and a Ponytail

AN ASSASSIN TRIED for me four times. Cobbler's Wax was prescient when he warned of palace conspiracies and jealousies. Over two thousand people—eunuchs (who were the cooks, gardeners, seamstresses, stablemen and so forth), guards, courtesans, concubines, and the dowager empress' family—had a precisely prescribed spot in the palace's pecking order, and when I arrived, enjoying the dowager empress' confidence like I did, virtually every one of them two thousand folks was bumped down a notch. Some of them didn't take to it kindly. One in particular.

The first attempt occurred during my morning constitutional. After each sunrise audience in the throne room, I had taken to going on a morning stroll, usually around the southeast corner of the grounds, always accompanied by Cobbler's Wax. Most of our route was among cherry and plum tree groves but we also passed the milliner's shop, stables, and the pension for the eunuchs who were in the snares of opium, so many addicted eunuchs that a second pension was under construction. One day as we passed this new construction, a wall fell on me. The whole of it: brick, plaster, and window frames. I leaped out of the way, and suffered only a bruise on an arm from a brick. I ran into the building, intent on bawling out some careless worker. But no one was inside, at least, no one I found. The bricks entirely missed Cobbler's Wax. So at first I thought this an accident, maybe due to the wind, and didn't recognize it for what it was—a try on my life—until the pattern became clear.

I was at the empress' side during all audiences with Westerners, who since the Boxer Uprising frequently visited the Summer Palace to gain more and more concessions from her. She always sat behind the yellow curtain with me beside her. Cobbler's Wax rendered the empress' whispered questions to me into English. Standing near the throne on the other side of the curtain, Prince Tuan translated back and forth. The empress did not make a single decision regarding the foreign devils without consulting me.

She was sorely vexed by the United States' insistence that China admit missionaries, but she had some leeway on which ones, and so looked to me. When approached by a group of Roman Catholics for permission to open a church in Peking, Old Buddha asked me what I knew about Catholicism.

I replied, "The only thing I remember about my Catholic education is Sister Margaret's little poem she'd recite over and over again at the lavatory door, 'Shake it twice to clear the bore. Shake it thrice and you've sinned some more.'"

So Old Buddha didn't see any threat from the Catholics, and granted them admission. And she let in the Episcopalians because I told her that they were really Roman Catholics though they pretended otherwise. But I advised that the Presbyterians be turned down because they like to argue things to death—every one of them having the pinched soul of a lawyer—and the empress agreed the Middle Kingdom needed no more of that. And she turned down the Methodists when I told her they were founded by the gunfighter John Wesley Hardin. We let in the Baptists just to see what kind of hell they'd raise, for our own amusement.

The second attempt on my life was made about a week after the first. I was eating dinner, and was on course twenty-eight, which was rice served with river leeks. But as I brought the first bite to my mouth, I smelled almonds, which I had learned to detest in the Sudan. So I fed the entire plate to my guard dog Wi, who gobbled it down in two swallows and promptly dropped dead. I learned later that cyanide smells like almonds.

On occasion I would invite Prince Tuan and Cobbler's Wax to join me for dinner. We'd eat everything from birds' nests to squid tentacles. One time I said, "Before I got to the imperial court, I weren't always viewed as so smart."

Prince Tuan and Cobbler's Wax glanced at each other, and Prince Tuan tried without success to dampen a grin.

I ventured, "Why is it, do you suppose, that Old Buddha looks to me for advice? I'm a foreign devil, last time I looked at my eyes."

"If I may be forgiven, Hairy One," Prince Tuan said, "but it has nothing to do with how wise you are."

"No?"

He shook his head. "You are Old Buddha's talisman, her protective charm."

"Like a rabbit's foot?"

"You saved her life. She follows your advice not because it is intelligent but because you are lucky."

"I've never thought of myself as lucky." Eight years shoveling dervish dung should testify to that.

Another smile from Prince Tuan. "But you are, exceedingly. That cyanide was meant for you, yet your dog died instead."

"And the pension's wall just missed you," Cobbler's Wax added. "Truly lucky, I'd say."

I believed in luck like I believed in the new doowillie that had become the rage in Boston just before I left, the Ouija Talking Board, but I weren't about to tell them that.

The third attempt on my life was made the night of that conversation. I had taken a shine to bathing. Them women would scrub me up and down, inside and out, then rinse me with fresh water from nearby buckets. That night I decided to linger in the tub for a change, so I waved away them two ladies, and I sat in the hot water an hour, watching the steam rise, dipping my mouth into the water to blow bubbles, and anything else I could think of, just passing the time luxuriating in that water. Then I clapped my hands, and the old women entered again for my rinse and toweling.

That night, though, when one of the ladies lifted a bucket of rinse water, the bucket suddenly fell apart. The bottom stayed on the floor and the staves rattled all apart, and only the wood handle came up in the old lady's hand. She screeched and jumped aside, swatting at her legs. The bucket's contents splashed all over the floor.

I hollered for Cobbler's Wax, and he procured Prince Tuan, and between the two of them they figured out that acid had been in the bucket instead of rinse water. The would-be assassin's plan had been for the unwitting old lady to rinse me in acid. But because I had lingered in the tub, the acid had eaten away the bucket before she could do the deed. The old lady had danced mostly out of the way, and suffered only a few pea-size burns on her feet.

Prince Tuan said that night, "You see? You are lucky."

One day not long after that, I said to Cobbler's Wax, "Old Buddha told you to serve me. Is my memory correct on that?"

"It is, Hairy One."

"Well, I'm tired of all my food being chopped up into little pieces. My teeth need something to do. Can you get me a steak?"

"Of course." He bowed low. "If you will only tell me what a steak is."

I explained, and for dinner that night, course number sixteen was a prime rib steak that weighed two pounds.

The next day I said, "Now, Wax, I noticed that the giant who sapped Colonel Frawley . . ."

The eunuch suddenly held up his hand and whispered fiercely, "Do not talk about Zhou. It is too dangerous. These walls have ears."

I put my mouth almost on his ear. "Are them diamonds in his teeth?"

Cobbler's Wax had begun to tremble. He whispered, "A diamond for every person Zhou has killed, so it is said. Old Buddha gives them to him."

"I've never seen a diamond up close." A small fib. I'd seen Diamond Jim's diamonds, and Victoria's that night in the Cairo hotel room. "Can you get me one?"

The topic having left the giant, Cobbler's Wax settled down some. "Old Buddha said I am to serve." He smiled in that superior way he had. "Just one?"

I thought I'd test him. "Yes. One bucket of diamonds."

He didn't hesitate a fraction. "Of course."

He backed out of the room—I never figured out why he never turned around and walked out like a normal person—and returned in less than an hour.

He held out a wood bucket that shimmered with diamonds piled high. I dug into them and brought out a handful, then let them cascade back into the bucket. They reflected iridescent blues and frost whites, and none was smaller than a garbanzo bean.

"Imagine the things I could buy with these," I breathed.

"You don't need to buy anything. Old Buddha has made clear that everything you want is yours."

I thought about that a moment. "Then why would I want these diamonds?"

"I am clueless."

I returned the gems to him. "Take them back. I don't need them."

He was halfway out of the room, bucket in hand, when I said, "You are a eunuch, Cobbler's Wax."

"I am well aware of that, Hairy One."

"You have lost certain desires felt by those of us who have all our parts."

"A woman, is that what you desire?"

"It's been a long time, if I may be frank."

"Do you have a type of woman in mind?" he asked.

"A type? There's more than one type?"

"Of course."

"Well, Cobbler's Wax, you may have thought I have a lot of experience in these matters, but in truth . . ."

"There are Han women, Mongol women, Huis women, Yis women, Miaos women, Manchus and Uigur, and Pu-is."

I nodded.

"They are all delicately different, I am told. Each will delight you in subtly different ways."

Why not test him again? "I'll have one of each."

I give Cobbler's Wax credit. He didn't even blink an eye. "Of course," he said. "It will take me two hours. Do you think you can wait that long?" Perhaps there should have been a note of disapproval in his voice, but I heard none.

"I'll try."

I polished off 114 courses in them two hours. And right on time, Cobbler's Wax returned. He led eight women into my room, and they didn't have a pound of clothing on between them.

The eunuch lined them up against a wall. A few cast their eyes on the floor, others stared at me steadily. I took Cobbler's Wax at his word that one was a Manchu, one a Han, and so forth, but I couldn't tell one from another. Most of them wore their hair in loose knots at the back of their heads, but two had tresses down to their shoulders. They were wearing lilac and honey and pink slips of silk so tiny that a French madam would have blushed. Them girls were bountiful, every one of them. A wall of girls, shimmering in front of me, waiting for me. Eight bare belly buttons, all in a row.

I asked, "Where's their clothes, Wax?"

"Clothes?"

"It's drafty in here."

"These nubile young maidens are all highly skilled. All you need do is snap your fingers, and they will take you to the seventh level of heaven."

"I've been there once." I was thinking of my night with Victoria Littlewood. "It's a lot more work than you'd think, you being without testicles and all."

"What then should I do with these girls?" he asked, his expression pained.

I scratched my chin. Once I knew I could have all them girls, the lead went out of my pencil. "Do I still own them diamonds?"

"Of course."

"Give them each a handful, then take them back wherever they came from, with my thanks."

He was still incredulous. "You don't wish to beckon these young women to do your every bidding?"

"Wax, I hardly know what to do with one woman, let alone eight of them. Take them away."

At the eunuch's signal, they softly padded out. I couldn't tell whether they were relieved or disappointed. But I was relieved, I knew that much.

TEDDY ROOSEVELT MUST have learned where I was, because I received a letter from him. It said only, DETERMINE SUMMER PALACE DEFENSES AND REPORT BACK. I tore up his letter and tossed it out a window.

Old Buddha smoked an opium pipe every afternoon, and she often bade me sit by her as she puffed away. She'd begin each of these visits by rapidly rubbing my arm, back and forth like she was shining me up. She was gathering up some of my luck so she could use it. But she'd mostly sit there, her eyes focused on the middle distance, and she'd chat away, with Cobbler's Wax or Prince Tuan translating.

I seldom spoke, other than to give her that day's wise saying, and I never failed to produce one. I quickly exhausted my recollection of Ben Franklin, such as, "Early to bed, early to rise . . ." So I went through my memory of the U.S. Cavalry manual: "Check the cinch before putting weight on the stirrup." Then sayings from my mother: "Don't eat like a Geordie." And my father: "Never let your peter do your thinking."

Each day she would accept my wisdom with a nod and another rub of my arm for good luck.

Old Buddha consulted with me on matters great and small. When called on to arbitrate a border dispute between the United States and Germany regarding their spheres of influence, I advised her to side with the Americans, and thereby expanded the United States' sphere in Manchuria by half a million square miles, for which I never got any thanks from my countrymen. Many times she asked me to pick out her earrings, which took some time because she had thirty boxes of jewelry. So, like I said, the great and the small, she followed my advice on it all. I ruled China by proxy.

Prince Tuan began coming by my room just to talk. I believe the reason was mostly to practice his English, which was already good. Cobbler's Wax always joined us. The prince was as handsome as the heathens come. He was tall, with long limbs and graceful movements. His features were delicate without being weak, with something of his mother in them. He smiled easily, but usually with cynicism. His nose was straight with tiny nostrils, and his chin was delicately carved. He coughed frequently, and told me he was suffering from consumption that he had acquired during the five years he was addicted to opium, when he would often wander the Forbidden City in winter, too addled to wear enough clothing. He had managed to overcome his addiction, but he said few could.

He was a dog with a bone on the subject of opium. The Celestial Kingdom's fondness for it had led to the admission of the foreign devils, who brought the opium to China in their great ships and traded the drug for silk and jade and spices. China's dependence on the opium had led to the treaties of Nanking and the Bogue, which ceded Hong Kong to the British and opened the treaty ports of Canton, Shanghai, and others. With the pleasures of the opium pipe so readily available, Prince Tuan's people had become timid and helpless. Even Old Buddha was under its spell and doing irrational things like taking advice from a foreign devil. No offense to me, the prince added. He fervently told me the only thing he wanted in this life was to strike a blow against the opium trade.

I picked up some of their language. That gagging and hawking and whistling that passes for talk in China actually becomes understandable after a fashion. I got pretty good speaking it, too. Clacking my teeth and hissing and yodeling. As I got better, Wax and Prince Tuan would often speak with me in their language, letting me learn.

I told them of Teddy Roosevelt and Diamond Jim Brady, of Lady Elizabeth Coleridge—she of the jagged piece of glass—and Lady Twig-Smathers, of Amy Balfour and her brother Dickie, and of Victoria Little-wood. I tried to be gallant by not mentioning the steamy details of my night with Victoria but Prince Tuan and Cobbler's Wax got it out of me, using their heathen wiles. Prince Tuan said that men are blessed with such a night only once or twice in their lives.

The prince was fascinated by my cavalry experience. He was unfamiliar with the term corporal, so I told him it was short for corporal general, the rank below major general, which was a mistake because he then assumed I knew something about military tactics. The only tactics I'd ever seen had been from the rear, sitting on a wagon loaded with beans and hardtack. I demurred to his questions about military operations, saying United States cavalry officers were sworn to secrecy. As a sign of respect, he and Cobbler's Wax started adding my rank to my name, calling me Corporal General Hairy One.

The fourth attempt on my life revealed who had done the first three. Cobbler's Wax and I were walking our daily route, strolling through the hydrangea gardens, passing a fifteen-foot-high limestone Seated Buddha, and then into the Three Well Plaza. The plaza was perhaps eighty yards across. Entrance to the cobblestone square was gained through a wood gateway, two slightly curved horizontal crosspieces on leaning pillars. At each corner of the plaza was a post-and-lintel building. Three water wells were positioned as if at the points of a triangle in the center of the plaza. The wells' crosspieces had ropes wrapped around them, and the ropes descended into the wells. I presumed there were buckets at the end of the ropes to haul up water. The crosspieces had handles on both ends.

Cobbler's Wax and I were halfway across the plaza, passing between two wells, when we noticed a palace guard step from behind a building. He was followed by another, and another, finally a stream of them, who took up positions between the two northerly buildings, blocking us. I glanced over my shoulder to see more guards flowing out from behind the buildings and forming up to prevent Cobbler's Wax and me from leaving the plaza in any direction. They lined up like fence posts, and each had a club in his hand resembling an ax handle. Wax and I were hemmed in.

"What's going on, Wax?"

"I am at a loss."

"This isn't one of your Chinee rituals, is it?"

My question was answered when the giant bodyguard, Zhou, stepped between two of the guards and entered the plaza. The sun gleamed off his head and his belly. As he walked toward us his ponytail swung from side to side, so long it almost brushed the cobblestones. In his hand was a maddhoge. He was smiling, a wicked leer, and his diamond-studded teeth reflected tiny brands of light.

A maddhoge? That's Irish for dagger. This one looked sharp enough to shave a sleeping mouse.

In the giant came, almost to the first water well. The dagger was held in front of his belly, blade up, which told me he knew how to use a dagger.

When I held up my hand like a traffic cop, the giant stopped four feet from me. I said, "Wax, find out what he wants."

"Is that not apparent, Corporal General Hairy One?" Wax's voice was unsteady.

"Maybe so. Ask him what I have done to deserve being knifed."

They spoke briefly, then Cobbler's Wax said, "Zhou believes you are now the number one bodyguard and that he has been demoted."

"Tell him I am Beneficent Counselor, not a bodyguard."

When the eunuch translated, Zhou jabbed a finger toward the scar on my cheek, and spoke in guttural barks.

"He does not believe you," Cobbler's Wax explained unnecessarily.

Zhou would have flattened the scales at three hundred and fifty pounds. He filled my vision, leaving little room for sky or cobblestones. His big belly extended straight out in front of him, filling the space between us. He wore red pantaloons and an embroidered vest. The day was hot, and a rivulet of sweat rolled down his chest. The dagger had an edge on both sides of the blade.

I put an expression of utter humility on my face. I spread my hands in a gesture of understanding and surrender. I started to bow. I said sweetly, "The curse of Cromwell be upon you."

And I swung at the giant with all my strength. I put years of boxing and years of physical hardship into that punch. It started at my feet and ended at my knuckles, every muscle in my body propelling my balled hand at Zhou's face.

My fist hit him right on his nose. The sound was of a gunshot. That strike would have killed a grizzly bear. But the giant merely staggered back, a puzzled look on his face, his flat nose a bit flatter.

I walked onto his shadow, and I wound up a left hook John L. would have been proud of. It sprang from my gut, and I unwound my arm and fist in a blur. My knuckles rocketed into his ear. The flat crack filled the plaza. That blow would have turned most men's brains to jelly, and would have laid them out on the cobblestones in quick order.

But all the giant did was totter backwards toward the water well, his knife still in position near his navel. He blinked a few times, was all.

Well, if he wouldn't go down, I weren't done with him. I plowed into him, feeling like I'd hit the side of a building, and managed to shove him back a few feet more. He grunted.

He jerked the knife up, the point plunging through air where my breast bone should have been. But I had stepped to his side. I grabbed his long ponytail, climbed onto the brick well wall, and yanked Zhou's tress like a sailor hauling in a sheet.

He howled, his back to the well wall. He dropped the dagger to grab over his head at his ponytail. I wrapped that long length of hair once around the well crosspiece, right around the rope coils, then tucked the end under several coils.

Then I stepped to the end of the crosspiece and slowly worked the handle. The supports groaned with the giant's weight as he was bent backward farther and farther over the well wall's rim. I cranked. He was lifted by his ponytail. His feet left the cobblestones, then scraped along the well wall, up and up.

I turned the handle. Zhou was pulled over the well rim, so that he was suspended over the black hole. He flailed his arms, catching only air. I cranked another quarter turn so that he had to go up on his toes to prevent swinging out over the void. He tried to grasp the crosspiece but his fingers were about three inches too short.

So he hung there, toes on the rim, queue wrapped tightly around the crosspiece, big enough, it looked like, to plug the well if he fell.

Cobbler's Wax's placatory half-smile was in place, and he was now perfectly calm. The guards at the edge of the plaza held their stations. There had been enough fear among the guards to follow Zhou's orders to line the plaza, but no loyalty, and so none of them rushed forward with their ax handles to save the giant's life.

"Hand me his dagger," I ordered.

Cobbler's Wax passed it up. The blade gleamed evilly in the sun.

Zhou's face was skyward, and blank. He would accept his fate calmly, it appeared.

But when I brought the dagger to the base of his ponytail, Zhou cried out in terror. He shook his head, more a rattle, his melon cheeks billowing back and forth. "No, no, no," he shrieked.

I later learned he knew one English word, and that was it.

"Not your ponytail?" I asked politely. "You must hold your hair in high regard."

Looking at me with beseeching eyes, he brought his finger across his throat. He was asking me to slit his throat rather than slice off his ponytail. He did not want to be disgraced in death. He didn't want to plunge to the bottom of the well without his long braid.

I scratched a mosquito bite on my arm, apparently deep in thought, weighing the possibilities. Then I put the dagger under my robe and cranked the handle backward. Zhou's braid unwound, and I pushed him back—no small task—so that he found his balance on the rim. The queue came free of the crosspiece. He jumped down to the cobblestones, so much weight the ground shook.

He instantly fell to his belly, kowtowing to me, his arms outstretched, his nose and jaw on the warm stone, a huge prostrate lump.

Cobbler's Wax said only, "He's yours."

And so he was, until the end of his life. Over the next five decades I weren't more than twenty feet away from Zhou but a handful of times, and most of them were at my wife's insistence on our honeymoon.

"YOUR MEN KNOW what to do?" I asked. "Do they know the signals?"

"They'll be there." Prince Tuan trained his binoculars on the ships. "You think one will do it?"

"One will be enough."

The prince lowered his binoculars. "You look ridiculous, by the way."

"You couldn't find a French or English soldier's cap?"

"German was the best we could do."

I had told Prince Tuan that I would have nothing to do with this operation if involvement by the United States could be traced. I required a disguise, I said. He had produced a German cavalry officer's pickle helmet. You've seen them, a black metal helmet with a curious point on top. The prince had also found black jackboots. The rest of the uniform was fashioned out of trousers and a pea coat. I vaguely resembled a German cavalry officer.

The giant, Zhou, stood next to me, as he had for weeks. He was always behind me, always alongside of me, he slept in the hallway outside my door at the Summer Palace. It was like having a bull follow me around. If I turned around suddenly, I bumped into him. He was wearing a Western coat, sorely strained at the seams, and pants that hung only to his calves. Under one arm he carried a black canister with what appeared to be a string dangling from it.

"Give the first signal," I ordered in a tone appropriate for a corporal general.

Cobbler's Wax was holding a railroad lamp with red glass on one side and green on another. The moonless night offered no light, and he fumbled a moment before he opened the lamp. He struck a sulfur match and put the flame to the wick. He held the lamp high and swung it back and forth exactly five times, showing the green side to sea. Then he spit on his fingers and doused the wick.

"You sure you've rowed a boat before, Wax?"

"Many times in the palace's lake."

"Let's go then."

Before I could set off, Prince Tuan grabbed both my biceps and squeezed them. For a moment I thought he was going to kiss me, but he just gave my arms a shoggle and let me go. His eyes were damp. I only nodded at him.

We had been standing between two godowns across a dirt road from a pier. Cobbler's Wax and Zhou followed me across the road and onto the pier, where several dozen lighters were moored. The vessels—each twenty to thirty feet long—usually ferried cargo from ocean-going vessels to the pier's ships because the harbor was too shallow for large vessels. The lighters had green-and-red eyeballs painted on the sides of their bows so the boats could see danger in the water below. Ten of the lighters had Prince Tuan's soldiers sitting in them, six men to a boat. They wore black pajamas, and were almost invisible in the night. Them ten boats also contained large wood casks with wood bungs in them. Also moored at the dock was a small fishing boat, with nets and buoys arranged on the deck. Three of the prince's soldiers manned the fishing boat, dressed in the blouses, short pants and straw hats of fishermen.

The pier creaked under our weight. I was carrying a bottle of gin. Not being able to see much beyond my hand, I stepped gingerly, hoping the pier weren't rotted through anywhere. When we came to the rowboat at the end of the wharf, I grabbed a mooring cleat to lower myself, careful to place my foot in the middle of the boat so it wouldn't rock. I took the seat in the bow. Cobbler's Wax manned the oars. The oarlocks were rope, rather than iron, so they wouldn't squeak. Zhou plopped into the stern, almost swamping the boat. Water splashed over the stern. He untied the line and cast off.

I pulled the cork on the gin bottle, poured some into my mouth, swished it around, then spit it on my coat. "I'll smell like I'm drunk, anyway." I sprinkled a little more onto my sleeves.

I held up the bottle. "And you're sure there's enough in here?"

Cobbler's Wax nodded. "Enough to fell an elephant. Don't swallow any of it."

The eunuch pulled at the oars. We headed out to sea, leaving the lighters behind. Because headlands to north and south acted as breakwaters, the bay had little swell. An indifferent breeze blew cat's paws across the water. Cobbler's Wax rowed steadily.

We slipped away from the shore and the lights of Shinha, a village south of Tientsin. The village was not one of the treaty ports but because Western opium vessels moored offshore and used the lighters to offload cargo, the Westerners claimed not to be actually using the port. So not only had the foreign devils imposed draconian terms on the Middle Kingdom, they cheated on those terms. A few lights showed in the town, most of them from the three sailors' saloons on the waterfront. Drunken sailors' laughter and other sounds of their carrying on drifted across the water. The steep hills behind the village were hidden by night, except for a faint purple line at their crest, the last suggestion of the dying day. Cobbler's Wax aimed our rowboat toward a small light in the bay that seemed eerily suspended above the water.

It was a ship's light, and then another light was visible, each at the bow of a ship, The vessels slowly emerged from the night, their masts towering over us. The hulls were vast black expanses, and we could hear the creaks and groans of the lines and blocks and tackles. The ships were moored to buoys fore and aft, and although I couldn't see them, I knew the vessel we were drawing alongside flew the Union Jack on its stern, and the other ship a German flag. These were hybrid vessels, coal-powered steamers that carried auxiliary sails. The British ship was about three hundred feet long. Pirates were plentiful along the China coast, and this merchantman showed six-inch guns through three portals above us. The vessel was wood hulled, and named *Princess Eugenia*. It carried eighty tons of opium in its hold.

Cobbler's Wax guided the rowboat alongside the cargo ship's hull to the companion ladder. I put the bottle under one arm, stood unsteadily, and climbed up the ladder to the *Princess Eugenia*'s deck. Zhou came behind me.

Prince Tuan's informant—a saloonkeeper—had said that only two men remained on guard on this ship. I walked forward, past funnels, rolled line, ratlines, winches, scuppers, and the forward wood superstructure, then up a ladder to the forward peak, Zhou a dark shadow behind me. The masts and booms and rigging were high overhead.

A sailor sat under the lamp near the bowsprit, idly whittling a piece of wood with a small knife and whistling a song I didn't recognize. When I held up my hand, Zhou retreated a little, to stand near a hatch to the forward quarters. Light came through brass portals on the superstructure.

I abruptly called out, "Goot Gotten, mine frienden. Vat youse doing here on de Kaiser's burtday?" Well, it sounded fairly German to me.

The English sailor started, half rising from his perch on a cleat. He wore a shirt with a V-neck held together with black ribbon, and black pants with white stripes. His mustache hid his mouth.

"Who are you?" he demanded. He looked at the pocket knife in his hand, perhaps wishing it were larger.

I waved the bottle cheerily. "Nobody should verk on de Kaiser's burtday. I come to trinken a toasten."

"How the bloody hell did you get on this ship? Where'd you come from?"

"Mine boaten ist de *Saxony*. Vee Deutchen sailors all be celebrating de burtday."

He glanced at my bottle and licked his lips. "I didn't know you German tars were sociable."

"Vee feel sorry for you, not trinken on de burtday. So I comen over in my tender, bringen de bottle. But I go backen, if you vant."

He wiped his mouth with the back of his hand, his eyes on the bottle.

"Now, don't be in such a hurry, mate. It's dry duty, it is, standing watch on this boat."

I popped the cork, took a pretend pull on the bottle, and passed it over to him. I sat down on a spool of cable.

The limey sniffed the bottle. "I didn't know you pig-footers drank gin." He took greedy swallows, six or seven of them, then reluctantly passed the bottle back.

The pickle helmet was a size too small, and pinched my head. I went through the motion of taking another swallow, then smacked my lips. "Knowing you der Kaiser's burtday songen?"

He shook his head and held out his hand for the gin. "We don't bloody well sing to the Kaiser in Falmouth."

To the tune of "My Darling Clementine" I drunkenly sang, "Oh der Kaiser/ Oh der Kaiser/ He be marching off to war/ Into Holland or maybe France/ Vee hopen he takes his pants."

The English sailor slurred his words. "That ain't much of a birthday ditty."

"What's going on here?" came a voice aft.

Another sailor walked into the lamplight. He wore a striped skivvy shirt and flared trousers.

The first sailor said, "We're celebrating the Kaiser's birthday, Hardy, me lad. Join us for a song."

"Who's this man here?" the second sailor demanded. "With the goddamn helmet."

"A sauerkraut who brought us a bottle of gin." The whittler giggled. "But it's half gone."

The bottle dampened any more questions Hardy might have had. All their mates were ashore, happily crapulent after a long voyage, and these two had been left on watch. Hardy held out his hand for the bottle. He eyed me suspiciously, but the scent of gin overcame all caution. He drank quickly, as if his mate might yank the bottle back from him.

The gin had been laced with laudanum, a tincture of opium, and plenty of it. We all sang "Oh der Kaiser," twice more, and then "God Save the Queen" three times, and then toasted the new century, and then to the certainty of a century of German-British friendship, and by then the whittler was asleep, slumping back against the guardrail, and Hardy had begun to stagger. I grabbed him before he collapsed.

Zhou stepped from the shadows and threw Hardy over his shoulder like an empty gunny sack. I dragged the whittler aft toward the companion ladder, the heels of his boots skidding along the deck. By the time I got to the ladder, Zhou had returned from the rowboat. He lifted the whittler under one arm, and descended the ladder again.

Still at the oars, Cobbler's Wax relit his lamp and swung it back and forth, the signal for the soldiers in the lighters to set out. The two English sailors lay at the bottom of the rowboat, breathing easily, passed out. Zhou brought the canister up the ladder. He followed me into the rear superstructure below the bridge. This was the galley. We found a ladder and descended to the deck below. It took only a few minutes to make sure no other Englishmen were aboard, and then to find *Princess Eugenia's* powder room. Shells were stacked in even rows, and casks of powder. The room was also the merchantman's armory, and carbines lined one wall on racks.

I lifted a sulfur match from my pocket, struck it against the instep of my boot and lit the fuse. It popped and snapped, flickering with yellow sparks. The canister contained ten pounds of explosives. Prince Tuan had assured me the fuse was slow and carefully measured, and that we would have fully twenty minutes to get away from the vessel. I lay the canister near the powder kegs, and set the fuse out along the deck so that it touched none of the shells or kegs.

I nodded to Zhou and led the way topside. We went down the ladder and into the rowboat. Hardy was snoring. After Zhou dropped into the boat, it had only four inches of freeboard. Cobbler's Wax pushed away from the hull and began his work with the oars.

I peered through the darkness. The *Saxony* was an indistinct smudge a hundred yards away. And through the night I could see suggestions of movements, black on black. The lighters were silently sailing back and forth, powered by oarsmen. The casks had been opened, and lamp oil was spilling out onto the sea. John D. Rockefeller had given away eight million Mei Foo (good luck) lamps in China to encourage use of his lamp oil. This oil belonged to Rockefeller, taken by night from his tanks at Tientsin.

I let five minutes pass before I motioned for Cobbler's Wax to relight the lamp. He held it high, swinging it back and forth, the call to retreat. The lighters turned back to shore, our rowboat among them.

Just as our boat reached the dock, the *Princess Eugenia* blew apart. The vessel ruptured midships, and the masts and booms shot into the air. A roiling ball of flame engulfed the ship, lighting the harbor in yellows and reds, and starkly illuminating the *Saxony*. The blast pushed concentric wave rings away from the vessel. The sound reached us a few seconds later, more a pulse than a noise. Fragments of the ship splashed into the sea. Sails had been tied to the booms, and flaming pieces of them landed on the water.

The lamp oil caught fire, and quickly a wave of flame spread toward the *Saxony*. The fishing boat lingered near the German merchantman, and when three German sailors rushed to the davits, Prince Tuan's soldiers yelled at them, motioning them to their boat. The Germans abandoned their attempt to lower their lifeboat and scrambled down their ladder, jumped into the sea, and swam toward the incoming fishing boat. The Chinese soldiers lifted them from the water, and the fishing boat started toward the shore.

The flames spread across the water and soon found the *Saxony*. The German ship was quickly surrounded by flame. Then fire crawled up its hull.

Down the roadway, sailors emerged from the saloons. They pointed and whooped and reeled. A few of the more sober ones started for their tenders, but saw there was nothing to be done, so stood on the beach and watched the fire.

Princess Eugenia's back had been broken, and she slid under the water in two parts, the fire abovedecks hissing and sending white clouds of steam skyward. She sank in less than five minutes, and all that was left of her were burning, smoking booms and other detritus floating where the ship had once been. And in them few minutes the *Saxony* caught fully afire, a huge and roaring torch, lighting the village and even the nearby hills. Soon the fire found the ship's magazine, and the deck bucked and bowed, and the hull ripped open. The *Saxony* settled into the sea.

Prince Tuan had been aboard one of the lighters. He found Cobbler's Wax and Zhou and me near the godowns. Zhou had carried both English sailors, one over each of his shoulders, and he lay them gently on the ground, their backs against a warehouse wall. When they awakened they would report that a drunken German had visited their ship, and would be able to report nothing else. The German sailors would say they had been rescued by brave Chinese fishermen who fortunately were in the area.

I asked dryly, "Are two opium ships enough for one night, do you think?"

"It is a start, corporal general." Prince Tuan smiled. "But it is only a start."

EIGHTEEN

The Descent

FROM HEAVEN TO hell in less than an hour. That was my dreadful route. I'll modjitate about the Seventh Level of Hell after a fashion, after I work up the courage to stir my recollection. Nowadays an entire day might pass when my cruel memory doesn't flash forth Hades and I sweat in fear yet again. But it has taken decades for those torments to recede. I shudder again, right now, at the prospect of revisiting that place, if only in my head. Let me first say one or two more things about heaven, Old Buddha's Summer Palace.

Heaven was idyllic, with its ponds and fountains and statues and vast expanses of blooming flowers. But it was more than that. To those of us who've given religion any thought, it's perfectly clear that heaven is also a place where you can have anything you want. Otherwise, why toe the line all your mortal life? At the Summer Palace, my slightest whim was some servant's command. In fact, Cobbler's Wax anticipated my fancies usually before they fully formed in my mind. I'd be sitting in my room staring out the window, vaguely thinking I'd enjoy some sort of tart fruit and also something to occupy my mind for a spell, and in would trot Cobbler's Wax with a pomegranate, thus fulfilling both nascent wishes.

By the way, have I mentioned that later in life, after I was wealthy, I attended Yale? I bought my way in, and I had to buy my way out. But that's where I learned words like "nascent." "Titular" is a good one, too.

Now, what I'm going to tell you—about how I spent my time at the Summer Palace—doesn't reflect too well on yours truly. I was an idler and a glutton. So before I lay out my excesses, let me come to my own defense by mentioning one kind act. I sent a Third Level Imperial Bailiff along with ten thousand silver taels to that burned-out orphanage I had passed while chasing Old Buddha that day. I told the bailiff that his new profession was looking after them children. How did I obtain those funds? Old Buddha allowed me to issue Vermilion Rescripts over her name. Vermilion Rescripts were personal directives to be issued only by the dowager empress. I checked on those orphans once in a while, and they did well with them taels. New dormitory and school, full pantries, new clothing, and a dozen fretting, hovering, loving old amah to look after them. Doing as well as orphans ever do, given the sucker punch that finds them early in life.

But that aside, I was a goldbrick and a trifler. Three times a week I enjoyed a Transcendent Fingers of Radiant Harmony massage. You've never had one? I would lie on a board padded with ostrich leather. Three women on each side of me—that's six total (See what a Yale education can do for you?)—would work me from my scalp to the bottom of my feet. First all six would stroke my shoulders and back and buttocks and legs with the tips of their fingers, choreographed movements where each lady drew Pai and Lai, the gods of Lucky Weight and Full Measure. Those drawings on my skin couldn't have been too accurate, what with all the scars. Then them six ladies donned gloves made of the rough surface of camels' tongues, and would vigorously rub me up and down, fairly pummeling me. Then—and this I found most curious the first time—one of the masseuses would place a house cat on my shoulders. This cat had been specially bred for this purpose, and was called a Wei Long cat. The masseuse would slowly pull the cat's tail, so that it was dragged along my body. Of course, any cat pulled backwards immediately extends its claws to dig into the flesh. So the cat left trails of thin scratches. Then an unguent that smelled like peppermint but stung like iodine was spread on those small wounds. The lotion smarted for only a moment, and then a warm flush penetrated my skin, working into the muscles, all the way through me. That liniment—I never learned precisely what was in it—made me gasp as it seemed to squeeze all my muscles and innards all at once, and then released me in a long and exquisite ebbing of muscular tension. I would then lie there panting, as the women sponged me with chilled water. This whole process took two hours. I never tired of it.

The Summer Palace had many statues in the gardens, usually of Buddha or one of the heathen gods such as the moon goddess Chang E or the god of longevity, Shou Hsing. I was a bit lonesome for Boston, so I commissioned the Imperial Art House to create a statue of Paul Revere.

The Number One Artist, Shan Yu, had never heard of Paul Revere, if you can imagine, so I sketched the great patriot from my memory. I'm no artist, but Shan Yu helped me some with the human form, and I produced a passable likeness of Paul Revere for Shan Yu to work from.

The resulting bronze statue stood eighteen feet high, and showed Paul Revere in a long coat, wearing a tricorne hat, holding a flintlock rifle in one hand and shading his eyes with the other. A noble statue, I must say, as fine a representation of the man as ever graced a New England town square. I was as proud as a whitewashed pig. I made one mistake, though. I'd forgotten exactly when wristwatches were invented, and I had Shan Yu put a wristwatch on Paul Revere's right hand. So just above his coat cuff is an Elgin. Now, after my descent to the pit of hell, Old Buddha had that statue thrown into an abandoned tin mine, where archaeologists of some future generation will unearth a bronze Paul Revere wearing a wristwatch, right in the middle of China, and they'll use up a lot of grant money figuring *that* one out.

I have never worn jewelry, not wanting to appear the fop. But I'd had such success with the statue—even Old Buddha would pause in her morning strolls to squint up at it and shake her head in wonderment—that I decided to try my hand at jewelry design. Zhou the Giant hung on me like a burr on a sock, as I mentioned. Sometimes he could be handy, such as when I had to crack open a filbert, which he could do between his fingers. Other times he was a bother, such as when the Pearl Concubine, dressed in a diaphanous robe that hid utterly nothing, knocked on my door late one evening, I suppose to thank me for saving her life. She came into my room with an inviting smile on her face, but out of a dusky corner stepped the hulking giant who counted killings with diamonds in his teeth. The Pearl Concubine shrieked and fled the room.

So, not wearing jewelry myself, I decided to design a piece for Zhou. I drew a design on a piece of paper, and Summer Palace jewelers crafted the piece. And quite a sight it was, too. The base was six inches across and made of solid gold. Two sabers crossed the front. The blades were inlaid rubies, more than a hundred for each blade, while the saber handles were single emeralds, three carats each. The field was of a thousand small diamonds. I couldn't think of any reason in particular to grant Zhou a medal, other than he was always around. So below the crossed saber blades was the word PROXIMITY spelled out in rubies. When I presented this medal to Zhou, along with a gold chain so he could hang it around his neck, he kowtowed to me, and he never took it off, not once for the rest of his life.

I had Shan Yu's artists paint eleven portraits of me, one after the other, because they never got my eyes right.

I tired of the view out my window, so I ordered the gardeners to transplant a forest—over three hundred trees—a quarter-mile to the south, thereby opening my view to the road to Peking.

Old Buddha was fascinated by clocks, and there were over a hundred of them at her residence at the Summer Palace. So I had one constructed for her, an anchor escarpment clock made of silver that was ten feet tall and weighed over two thousand pounds. When it struck the hour, a one-foot-high mechanical Woodrow Lowe marched out of a door and banged a gong with a hammer. A mechanical Zhou followed right behind me, just like in life. The dowager empress was quite tickled to see this contraption, and added it to her collection, though it fell through the floor of her hallway when workers tried to move it in. The foundation and floor were reinforced, and the clock placed in an honored position.

About now you are expecting me to announce some enduring moral lesson. With my every wish granted at the Summer Palace, with all my whims howsoever exotic quickly fulfilled, I must have been bored and restless, and searching for the deeper meaning of it all. You are anticipating I'll lecture about how happiness cannot be found in great wealth.

Nonsense.

If a man ever had a better time on this earth than my visit to the Summer Palace, I've never heard about it.

And then the men in black robes came for me, and I was carried to the center of the earth.

YOU ASKED A question, did you? How did I buy my way into Yale? Well, before I describe the Seventh Level of Hell, I'll tell you how.

I met with the president of Yale. This was much later in my life, when I was truly wealthy. Yale's president was Crofton Culpepper III, and he rose from behind his desk to meet me, surveyed my face, then reluctantly extended his hand in greeting. A letter was in his other hand.

"Mr. Lowe, I have received a message from my friend Theodore Roosevelt asking me to meet with you." His voice was so deep and resonant that it provided its own echo, like he was speaking into a bucket. "How is Teddy doing in his retirement?"

"Just fine, sir. Spends most of his time at Sagamore Hill."

After I let loose of his hand, I looked around his office. The massive Queen Anne desk had scroll legs and claw-and-ball feet. Behind it was a Windsor chair. An enormous globe mounted on a gilded statue of Atlas—his face twisted by his effort—occupied a corner. A caned satinwood settee was against a wall under a landscape by John Constable, identified by the small plaque on the frame as *A View of the Severn*. A bookshelf lined another wall, and all the books had leather bindings with gold-leaf titles. Windows looked out onto a commons.

Crofton Culpepper III returned to his chair. I sat opposite him on a Gothic chair that had velvet upholstery but not much padding so that it didn't invite long visits.

"I've also received your application for admission to Yale, Mr. Lowe." Culpepper accented each word with a slight lift of his nose. "And I must tell you that despite Teddy's perfervid recommendation of you, we cannot admit you. I'm afraid you simply aren't qualified."

"Not qualified? What am I lacking?"

"High school." He peered at me over his fingers that were arranged in a steeple. Culpepper had a cold face and an enameled complexion. His grin was fixed and his eyes were green and merciless. He was wearing a gray silk tie and a silver collar pin. A key from some honorary society hung from his watch chain.

"I wondered if not going to high school would complicate things," I observed. "But I promised my mother I'd go to college." Teddy's letter had gotten me into the Yale president's office, bypassing several deans, but no further.

I rose quickly from the chair. Culpepper was alarmed, lurching back in his seat. But I just walked to a window overlooking the grassy square. "Mr. Culpepper—"

"It's 'Doctor Culpepper,'" he interrupted, perhaps to compensate for being frightened when I stood.

"Of course it is. Would you come over to the window and look at this building. I'm just wondering what this lovely new building is."

Maybe he thought humoring me would get me out the door more quickly. He stepped around his desk, around a miniature marble Pietà on a pedestal table, and stood next to me, peering out the window.

"To which building do you refer?"

I had lived my whole life without starting a sentence with "to which." I replied, "The new building, right next to that sandstone one."

He bent closer to the window. "Well, the sandstone building is Thackeray Hall, a dormitory. But next to it is a grass field."

I shook my head. "Next to Thackeray Hall is the new four-story liberal arts library. Can't you see it, Dr. Culpepper? It has a series of marble columns in front of it, wide windows, balconies near the roof. Nicely landscaped, with Japanese maples and English topiary. And next to the door is a slab of stone with CROFTON CULPEPPER III LIBRARY etched into it. I'm surprised you can't see it because it's as plain as day to me."

He studied me a moment, then turned back to the window. "You mean the building with the Italian marble arch over the door, and the marble facing stones, and the greenstone walkway? And a gargoyle or two?"

"That's the one."

"The building with the Preconi fountain in front of it?"

"That's it."

"But it appears to be six stories," he said. "Not four."

"So it is. My mistake."

"Yes, I do see that new library after all, right there next to Thackeray Hall." He put his hand on my shoulder. "Welcome to Yale, Mr. Lowe."

And how did I buy my way *out* of Yale? Five years later, I met again with Crofton Culpepper III. Same office. Same imperious gaze. I had not spoken to him since the dedication of the new Crofton Culpepper III Library during my second junior year, having had a bit of trouble with calculus during my first junior year. Now Dr. Culpepper glanced at the page in his hand, then turned it over to look at the back of it.

I was sitting on that same velvet chair. "I can't graduate next week unless I get a passing grade in my last class, the philosophy of logic. I've already been at Yale too long. I've got to graduate."

"I have your test paper in front of me, Mr. Lowe. It is blank, except for your name in the upper right-hand corner. You went to the test, and then handed in a blank piece of paper?"

I nodded. "Except for my name on it."

"You didn't attempt to answer any of the questions?"

"Logic has never been my strong point." If he only knew.

"Well, Mr. Lowe, I'm sorry to say that you don't have the credits to graduate from our university because you have failed this examination."

"Don't I get any points for getting my name right?"

"This is Yale, Mr. Lowe. Not Princeton." He rose from the desk and walked over to that same window. "Mr. Lowe, look at the new Crofton Culpepper Library. Do you see it?"

"Of course."

"Do you see the even newer west wing?"

"The west wing?" That damn building had no west wing. I had paid for every square foot of the Crofton Culpepper III Library—and every square inch of Lathiti marble Culpepper had insisted on—and I well knew there was no west wing.

"Yes, right there." Dr. Culpepper pointed. "To the side of the building, in the direction of Thackeray Hall." He held up my blank test paper, lest I miss the point.

Which I didn't. "Well, now that you mention it, I do see the new west wing. And a mighty fine structure it is, too."

He put his hand on my back to guide me to the door. "Do bring an umbrella to the graduation ceremony, Mr. Lowe. Weather at this time of year can be chancy."

And that's how I bought my way out of Yale. When I showed my degree to my mother, she sank into her knitting chair, and tears rolled down her cheeks as if her plumbing was broken, even though the degree was printed in Latin, Latin being somewhat sparse in the Lowe household. To see my mum hold my degree like it was a piece of the true cross made them years and that library and its west wing cheap at the price.

NOW, BACK IN time again, to when I was younger and still in China. To the Seventh Level of Hell.

I never heard a thing. To this day I do not know how the men in black robes overpowered Zhou on his cot outside my door. Zhou never figured it out, either, and it was a matter of considerable embarrassment to him later, much later, after he had healed sufficiently to care about anything but physical pain.

One moment I was asleep, dreaming about the quarter-scale railroad I was going to have built on the Summer Palace grounds, and the next moment I was suspended in the air, wrapped in brown oilcloth that pressed in on me on all sides. Chains were thrown around me, at least a hundred pounds of chains, from my ankles to my shoulders. With the oilcloth over my head, I couldn't see anything. I tried to cry out, but before the first sound escaped my lips, a club came down on my temple. I might've blacked out a moment, but I couldn't tell due to the thick black cloth cutting off my sight. All was black. The cloth suffocated me. I wheezed and coughed and gagged, fighting for breath.

Many hands lifted me, at least six men, and I was carried on their shoulders. The only sounds were of the swish of their clothing and the clink of chain links.

Again I tried to speak. "What's—"

The club struck me again, and this time I was out for sure.

When I came to I was in a cage on an oxcart, a prisoners' wagon. The bamboo bars were lashed together with hide strips. My chains had been removed. Zhou was lying next to me, unconscious. In the back corner of the cage, Cobbler's Wax sat with his head bowed. Blood seeped from his nose onto his bare chest. He wore only black pajamas.

Morning was leaching the eastern sky, sending meager streams of blue light across the land. The cart was on a stony road, headed west, and was nowhere within the Summer Palace grounds. Three men in black robes walked on each side of the cart. Hoods hid their faces. Their hands were lost in long sleeves. The robes almost touched the ground, so they appeared to be floating rather than walking. A teamster, also in black, walked alongside the ox, flicking its flank with a quirt.

My head was filled with pain, and each time the cart rolled over a rock, I was pounded by agony behind my eyes. Dried blood matted my hair.

I tapped Zhou's cheeks, trying to revive him, but his eyes remained closed. His proximity medal was still around his neck. I searched for his pulse in his wrist. The giant was alive. I was relieved. I had come to believe I couldn't be harmed as long as Zhou was by my side. That was shortly to be proved wrong.

The road was flanked by steep, barren hills, as bad a land as ever a crow flew over. The cart passed a few poor huts. Peasants ducked into their homes and closed their doors and windows. They knew who the men in the black robes were. Zhou moaned and brought his hand to his forehead. I helped him sit up. His eyes rolled in their sockets and his jaw hung loose, but he bared his diamond teeth, glad to see me.

We came to a palisade of tree trunks, the trunks having conical points. The palisade hid the base of a steep hill. A wood gate hung on massive iron hinges. When the gate swung open, the teamster swatted the ox, and we trundled in.

A dirt courtyard stood before a cave. About a dozen more men in black robes stood there, carrying long pikes and apparently waiting for us. All around the square entrance to the cave gargoyles had been carved from the sandstone hill, each the size of a man. Their features were contorted in rage and pain, tongues lolling out, pointed ears, twisted mouths, cruel eyes. Beckoning claws and barbed tails and cloven hoofs crowded the entrance. These were the gods of Suffering, Agony, and Wretchedness, and lesser gods, such as the God of Suppurating Eyeballs, the God of the Leaking Black Bubo, and the God of Impalement.

A black robe opened the cart's cage, and motioned us out. Cobbler's Wax and I jumped down, but Zhou was too weak to move, so he was shoved off the cart to land on the ground in a pile. Four robes lifted him and struggled with his bulk toward the cave. Cobbler's Wax and I were prodded toward the mouth of the cave.

I whispered, "Wax, do you know what's going on?"

"I have heard dark rumors of this place for many years, corporal general." His voice fluttered with fear. "But I thought it was a myth. All of us at the Summer Palace thought it was a fable, spread by Old Buddha to quell thoughts of mutiny."

"What is this place?"

"The Seventh Level of Hell." Trepidation weakened Wax's legs, and he staggered. I grasped his arm and helped him to regain his feet. He said faintly, "We are lost."

A pike jabbed my back, prodding me along. We approached the hideous statues. I felt cool air coming from the cave.

Cobbler's Wax said, "You have strong hands, corporal general."

"I suppose I do."

"I beg of you—I call on our friendship and all my loyalty to you—end it for me now. With your hands, rip out my jugular vein. Do not let me enter between those gargoyles."

"Now, Wax, I couldn't do that."

He sobbed. "I beg of you, colonel general." He craned his head back, exposing the full length of his throat. "I beg of you."

The robes must have guessed Wax's plan, because we were roughly parted. We left the morning sun behind us as we marched through the gargoyles, surrounded by the men in black robes. The cave was chilled, a stepmother's breath in the air. Soft sand was under our feet. Burning oil lamps suspended from the rock walls by metal brackets lit our way. The flames bent in the breeze coming from the belly of the cavern.

A few more steps and we came to a high desk manned by a fellow dressed in red satin. On his nose was the first pair of spectacles I'd seen in China. Two fire pots with rush wicks were on his desk, and his face reflected the flames' streaking reds and yellows. The man's face was twisted in concentration. His forehead was high, was most of his face, as his white hair had receded to his crown. His lips were professionally pursed, and his eyes were lost in the glint of his spectacles. Dewlaps wagged under his chin. He was perhaps sixty years old. His skin was swan-white for lack of sun. He bent over a massive leatherbound book, making entries with a quill, not looking up at us for a moment. I was to learn his title was Gatekeeper.

Zhou was finally able to stand unassisted. His eyes were wide with fear. He and Cobbler's Wax leaned into each other for support.

Behind the desk was a side room dug out of the rock. I could see rows of floor-to-ceiling rosewood cabinets inside. More oil lamps sputtered inside this room. Dressed in black, clerks hustled back and forth, bringing out scrolls and unrolling them in front of the white-haired man. Gatekeeper would check something from the scroll, then make another entry into the huge book. Stationed behind the Gatekeeper was a man who held a tiny knife, and who had but one duty. When the Gatekeeper absently passed his quill over his shoulder, this fellow quickly snigged the quill's point with his blade, then returned it to the Gatekeeper. Near the leather volume were three inkpots and a silver bell with a bone handle.

When the old man finally looked up, squinting at me behind his specs, one of our escorts pulled out a rolled document from under his black robe. The document was scarlet. A Vermilion Rescript. We had been brought here on Old Buddha's orders.

The scarlet roll snared the Gatekeeper's attention. He leaned forward and snatched it from the black robe. He untied a black ribbon to unroll the document, peering at it intently, nodding and pushing out his lips even further. He glanced at me over the top of the spectacles, then back at the rescript, then at me again. Finally he reached for his bell and fiercely shook it.

From the shadows further into the cave came two men, almost identical, and almost as big as Zhou. They were both naked from the waist up. On their chests were duplicate patterns, skulls drawn not with the tattooer's ink but in raised scar tissue. Like Zhou, these men had bald pates, and were hefty. One was missing both ears, leaving dark holes in the sides of his head. Their pantaloons hung only to their calves. These fellows were barefoot. As quick as I can relate it, these two bracketed me, and half-lifted me by my shoulders to propel me further into the cave.

I was beginning to worry, frankly.

Four more of these minions—all with scar skulls on their chests— came for Zhou and Cobbler's Wax. Zhou shrugged them off, sending two crashing into the cave's wall. The Gatekeeper rang his bell again, and four more scar skulls sprinted into the light. They pounced on Zhou, and after a struggle managed to subdue him. Cobbler's Wax moaned in fear.

I was taken about fifty yards farther along the dark path, and there the cave opened into an enormous vault the size of a cathedral, rising high over our heads. Spaced evenly along the walls were fire pots, these resembling thirty-gallon drums, with bonfires roaring in each of them. As the walls rose, they leaned toward each other as in a dome, but the roof was lost in the high darkness. The cave contained no stalagmites or stalactites, and was uniform in length and breadth, which indicated the entire subterranean structure had been hewn by men out of the living rock. I heard the distant piping and rustle of a waterfall.

Not only did the cave rise above, it dropped below. I was standing on a rock ledge that circled the entire cavern at entry level.

So massive was the stone statue across the pit that it at first failed to register on me, so improbable in scale and terrifying in design. The statue was sixty feet high, and grew out of the cavern's far wall in harsh relief. The head was more a skull than a representation of anyone alive, with bony plates and zigzagging fissures, and a triangular hole instead of a nose, yet the eye sockets weren't hollow, but rather contained shimmering, faceted red stones. Skin was depicted around the mouth, with lips turned down in an eternal snarl. All the teeth were pointed, and the canine teeth curved over the lower lip. Massive, ribbed ram's horns protruded from the sides of this visage and swept out and down as far as the chin. The chest was muscled and immense, and the stomach striated with muscles. Its left arm hung at its side and held several stone chain links. The other arm was upraised, near its head, and the hand was balled in a fist. Instead of fingers, long claws gripped the full-scale form of a human, whose face showed utter horror. The monster's hips and stunted legs were those of a goat, and instead of feet the monster had cloven hoofs. I learned later this was the Second Demon of Eternal Anguish. I never met the First, thank Allah for eternal mercy.

I was propelled forward again, toward a stone staircase that descended into the well of the cavern. That waterfall sound grew louder, and then divided itself into numberless wails that echoed back and forth in the cavern, and then slurred together again, as if all an organ's keys were pressed at once. The ceaseless sounds of anguish, the howls and moans and cries rising from below.

The stone staircase clung to the side of the pit, winding down into the depths. Like the giant statue, the stairs had been carved from rock as the hole was dug. I glanced over the rail. Rather than a solid wall down into the abyss, seven stories had been dug into the pit's sides, each layer ringing the chasm all the way around and disappearing behind the Second Demon of Eternal Anguish. I was still too high to peer into these recesses, but lights flickered from them all.

Prodded from behind every few steps, Zhou and Cobbler's Wax and I descended to the landing at the first level. At the back of the landing was an open area flanked by a raised stone bed of fire. Two men worked a bellows shaped like an accordion, blowing air over coals. The flames sparked and flared when the bellows came down. Dressed in a white vest and baggy pants, a fellow was bent over the table applying a glowing brand to a pile of raw meat. At least, it looked like uncooked meat, but I admit to not looking at that operation too long.

Ranging along this level were cells, one after another, pens chipped out of the rock. The cells were barred with bamboo floor to ceiling. Most inmates lay on mats inside. Some stood in front of the bars, their arms outstretched, hands clinging to the bamboo.

I was shoved along, down the next flight of stairs to the second, then third and fourth levels. Each had the same arrangement; the fire bed and bellows behind the landing, and a row of cells circling the pit, all the way around to the Second Demon of Eternal Anguish.

We came to the lowest tier of cells, the seventh. The pit was another fifty feet deep. The bottom was covered from wall to wall with human bones. Thousands of skulls. Hip bones, long leg bones. Grasping hands. Stripped of all flesh. Many skeletons were whole. Others had been pulled apart. And when I say the pit was another fifty feet deep, I mean this was the distance down to the bone pile. I never learned how deep the bones went, and perhaps no living soul knew.

Doubtless prompted by perversity, our escorts let us stare at this grotesquery a moment. From level two, a body was thrown into space by two black robes. It plummeted down to land with a rattle on the mass of bones. The bone pile instantly came to life with movement. Rats—hundreds of them—scurried up from the bones to attack the body, which was quickly buried under a churning mass of black fur. A moment later, the tide of rodents receded. The body was entirely flensed. Nothing was left but sparkling bone. The skeleton stared up at us with its newly hollowed eye sockets, an expression of astonishment on its chalky face.

We were pushed toward the alcove where, here too, men worked a bellows handle. Coals glowed in a raised bed. Cobbler's Wax cried out when he was pushed away from me toward the cell row. Zhou struggled, but a bludgeon cracked his head, and he was towed away by his arms. I was led to the stone table, a massive structure resembling a sarcophagus. Carvings of evil imps with rictus smiles adorned the table side. Nothing was on the waist-high table but three bolts along each side. The top was stained in colors from rust to brown.

Near one wall of the alcove was a sideboard on which were five hourglasses, all mounted on the same axle. I guessed these sand-filled glasses ranged from measuring three minutes to one hour. Near them was a wood rack of skeleton keys on pegs, perhaps fifty keys in all.

The black robes lifted me by all my limbs and placed me none too gently on the table, spread-eagled and belly up. From somewhere they produced chains and cuffs and anklets.

My view was of the alcove's stone ceiling twenty feet over my head. Painted in red and white and black, another Second Demon of Eternal Anguish stared down at me, the sharp tips of its horns aimed at my heart. I desperately yanked on the chains securing my wrists, doing nothing but creasing my skin under the iron bracelets.

I closed my eyes a moment, trying to sort out the morning's dizzying events and trying to rein in my fear, which I confess had the best of me. I was trembling from cuff to anklet. And when I opened my eyes, it

MAN OF THE CENTURY

seemed the Second Demon of Eternal Anguish above me had been transformed by sorcery into a stunning woman.

A Manchu woman. She had drifted into my sight over me. She was reading the same Vermilion Rescript as had the Gatekeeper. Her brows were furled, and her lips moved silently, as if tasting the words on the rescript.

"Number twenty-two," she said finally.

"Twenty-two?" I croaked in Chinese.

"Old Buddha has selected number twenty-two from this first column of our bill of fare." She nodded approvingly. "And number six from the second column." She stared down at me. "You must have caused her a river of difficulty."

"There's been some mistake, and I can't figure out . . ."

She held up a hand and purred smoothly, "The luxury of concerning myself with my patients' excuses is something I must do without. There are only so many hours in the day." She ran her tongue along her lower lip, which in any other circumstance would have been provocative. "My, my. Number twenty-two and number six. This will be quite a challenge."

Let me offer as dispassionate a description of her as I can. Even after all these years, I cannot think of that lady without attaching the devil's horns to her head, without sharpening her teeth, without transforming her eyes into burning red coals, and without twisting her mouth into a harridan's malicious grimace. Without making her resemble the Second Demon of Eternal Anguish.

But in truth she was exquisite. Her eyes were the color of smoke. Her nose was narrow and retroussé. Her lips were plump and finely turned, and revealed teeth that were even and eggshell white. Like the Summer Palace courtesans, she wore dramatic makeup, highlighting her eyes in black and making her cheekbones seem even more pronounced. Clusters of pearls hung from her ears on thin silver chains. Her head was the shape of a perfect oval, with hair pulled loosely behind in the Manchu fashion. She wore a crimson satin garment trimmed in black and tied at the waist with a sash.

"What's your name?" Maybe if I was friendly.

"I am called the Demon's Daughter."

"What do your friends call you?"

She didn't answer. She paced back and forth a few times, her mouth compressed, her eyes unfocused, apparently lost in thought. Her movements were those of the gazelles I had seen along the Nile River. She might have been a dancer, had she not somehow been sidetracked into being a demon's daughter.

When she clapped her hands, two scar bellies appeared. She issued orders in a low voice. One of the scar bellies disappeared from my view along the walkway.

Then she said to me, "Just a taste today, then."

The scar belly returned, carrying a foot-square wire cage by a wood handle. On one end of the cage was an odd leather harness made of four hide straps. A sliding panel was on that same end. At Demon's Daughter's direction, he turned the cage so I could see its contents.

A rat. A wharf rat as big as a cat, with a foot-long tail thick at its base, and quick black eyes. The animal turned in tight circles in the cage, which was not much larger than it was. The rat seemed to smile at me with its mouthful of teeth like white razors.

Demon's Daughter announced, "This is going to be a bit uncomfortable."

As she stepped to the bank of hourglasses, the two scar bellies used the harness to strap the cage to the bottom of my left foot.

"Let's begin, shall we?" Demon's Daughter asked.

When she tipped over the smallest hourglass, a scar belly lifted the panel separating the rodent from the sole of my foot. And that rat knew where the food was. He leapt at my skin, and began to tear away at it with its teeth. The sands began draining into the hourglass's lower chamber.

Now, I realize that few who will hear my story have ever had a rat eat the bottoms of their feet. So let me tell you that it hurts. And I don't mean it hurts like barking your shin or biting your tongue or cutting your finger with a paring knife while peeling an apple. The idea of the rat munching away is so revolting, and the pain is so vast, that agony envelops and invades your entire being. I bucked and screeched. The rat bit off a hunk every few seconds, working its way into my foot. I yanked my leg so hard that I tore the skin on my ankle. The rat sank its incisors into me again and again.

The Second Demon of Eternal Anguish on the ceiling dispassionately stared down, and the Demon's Daughter leaned in and out of my view, so that my careening mind could no longer distinguish the demon from the daughter. I struggled against the chains and cried out and sobbed and cursed. The rat ate its dinner.

Then the sand ran out. A scar belly slapped down the cage panel, forcing the rat back into its cage. The scar bellies unfastened the cage from my foot.

Demon's Daughter came into my view above me. "You see, everything ends. My patients learn to watch the hourglass closely. And an upright heart does not fear the demon."

Tears of pain streaming down my cheeks, I was unshackled and lifted off the stone table by the scar bellies. They carried me from the landing along the catwalk to the first cell, where they dropped me onto a straw pallet. I was fading in and out, my whole body aflame with pain. A scar belly locked the bamboo door with a brass key and a square padlock.

A few hours later—it might have been a week for all that I could judge or cared about passing time—a scar belly delivered to my cell a large bowl of rice with snow peas and sizable chunks of beef. I ate, despite the pain.

Night from day was impossible to ascertain in the pit, but all things, even hell, have rhythms, and the next day—so it must have been—the scar bellies came for me again. Not the same two fellows, though. The new ones looked similar, with their black vests and artful skulls in raised tissue on their stomachs. Perhaps the first couple had went on holiday. I was hauled from my cell along the stone mezzanine, the giant statue of the Second Demon of Eternal Anguish glaring without pity down at me, to the table where I was strapped down again. My foot had been in such agony that I had no mental reserve to be afraid. I should have been.

Demon's Daughter was waiting for me, dressed in red and black again. This outfit was almost transparent, a glass toga, as the Romans called their flimsy silk robes. It was lined in black beading. In her black hair was an ebony barrette inlaid with emeralds. For a torturer, she had a fine sense of fashion.

She spread her arms and turned a full circle. "Do you like it?"

Her curves were readily visible beneath this suggestion of wafting silk.

"It's enchanting," I replied.

She seemed pleased. "According to heaven and according to fate, not according to man." She turned an hourglass.

Two scar bellies gripped my head, their meaty hands surrounding it entirely. Demon's Daughter appeared above me, smiled winningly, then dashed a handful of cayenne pepper into my eyes.

She might as well have used an ice pick. My head exploded in pain, a red wash of agony that spread from my eyes in a ring to every fiber of my being. My eyeballs were a pump of agony, sending burning spears down my frame. Everything in the cold universe was pushed away from me, leaving only a well of blinding suffering in my head.

Time had no meaning, only the searing pain. An instant or an eternity later, a scar belly forced my eyelids open so he could flush my eyes with water. The pain subsided a little. He poured more water from a ceramic pitcher. After a moment I could see again, though my head ached mightily, and my sockets felt full of gravel.

Demon's Daughter said, "This is day number two. I will so mark it in my ledger."

I gasped, "Why am I down here?"

"While you coveted another man's horse, you lost your ox."

"What does that mean?" I pleaded.

She smiled sweetly, soothingly, in all appearance immensely concerned with my well-being. She patted my shoulder. "You must think of me as your physical and spiritual physician. I will cure you of all your ills, those of the body and those of the mind and those of the soul, but it will be a long journey."

"How long will I be down here." My eyes were shedding water like a cloud, and she swam above me.

"You are mine," she cooed. "Forever."

"How can you do this? You don't—"

She shushed me with a long and painted finger to her lips. "I eat my rice with my gaze on the heavens."

I was hauled back to my cell, where I lay on the straw mat, my eyes still pockets of fire in my skull. So all-consuming was the pain behind my nose that I forgot my damaged foot, and so overwhelming was the anguish that my name was called several times before it made its way through the wall of torment to register on me.

"Corporal General Lowe."

I moaned, my palms pressed into my wet eyes.

"Corporal General Lowe. It's me. Prince Tuan." English words.

I blinked away the tears. There he stood, on the other side of the bamboo bars. He was naked except for black trousers, and his hands were locked in iron fetters attached to a heavy wood yoke around his neck. Much of the skin of his chest had been stripped away, and he was seeping blood.

I hobbled to the bars and put my hands through so I could touch him. I held him by the sides of his head, trying to give him strength and receive strength. Two scar bellies stood behind him on the mezzanine. They had apparently been ordered to let him pause in front of my cell.

"Prince Tuan, what has happened to us?"

His voice was fogged with pain. "Old Buddha discovered we sank the opium ships."

I groaned. Of course.

He said, "Because of my royal blood, I have been spared your fate."

"What is my fate?"

"An eternity before the Second Demon of Eternal Anguish."

"I won't live long, your highness. Not down here, not with the Demon's Daughter."

"You will." He staggered under the yoke's weight, but caught himself. "Demon's Daughter won't let you die. Never. You will be fed well. You will be shaved every day, and your clothes will be washed. You will be given medicine for any disease. Serious wounds will be addressed. But every day you will return to the Daughter's table for more treatment."

"What's to become of you?" I asked.

"I have been stripped of my rank and titles, and am being sent to the northwest to be a slave to a frontier guard."

My voice rose like a stormy wind. "Prince Tuan, I've got to get out of here."

"There is nothing I can do. Not for me. Not for you. Not for Zhou or Cobbler's Wax."

"Where are they?"

"In the two cells nearest yours."

I cast about for an idea, anything that would offer a thread of hope. "Prince Tuan, you may at some time have a chance to send a message for me."

He tried to shake his head, but it was clamped in the yoke. "I'm sorry, corporal general. I will be a slave on the frontier."

I gently squeezed his head between my hands. "You might. You just might someday be able to help me." I searched my memory, trying to withdraw anything useful from the web of pain. "Send a message, a letter to anybody who knows me, to those people I've told you about. A letter, I beg you. Try."

The scar bellies came for the prince. One pulled roughly on a lead attached to the yoke. The prince stumbled away.

He called in a weak voice, "The peace of Buddha be on you, corporal general. Goodbye."

I sank back onto the straw, lost and suffering.

Next day, the scar bellies came for me again, and they came every day for 368 days. I know the precise number because I left a mark in blood on the rock wall of my cell each time I returned from the table. No two tortures were alike. I will not catalogue the suffering I endured.

Yes, I will. You've been along for the good, such as my rapturous night with Victoria Littlewood. So you might as well hear of the bad.

On one occasion, Demon's Daughter brushed a patch of lye paste onto my back. To say this merely burned is to say a rose is merely pretty. My back felt like a field of fire. On another day, nails were driven through my hands and feet. Another time, swamp leeches were attached to my testicles. One time my thumb was snapped back against my wrist, broken like a stick of ceiling wax. Some of the treatments were clever: 500 leaf cutter ants were put into my mouth and my lips then sewn shut with a sailmaker's needle. Others indicated a certain mental laziness on the part of the Demon's Daughter; one day she just had the scar bellies yank the hair out of my scalp. Some didn't hurt too badly, at least by comparison; needles pushed through all fingers, sideways below the nails. Others made me faint dead away; a bead of heated, molten gold dropped down my throat.

So that year passed. Never did the moaning and screaming and wails of lamentation from the cells abate, and much of it was my own. Never did the Second Demon of Eternal Anguish, who could peer into almost all the cells, shed a tear of compassion.

Visitors occasionally came into the pit, mostly Buddhist and Taoist monks who would perform such rituals as the Prayer for Bountiful Supply of Provisions for the Departed, and Thanksgiving by the Use of Cakes. I saw a few Anglos, one a Catholic priest in a black robe swinging an incense lamp. I cried out to him, but my entreaties were lost in the moans and the echoes of moans. Same with a team of five Catholic nuns, in their black and white habits, faces hidden under sweeping hoods. The missionaries were escorted by the Gatekeeper, who shooed them quickly along. Old Buddha visited once. I saw her on the edge of the top mezzanine. She threw a bucket of salt down onto the Second Demon of Eternal Anguish. All the scar bellies kowtowed to her, hundreds of them lining the mezzanines.

Those interruptions were the only relief from the dull dread of every new day's visit with Demon's Daughter. The fear was as monotonous as the path of a pendulum. After several weeks in the pit, my mind began to lose its grip, and I would wander along in absurd hallucinations. And when I was lucid, some new part of me was always in agony, thanks to Demon's Daughter. Hopelessness and despair and pain were my companions.

The scar bellies came for me on my 368th day in the pit. I dragged myself off the mat, and met them at the cell's door. They no longer had to push or carry me to the table because I was resigned to my daily ordeal. That day, number 368, I climbed onto the table, looking at Demon's Daughter to see whether I should lie face down or face up. With an alluring smile, she indicated up, so I lay on my back. The scar bellies shackled my hands and feet.

She instructed, "Under a plum tree, do not lift your hand to adjust your cap."

I had no clue what she meant. I almost never did.

She hovered over me a moment, a four-inch blade in her hand. I vaguely wondered which part of my body she would slice.

She said, "A covetous heart is never satisfied."

Demon's Daughter was about to bring down the knife when she abruptly righted herself and asked, "Yes? What is it, Gatekeeper?"

I unscrewed my eyes and raised my head. The Gatekeeper was escorting another missionary on a tour. The missionary was Eastern Orthodox or some such. He wore a brown wool robe with a hood that hid his features in shadow. A silver cross hung from his waist on a chain.

The Gatekeeper said, "I have explained to this foreign devil about the health benefits of bloodletting, and that your patient"—he nodded in my direction—"has a heart murmur that requires the extraction of a small measure of blood."

"Of course." She dipped her chin at the missionary. "And then you can explain to me why Old Buddha inflicts these long-noses upon our establishment. And inflicts our own monks on us, too."

"Old Buddha has the spiritual welfare of all her subjects at heart," the

Gatekeeper said. "Westerners deserve Western spiritual guidance, she believes."

"Get rid of him as quickly as you can," she ordered. "Let me resume my therapy."

And then I began hallucinating again, surely. For at that moment, the missionary brought out from the robe a large revolver, a British pistol, a Webley .44. At the same instant, the missionary stepped toward the Demon's Daughter.

The mouth of the gun barrel touched her nose. The Webley fired. Gray matter and bits of bone shot out the back of the Daughter's head to splash against the stone wall. Her head now just a mask, with nothing behind her lovely features but red and gray mash, Demon's Daughter collapsed to the floor.

With mechanical efficiency, the missionary swung the pistol toward the Gatekeeper, who opened his mouth to protest, but caught a bullet in it instead. He, too, was sent to the floor.

The smoking Webley arched toward the scar bellies, but they had already turned and were sprinting along the mezzanine.

Them 368 days had destroyed my mind, had they not? Certainly. And now here was the incontrovertible proof. At that moment, the utterly impossible presented itself as reality.

Victoria Littlewood pulled the hood off her head and smiled at me.

NINETEEN

The Silk Road

THE FIRST LIGHT of a new dawn stole down the slopes. Black gloom gave way to shades of gray. The mud hut was slowly brought from darkness. An old peasant with a white beard tipped with yellow like a goat's sat on the dirt floor, his conical straw hat on the floor next to him, his hands clasped together, his eyes round with fear. We trespassers filled his home.

Victoria Littlewood cradled Cobbler's Wax, his head against her bosom. She tenderly dabbed a cloth at his forehead, cleaning wounds Demon's Daughter had put there with fish hooks. Though he had been conscious a few times since our escape from the pit, he was out cold now, which was fortunate for all of us. Every time he was awake he dribbled and ranted like a madman.

His arms crossed in front of him, Zhou leaned against a wall. The giant had been treated as roughly as Wax and me, and his skin from scalp to toes resembled a rocky field. But he was indomitable. He had carried Cobbler's Wax out of the pit, then for another two hours until we found the hut, held Wax tenderly but firmly when Wax raised his deranged ruckus.

In a low voice, Victoria told Cobbler's Wax of her school in England, as if her words might comfort him even in his darkness. She dipped her finger into a pot of crushed wild rhubarb, then opened his mouth and wiped the paste on the back of his tongue. The rhubarb would fight his fever. After a while, she carefully lay him on a straw mat, then crossed the tiny room to Zhou. She dipped a new corner of the cloth into a water bowl. She found an infected wound on Zhou's arm, a deep puncture. She used the peasant's knife to scrape the yellow scab from it, then sliced open the pocket. Zhou kept himself from flinching. She kneaded out the pus, wiping it away before it leaked down his arm. She sliced the

275

wound open further. She swabbed root soap onto the rag, and cleaned the wound, pausing to cut away bits of purple dead flesh. Beads of sweat formed on Zhou's head. She spoke softly to him, even though he knew almost no English.

With an effort that made me tremble, I pushed myself to my feet and bent low to leave the hut. I wanted nothing more than to watch the advent of morning, my first in more than a year. And it was a majestic daybreak. First came a drifting haze of purple light, then a rising ruby luster, then the full blue tide of morning, sweeping away the stars east to west. Shafts of honeyed light streaked the heavens above, and then the waxing sun flooded the hills with a golden sheen, and the rays found my hoary skin, stroking it with warm and healing fingers. I raised my arms and spread my fingers, making a sail of myself, catching the gilded sun. A sunrise made by God. I stood there many minutes, the new sun working on me.

Then I turned to peer through the window. Victoria was still tending to Zhou, now with salve from an earthen bowl. She applied it to his palms, where the skin had been burned off several days before. Zhou stared at this lovely foreign creature, gratitude and adoration on his rough face.

She was lovely, but she was tough, I'll guarantee you that. The day before, after she had put holes in Demon's Daughter's and the Gatekeeper's heads, she had quickly unshackled me. As she was opening a cuff around my wrist, a scar belly rushed her from the mezzanine. I hollered, and she spun and cut him down with a bullet through the throat. After I rolled off the table, I gasped out that two friends were in cells down the walkway. The keys on the pegs were arranged to correspond with the cells. We opened the giant's cell door. Without a word (he seldom spoke, his visage doing his talking for him), Zhou came out and stepped with us to the cell where Cobbler's Wax was held. We found Wax lying on a straw mat, unconscious. Zhou threw the eunuch over his shoulder, and we made our way up the stairs to the Gatekeeper's desk. There Victoria put a bullet into a scar belly who hesitated getting out of our way. Then for no other reason than to announce we weren't to be quibbled with, she gut shot a black robe who was standing at the cave's mouth.

With five stock-still black robes staring at us, we pushed through the palisades gate and onto the road. Zhou and I were blinded by searing daylight, and I put my hand on Victoria's shoulder, and Zhou's hand was on my shoulder, so she could lead us out like a locomotive.

We weren't killed and we weren't caught, and there's an explanation for both them startling circumstances. No firearms were allowed within the palisades or down in the pit because of the danger of a patient getting hold of one. So we walked out with just the persuasion of Victoria's revolver. And we weren't caught, despite what I later learned was the largest manhunt in the Celestial Kingdom's history, because at a crossroads a hundred yards from the palisades, we turned west and pointed ourselves at central Asia, rather than east toward the nearest port. That we might venture further into the kingdom did not cross the hunters' minds. We walked what I guessed was five miles, and found the peasant's hut.

Sun hot on my arms and shoulders, I stared through the window at Victoria a moment more before entering the hut again. Zhou had taken out his dentures and was using the peasant's knife to pry out a diamond. He spoke quickly to the fellow, then handed him the gem. The peasant held it in his hand for a long while, as if afraid to touch it with a finger. He might never before have seen a diamond. Then he slowly and reverentially closed his hand over it. He rose, nodded to Zhou, and disappeared from the hut.

Cobbler's Wax began sputtering, his hand squeezing his throat. I went to him and peeled his fingers away, then held his hand. Victoria spoke to him quietly. His eyes bobbed left and right. I don't know if he was seeing us. His words were broken and strange, neither English nor Mandarin. Victoria dipped her hand into a bucket of water to wet his brow. Wax's eyes closed again.

The peasant returned with a pot filled with rice and nims of pork and small red peppers. I don't eat pork, of course, and in fact I don't eat anything mixed with pork, and I don't touch a knife that's cut pork. When the fellow saw this, he produced a flat bread, so I didn't go hungry. I don't favor peppers either, by the way, because they repeat on me. Zhou ate his meal with his dentures back in place, one sparkler less than usual.

We stayed with that old fellow five days. During that time Cobbler's Wax started to come around, and would sometimes say a sentence or two that made sense. He held a hand to his left ear most of the time, as it was in considerable pain. Night and day Victoria nursed us. On the fifth day, we bid our host goodbye and started southwest. Zhou carried Cobbler's Wax piggyback much of the first day, but Wax could walk thereafter. Wax was the smartest fellow I'd ever met—Teddy Roosevelt would take offense but it's true—and I was pure glad when a few days later his mind seemed to be all the way back. He still cried out at night, though. We all did, except Victoria, who was always there when we did.

We didn't talk much, just tramped along. I do believe now, looking back, that the three of us dared not utter a word about the pit, lest it somehow snatch us back. We had escaped but to speak of the cursed abyss would tempt capricious fate.

After four days of walking, Zhou pried another diamond loose, and purchased a cart and mule. We took turns walking alongside the animal, while the others rode. Victoria always insisted on her shift as a skinner despite Zhou's entreaties that he be allowed the honor of taking her shift. A rough glass bead, shoved in by Demon's Daughter, finally worked its way out of Wax's ear, and his earaches left him.

A full week passed before I could gather the mental stamina to ask Victoria how she had come to China. We were walking on a rutted road past a dusty landscape, nothing but yellow brown in all directions, earth and sky. Yesterday's sandstorm still ringed the sun and made the distance a dun haze. To our left was a village carved out of loess cliffs. The cave dwellers made a sparse living by selling weak lemonade and rice pilau to travelers. Victoria was still wearing her brown robe.

She said, "Even though my parents have lost all their money, my father still has influence with our Church of England bishop."

"I thought your folks had enough money to grease the fat sow's lug. They lost it all?"

"Mother and father are almost penniless. They have had to let their manor house, and they've given papers to all the domestics. They've moved from the country into a commonwall house in Hyde Park, a small thing with a garden out back hardly big enough for a tree. Father has had to join a bank. They've had to sell their winter villa in Tuscany and their interest in the African coffee plantation."

"How'd that happen?"

She hesitated. "A bad investment. Poppa saw a chance to triple his wealth, and so he went out on a limb." Victoria brushed a tear from her eye. At least, I thought she did. Her face was under the hood. "The limb was sawed off behind him."

"What'd he invest in? What could have proven to be such a terrible risk?"

"I'm quite embarrassed to talk about it. It's so unseemly."

"I don't mean to pry."

"Opium, Woodrow."

"Opium?"

"My father came into league with a promoter of Far East trade. At the promoter's direction, my father paid for a ship to sail from England to the Far East. Poppa invested all he had in that ship, even mortgaged his Scottish hunting lodge. When the vessel sailed down the Thames, her cargo was English manufactured goods, which it traded for opium in Siam. And then it sailed for China to trade the opium for silk and spices. Fantastic sums were to be made. But the vessel never offloaded its cargo. It was a total loss."

My stomach rolled over. "What was the name of your dad's ship?"

"The *Princess Eugenia*. When she burned in Shinha harbor she bankrupted our family."

Oh, Lordy.

"But my father still had a few chits with the bishop. I told Poppa that I wanted to go to China as a missionary. In any circumstance but penury, father would have railed against his daughter's insanity, but he was broken in spirit, and he let me go."

"Did you know I was in China? Being held a prisoner?"

She gazed up at me with her pale blue eyes. "Woodrow, why else would I come here?"

I felt a curious heat rising from her as she stared at me.

"How'd you know where I was?"

"I received a letter," she explained. "Such a letter, all soiled and crinkled, and written on bark paper. I knew before even opening the letter that it had made a long and desperate journey. And when I tore it open, I saw that it had been in transit eight months. From your Prince Tuan. Written in the queen's English, and addressed to me as if you and he and I were a family who knew no comfort but each other and could rely on nobody but ourselves."

Oh, my. Now a slave in the mountainous frontier, the prince had sent a message to Victoria. Who could calculate at what risk and cost? May the Merciful One bestow peace on my eternal friend Prince Tuan.

I was to learn later that the prince had also sent letters to Theodore

Roosevelt and Diamond Jim Brady. Them messages never arrived. Only Victoria's made it through.

"So I visited the bishop," she continued. "I told him I wanted to go to China. He asked rather pointedly why I didn't visit the Cunard office rather than a house of God. I set out my dilemma. Not only did I need to get to China but once there I needed to visit a place where only people of God are allowed in. And, in light of my father's past support of the bishopric, the bishop commissioned me a missionary, with all the proper documents, made out, at my request, to Victor Littlewood."

"You disguised yourself as a man?"

"Only after I reached Shanghai. No Anglican missionary wears a hooded robe but the Chinese never questioned it. I darkened my skin a little with crushed pencil. I didn't really resemble a man but under the hood my face was hard to see."

"And how'd you get into the pit?"

"I traveled to Peking on the train with several American missionaries. I kept to myself, and I think those Americans thought I'd taken a vow of silence. Prince Tuan had written that the Third Assistant Commissioner for Internal Rescripts was the bureaucrat to negotiate with. I found him in his office near the Forbidden City's Dragon Gate."

"Negotiate?" I asked. "What did you have to negotiate with?"

"Such a question would make any one else blush, Woodrow," she said in an iron voice. "I was penniless but I have seen too much and endured too much to allow a venal bureaucrat to deter me. I offered the only thing I had."

Enough said on that subject, I suppose.

"He accepted the offer," she said, "and shortly thereafter, he issued me the documents and—"

"How shortly thereafter?" I blurted.

She beamed at me. "Do you remember how skilled I am, Woodrow?"

"I almost died that night, thanks to you."

She laughed gaily. "It was a matter of a moment, and the Third Assistant Commissioner didn't even get out of his trousers, he was so excited. He soiled his pants instead of me. He was red with embarrassment, and quickly issued papers allowing me to enter the Shalin Subterranean Hospital for Incurables, for that is what your pit is officially called."

I reached for her hand. I never really thanked Victoria Littlewood for rescuing me, by the way. Not for lack of trying. Her pluck and boldness were so grand and my plight in that pit so horrendous that any words I thought up were wan and insufficient. I just held her hand a lot, and I think she understood.

THE TOWN OF Lanzhou, along the banks of the Yellow River with brown hills on both sides, was ringed with orchards, and when Zhou pried out another diamond from his choppers we feasted on apples, dates, walnuts and grapes. We sold the cart, for the road—which would not be paved for another forty years—had become too rough. That same diamond also purchased four mules broken for riding. We found ourselves in a long line of mules with tea leaves and rolls of silk strapped to their backs. The tea and silk had arrived in Lanzhou on animal-hide rafts but now travel for the traders was to be overland. Some traders had no pack animals. They wore tightly bound clothing with pistols in their belts. We knew them to be carrying gems in purses around their midriffs. With the Qilian Mountains to the south, the caravan made its way along the Hexi Corridor toward the Taklimakan Desert.

At Anxi, at the edge of the desert, we camped with several dozen Mongols who were headed in the opposite direction with their camels laden with carpets and cotton and wool. These were two-humped Bactrian camels, which could each carry 500 pounds, and which were favored over the single-hump animals which couldn't match the Bactrians' pace. The wind was blowing bitterly, as it always did at Anxi, carrying grit from the desert. The Mongols let us share their oxhide wind shelter for the camels and mules. We pitched a tent of hides, which we purchased from them for a diamond. Zhou was beginning to look a bit gaptoothed.

We had eaten a meal of mutton shashlik. Zhou and Cobbler's Wax were asleep in their bedrolls, and Victoria sat near our fire's crimson embers. The wind piped around our tent. She asked, "Woodrow, have you ever examined your life?"

"Examined my life? What's to examine?"

"Have you ever wondered why your life is such a careening odyssey?"

"Bad luck?"

"You aren't much of a philosopher, are you?" she asked sweetly.

"The small measure of brain that was granted to me has been entirely occupied with keeping myself alive, Victoria. I've never had any gray matter to spare to wonder much about my life. But mostly I think my peculiar journey was because of a woman."

"Me?" she protested with a smile. "Surely not me. Your travails began long before you met me."

"Not you. Another woman."

She looked disappointed for some reason.

I explained, "A woman—she was just a girl back then—I met in Boston. I didn't actually meet her. I met her horse."

I told her all about Amy Balfour. About our first meeting outside Joe Lowe's Museum and Sporting Palace, and how, after a few missteps involving her, I ended up in the cursed cavalry. Then about her wedding, and how I'd poisoned her and all her guests, and how I found myself on a ship to Europe. Then how I ran into Amy again in Buenos Aires, and how she had duped me into entering the bullring.

After I concluded this sorry tale, she said, "Well, there's a simple explanation for your troubles, Woodrow."

"Yes?"

"You are an utter moron."

"I've been told that before."

"How could you do this to yourself? A proud man like you, humbled again and again before this Boston woman?"

I shook my head. "How could I do it? I've always found it rather easy."

"What hold can she possibly have on you?"

Again I wagged my head. "I concluded long ago that my attraction to her was nature's way, and so inevitable. I can no more resist making a demonstration in front of her than water can resist turning to ice."

Now it was her turn to shake her head, and she sighed loudly. "Woodrow, you need to forget that awful woman." She rose from the fire and stepped to her bedroll.

I put away my spoon, and looked for my blankets. But they weren't where I had placed them. I looked around the small tent. They were gone.

Under her blankets, Victoria said, "I threw out your blankets. They were filthy, and probably had lice, knowing you."

"Where am I to sleep?"

She lightly stroked her chin. Her eyes were alight, reflecting the red embers. "Well, let's use your pittance of gray matter on this, shall we? There are still three bedrolls here. Zhou is in one of them."

I wet my lips. I think Victoria was enjoying herself but I couldn't be sure. The tent was now too dark for me to see her expression.

"He's too big to share a bedroll with," I said. "And he'd roll over and crush me, most likely."

She said, "And then there is Wax's bedroll."

"He's a eunuch. I wouldn't know what to expect."

"And so there's my bedroll."

"Yes?"

"There's lots of room in here, Woodrow." She moved to one side and pulled back the top blanket.

"I'm still weak from my time in the pit, Victoria."

"I'll be gentle."

I removed my clothes, turning my back to her as I did so, of course. And then I slid between the blankets next to her.

She roughly grabbed my head. "Even though I've never met her, I detest that red-haired Boston tramp, Woodrow. And I'm going to make you forget her."

And she did, for a while. I like to think I'm the strong and silent type but some of the Mongol men who had been in nearby tents cuffed my arms the next day, grinning knowingly. Zhou and Cobbler's Wax were ever chivalrous, and never let on they were anything but asleep. Except that Zhou smiled and nodded at us all the time. I think he approved.

THE SILK ROAD branched at Anxi. We enjoyed Mongol company, and so chose the northern route, where we'd see more of them fine people. The journey from Anxi to Hami took twelve days. I rode my mule, slumped over, often asleep, too tired from my nightly visits to Victoria's bedroll to stay awake. We made way for herds of small, hardy horses headed toward the Middle Kingdom, prodded along by Mongol traders.

Our route was along the northern edge of the Taklimakan Desert, hard against the Tian Mountains. Between Turpan and Korla is the Dry Ditch, a narrow road between ochre and gray hills. In many places the road had been washed away by flashfloods that had poured down from the barren hills. It is said of the gulch that the God of the Flaming

Mountains rescues the worthy by scattering pearls along the path, which turn to thirst-quenching Turpan grapes.

One night, after a dinner of mutton dumplings and unleavened nan bread, Victoria asked me, "What are you going to do when you get back to the United States?"

Our tent was among the tall grass on a soda-whitened marsh near Baghrach Lake. Sharp blades of grass tapped the tent, sounding like rain.

"I'm going to Anguilla."

"Where is that?"

"It's an island in the Caribbean Sea."

"Why go there?"

"I'd tell you, but you'll call me a moron again."

She arced her eyebrows invitingly. "I won't. I promise."

"You really promise?"

"Trust me."

So I told her about Bruce Twig-Smathers, and his grandfather, Captain Twig-Smathers, and the captain's ship, *The Golden Ram*, and how I'd come across the map, and how the treasure awaited me in the cave on Anguilla.

Finally she exclaimed, "Woodrow, you are a moron."

"You promised . . ."

"The story you told me—and your astonishing credulity in believing it—suspends any promise I made. How can you possibly believe that nonsense? How can you possibly arrange your life according to such a fairy tale? I'm traveling with a fool."

That night she tossed me a blanket, so I had to sleep by myself. I couldn't tell her how that treasure had sustained me during my time in the pit—how it was a tiny glitter of hope in a bleak world—and that how, even now, that buried fortune urged me on across Asia.

Next day she dug her heels into her mule and rode on ahead, which put Zhou into a quandary. He didn't like being far away from either of us. So he clicked his mule, and divided the distance, riding along the rest of the day precisely halfway between us.

She had calmed some by that evening. And after I washed my spoon in the sand, I braved a glance toward her. She was lying between the blankets, and she pulled down the top one for me. She smiled. I was relieved.

Day after day, week after week, we traveled. Then we spent a snowy

January with the Kirghiz in the Pamir Mountains, the Roof of the World, where for several diamonds the tribesmen rented us a white yurt that resembled an enormous mushroom, and filled it with felt rugs and reed mats decorated with dyed wool thread. We ate sun-dried cheese balls and bread made from mutton fat and flour.

Victoria and Cobbler's Wax and Zhou occasionally drank fermented mare's milk wine, and had lively parties, telling stories and laughing. I forewent the alcohol, of course, following the Holy Strictures, which was damned hard on this Irishman, if I may be frank. Laughter isn't forbidden, though, and I had my share of it. One night, Victoria, a little tipsy, performed a veil dance for us. Zhou and Cobbler's Wax stared at her with open mouths. Rather than wait for the fire to die down, which was usually the signal to head for our bedrolls, I threw water on the fire, and scrambled between the blankets, and waited impatiently for Victoria to slip out of her clothes and climb in next to me, and I was rewarded hugely. Something about a veil dance had an effect on both of us.

We decamped the Pamir Mountains when the bitter winds subsided, and marched through Samarkand and Bukhara and Merv, and on into Persia. The rigorous walking and riding transformed Victoria. She had begun our journey looking like a proper British lady, delicate features on a porcelain face, with thin arms and lean legs. But in them months she took on a bronze color and became muscular. Often she would ride with her gold hair trailing behind her. She was an accomplished rider, even on a mule. She made that cantankerous, bony mule look graceful. She would catch me staring and grin at me, her teeth flashing in the sun. She was a delightful mirage, a tonic to the desert.

In Persia we made a mistake. For centuries the Silk Road has been littered with the bones of them who had made such errors. We were passing Persian merchants, whose cargoes included oils from frankincense and myrrh, indigo dyes, and purple mascara from murex shells. We were in the foothills of the Elburz Mountains, just south of the Caspian Sea. I asked Cobbler's Wax why his ruby ring and Zhou's proximity medal and his diamond dentures hadn't been stolen during their stay in the pit.

Cobbler's Wax brought up his ring to study it and to compose his answer. Finally he replied, "I believe that even hell has its ethos. Demon's Daughter was empowered to strip us of our flesh and our humanity but it was against the rules to steal anything else. The pit was run according to a daft logic of its own."

Riding along next to him, the giant Zhou nodded. He was now under-standing English. The giant had been wearing the medal under his shirt so as not to tempt bandits. He pulled it out and let it glint in the sun. I knew he was praying that his enamel teeth would issue forth sufficient gems to take us all the way west. He loathed the thought of having to dig into his medal, and I hoped I'd never have to ask him.

Certain eyes on passing horses also caught the reflection of the medal.

That night we lay close by a fire as it was frosty. How the desert could be so cold at night was something I never understood when I was in the welt-raising cavalry. But I had learned a few other things in the cavalry, and one of them was to post a sentry. I hadn't bothered when we were among the Mongols and the Kirghiz, as they were trustworthy folks, and we were among so many of them. But in the desert, the caravans were stretched out, and on many nights, our group bivouacked alone. This was one of them. And them endless sands were filled with people who'd steal the cross off an ass's back.

I heard a faint clicking. My eyes came open. Cobbler's Wax was at his post twenty yards from the fire and was making a cricket's noise with his tongue. I nudged Victoria, who came awake instantly and reached for the Webley in the blanket she had rolled up for a pillow. Keeping my profile low, I rolled out of the bedroll and tapped Zhou's shoulder. His eyes opened but he lay there flat, looking at me. I motioned in the direction I thought I heard soft pads on stone and sand. His bald and tattooed head gleamed in the firelight.

With a sudden whoop, the bandits came in at us, five of them, daggers glinting like beacons in the firelight. One moment the night was black, the next it was filled with cutthroats looking for Zhou's proximity medal. Victoria shot one through the belly but before she could fire again—and she was mighty quick on the trigger, if you'll remember—Zhou rose from his blanket like a rake that's been stepped on, shot his fingers into a bandit's throat just below the man's Adam's apple, grabbed that same robber under his chin with his other hand, and ripped the fellow's head off.

Now when I say he ripped his head off, I'm not talking in slang. I mean Zhou separated the robber's head from his spine so that there was air between the two. Then Zhou held up the head like a prize. It dripped blood and gore in the firelight.

Just as quickly as the bandits had come, they fled again, vanishing in the night, wailing in fear. The dead remained at our feet, of course.

That next morning, Zhou mounted that head on a stick and carried it above him like a banner, and he did so until we were out of Persia. We were never bothered again, needless to say.

We arrived in Beirut on January 26, 1905, after seventeen months on the Silk Road. At the time, Beirut was run by the Turks, who are enormously hospitable if paid enormous sums. Fortunately, a few diamonds still remained between Zhou's gums.

Just before we boarded a boat for Athens, I was told by the manager of the Beirut Hotel that Teddy Roosevelt was president.

"President of what?" I asked blandly, thinking maybe the Lower Manhattan Order of Elks.

"President of the United States of America."

I laughed and dug my elbow into the fellow's ribs, for which most Turks will slit your throat. But the manager was accustomed to strange travelers. He showed me a half-year-old copy of the New York *Post*, and there was Teddy Roosevelt, splintering a magnum of champagne over the prow of a new Navy ship. The caption began, PRESIDENT ROOSEVELT ARRIVED FROM THE WHITE HOUSE TO LAUNCH . . .

That mouth-full-of-teeth was president of the United States? I could scarcely credit my eyes. How in the world had that happened? And I was traveling back there? Later in the day Victoria and Zhou and Cobbler's Wax had to fairly carry me up the gangplank onto the boat.

TWENTY

The Treasure

THE RESIDENCE HAS been called the White House ever since Theodore Roosevelt became the first president to engrave the name on his stationery. I told the guard at the White House gate my name, more for curiosity than anything else, and was surprised when he immediately waved me through and pointed up the drive.

I had to convince him to let Zhou in, who despite his Western clothes still looked much the heathen, with his bald and tattooed head and his sloping eyes. I had noticed since returning to the United States that people gave me a wide berth—that is, even a wider berth—due to the mountainous and brawny Chinee who always walked on my heels. We strolled up the drive, then under the porte-cochere on the north side, passing high Ionic columns.

We were shown into the Green Room, and I guess I didn't really believe he was president until that moment. Teddy Roosevelt paced back and forth in front of two Empire chairs, dictating to a secretary who stood to one side holding a notebook. Teddy gripped a piece of paper as if he were choking the life out of it.

He looked up at me, but he didn't break his pace. "Woodrow, I want you to keep these nuts off me. Look at this letter." He slapped the paper in his hand. "I've made some formidable enemies in my time. Standard Oil. The Spanish. Mark Hanna. And now it's the New York apple growers who threaten me. They say they're going to raise a ruckus at my inauguration. Damn their impertinence." He fairly threw the letter into my hands. "You keep them away from me."

He paced another moment, lost in thought. He was wearing a formal black coat and gray trousers with black piping. A top hat was on the table between the Empire chairs. It was March 4, 1905, the day of Teddy's second inauguration. He stopped, his eyes finding Zhou.

"Who's the giant, Woodrow?"

"He's my bodyguard. So he tells me."

Roosevelt barked, "You mean, my bodyguard has a bodyguard?"

"I'm afraid so, sir. And I'm a lot better protected than you'll ever be."

He laughed, grabbed his top hat, and started out of the room with that curious stiff-legged rooster's gait of his. He called back, "Be on the portico in ten minutes. And if that big fellow has to come along, get him a hat so my wife doesn't burst an artery when she sees the tattoos on his head." His secretary followed him out of the room like Zhou follows me out of every room.

Now, does it strike you as strange that Teddy acted as if he'd just seen me the day before, when in fact he hadn't laid his bottle-bottomed eyes on me since the charge up San Juan Hill, six and a half years before? Might he have asked where in thunderation I'd been all that time? And how a tattooed giant Chinee had come to adopt me? Didn't seem to cross Teddy's mind. Well, he had a lot on his mind, I'm sure, what with the apple growers upset at him.

Zhou and I found a cart of tiny sandwiches with the crusts cut off on a tray out in the hallway. I ate six of them, and Zhou ate six pounds of them, and there weren't a single sandwich left when he finally licked his fingers clean. Then he resumed his principal occupation of the morning, other than watching me, which was tugging at his collar and necktie.

A few minutes later Zhou and I appeared at the portico, where I was told by some colonel that I was to walk alongside the president's carriage and keep everybody away from it. Sounded simple, and so it was. Teddy bounded onto the carriage, then turned to give a hand to Edith, and then his daughter Alice, a genuine looker. The driver swatted the horses, and off we went, Zhou behind me, felt hat on his head. A military escort—two hundred horsemen and marchers—picked us up at Lafayette Square.

About halfway to the Capitol Building, huge crowds cheering all along the way, Teddy looked down at me from the carriage and asked, "Have you found your fortune, Woodrow?"

"Not yet, sir."

"A wife?"

"No, sir."

"Then what precisely are you doing each time you disappear?"

So he had noticed my absence after all. "I scarcely know, sir."

"What happened to your thumb?" the president asked. "It's crooked."

"A lady broke it." The Demon's Daughter.

"Same woman who cut your cheek?"

I hadn't ever told him about Lady Elizabeth. I wondered how he knew. "Different lady, sir."

"You want me to chaperone your next date, Woodrow? Maybe I can help prevent some of this damage."

I suppose he was being funny. He turned to wave at the crowds. The cherry trees were blooming, and a warm spring wind ruffled my coat. Back then presidential inaugurations were held in March. Teddy looked just like I'd last left him. A few new lines around his eyes, the hair a little gray. But the essence of Teddy Roosevelt had always been his energy. Were you not to know better, you'd swear he was an eighteen-year-old buck up on that carriage. He was as animated as ever. He stood in the carriage, waving, signaling, giving the thumbs up and the V-for-victory signal, dueling the sun with his immense smile.

Half an hour later Teddy was sworn in on a podium in front of the Capitol Building. I stood next to him, watching the crowd, just as he'd told me to do. That's when that photograph you have was taken. Zhou was behind the podium, making sure nobody snuck up on me, so he's not shown in your photo.

Later that afternoon, Theodore Roosevelt greeted well-wishers at the White House. The line of people who wanted to pump his hand ran along Pennsylvania Avenue as far as Seventeenth Street, then turned south for another half-mile. At the head of the line were the foreign potentates; viscounts and barons bringing greetings from their sovereigns. Then came military officers, with their handlebar mustaches, plumed helmets, gold braid and medals. Then came the Supreme Court justices and members of Congress, and finally the rabble, for which Teddy increased the pace of his handshaking, and I counted fifty shakes a minute.

"How do you do? How do you do? How do you do?"

Nobody in line got a chance to answer to Teddy's face because officers of the White House detail pushed the line along at a brisk pace.

I was watching these well-wishers, fairly mesmerized by the unending line of passing folks and Teddy's steady "How do you do?" when sud-

denly one of the greeters shouted, "Keep Canadian apples out of the
United States," and hurled an apple pie at the president.

Sometimes I'm regrettably swift afoot. I stepped between Teddy and
that fellow, and caught the apple pie full in the chops.

I coughed and gasped, and wiped the pastry from my face. I finally
cleared my eyes of apple goo, and saw that Zhou was holding the pie
thrower by his shirt, a dagger point a quarter-inch from the fellow's eye.
Zhou's face was contorted with rage, his bulbous neck quivering and his
mouth pulled taut. He was looking at me, his black eyes resembling
bullets, waiting my signal to carve the man's eyeballs out. The pie
thrower hung there, feet entirely off the ground, his hands around
Zhou's wrist to no effect, whimpering in fear.

I couldn't say anything because my mouth was full of pie. It was tasty
but could have been a tad sweeter, as I recall. I held up my hand, and
Zhou reluctantly lowered the orchardist. Officers of the White House
detail hauled the pie-thrower away.

"How do you do? How do you do?" Teddy was a metronome. I don't
know if he even saw the pie-thrower or his product. Someone handed
me a handkerchief, and after a fashion I was able to resume my
bodyguarding duties.

Later that day, Teddy reviewed a military procession from a grandstand in front of the White House. And that night he, Edith, Alice,
Zhou and I attended the inaugural ball at the Pension Building. Zhou
was a curiosity at the ball, where crowds gathered around and pointed at
his bald, tattooed head.

That evening, Teddy found himself with no hands to shake for a
moment, so I asked him, "Sir, am I still in the military service?"

"Of course. Why do you think your army pay has been deposited at
the Morgan Bank in New York all these years?"

"I have a bank account? With some funds in it?" Victoria and Cobbler's Wax and Zhou and I were staying at the Hastings Hotel in Washington, and a week's lodging had cost us the last diamond in Zhou's
mouth. "Six years of corporal's pay?" I tried to figure it in my head.

The president said, "Four years ago I promoted you to sergeant in
absentia."

Sergeant in absentia? I'd never heard of that rank. Was it something
like corporal general?

I asked, "Will that money get me to Anguilla?"

"Woodrow, are you going to desert again?"

"I've got one more journey in me. To Anguilla. Me and my entourage."

"No fortune, no wife, but an entourage?"

I nodded. "Something like that."

A diplomat with a pointed beard and his bejeweled wife stepped between Teddy and me. I glanced around. Long ropes of pearls had come into fashion, and the ballroom must have had a mile of them. I thought of Old Buddha and her pearl ropes. Perfume hung in the room like Cuban swamp gas. There weren't a callus or scar or tattoo in the entire room, save for Zhou's and mine, and we had plenty.

"How do you do? How do you do?" At another pause, Teddy said, "I don't suppose it'll do me any good to order you to stick around."

"I've got to get to Anguilla." My words carried more emotion than I ever cared to reveal.

He looked at me, a puzzled expression on his face. Then he said, "Go to Tampa. I'll order a revenue cutter to take you and your entourage to Anguilla. Report back on the state of that island's defenses and navy."

Then he was off, hand outstretched, and was instantly surrounded by congressmen and diplomats and other bootlickers.

It was a kindness, but he was gone before I had the chance to thank him.

FROM THE HIGHEST point on Anguilla, the island of St. Maarten is visible ten miles to the south. Our eyes weren't on St. Maarten, though.

I recited, "One mile south of the island's highest peak is a pool."

We descended the slope, hardly a peak, not even much of a hill, called Flag Hill. We pressed through guava thickets. Below us to the west, in an area called Sandy Ground, were twenty or so thatch huts. Our cutter was moored in the bay there, patiently waiting for us, black smoke rising from its stack.

I counted each step, figuring that at about four feet per step I would reach the pond at step thirteen hundred. I had to walk around several yagruma trees, with their two-tone leaves that make it look like snow has dusted the trees. A killdeer's piping and the scent of jacaranda carried to us in the idle wind. We passed a bank of wild avocados, then a spate of mango trees. We had to dodge guava thickets.

"Woodrow, are you prepared for the worst?" Victoria asked, two steps behind me.

"Questions like that will make me lose my count."

She was wearing a wide-brimmed straw hat held in place with a blue ribbon around her neck, a khaki shirt and army trousers. Zhou and Cobbler's Wax followed, ducks in a row.

She asked, "You know this mission is folly, don't you?"

"I'll find out for sure in short order."

"Woodrow, I'm worried about you." She caught up to me and turned me by my shoulders. Her eyes were the color of the sea. "You have planned and dreamed about this mysterious treasure for so long. What if nothing is in that hole? What are you going to do then?"

"It's there, under that rock."

I tried to start down the incline again, but she reached for my hands and brought them up and gently held them. "I want you to know that no matter what is under that boulder—something or nothing—you'll still have me."

I dipped my chin. "It's there, Victoria. It has to be."

Faith is a bizarre phenomenon. My faith in that treasure had grown over time, as my circumstances had worsened. Evidence of the treasure's existence was no stronger now than when I had first heard of it. Yet I had traveled the intellectual pilgrimage of a convert to a faith: from scoffing to skepticism to hope to rabid certainty. So confident was I that jewels and pieces of eight lay under the stone with the hourglass mark that I had mentally spent the money. Victoria was going to love her diamond necklace that, as immense as them diamonds would be, could not outshine her blue eyes. I was going to replace the gems in Zhou's teeth. And a hundred other noble expenditures.

I tramped on, counting steadily. The ground was stony and dry. Behind me, Victoria sighed loudly. The sun was weighty and brilliant, high over head. Sweat slipped down the side of my face. I looked back at Zhou and Cobbler's Wax. They, too, were sure I was on a fool's errand. But they hiked along behind me, mopping their brows and passing a water jug back and forth. Zhou carried a prybar and Cobbler's Wax had a short-handled pickax over his shoulder, both borrowed from the cutter's tool locker. Zhou was embarrassed by his dentures, which now contained only holes instead of gems.

I smelled the pool before I saw it, a fetid, brown scent that came in the wind. My mind had visited this pool many times over the years, and had painted it in lush blues and greens, with tropical ferns, orchids, lilies and goldfish, maybe a swan or two. Instead, we came to a pocket of mud with a sheen of water across it, perhaps twenty feet across, with banks of pea gravel and some larger stones, and not a plant of any sort except one royal palm that had shed several dry fronds onto the banks near a half-submerged, rotted fruit crate.

I walked around the pond and said from memory, "One hundred thirty yards farther south is a two-man stone with an hourglass mark. Under the stone."

Again I began to count. A grove of belly palms, with bulges on their trunks where water is collected, blocked our way, so I interrupted my count to walk around the palms, then resumed the count. "Fifty-five, fifty-six, fifty-seven . . ."

At pace number ninety we came to the top of a spink. To the south I could see the huts of Blowing Point, and Rendezvous Bay's gentle curve of white beaches.

Spink is Irish for a precipice, to save you from asking.

There weren't any bushes to gain handholds, so I climbed down slowly, gripping the corners of sharp rocks for anchors, my boots slipping on the boulders that formed the bluff. This bluff weren't much of an edifice, maybe fifty vertical feet. Patches of prickly pear and salt grass clung to purses of soil between the boulders. I looked above me. Victoria and Cobbler's Wax and Zhou were backlit by the high sun, their faces lost in the dark contrast. Victoria started down after me, loosening some scree with her shoes. At the bottom of the precipice was a stony field with a few banana trees and pineapple plants.

Near the base of the bluff the boulders were larger, many the size of desks. I figured I was now about 130 yards south of the mud puddle. I searched the boulder under my hands, then the stones to the left and right, not finding the hourglass. Zhou and Cobbler's Wax also searched. Victoria sat on a rock and stared down at me, her elbows on her knees, an expression of infinite compassion on her face.

I confess to having worked myself into a lather by that point. I had learned of the treasure in 1889, sixteen years before. In all my years in the Sudan and in all the time in Daughter's pit, my knowledge of the treasure was the only thing of value left to me. In those dark times, the prospect—no, the certainty—of the treasure had given me something to live for, had given me strength when otherwise I might have listened to the pain and despair and allowed myself to slip away from this life. My hands shook as they brushed aside dust and twigs. I frantically searched for the hourglass, breathing the sweet air of imminent redemption and victory.

I found it. I found the hourglass mark, there under my fingers, no larger than a swallow, chipped out of the rock with a sharp instrument, just a shallow mark, something the unknowing eye would pass over.

"It's here," I called in a voice I strove to render firm. "Zhou, bring the prybar."

I glanced up the bluff to Victoria. I asked with unabashed pleasure, "What have I been saying for so long? Do you believe me now?"

She might have shaken her head, I couldn't tell in the sun.

The giant scurried along the rock to me, then wedged the bar's tip between the hourglass rock and the neighboring boulder. Zhou grabbed the bar high, then brought his weight down on it. The stone budged, but just enough to loosen some dust at its edge. Cobbler's Wax positioned himself on the bluff above Zhou to plant his feet on the top of the stone, while I stood next to Zhou and grabbed the bar just below his hands.

I called, "One, two, three, heave."

We grunted in unison. The rock shifted. Zhou and I stabbed the bar deeper into the resulting crack, and we pulled down again. The stone inched away from the other boulders. Wax's face was red from his effort pushing with his feet.

The stone was about as big as Zhou. We quickly positioned the bar again, and heaved away. The boulder slowly rose from its slot, and teetered on the stone below it. With an effort that made the cords in his neck stand out, Cobbler's Wax shoved with his legs, and the boulder slowly swung out into space, then rolled loudly down to the base of the bluff, leaving a trail of dust in the air behind. The boulder came to rest among dozens just like it, and the instant the stone stopped moving it was difficult to distinguish from all the others.

Revealed to our gaze was an excavation little wider than my shoulders, and about four feet high. My eyes were accustomed to the incandescent tropical sun so they couldn't make out anything inside the hole. I held a hand out in front of me, and slowly crawled into the cave. The air tasted of the ages. I scraped along for several feet.

And before I was entirely inside the cave, my hand hit against the far

wall. I felt around. Stone wall was close at hand on all sides. The excavation was less a cave than a pock. My eyes began to reveal the inside of
this small pit, no larger than the inside of an armoire.

My hand brushed something on the floor of the pit. I reached for the
object, and it was instantly and dispiritingly familiar. A bottle. I gripped
it by the neck and held it up to my eyes. No markings were visible in the
dim light. I passed it back to Cobbler's Wax. Now my eyes could make
out the entire vault. Nine more bottles were lined up against the back
wall. I handed them back one at a time to Cobbler's Wax.

Bitter disappointment rose like bile in my throat. I asked for the
pickax, and when it was shoved to me, I chipped away at the rock floor,
then on the far wall, then to both sides, thinking perhaps something
more might lay behind an artfully concealed wall of masonry. I hacked
away desperately, my dreams of fortune painfully receding.

Not until the floor of the pit was littered with chips hewn from the
wall with the pickax did I surrender all hope. I was covered with sweat,
and grains of rock clung to me. Air in the hole had become thick with
my exertions.

Disgraced and defeated, I would have stayed in that hole forever, but I
knew Zhou would drag me out, so I backed out, the pickax in hand. The
sun greeted me at the mouth of the cave, and for a few seconds I
couldn't open my eyes.

Victoria and Zhou and Wax were waiting for me, sitting on boulders
to one side of the cavity. Victoria held an open bottle in one hand, the
stopper in the other. I tried to speak, but my throat closed down, and
only a small groan escaped me. I dropped to a rock next to Victoria and
held my head in my hands.

"It's rum," she said quietly. "Ten bottles of rum."

I shook my head, my hands over my eyes. God, I didn't want them to
see me weep.

Victoria put her arm around my shoulders. "We aren't any worse off
than we were an hour ago, Woodrow."

I stared into my hands.

She said, "And just like I said, you've still got me."

Cobbler's Wax added, "And me. And Zhou."

I found Victoria's hand and gripped it fiercely.

We sat on them boulders half an hour. And during that time my heart
calcified. I have no other word for it. When I at last rose and started

back up the precipice, I was capable of things I would never before have dared. Cruel disappointment and frustration had in those few minutes made me as hard as the Rock of Cashel.

"Where are you going, Woodrow?" Victoria called. She and the others scrambled up the slope after me.

"I am going after my fortune."

"Woodrow, listen," she said as she tried to catch up. "Don't you think . . ."

"And this time," I growled, "I damn sure know where it is."

TWENTY-ONE

Amy Again

THE BUTLER—THAT same snoot named Edgar who I last saw in Buenos Aires—opened the door.

I gave him my card. He looked at it closely, perhaps judging the quality of the print and paper. Then he looked over my shoulder at Cobbler's Wax and Zhou.

"She is expecting you," he said finally. "Do come in."

He held up his hand to stop Cobbler's Wax. "Your servants will have to wait on the porch, sir."

"I certainly understand your concern about servants in the house. But I will wait on the porch with them. And your missus will have to meet with us on the porch."

Biting his lower lip, he weighed the alternatives. "Perhaps they can enter, then."

I stepped by him into the hallway, removed my white gloves and hat, and passed them to Edgar without looking at him. I had never before been in this home, though trying to break into it had cost me all them years into the ball-busting cavalry.

"If you will have a chair in the sitting room," Edgar said with his vaguely British accent, "I'll call Mrs. Malcolm."

I entered the sitting room, Cobbler's Wax and Zhou close behind. I was wearing a silk jacket and calf shoes. The cufflinks were diamonds. The nosegay pin in my lapel also sported a diamond, this one only a little smaller than my cauliflower ear. The pin held a small red rose in place.

Wax placed a one-foot square of silk on a fanback chair, which I sat on. The chair was near a green marble fireplace mantel on which was a two-hundred-year-old kingwood bracket clock and three crystal candlestick holders. Matching Grecian urns were stationed on the floor at the ends of the mantel. Cobbler's Wax dutifully stood at my elbow while Zhou positioned himself opposite me, to the left of the door, out of sight of anyone entering the room.

I surveyed the room, the place of so many of my youthful fantasies, dreams of me on one knee, asking for her hand. In one corner was an ebony grand piano under an orange-and-green leaded-glass lamp. One of them new telephones was on a pedestal table near a leather wing chair. To my right was a japanned cabinet-on-stand made of rosewood with silver hinges. The Persian rug was large enough to fill the room to the corners, and was in reds and lime green. Two red leather club chairs were around a table in another corner. Red draperies were heavy and swooping, with long matching cords with tassels tipped in yellow thread. The fireplace had no ashes in it, and the three Chinese vases had no flowers. The sitting room was seldom visited, it looked like.

"Mr. Lowe, how kind of you to visit." Amy Balfour Malcolm swept into the room.

She was wearing a beige walking dress, with large buttons all down the front. The waistline was high and emphasized her bosom. Her hair was still afire, still that befuddling swirl of red and gold, and was held in place with a pearl-studded turtlewood barrette. She was about forty years old now, but her vibrant red hair and luminous smile made her seem younger. Webs of tiny lines were at the corners of her eyes, but they only added maturity to her beauty.

"It was gracious of you to receive me, madam."

"How could I refuse, after your gallant gift." She held out her right hand to display a two-carat diamond ring in a white gold mounting. "I fairly had the vapors when I opened the box the messenger brought. So gracious of you." On her other hand was her wedding ring, even larger than my gift.

"It was the least I could do, I assure you. After the favor you and your brother did for me . . ." I waved away further comment on that subject. "Did you have the opportunity to contact him? I would like to thank him in person, also." I patterned my accent after Teddy Roosevelt's. I was less Boston Irish than I had ever sounded in my life. I imitated a New York Brahmin. And if it sounded forced—like the butler's phony English accent—all the better.

Dickie Balfour walked in, twirling a walnut walking stick with a silver head inlaid with a dozen small diamonds. "And I thank you too, old chap." He held up my gift to him. "Diamonds in a walking stick. Some of the old windbags at my club have ivory and silver tipped sticks, but no diamonds. I'll have one-upped them this time." He chortled.

He hadn't gained a pound, was still as thin as a firehose. He was wearing black slacks and a shirt with French cuffs but no tie. His hair was slicked back as always, but was now parted to one side—more the fashion—instead of in the center. His pencil mustache was even smaller now, clipped above his lip. Time had not treated Dickie Balfour as well as his sister. Pink veins lined his nose, and gray crescent bags were under his eyes. A nick was on his chin from shaving that morning. His hands shook, just a little. He had the look of a dissolute. Too much whiskey, too many women, and all too late at night.

I held up a finger apologetically, and opened my mouth, my eyes squinting, about to sneeze. Cobbler's Wax instantly stepped forth and held a silk handkerchief to my nose. I sneezed into it.

His eyebrows high on his forehead, Dickie asked, "This fellow catches your sneezes?"

"A custom in the Orient. A gentleman does not concern himself with the nose's effluent."

"Is he your man?" Amy asked. She sat on a tête-à-tête near me.

"Yes, one of a few I picked up in China." I pointed over their shoulders. "So is he."

Amy and her brother turned, and for the first time saw Zhou. Amy's mouth opened involuntarily, and Dickie gasped aloud.

"Who is he?" Dickie almost yelled.

"My bodyguard. I find that I cannot go about town, dressed as I please, without a bit of protection."

Zhou was wearing pajama bottoms and a black vest with a skivvy underneath, and satin moccasins on his feet. His arms were crossed. His head was bald and inked. He smiled, and his false teeth had new diamonds in them. I imagine Zhou was as foreign a personage as either Amy or Dickie had ever seen, perhaps had ever imagined. And Zhou was immense, with biceps the size of Dickie's waist.

"My God," Dickie exclaimed. "He goes wherever you go?"

"It is required by the times, don't you know? What with vagabonds roaming the streets." I crossed my legs and swatted at a particle of dust on my pant cuff. "A simple precautionary measure."

"And this other Chinese fellow, the smaller one?" Dickie pointed at Cobbler's Wax as if he were a cigar store Indian. Wax was wearing Mandarin red silk with a sash around his waist and satin slippers. He was almost as exotic as Zhou.

"A manservant, is all," I replied. "He is most useful with his silk squares." I flicked the corner of the silk patch I was sitting on.

"Silk squares?" Amy asked. "Is that a Chinese custom?"

I chuckled merrily. "No, not at all. It's just that my years in the Orient gave me a preference for silk over leather. I choose to sit on silk, and so my man here"—I indicated Cobbler's Wax with a toss of my hand—"puts a square of silk down on any leather chair before I sit in it. It's quite a luxury."

"That's all this fellow does?" Dickie asked. "Puts a piece of silk on a chair before you sit on it? And holds the hankie while you blow your nose?"

"I have other servants for other tasks."

"I don't mean to pry," he pried, "but how in the world can you afford to pay a man for such a small duty."

I smiled with the benevolence of superior knowledge. "I don't pay them anything, of course."

Amy asked, "How then . . ."

"They are—ah, how should we say?—indentured to me."

"Indentured?" she asked. "Like the early Irish who came to this country? Seven-year indentures?"

"Ninety-nine-year indentures," I corrected her.

Dickie narrowed his eyes, calculating. "That's slavery, isn't it? I mean, ninety-nine years?"

I held up my hands in a gesture of utter reasonableness. "Such a tawdry word, my dear man. They are indentured, I assure you. I even have the documents. Somewhere."

"You can do that? Slavery? I mean"—Amy quickly corrected herself—"a ninety-nine-year indenture?"

"Under the laws of the Celestial Kingdom of China, many things are possible. But enough about my servants, if you will. I came here merely to thank you, and I have done so."

I gathered my pant legs to rise but Amy held me in my chair with a gesture. She said, "I am grateful for the lovely ring. But I am puzzled. What did my brother and I do to earn your gratitude, Mr. Lowe?"

I laughed again, a trill of delightful boredom. "Forgive me, Amy. May I call you 'Amy'?"

"Of course." She paused, then added, "Woodrow."

"How could you have put two and two together?" I took a long breath and smiled at each of them in turn. "You remember the last time we met, perhaps? It was an evening of little consequence to you, I fear, but for me, it was the first step toward my fortune."

She was hesitant. "In Buenos Aires?"

"In Buenos Aires." I happily patted my knee. "If you'll recall, you entered me into a bullfight, of sorts, and I survived it, thus winning you both small sums."

She slowly shook her head. "I have always wanted to offer you an explanation."

"Me, too," Dickie chimed in.

She glanced at her brother, inventing on the spot, no doubt. "We looked for you after the Dequella, but couldn't find you. I was rather distraught."

Dickie nodded fervently. "She was. Distraught. I remember clearly."

"That touches me deeply, and thank you. My wounds were none of your concern, of course." Once again, I made a dismissive gesture with a hand. "But let me continue. I found myself without funds—beggared, to be precise—so when I had regained my strength I boarded the next ship that left Buenos Aires. It happened to be a particular merchantman, and when I reached China, I started to work in that trade." I glanced modestly at the floor. "You can see, I did rather well, and rather quickly. It seems I have a gift for the trade."

"What trade?" Amy demanded, a bit of steel in her voice.

The telephone rang. The butler raced into the room to answer it but Amy reached the phone first.

"One of her boyfriends, I'm sure," Dickie snickered. "Lord knows which one, she wears them out so quickly."

"She is no longer married?" I inquired.

"Her husband John passed away of a heart condition." He leaned toward me confidentially and laughed. "She ground him down to nothing, so he died."

"Oh, my word." Amy gulped, an inordinately unsophisticated sound, considering its source. "It's for you, Woodrow."

I snapped my fingers at Cobbler's Wax, and he started for the phone.

Amy's fine features had formed an incredulous gape, maybe the first of her worldly life. "It's the president. Of the United States. President Roosevelt. On the telephone. For you, Woodrow."

Dickie scoffed, "You bet, sister."

She held the phone out to me. "Dickie, the caller said he was the president, and I know that voice. I've heard him speak three times at those horrid rallies Malcolm used to take me to. It's Theodore Roosevelt on the telephone, calling from Washington."

I put the receiver to my good ear, slowly, so as not to show awkwardness with the instrument. I'd used a telephone only six times in my life, all in the last few days. "Why, hello, Mr. President . . . Of course, sir. I would be delighted. I'll check with my scheduler and call you back tomorrow . . . Goodbye, then."

Amy placed the receiver on its tall cradle.

"I apologize profusely for the intrusion," I said. "I knew the president was going to try to contact me in Boston this afternoon so I gave his secretary your name. He's quite the chum." I dug into my suit pocket. "Here's a photograph of the president and me, taken just six weeks ago at his second inauguration."

Dickie leaned toward his sister to view the photo. It was the same one heretofore mentioned, taken on that day outside the Capitol Building, Teddy giving the oath, his hand on the Bible held by Mr. Justice Fuller, me in the background.

After a while studying the photo, they gave it up, and I stepped toward the hall.

"What trade, were you saying, Woodrow?" Amy asked.

"Importing and exporting. I wish I could be more specific." I sighed heavily. "But it is a tad unseemly. I wouldn't want it to—how shall I say?—catch up with me."

Amy reached for my lapel, the one opposite the nosegay pin. "Diamonds suit you, Woodrow." She ran her finger along a lapel pin made of five two-carat diamonds mounted in silver.

"They are but bagatelles on a piece of metal." I clicked my fingers at Cobbler's Wax.

He quickly opened the lapel pin and removed it from my suit. He handed it to me, then deferentially backed away.

"Will you honor me by accepting this pin? In light of my good fortune, that chip on your finger I gave you seems so inconsequential, the more I think of it."

"Now, now, Woodrow." She tapped the pin. "I couldn't possibly."

I shrugged and slipped it carelessly into my pocket.

She said, "My brother and I are unworthy of your gifts. We did nothing, really."

I vigorously shook my head. "I believe in fate, Amy. The only reason I boarded that ship to China and found my fortune in that distant land was because I was wounded and desperate in Buenos Aires, and emerged penniless from the hospital. I was all of those things—wounded, broke, and desperate—thanks to you two. I had no choice but to get on that ship. Only a cad would not be grateful."

We made our way to the hallway, Zhou and Cobbler's Wax following. Amy and her brother exchanged meaningful glances, then she nudged him.

"What do you say, Woodie, to getting together, you and me, maybe tonight," Dickie offered. "I know a few spots in town."

Edgar the butler opened the front door.

"I couldn't possibly. I have a dinner engagement tonight." I hesitated on the top step. "But perhaps later? You could join me at the club at ten, Richard." I wagged my finger naughtily at Amy. "Men only, of course."

"What club, Woodie?" Dickie asked.

I pursed my lips, my eyes alight, about to reveal a secret. "The Fortune Club."

"The Fortune Club?" he echoed. "I've never heard of it. And I know all the clubs. I'm a member of most of them."

I smiled tolerantly. "One must have a fortune to belong, Richard. To even have knowledge of the club."

Intense anxiety crossed his face. He opened his arms to encompass the house. "We have a fortune, Woodie. My sister lives here—look at this place—inherited from our parents. My house is down the street. It's just as grand. We've got the funds."

I clucked my tongue. "Richard, there's wealth." I indicated Amy's mansion and the grounds—with the Corinthian columns, the white stone balustrades, the fan window above the door, the flagpole with the red griffin flag—then flicked it all away with a finger. "And then there's wealth."

I stepped to the carriage, a Heritage three-seater with four brown

Belgians, majestic in their traces. The Heritage was trimmed in silver, and the wheel spokes were silvered. Cobbler's Wax opened the door for me, then leaped up to the driver's seat. Zhou climbed to the boot behind the rear window—the carriage sinking under his weight—and grabbed the handholds.

I withdrew a card from my suit pocket, scribbled on it with a pencil, and held it out through the window. "Here's the address. Remember, mum's the word, Richard."

He grabbed the card like a lawyer grabs a check. Cobbler's Wax shook the reins, and the carriage started forward.

"Ten o'clock," Dickie called. "I'll be Johnny-on-the-spot, Woodie."

I glanced back through the rear window, leaning to see around Zhou. Amy was caught in a spotlight of sun coming down through the elm trees that surrounded the Balfour mansion. It lit her up. She was gilded and shimmering in them hot rays. Perhaps knowing I would be looking back at her, she smiled at my carriage, a smile of a wattage Mr. Edison would have admired.

I smiled, but to myself. The carriage rolled down the driveway. I wondered which of the branches overhead had coldcocked me that day so long ago.

NEAR THE LEWIS Wharf was the American Eagle Salvage Company. I pushed open the company's front gate, then slammed it behind me just to see if Zhou was alert. He caught it easily. With a chuckle—which sounded like most people's grunts—he closed it gently behind us. He followed me onto the salvage company's grounds. He was wearing Western clothes, including a hat. No sense drawing a crowd.

We were met with the sounds of sledgehammers and prybars. No one was in the small clapboard office, so we stepped around back toward the yard and the bay. Masts and yardarms were above us. Six workmen were tearing apart a seventy-foot mosquito ferry that had served its time carrying passengers, perhaps to Crow Point and Plymouth. The workers ripped and pulled at the hull, peeling back the boards. Some of the wood was loaded onto mule carts in the yard, others—too rotted to be reclaimed—were tossed into a fire pit that sent a tower of black smoke skyward and out over the water. Three other ships in various states of decrepitude awaited the workmen's attention.

A fellow smoking a pipe and wearing a dusty bowler hat and suspenders approached Zhou and me, pausing only a second when he noticed Zhou.

He asked, "May I help you?"

"I'm looking for a vessel. An old one. Two hundred feet long or larger."

"You've come to the wrong address, sir. This is a wrecking yard, a salvage company. You require a ship broker. I can recommend a good one at the head of Foster's Wharf."

I shook my head. "The ship I have in mind must be a floating wreck. I need no sails or lines, no boilers, no navigation equipment, no blocks and tackle, nothing belowdecks. All she need do is float."

He scratched his head. "You require no propulsion?"

"None, sir."

"Well, the *Lily Arlene* is right here." He pointed at a cargo vessel rafted to the ship being dismantled. The *Lily Arlene* was battered and drooping, its masts a tangle, its hull blackened with rot, and the ship was already stripped of its brightwork. "It is scheduled to be taken apart beginning next week."

"How much for it?" I asked.

"For the *Lily Arlene*? Sir, you will be purchasing a hulk. This ship is beyond refurbishing"

"I fully understand."

He scratched his chin. "I paid one hundred dollars for it, and it would have cost me another hundred in labor to take it apart. Then I could have sold its salvageable parts for about three hundred dollars. So I had hoped to profit by one hundred dollars on her."

I brought out my wallet and removed the bills. "I'll pay you three hundred dollars for the *Lily Arlene* right now."

He smiled. "Done. And a poor bargain you've made, if I might say without souring the deal."

"A poor bargain, perhaps." I joined him in the smile. "But I doubt it."

DICKIE BALFOUR WAS waiting for me outside the club on Waxford Street when my carriage rolled up to the curb that night. He started bumping his gums at me before I stepped down from the carriage.

"Woodie, are you sure this is it?" He pointed at the modest green door

in the three-story brick structure. "That sign near the door says, ADAMS
BAKERY."

I was wearing a dove-colored cape, a vest with tiger stripes, a high-
collar shirt, and an evening coat. I peeled off my white gloves while
Cobbler's Wax knocked on the green door. Three raps, then two, then
three again.

"Do not let appearances deceive you, Richard."

The door swung open. The scents of cigars and leather greeted us. I
stepped inside, Dickie close enough so that I could feel his breath on my
neck. A butler dressed in black except for white gloves helped us out of
our coats. Dickie stared all around, at the crystal chandelier overhead,
and the tapestries on the wall, at the gold-rimmed ashtray near the
reception desk. We stepped across a thick Karbhola rug to the desk.
Cobbler's Wax and Zhou came behind.

The desk attendant was formally dressed, the front of his shirt ruffled,
and the collar held together with a silver stickpin. "Mr. Lowe. We have
been expecting you. Your room is ready, of course."

A waiter appeared, and placed snifters of brandy in Dickie's and my
hands. Dickie drained half the glass in one draught. I pretended to sip
mine.

"May I escort you to your room?" the deskman asked.

I waved him off. Dickie and I walked down a short hallway. On the
wall was a florid French painting of winged cherubs feeding grapes to a
buxom woman reclining on a bearskin and wearing nothing but chiffon.

The murmur of voices and low laughter and the clink of glasses
reached us.

I explained, "At the end of the hall is the club room, but I've got
something a bit special planned for us tonight, so we'll retire to my
private chamber."

The hall opened to a foyer where curving stairs rose to the second
floor. Dickie craned his neck as we climbed the stairs. At the top was a
risqué marble statue of two lovers embracing. I pushed open the first
door on the right, and Dickie followed me in, and so did Cobbler's Wax.
Zhou remained in the hallway, a sentinel by the door.

"Take off your shoes," I commanded, bending to untie my new Mc-
Morrow brogans.

"My shoes?"

"Oriental courtesy."

He flipped them off, then stared gape-jawed at the room. Chinese silk tapestries hung on two walls, and on another was a copy of Ingres's harem painting, *The Great Odalisque*. Instead of chairs, enormous pillows lined one wall. An ice bucket with champagne was near a brass gong on a cherrywood stand. A folding black lacquer screen with a pattern of inlays hid one wall and a second door. On the floor in front of the screen were three oil lamps with polished metal reflectors that threw soft light up toward the screen. An Oriental carpet covered the floor. In a corner was a tree made of jade. Veined pink jade for the trunk, and hundreds of green jade leaves.

I lowered myself to a pillow. Cobbler's Wax rushed over to plump it behind me. Then from behind the screen Wax brought out a brass-and-glass Turkish water pipe. Dickie sank into the pillow near mine. Cobbler's Wax lit the pipe, primed it, then passed it to Dickie, who probably had never seen one before but was game for any indulgence. He sucked on the pipette as hard as his meager chest would allow, blowing out the cold smoke through his nostrils. When he passed the tube to me, I held it idly a moment without using it, then passed it back. Cobbler's Wax brought out a bottle of brandy and refilled Dickie's glass.

I struck the gong with a padded stick. Dickie lay back, a rapturous expression on his face, ready for anything.

But he weren't ready for Victoria Littlewood. Wearing bells on her wrists and ankles, and translucent slips of silk, she glided from behind the lacquer screen. Around her waist was a string of pearls. She wore only a tiny triangle of silk below her navel. Flowing veils were in both hands. Her breasts were barely held in place by a harness of silk. Her saffron hair flowed around her neck. Her lips were painted sunset red, and liner on her eyes gave them the cast of a tiger's. She moved her hips to the pulse of her bells, her arms moving the veils in front of her, her half-closed eyes on Dickie. On her forehead was a singular emerald hung on thin silver braid around her head. Light from the floor lamps accented her curves.

"Oh my God," Dickie exhaled. "She is exquisite."

Victoria wet her lower lip, then pursed her mouth erotically, then slowly smiled at Dickie. She danced languidly, turning her back to us, provocatively wiggling her derriere. When she turned again to face us, the silk brassiere was gone, and Dickie was faced with Victoria's amplitude. I glanced sideways at him. His face was red, his mouth was open, his eyes were glassy, and he was breathing like a runner. He looked ready to explode.

He stammered, "Where did you find her, Woodie?"

"In the Sudan. The abdullah showed me a row of a dozen women, and after close inspection, I chose this one."

"Is she . . . is she . . . ?" So delicious was the thought, he could not finish the question.

But I did. "Is she indentured to me? Why, yes, of course. She is one of four dancers I've picked up in my travels. I'm partial to this blonde, but the others have their qualities."

Victoria cast me the smallest of glances.

I embellished my account. "I keep one of these lovelies at each of my homes. This one traveled with me from France on this trip."

"Woodie." Dickie gulped his brandy. "Woodie, I must ask. How much did that, ah, indenture cost you?"

I smiled narrowly. "You ask that I be indiscreet."

"I know, I know. But tell me anyway."

Nothing covered Victoria's breasts but a veil. She pushed her breasts up with her arms. His eyes locked on the deep cleft between her breasts, Dickie moaned quietly, swaying left and right in sympathy with her movements.

I whispered the amount into his ear.

It sobered him. "My Lord. That much? I could purchase a home for that amount."

I shrugged. "Look at Melonica closely, Richard."

"Her name is Melonica?" He moved his mouth, chewing the delectable name.

"I am prepared to state that she is the finest example of her gender in this hemisphere. Perhaps in the world. Have you ever seen anyone like her?"

"No, no." He was adamant. "Never."

"So how could you think she would come cheaply?"

"No, of course I didn't. But . . . that much? And you have three others like her? All that money just for dancers?"

"Dancing?" I laughed contemptuously. "Richard, dancing is just the ribbon on the package, if you know what I mean."

"The ribbon?"

"This little veil dance is the least—the very least—of Melonica's talents."

He sucked in air through his teeth, making a feeble whistle. "What are her other talents?"

"A man of the world such as you already knows the answer, Richard. A night with Melonica is as close to nirvana as can be found on this earth."

He wet his lips, his fevered gaze on her. Victoria moved slowly and rhythmically, the veils wafting, her hips rising and falling, the bells chiming.

"And she's yours? For ninety-nine years?"

"Mine. And she will do anything I tell her. Utterly anything."

I thought Dickie might pass out from this revelation. I let him luxuriate in fantasies of Victoria and the things—the utterly anythings—she would do on command. Then I hit the gong, and she drifted from our view behind the screen.

"I have another appointment in a few minutes, Richard." I rose to my feet. "Meeting a few friends."

He struggled up, adjusting his pants to hide himself. He ran a hand across his mouth. "I never imagined . . ."

"Few do." I laughed quietly. "But wealth—true wealth—allows me these little fancies and whims."

He followed me out of the room and down the stairs, my Chinese entourage trailing after us. I nodded to the deskman on my way out.

At the curb, I said, "Goodbye then, Richard."

I entered the carriage and it began down the street, its steel-rimmed wheels clattering on the cobblestones. And once again I peered out the rear window. Dickie stood on the sidewalk, both hands in his pants pockets, his eyes still swimming and his chest still pumping from all he had seen and learned this evening.

"I AM DELIGHTED you could join me, Mrs. Malcolm," I intoned. "Such choices confound me. Your advice will be hugely appreciated."

"It's Amy," she insisted. She bent over the display cabinet with me, careful to brush my arm with her breast. We were visiting Trencher's Jewelry Shop near the Museum of Fine Arts. She had met me there, responding to a note I had sent her an hour before.

Mr. Trencher lay before us three necklaces. Each was grander than the other two. One was set with alternating emeralds and diamonds. Another was a vast swath of rubies and diamonds. The third was just diamonds, a wide path of them. They glittered blindingly on the black velvet. A loupe in one hand and his spectacles in the other, Mr. Trencher beamed at me. Zhou stood near the doorway.

"Why did you say you are buying a necklace?" Amy asked. She was wearing a green pleated dress the color of the emeralds. In her hand was a rolled sun parasol. She wore matching green laced boots that disappeared under her dress.

"During my last visit to China I was the guest of the dowager empress." From a pocket I pulled a copy of a photograph showing Old Buddha sitting on her throne, with me in Mandarin clothes sitting at her feet.

"This is the empress of China?" She held the photograph to her eyes. "And you sitting with her? It is, isn't it? My Lord, look at the pearls around her neck."

"She is known as Old Buddha," I said. "A delightful lady. I stayed at the Summer Palace with her. She showed me one kindness after another, and a gift for her would be appropriate but I simply do not have your sense of taste, if I may admit."

If I had to talk like this much longer, I'd most likely become a sissy. If that old teamster Bo Latts or John L. or my pa had ever heard me talk this way, they'd have slapped me around some, trying to bring me out of it.

"Which, do you think, Amy? Perhaps the one with rubies?"

She laughed. "An empress deserves them all."

I laughed with her. "Of course. Mr. Trencher, I'll take all three."

His eyes opened. So did hers.

The jeweler sputtered, "All three, Mr. Lowe?"

"Wrap them up."

He pulled a notebook and a pencil from a drawer, then did some figuring. He passed me the pad. "This is your cost, Mr. Lowe. I realize it seems high . . ."

Out came my wallet. "Is cash too inconvenient?" I lifted out bills, a lot of them, and passed them to the jeweler. His hands were trembling as he latched onto them.

Amy watched this transaction with delight but also with clinical interest, it seemed to me. Mr. Trencher placed the necklaces in a satin-lined box, and gave me the box. I casually tossed it to Zhou, who tucked it into his trousers.

As we left the shop, Amy gripped my elbow and leaned into me. "Woodrow, I want you to come to my house again. Right now."

I pulled out my pocket watch. The fob was a diamond as large as my nose. "Well, I had promised . . ."

"We need to talk, Woodrow. You won't regret a visit. Come now. Let's take your carriage."

"I won't regret it?" I asked. "But what if you do?"

Her laugh was salacious, and it climbed the scale of notes. "Nonsense, Woodrow. Nonsense."

EDGAR THE BUTLER saw us coming, and opened the door. I made to step into the sitting room but she took my hand and led me to the staircase. Boston ferns on cherrywood stands were on both sides of the lowest step.

"I must show you something, Woodrow. Come with me."

She led me up the wide stairs, along a hall, and into her bedroom.

How many times had I dreamed of her bedroom? More times than the normal mind can imagine.

The four posters of her bed had cupids carved into them. The bedcover and the canopy were in matching red and blue flowers. A Boston rocker was in one corner and a chesterfield lounge in another. A silver comb and brush set was on a satinwood dresser, along with about twenty crystal perfume bottles. Above the dresser was a carved and gilded pine-framed mirror. Hanging in the center of the room, a fan idly pushed the air.

Still holding my hand, she led me to the lounge, where I sat down, adjusting the crease of my trousers.

She walked back and forth in front of me a moment before beginning. "I know who you are, Woodrow. You think I don't, but I do."

"Yes?"

She lowered her lashes at me. I had told her brother that Victoria—rather, Melonica—was the finest the hemisphere had to offer. Amy was a close second. She was red and radiant and commanding and . . . and devious. Always devious.

"You are the little boy who saved me from that despicable oaf who hit my horse. Outside a saloon in the Roxbury district. It must be twenty-five years ago." She smiled. "Can you deny it?"

I took a moment before answering. "No, I guess I can't."

"The same lad who tried to break into my house to find me. And who was banished to the cavalry by a court of law."

"That's me, all right."

"The same fellow that broke the watercloset door down at my wedding, as you admitted when you arrived at my home in Buenos Aires. You didn't think I recognized you in Buenos Aires, but of course I did."

I nodded.

"And now you have come back to me. You cannot stay away. I am sure that your common sense has warned you about me. Perhaps friends and family have warned you. Perhaps President Roosevelt has warned you. But you cannot stay away."

There was some truth to everything she said.

She lowered her voice and stepped near to me. "I am an intelligent woman."

"Doubtless." Teddy would say "doubtless," wouldn't he? Instead of "You bet"?

She took my hand in hers. "I know the power I have over you, Woodrow."

"You do?"

"I know that my shifty little brother Dickie lied at your trial many years ago, that you didn't try to kidnap him at all. He still laughs about it. And you are being gallant about the Dequella in Buenos Aires but it was a filthy trick Dickie and I played on you. We punish you, and you keep coming back for more. Do you know why?"

I shook my head.

"You are helpless before me, Woodrow. You are mine to do as I will. That is as clear to me as it is to you." She drew her fingers along the back of my hand. "Can you deny it?" She pulled me to my feet and she stepped close to me. "What do you suppose is the source of my power, Woodrow?"

I said nothing.

"Do you think it is my appearance in general?" With her other hand, she began unbuttoning her dress at the neckline. "Or is it some particular part of me?"

"There's a lot of fine parts, I'd wager."

When the buttons were undone down to her waist, she guided my hand inside the dress and placed it over a breast.

She held me with her eyes. "Woodrow, undo the buckle at my waist and pull the dress off my shoulders."

I did as ordered.

"Do you see? You will do anything I tell you. Now run your hands along my shoulders. Do you like the skin there?"

"I do."

"And my breasts. Are they full enough for you?"

"They are."

"Do you know why I am giving myself to you, Woodrow?"

"I've got my suspicions."

"And you are right." Her voice was as smooth as her skin. "You are going to tell me how you made your fortune. All about your China trading. And you are going to help me increase my fortune. Do you understand the nature of our bargain?"

"I do." I tried to control my voice but it sounded like a stormy wind.

"And I will be yours tonight, and every night, until my ship comes in. You will have me in person, instead of in your fantasies. All those years of wild and hot dreams about me. Now they are going to come true."

I nodded.

"Tell me what you trade in."

I hesitated.

She made me squeeze her nipple, pushed it between my fingers and made me knead it. "Tell me."

"Opium. I made my money in opium."

"Will you show me how?"

A long exhale, a sigh of desire. "I will."

"Enough of this sad and tiring business chatter, Woodrow. My dress. Slide it down to the floor. And linger along the way. Linger all you like. Fill yourself up with me, Woodrow."

"Oh Lordy." I began with her dress.

Just then someone hammered at the door. Amy started. I don't mean it was a knock. I mean a battering. Again and again.

She quickly composed herself. "Ignore that, Woodrow. It'll go away."

But the pounding continued. And then the door opened, and Zhou rushed in, all of him, an ox of a man. He hustled up to me, out of breath.

He seldom spoke, but he did now, in broken English. "Sir, an emergency. You come. Right away."

"Zhou, for the love of God . . ."

"No time to lose."

"Whatever it is can wait, and if you'll just . . ."

He lifted me bodily and lay me over his shoulder, just as he had done with Cobbler's Wax down in the pit of the Demon's Daughter. My hand slipped out of Amy's dress.

Zhou hollered, "An emergency, sir. You must come."

He carried me out of her room and down the stairs past a bewildered Edgar, then out the door, where he tossed me into the carriage.

"Zhou, you'd better have an explanation."

He smiled, his choppers flashing. Now he spoke in Chinese. "Miss Victoria ordered me to retrieve you if you were in the red-haired woman's bedroom longer than five minutes."

"Victoria ordered you?" I blustered. "Who do you take orders from, anyway?"

He climbed up to the driver's box and called down. "Depends if I like the order. I liked this one from her."

The carriage rolled away.

How can I tell you, and have you believe me, that I sank back into the carriage seat hugely relieved, though I had hidden it from Zhou? And later tried to hide it from Victoria, though she saw through me like glass.

I had convinced myself that Amy Balfour no longer had me mesmerized and stupid. But a session in her bedroom might have changed that, might have thrown me back to the days when she filled my hopes and dreams, when she was that lustrous star seemingly so close yet so far out of reach. Just then in her bedroom I had felt my resolution slipping away at the same rate I was slipping her dress down over her hips. Then Zhou burst in. As I once again rode down Amy's driveway in the carriage, I was happy not to have been truly tested. I was happy that Victoria had rescued me. Again.

TWENTY-TWO

Ship, Captain, and Crew

"THE SHIP IS entirely marvelous, Woodrow." Amy stroked my arm as we walked along the Western Dock. The ship rose above us, its masts and booms and sheets and sails a vast web in the sky.

Dickie was on the other side of her. "The Balfours are a yachting family, Woodie. I dare say I could skipper this ship around the Horn without much trouble."

"That's lovely lettering, Woodrow." Amy pointed at the yellow script on the ship's stern, *Golden Ocean*.

"I had the paint freshened yesterday to honor your visit." I nodded to two stevedores who lifted a box of window glass from a mule cart, and who started up a gangplank.

We walked on the dock the entire length of the *Golden Ocean*'s hull, all 350 feet, from bowsprit to stern pulpit, dodging horsecarts all the way. The ship was being loaded at a hectic pace. A hundred stevedores trooped between the carts and the ship. Fore and aft derricks lifted cargo too heavy for the stevedores. Several other vessels were loading at the Western Dock, but the *Golden Ocean* was the largest, and was being served by more mule and horse wagons.

I escorted Amy and Dickie up the gangplank. Zhou followed. Cobbler's Wax was off doing missions at my direction. The ship's captain met us at the top of the gangplank. He gallantly saluted Amy and Dickie.

"I am Captain MacDougal, at your service. May I say that you have purchased and provisioned a worthy ship. And may I give you a tour?"

Amy nodded. A stillness spread over the ship. Stevedores and riggers and chandlers all stopped their labors to gaze on Amy Balfour Malcolm. She smiled, accepting the silence as her due. Her beauty was regal. None

316

of the workers dared whistle at her. Or they might have been staring at Zhou.

Captain MacDougal's face was hidden by a white beard. His nose and cheeks were bright pink from years of apprenticing behind the wheel in hard weather. He led us toward the forepeak. The cargo holds were open, and manufactured goods were being lowered into them. Rifles and carbines and ammunition, cases of binoculars, a locomotive and coal tender and many railcar trucks, carriage wheels, printing presses, grandfather clocks, brass door hardware, pots and pans, drill presses, lumber saws, steam engines, saddles, eyeglasses, dental drills, and dozens of other items. All flowing down into the holds.

His hands clasped behind his back, Dickie exclaimed, "How I enjoy watching men work."

Captain MacDougal pointed out the carved taffrail, the gleaming winches, the burnished decks and superstructure, the polished brass portholes, the new sails and stays, the lines wrapped in perfect coils on the deck, a glittering binnacle.

"Though commissioned fifteen years ago, the *Golden Ocean* has been refurbished to the finest standards." Captain MacDougal raised a hand to encompass the three masts. "Better than new. Madam, you are to be complimented on your financial commitment to the vessel."

"A commitment that will be rewarded," Amy said.

We paused to watch the loading of a container of Singer foot treadle sewing machines. Two booms were used, one plumbing the hatch and the other rigged out over the side to plumb the dock. Cargo whips from the hatch and yard winches were rove through their respective heel and head blocks and shackled to the same cargo hook. Workers manned the winches and topping lifts. One intoned, "Steady, steady, steady."

"May I toast you in my cabin?" the captain asked.

Amy asked, "Do you have a desk in your cabin, captain? My banker is meeting us here."

"Of course."

We followed MacDougal down a ladder and along a companionway aft, then into his cabin. An inlaid desk with rails at its edges to prevent spills during rough weather was in the center of the cabin. A brass barometer and temperature gauge were on the bulkhead behind the desk. A brass speaking tube running to the wheel topside was mounted to the desk. The room was paneled in mahogany. The captain's bed was in a nook to starboard, and a washing and dressing room were to port. The cabin also contained a liquor cabinet and a gun rack. On a stand behind the desk was a three-foot model of the *Golden Ocean* in a glass case. Because of an overhead glass hatch, the cabin was bright.

The captain poured sherry into crystal glasses and passed them around. He was about to lift his glass in salute when a knock came from the hatch. A cabin boy opened the hatch and a gentleman in a black striped suit was shown into the cabin.

"Amy, here I am then." The fellow spoke in short bursts. "With your documents. But we should talk first."

Amy introduced Ernest Blankenship, senior vice president of the Massachusetts State Bank. Blankenship had a narrow, saturnine face with a turned-down mouth and forever suspicious eyes. He was a small man, but vigorous and certain, with choppy, energetic movements, not a man to joke or laugh, maybe never in his life, judging from his stern appearance. In his hand was a briefcase.

"Amy, Dickie, may I meet alone with you?" he asked, eyeing Captain MacDougal and me with mistrust, and Zhou with alarm.

"Mr. Lowe is my advisor, Ernest. I should not hide anything involving the ship from him."

He reluctantly nodded. Captain MacDougal excused himself, and Zhou left the cabin, but posted himself just on the other side of the hatch, knowing him.

The banker removed a sheaf of documents from his case. "I have not often questioned your investment positions in the past. Nor have I needed to. But this time, your hurried and drastic actions are a source of grave concern to me."

"Believe me, Ernest, we know what we're doing," Amy said, sipping her sherry.

"We'll be coming back to the bank with piles of money, Ernie," Dickie crowed.

Blankenship knew who made the decisions, and scarcely bothered to look at Dickie. "Amy, in the past three weeks you and your brother have withdrawn your every cent from the bank. You have sold your entire stock portfolio. You have instructed our real estate department to sell the Hawthorn Building, and it was sold at a deeply discounted price due to your haste. And you have sold your father's yacht, the *Empire Princess*. And for what?"

Dickie had been impatiently tapping his new diamond walking stick on the floor. "For this, of course." He brought up both hands to indicate the ship. The walking stick glinted in the light coming through the hatch. "For this vessel and its cargo."

Blankenship's eyes never left Amy. He spoke calmly, in the tones of reason and conviction and experience. "And now you have instructed me—both of you have ordered me—to prepare documents to mortgage your homes. In other words, not only have you used up all your assets, but you will be also going heavily into debt to invest in this venture."

Amy inquired, "And you undoubtedly brought the documents and the funds."

The banker inhaled sharply. "Amy, how long have I been your banker?"

"Since my father passed away."

"And I was your father's banker the last twenty years of his life. He and I worked together, and if you will allow me to be immodest, he took my advice on many occasions, almost always to his profit. He was a banker, yet even so he felt he needed the investment advice of another banker, me. He was a conservative investor, and a smart one. Now that he is gone, you and your brother are the stewards of his money . . ."

She cut him off. "The term 'steward' implies that we are only looking after the money, that it belongs to someone else."

His correctness grew on him. "I mean no offense, Amy. But your father's fortune was made in small and steady increments. Never once did he do anything so"—here he interrupted himself to mimic Dickie's expansive gesture, embracing the ship—"so risky as this."

"Tut, tut, tut," Dickie mewed. "Balfours have never been afraid of a toss of the dice. Have we, Amy?"

She ignored him, too. "Ernest, my father has been dead for years, yet you have never stopped thinking of Dickie's and my inheritances as anything but my father's treasure."

"That is not the case, I assure you."

Her voice could have chipped ice. "Then if you wish to continue as our banker, please proceed with the documents."

Blankenship wet his lips. "May I say that you have been warned, and that I stand apart from and am opposed to this entire adventure?"

"The documents, Ernest."

With a heavy sigh, he pushed the papers across to her. She lifted a pen from an inkwell on the desk.

She signed one document, and Dickie signed another.

"Now, the funds, if you will," she commanded.

From the briefcase, the banker produced two drafts, and passed one to Dickie and one to Amy. Both studied the sums indicated on the checks.

The banker instructed, "Sign the drafts, and I will deposit those borrowed funds into your accounts, and you will be able to write drafts on the accounts immediately."

She said, "Outfitting a ship, and buying the trading cargo is an expensive proposition, Ernest. More than we had anticipated, frankly. I had no idea what a locomotive cost. Or a hundred grandfather clocks. Or three dozen crystal chandeliers."

Dickie laughed. "We'll be fairly tapped out until our ship comes in."

Contempt deeply lining his face, Blankenship glanced at Dickie for the first time. "Do you know that all you have left is the trust your father set up? By your standards, it is an insignificant sum, providing a small annual stipend, not enough to keep you in cigars, Dickie. If you two lose everything in this adventure, you will be living in drastically reduced circumstances. Circumstances that you will find entirely foreign and entirely disagreeable. Circumstances your father spent his life clawing up from."

"In a few short months, I will reappear at your desk at the bank, burdened by the money I'm carrying." He laughed uproariously. "Be off with you, Ernest."

Stitched taut with disapproval, the banker issued receipts, and put the drafts and the mortgages back into his briefcase. "Goodbye then, Amy and Dickie. I sincerely wish you luck in this venture."

After he was through the hatch, Amy said, "My brother and I will continue to pay the suppliers and chandlers, and this afternoon will make the final payment on the *Golden Ocean*."

I had not drunk my sherry, of course. "I have explained this before, Amy, and I want to do so again. This ship will be an opium trader, and you cannot procure hull or cargo insurance on such a vessel. Lloyds and the English insurance clubs will not touch the ship. And even if you manage to obtain insurance under some pretense, the insurance will be declared null and void once it is learned the *Golden Ocean* traded in opium."

"I fully understand." She smiled sweetly.

"And the United States government will not investigate the loss of any ship involved in opium. You cannot count on the Coast Guard or Navy."

Another smile. "Then we will be quite alone in our escapade."

Dickie said, "Balfours have always been brave at heart, Woodrow. Don't fret about us."

I lowered my head in admission of the truth of Dickie's words. "The *Golden Ocean* sails on the ebb tide tonight. I trust you won't mind that I have arranged a small bon voyage party."

"A party?" Dickie was instantly alert. "Just tell me where and when."

I put the address down on a card. "It is a sea-going tradition. Investors in a shipping venture have a bon voyage and good luck party. Invite a few friends." I passed Dickie the card. "From this address, we'll be able to see the *Golden Ocean* just as it leaves the main channel, rounds Fort Independence and heads to sea. Captain MacDougal and his crew will salute us with white flares, his goodbye. Another tradition."

Dickie ran his tongue across his upper lip. "Will Melonica be at the party?"

"I can arrange it."

"Woodrow, have you ever considered selling . . . ?" He rephrased his request, "Have you ever considered transferring her indenture?"

"Believe me, Richard. Such a thing is not possible." I smiled. "At least, not until your ship comes in. And then I would have to insist on a modest profit."

"Of course, of course." Dickie stared at the barometer, his thoughts traveling up and down Melonica's body, no doubt.

"Dickie told me about Melonica," Amy chided. "She sounds quite the tramp. And she is the reason you are not availing yourself of your bargain with me, is she not, Woodrow?"

"After his nights with Melonica, Woodrow has nothing left for you, sis." Dickie cackled and chucked my arm.

I said in a mollifying voice, "My one percent commission on your profits will adequately reward me for my advice, Amy." I had made that arrangement with her a few days after Zhou carried me from her bedroom. It allowed Amy and Dickie to think I had a stake in assisting them.

"I cannot recall this ever happening to me before, this kind of rejection. I am hurt." She didn't sound hurt. "Tonight then, Woodrow. And do bring Melonica. I'll stand beside her, and you shall compare us. Then you will fully understand what you are missing."

That woman had a power of confidence, didn't she? She and her brother left the captain's quarters. I remained behind for a few more words with Captain MacDougal. I had a few final instructions for him, none of Amy and Dickie's concern.

IT WAS AN affair to remember, that night. At least, Amy and Dickie remembered it to their graves, I'm utterly certain. And as I recall that night now, after all these years, I still grin about it. Not a discreet grin, mind you. But a full-blown idiotic grin.

We met at the Cressy home, which I had rented for the evening, overlooking the sea to the east. A long and sloping yard gave us a fine view. Canapés and champagne were served at nine o'clock. Even though it was a fine summer evening, a wind had come up, and a tent had been erected on the lawn. Hors d'oeuvres were spread on a table in the tent. Champagne bottles were on ice in a silver bucket. The wind had begun to blow white horses across the water, which in the dark of night were just pale suggestions on the ocean. The light at Deer Island was visible to the east. Other than several fishing boats returning to Boston Harbor—their bobbing lamps seemed suspended out in the void—nothing was between us and Deer Island but the black sea.

"How will we see the *Golden Ocean* in this darkness?" Amy asked. She was wearing a white cotton high-neck dress with pearls sewn down the front and across the shoulders.

"I've asked the captain to show four lamps, displayed vertically. And then he'll salute us with flares."

Dressed in a blue dress ruffled at the shoulders and a small string of pearls, Victoria appeared next to me.

"See what I told you, sis," Dickie said proudly, daring to touch Victoria's shoulder. "Did I lie?"

Amy appraised her, taking fully a minute. I made no introductions, reinforcing their conclusion that Victoria was mere chattel. Victoria was careful not to slip her arm into mine, which she had been doing lately. Or goosing my bottom, which she found fun, so she said. Or pecking me on the cheek, even in public. Or just gazing at me for the longest time, which I didn't mind in the slightest, though I found it hard to stare back into her deep blue pools without getting agitated, if you know what I mean.

Finally Amy admitted, "She has her points. But I hope this doesn't mean you are no longer in my thrall, Woodrow."

"I am yours entirely, I assure you." I was becoming accomplished at this milksop talk, weren't I?

I had hired a brass band, twenty pieces, and they played "The Washington Post March" and other Sousa numbers. Though Amy and Dickie had invited a few friends, there were more bandsmen and waiters than guests. Torches mounted on poles lit the yard and garden. Zhou watched from the tent, eating sandwiches like they were free. Cobbler's Wax served champagne.

"Have you ever visited Marblehead, Woodie?" Dickie pulled a cheroot from his pocket, scraped a match with his fingernail, and lit the cigar. "When the *Golden Ocean* returns I'm going to buy a little hideaway up there. Nothing too ostentatious. Five or six acres on the ocean. Large enough for a staff. Twenty-five rooms, perhaps." The cigar glowed red in the night, casting Dickie's face in amber shades.

"Richard, I have mentioned the risks already," I said solemnly. "I am still willing to be partners with you both, to take a one-third share of the *Golden Ocean*. I can write you a draft right now, and become your one-third partner." I pulled out my bank drafts from a coat pocket. "That way, any loss will be shared by three, instead of just you and Amy."

Dickie's eyes narrowed in amusement. "But our gain will also have to be shared. No, thank you, Woodie. It's too late to try to muscle in on Balfour profits."

So I returned my checks to my coat. "Then the issue is closed."

"There she is," Amy cried, taking a few quick steps toward the planters that marked the lawn's edge at the beach. "Four vertical lights. Just rounding the head."

The vessel was perhaps two miles away, not distinguishable from the black water except for the four lamps on a mast. Amy and Dickie and their guests applauded. The band struck up "The Stars and Stripes Forever." The ship glided through the night.

I looked at my watch. "The flares should be sent skyward about now."

At my signal, the drummers began a snare roll, then the band trumpeted a fanfare. And right on time, a white rocket roared into the sky in a long and graceful arc. At its apex, the flare burst into a dozen balls of light that sank slowly back to the water. The cymbals crashed and the drums rolled. We all applauded mightily, except for Zhou who was too busy shoveling sandwiches into his yap.

Amy leaned into me. "Just thrilling, Woodrow. Just thrilling. My ship, my lovely ship. The *Golden Ocean*."

Another drumroll and fanfare. A second flare was sent toward the heavens. It rushed up into the night, then shattered into little fires and drifted back down. The crash of cymbals, more applause.

She turned to her brother. "We should have rechristened it *The Horn of Plenty*, for that's what it will be for us."

He chuckled, his cigar in one hand and a champagne glass in another. His glassy, pomaded hair reflected the flare.

A third rocket erupted from the vessel, headed to the night sky. For an instant. Then something went wildly wrong. The rocket wrestled with the vessel's rigging, ricocheting among the lines and masts, then it took off parallel to the water for two seconds before angrily plummeting into the sea, where it sputtered and died. But it had left its mark. Fire quickly crawled along the ship's rigging, curling and climbing and rushing, and within seconds the sails were walls of flame.

The vessel was too distant to see with certainty the pattern of the fire, but the flames seemed to expand in all directions at once, to the stem and to the stern, and within moments the ship was embroiled in fire. A small but providential boat—perhaps a tug—drifted into the circle of illumination provided by the blaze, and began lifting the crew out of the water. The big ship's masts were spirals of fire. Flame twisted out of portholes and wrapped around the bowsprit. Smoke from the burning ship was lost in the night sky. At this distance, the vessel was a glowing globe, a yellow moon, the reflection coming across the water to us. This was not the first time I had witnessed a ship burning to the waterline, if you'll recall.

Several small boats gathered near the burning freighter but seeing nothing was to be done, kept a respectful distance, and were just barely visible in the corona of light thrown off by the burning ship. The golden fiery orb began a slow descent into the water.

I turned to Dickie. "I'm beginning to be thankful I couldn't convince you to go partners with me."

He may not have heard me. He stared dully at the spot of flame, his cigar chewed apart, the burning end on the ground at his feet, tobacco leaves stuck to his lips and chin. His mouth was open, and he was breathing stertorously. He was as white as a fish belly.

He squeaked, "Woodie, what . . . what is happening?"

"As far as I can tell, your ship is burning to the water, and rather quickly."

"What . . . what . . . what . . . My money, my house . . ."

"This is a terrible turn of events, Dickie. I must console your sister."

But she was not standing there. Zhou had seen her start to tremble, then weave as if in the wind, then stagger, her knees giving way entirely. He had caught her with one hand—his other still occupied with sandwiches—and had laid her on the grass. I bent down to her.

She weren't weeping—I don't believe her physically capable of producing tears—but she was green, her face blending nicely with the grass. Odd that one sibling would turn white and the other green. Amy was making small sounds, rather like the braying of a newborn mule, though a bit softer.

She finally could form a few words. "I . . . I am ruined."

I patted her hand. "It can't be as bad as that, Amy."

"Ruined . . . ruined . . . ruined."

"Now, now, now." I can be a comfort, can't I?

Spittle was at the corner of her mouth. "My father's money . . . gone. And my husband's. All gone."

Her hair was splayed all around on the grass under her head. I tidied it up with my hand. Those flaming tresses.

The guests were pointing and speculating at the distant flames.

Amy breathed in gulps. "The bank will foreclose. I will have no place to live."

I thought for a moment. "The new Young Women's Christian Association on Beloit Street may have a room. They allow short stays."

Fortunately, she weren't listening. "I am impoverished. Destitute. How will I survive? How does . . . how does one be poor?"

I held her hand a few minutes more. It seemed to revive her. She struggled to sit up.

"Woodrow, you are awash in money." She offered a tempting smile. "Can you tide me through? A loan?"

"Of course. Callous of me not to have thought of it first." I paused. "May I be so forward as to ask what collateral you will offer?"

She studied my face—my beaten, scarred, long-suffering face—then sank back to the grass, turning her head to watch the last of the fire, and resumed making her peculiar bleating sound.

I left her on the grass. When I nodded to Victoria and Cobbler's Wax and Zhou, they followed me from the garden toward our carriage, Zhou five feet behind me, as always, though his belly was only three feet behind me, as always.

TWENTY-THREE

A Diamond Ring

"I DO," I answered, my voice weak.

"Please place the ring on her finger."

My hands trembling, I complied.

"Now by the authority granted me by the Protestant Episcopalian Diocese of Boston and by the State of Massachusetts, I pronounce you man and wife. You may kiss the bride."

I turned to Victoria. She looked at me with the same expression as when she removed her hood in the pit. I do believe that woman adored me. I kissed her full on the mouth. Then I took her by the hand and turned to present my new bride to the congregation.

They applauded mightily. It was only a small gathering. My mum and pa were in the front row, mom dabbing at her eyes with a hankie. A few of pa's friends from Joe Lowe's Museum and Sporting Palace sat behind him, probably wondering when the drinks were coming. John L. was there, too, fidgety because he hadn't had a cigar in fifteen minutes, but smiling anyway. Bedecked in gems from collar to cuffs, Diamond Jim Brady sat next to John L. A few of my old fighting opponents were in the pews. And so was Sergeant Rose, the old Indian fighter. Victoria's family hadn't been able to make it across the ocean. Or maybe she hadn't told them.

I shook hands with my best man, Cobbler's Wax, who was dressed in heathen finery. Zhou, my second man, also dressed in silk and slippers, smiled with his dazzlers, and took my hand in his and patted it and for a long moment wouldn't let go. Then I shook hands with my third man, the president of the United States.

Teddy proclaimed, "You found your fortune after all, Woodrow. And a lovely bride." He looked at her closely for the first time. "An astonishingly, an impossibly lovely bride." I believe he was about to ask how in God's green earth I had snared someone like Victoria, but he desisted. "I'm proud of you, Woodrow."

He couldn't take his eyes off my new wife, and I couldn't blame him. She was dressed in white, with much lace and finery, with baby's breath and tiny white roses in her hair, and no veil, which no doubt shocked my mum.

Teddy Roosevelt had journeyed to Boston for the ceremony. So when I say there was only a small gathering, I'm not counting the mayor, councilmen and bureaucrats hovering outside the church, waiting for Teddy to emerge from the church so they could do some fawning. They had been as surprised as I was to learn the president had arrived at the Southern Union Station on Dewey Square, where he had immediately made his way to the church. Word of his arrival had fanned across the city, and I could hear the crowd outside growing.

The ceremony was held at Trinity Church on Copley Square. Victoria and I walked down the aisle toward the door, Zhou close behind. I had hired the Masons' Hall down the block for a reception. Once out in the square my bride and I pushed our way through the arse-smoochers who were trying to sidle up to the president. Teddy's bodyguards funneled him toward the hall. John L. paused to sign a few autographs. So did Diamond Jim.

Once there, I toasted my bride, though not drinking any of the champagne. I might've been married at an Episcopalian Church at Victoria's insistence but that didn't mean I didn't still fall to my knees five times a day toward Mecca. We entered the reception hall which Victoria had decorated in green and white. A couple passersby bluffed their way in, and made straight to the refreshment table to join John L.

Victoria's hand in mine, I approached Diamond Jim and slipped him an envelope. "Here's your twenty-five percent commission."

He chuckled. "All those percentages added up over the years, didn't they, Woodrow?"

"Your services were cheap at that price, Mr. Brady."

He leaned toward Victoria, not quite believing his eyes, just like Teddy had done. I was by then accustomed to the reaction. Victoria's beauty stupefied men. That's the best way to put it. On numerous occasions in the prior four weeks—since the burning of the *Golden Ocean*—I had been walking along a Boston sidewalk, Victoria's arm in mine, when a man would approach us on the sidewalk, tip his hat to Victoria, and bang his head on a signpost behind us, which he hadn't seen because he had craned around to look at her. And my pa had almost spit out his bridgework when I had waltzed into Joe Lowe's Museum and Sporting Palace and announced the lady on my arm was going to marry me. Another time, after about fifteen minutes of eyeballing her, John L. had announced, "You're lucky I'm such a good friend of yours, Woodrow, or I'd beat you to a quivering pulp—like I did out in the Dakotas—and steal her away." Victoria always smiled grandly, accepting the ogling as compliments.

That day in the Masons' Hall, she affected Diamond Jim the same way. Finally he could block-and-tackle his gaze from her. He didn't bother looking at the draft in the envelope. He put it into his coat pocket. Zhou stood next to him, and it was a contest as to who was bigger.

"Your Chinaman friend has already returned to me the money and jewelry you borrowed." Diamond Jim paused, looking at my face, left and right, canvassing it. "Suddenly you have lots of money, Woodrow. A fortune, it seems. You care to tell me how you did it?"

"You are an upright man, Mr. Brady, and I would not burden you with such a revelation."

"I cannot be tainted with your scheme. I only loaned you the funds and the diamonds. I am an honest man."

It had been an enormous sum of money and a bag of diamond jewelry. When I had returned from Anguilla and had met Diamond Jim at the Waldorf, he had asked no questions and demanded no security when he passed me the draft and the jewels. He had said only, "That's another ten percent you owe me, Woodrow."

"I, too, am an honest man, Mr. Brady. But this woman, Amy, set me up to be killed in Buenos Aires, and when I didn't die, she left me for dead. Her brother Dickie perjured himself and was responsible for getting me convicted of a felony. Perhaps they thought I could forgive these things but I could not. And I did not."

"Who are these people?" he asked.

"A family named Balfour."

"The Boston banking family?"

"The daughter and son of the founder of the Massachusetts State Bank."

He smiled thinly. "Have your man there, the tattooed Chinaman, pass me some of his sandwiches."

I did so, and Zhou complied but not without a look of consternation.

Diamond Jim said around a mouthful of sandwich, "How did you set up the Balfours?"

"I chartered a cargo vessel named *Gladiator* for two months. A fine ship. Top of the line, three hundred and fifty feet long. That's where some of your money went, for the charter. I had the stern and hull repainted to say GOLDEN OCEAN."

"I chose the name," Victoria said. "It has a solid, prosperous ring to it."

I went on, "I learned of a First Street ship broker who would occasionally perform midnight deals. He took the leased *Gladiator*, now called the *Golden Ocean*, and put it on the market, and I guided the Balfours to it. Amy and her brother purchased the ship for their trading venture. The ship was enormously expensive but the broker insisted on cash."

"Yet the ship was only rented to you?"

"Two-month charter. Amy and Dickie's purchase money went into my pocket, less the cost of the charter and the broker's small fee. Then Amy and Dickie bought the goods to take to the Orient for their trading. At my suggestions, they filled the holds with high-priced goods. In fact, when the holds were finally filled, the cargo was worth twice what the vessel was worth. And they paid cash for all the cargo."

"Cash to whom?" Diamond Jim asked.

"To vendors and manufacturers and chandlers. All perfectly normal and legitimate. The Balfours spent every cent they had—and went deeply into debt—to buy the ship and provision it."

"Let me ask you something," Diamond Jim said. "It seems these two—Amy and Dickie Balfour—were acting in haste, and improvidently, even foolishly. You primed their pumps?"

"Victoria and I created great thirsts in both of them, overwhelming thirsts."

Zhou passed Diamond Jim more sandwiches, a plate of them. Zhou may have never seen anyone eat more than he could, and I think he was testing Jim, who finished off a sandwich every three bites.

I continued, "I arrived in Boston seemingly flush with funds and good fortune. But all of it was borrowed from you. Your money, your jewelry."

Victoria said, "He looked quite the gentleman in your diamond lapel pin and watch fob. You were even kind enough to ship him on the train your silver and leather carriage and your Belgian horses."

Diamond Jim grinned. "That wasn't kindness. It was included in my fee."

"And I did a few things to polish my image in the Balfour mind," I said. "Such as having the president of the United States telephone me at the Balfour home. I never told Teddy why he was to call, and he never asked. He did it as a favor. And after that phone call, Amy and Dickie never even thought to check my credit references, or even to doubt me."

"Entirely understandable."

"Dickie Balfour always had a taste for the fast and the loose. So I created the Fortune Club. Rented the hall, furnished it, hired a few people to be the deskman and waiters, even hired a few customers. Filled the place with expensive furniture and rugs, all rented. Dickie was frantic when he learned there was an exclusive Boston club he didn't belong to, hadn't even heard of. I took him there as my guest."

"Then I blinded him." Victoria laughed. "Just like I blinded Woodrow long ago, and continue to blind him."

"I can only imagine," Diamond Jim said around most of a sandwich.

I shook my head. "You can't imagine. Believe me. Victoria put on a little performance at the club that made Dickie desperate for the money to afford such a woman."

"A performance?"

Victoria quickly corrected the impression. "Just a little dance."

I said, "But a dance suggestive of so much more. Victoria, and the Fortune Club, the diamonds, the four homes I told him about, all were beyond him, and he thirsted for it all. Particularly for Victoria."

"He sounds like a child," Diamond Jim said.

"And he always will be. His sister was another matter. She has always been cunning and singularly dedicated to her own welfare. But there I was, returned to Boston, suddenly up from broke, impossibly wealthy, my fortune vastly eclipsing her own. I was casually giving away expensive baubles, and buying gem-heavy necklaces on a whim. Thank you for loaning them necklaces to me, by the way. The jeweler, Mr. Trencher, is a fine actor. So Amy was blinded, just like her brother."

"Those are the two components of a sucker, aren't they?" Diamond Jim accepted more food from Zhou. "Unbridled greed and a willingness to do the shady." He chewed a moment. "So what was the shady?"

"Opium trading. I had them convinced my fortune was made sending American manufactured products to Siam, where they were traded for opium, which was then sent to China to be traded for gold, silver, jade and jewels. Profits of five hundred percent each voyage, I assured them."

"But risks always accompany high return."

"Ship fires, for one." I laughed. "The night of their ship's departure for the Orient, Amy and Dickie thought they were watching the *Golden Ocean*, but the ship they saw burn was a hulk I had purchased from a salvage yard. It was towed out into the channel at night, too dark to see the towboat pulling it. Because my skeleton crew had doused the hulk with lamp oil, the hulk burned like a match. After a few minutes the towboat appeared as if by chance, and took the crew off the burning hulk."

"And where is the *Golden Ocean*, née the *Gladiator*?"

"She sailed later that night, down the coast to Savannah, where everything in her hold was sold. I took a small loss on some of the goods, made a small profit on others. And now the *Gladiator*—its rightful name back on its hull and stern—has been returned to its owner, just at the end of the charter."

"Woodrow, I hope you won't take offense," Diamond Jim said, preparing to give offense. "But this scheme sounds a little beyond you, the fellow who went to an island in the Caribbean searching for treasure in a hole."

"One of my acquaintances has proven to be an exceptional businessman." I smiled. "I would tell you who but you would hire him away from me."

Diamond Jim looked around the small crowd. A knot of people had gathered around the president, who was lecturing on some subject. "It's that Chinaman, isn't it? The smaller one. The smart-looking one over there."

Cobbler's Wax must have suspected the gist of the conversation. He was eating shrimp from a silver ice bucket. He smiled and bowed.

I shrugged, a nonanswer. But of course it was Cobbler's Wax. He had put much of my connivance together. He had a genius for commerce, turns out. Same genius that had allowed him to rise at the Summer Palace.

Diamond Jim pulled a wad of tissue from his coat pocket. It had a red ribbon around it. He held it out to Victoria. "This is for you. I didn't have time to get it wrapped."

She dug into the tissue and pulled out a silver B with diamonds mounted on it, about fifty diamonds. She hugged him, careful not to squash his sandwiches. She asked, "A 'B'? For Brady?"

"It's the only thing I had with me that was sufficiently grand. It can stand for 'beautiful.' "

Zhou had not kept up with Diamond Jim's appetite, so Jim turned toward the service table headed for more food, saying over his shoulder, "Let's do more business someday, Woodrow."

Teddy Roosevelt saw us alone, and broke free of the crowd to come over. "Where you off to on your honeymoon?"

"Between the two of us, we've been everywhere," Victoria said.

"And we didn't like most of them places," I added.

"So we're taking a hansom down to Rowe's Wharf," she explained. "And boarding a steamboat named *Myles Standish,* sailing for Nantasket Beach. We've got a little hotel room on the beach. And there's a roller coaster there. I've never been on one."

"Life with Woodrow will be roller coaster enough, I suspect." Teddy Roosevelt took off his spectacles to polish them with a handkerchief. "You are still in the army, Sergeant Lowe."

"I am?"

"And I'm your commander in chief." He smiled with teeth a horse would be proud of. "So report back to me on Nantasket Beach's navy and its defenses."

He walked to the door, where he was picked up by his bodyguards. He waved to the crowd, then left, aiming for the train station and Washington, D.C.

So you can see why I presume to call myself the spy of the century, with all the reporting Theodore Roosevelt ordered me to do all them years. Never mind I never did report.

NOW I HAVE one further incident to relate before I nod off and you go on your way, none too soon. And it explains why I went to such trouble to hide myself for so many years, and why you didn't find much record of me anywhere.

My honeymoon went like you'd expect with a woman such as Victoria

Littlewood Lowe. And I'm not going to rile you up like I did describing my night with her in Cairo. Let's just say she flat wore me down to nothing, and I never did try out that roller coaster because I didn't trust my legs to walk to it from our hotel. And why did I need a roller coaster when I spent my honeymoon sort of dizzy anyway, with all her attentions?

When I said earlier that my wife insisted Zhou keep his distance on our honeymoon, I did not mean to imply Zhou didn't accompany Victoria and me. He slept in the room across the hall from us, protesting it was too far away to do his bodyguarding.

One night—our fourth one at the Nantasket Hotel—I heard what I thought was a sneeze from the hallway, then the drip of water like someone had left a faucet on. So I got out of the bed, gripping the bedpost for support for a moment to get my wobbly legs under me, and—careful not to wake Victoria—walked across the room and opened the door.

Zhou stood there wearing only his briefs and his proximity medal, blood splashed across his body and the floor and the wall behind him. A head—a severed Chinese head—was planted on the banister knob next to him, gore dripping down, the face's expression one of a last unimaginable passion. Dressed in Western clothes, the headless body lay at Zhou's feet, and was still gushing blood from the neck. A second body, another Chinaman, was down the hall five paces, belly up, a puddle of blood widening across the wood floor. A revolver lay next to him.

I ran my hand across my mouth, then asked in Chinese, "Old Buddha?"

"She has a long memory. She must have sent these two killers for you. Perhaps to San Francisco, then across the country to Boston, then to here."

I stared at the bodies. "Lordy, that was close."

Zhou was affronted. "With me guarding you, this wasn't close at all. These men were dead the day they sailed from the Celestial Kingdom. They just didn't realize it."

"Can you clean this up?"

He nodded, then smiled widely, pointing to his dentures with his dripping dagger. "That's two diamonds you owe me."

"You'll get them."

I went back into the room and crawled into bed next to Victoria. She purred sleepily, "Something wrong, Woodrow?"

"Nothing out of the ordinary, my life considered as a whole. Nothing unusual at all."

AFTERWORD

THIS IS ME again. Truman Pease.

I hadn't intended my last interview with Woodrow Lowe to be the last. I was kept away from his Newbury estate by an emergency in my cubicle at the National Archives Building. A water pipe burst, and when one's office is 19.38 feet below the Potomac's mean high tide, a ruptured pipe is a thing of consequence. Water sprayed around my cubicle, and I rushed around scooping up piles of photographs and hurrying them out to the safety of the hallway.

Regrettably, my eight photographs of Marilyn Monroe—from her 1956 nude session with the now-deceased photographer Hap Joiner; extraordinary photographs never seen in public because I couldn't bear to share them with the world—were directly under the pipe, and were destroyed, and to my knowledge no negatives exist.

Almost a week was spent cleaning my office and cataloging the ruin, and when I returned to Woodrow Lowe's home in the first week of August, 1972, once again negotiating my way around the ample nurse with the warden's disposition, I again found Woodrow Lowe in his sunroom. But he was much diminished.

He opened his eyes and managed to roll them around to me, and only with effort could he lift his chin off his chest. The scar on his cheek had been badly shaved, and tufts of gray hair dotted his face.

His voice was the ghost of a whisper. "I staved off the grim reaper for 108 years but now I can feel him coming."

"You don't look any worse than the last time I was here," I said. "You'll probably live until you are an old man."

He snorted. "Where was I in my story? I'd better get to the end of it fast."

I was alarmed. "You're only up to your honeymoon. You've said nothing about the assassination of Archduke Franz Ferdinand, nothing at all. You've only taken me up to your forty-first year, not even halfway through your life."

He burbled something I couldn't understand. His chin lowered back to his chest and his eyelids closed.

I yanked on his sleeve. "Mr. Lowe, please. You've got to find the energy to tell me your story."

The baleful eyes opened. "Nobody tugged my sleeve when Zhou was around, I'll guarantee you that."

Distinguishing his voice from his wheezing was difficult. Profoundly distressed, I realized I might never hear the rest of Woodrow Lowe's story. So I decided I'd better wrap up those parts I knew.

"Mr. Lowe, whatever happened to Zhou?"

He clacked his dentures. "He lived to be an old man, eighty-five years old. He had a stroke on his eighty-third birthday, so I ended up pushing him around in a wheelchair for them two years, him insisting he was still my bodyguard." He chortled, a sound like stepping on dried twigs. "I may be the only person in history who had to push his bodyguard around in a wheelchair."

"Did Old Buddha ever try to kill you again?"

"She died in 1908, but her successors may have tried. I never felt safe from her or her successors until Mao took over in 1949. Old Buddha pardoned Prince Tuan after he'd been on the northwest frontier only two years. She could forgive him because of his royal blood, but she never forgave me, I don't think. I corresponded with the prince for a number of years until he died of consumption."

"And Zhou?"

"I buried Zhou with his diamond dentures and his proximity medal two days after his eighty-fifth birthday, and I don't mind saying it was a grievous day for me."

"And Cobbler's Wax?"

The old man tried to smile, but lifting the corners of his mouth was too much effort. "When I got done counting all the money I conned out of Amy and Dickie Balfour, I had one million, five hundred thousand dollars. That was after I'd given Diamond Jim his 25 percent. So there had been a draft for half a million dollars in that envelope I'd given Diamond Jim on the day of my wedding. But I had a million and a half left. That was back in the days when a million and a half was a sizable assemblage of cash."

With the slightest rise of a finger, he indicated a water glass on a TV table next to his chair. I held it to his lips and he swallowed a few drops.

He continued, his voice a soft piping. "I've only met a few geniuses in my life. Teddy Roosevelt was a political genius, that was for sure. John L. Sullivan was a genius with his fists. Well, Cobbler's Wax was a business genius. As my agent he doubled that million and a half dollars in three years, and doubled it again in the following two years. He imported and exported, and set up a trading company, several trading companies, with offices on both coasts and in the Orient. No opium, mind you. He made a vast fortune for me, and for himself, and even for Zhou. And he did it all without using my name because we were afraid of Old Buddha."

He coughed raggedly, his spindly body bucking. "Cobbler's Wax made me money every day of his life, and was doing so on the day he died in 1951 of a heart attack. Since then I've just mostly sat on my fortune, not trusting myself to do much with it. Only time I ever saw Zhou weep was when he and I lowered Cobbler's Wax into the ground."

"And Victoria?"

He said nothing for a moment, just stared into a wall of hothouse foliage. Then his words were serrated. "For many, many years, I asked God on my knees five times a day that He allow Victoria to outlive me, that I would never have to sit by her side while she slipped the fetters of this life. My prayers were not answered. Or maybe they were answered, and God said no."

"When did she die?"

He coughed weakly. "I can't say I was cheated of her, though. She lived to be ninety-two, a full measure of a life, compared to anybody but mine. As beautiful at ninety-two as she had been on our wedding day. And as feisty. And as smart. And when she passed on, she was gazing at me just the way she did when I put the ring on her finger so many years before at Trinity Church. I will join her soon, within days maybe, I am certain of that. I can't wait. It has been too long."

"And Amy and Dickie Balfour?"

"Dickie died of syphilis in 1909. Amy lived well into old age. Her little pension meant she never had to take in laundry, but she lived in a one-bedroom common-wall house in Roxbury—my old Roxbury—for the rest of her life. About once every five years I'd pass her on the street, and she'd feign not to recognize me."

"Do you think she ever figured out your scheme?"

"I can only hope she did."

Then Brunhilde the nurse came to shoo me away, as she did to end each session, her massive posterior barely fitting through the pathway of leaves.

Woodrow Lowe managed to hold up a hand in her direction, which made her pause. "Want to lose another twenty dollars, young man?"

"Not particularly."

"I'll wager you twenty dollars that you can't tell me how many faces are on Mt. Rushmore."

"Who is on Mt. Rushmore?" I was wary of his wagers, after losing the twenty dollars when he showed me his tattoo.

"Not who, but how many."

I stared into those yellow eyes. "It's a deal," I declared emphatically, reaching for my wallet. "There are four faces on Mt. Rushmore."

He shook his head, an almost imperceptible movement. "There are five."

"Hah," I jeered. "After 108 years, age and infirmity are finally beginning to show, Mr. Lowe. Any fool knows Lincoln, Jefferson, Washington and your old friend Theodore Roosevelt are carved into that mountain."

He tried another smile. His eyes were dug into mine. "On the longest day of the year, some June 21, when the sun is highest in the sky, I want you to be at Mt. Rushmore. You take a pair of binoculars, and you look at Theodore Roosevelt's granite mustache up on that mountain. The shadows are perfect only on that day each year, and only for a few minutes."

"And?"

"You will see yours truly, Woodrow C. Lowe, in the stone hairs of Roosevelt's mustache."

I scoffed. "Mr. Lowe, them stories . . . those stories about your life, well, they insist on a certain credulity, some of them. I have listened, not saying too much. But you have finally gone too far. To say that you are on Mt. Rushmore . . ."

"Theodore Roosevelt's sixty-foot-high head—twice as high as the Giza Sphinx, a fact I'm sure he would have relished—was being worked on in 1938 by the sculptor Gutzon Borglum. I approached him and offered him a nice sum if he would do this little favor. He did. And now no one ever knows about me being up there on that mountain, unless they are by chance staring at Teddy's rock mustache at just the right time, on just that one day a year."

"I find that impossible—"

He cut me off. "You will not be able to resist finding out if I am correct. And when you see me emerge in the shadows of Teddy's mustache, you march right back to my grave, and you tear up a twenty-dollar bill, and you sprinkle it over my plot."

"Enough for one day," announced the Hun nurse. "Out you go, you. And Mr. Lowe, you have your medicine." She was holding a pint jar of pills.

I stared a moment longer at Woodrow Lowe, and he at me. I look back now, and believe with that gaze he was saying goodbye, for he had counted down the days he had left, and they were few, and he knew he would never see me again. He called himself the spy of the century, which may have been his little joke, as he did no spying despite being asked again and again. But Woodrow Lowe may well have been the man of the century.

As I mentioned earlier, the old fellow died in August 1972. I was unaware of his passing until I visited his Newbury estate a week after the conversation related above, to see if he could continue the story of his life. I was surprised to see his mansion for sale, a large realtor's sign on the front gate. And when I inquired inside, the nurse—on the payroll until the end of that month—told me he had been laid to rest. Whether Woodrow Lowe was mourned by anyone at his burial is unknown by me.

Mr. Lowe's association with Archduke Franz Ferdinand will remain forever a mystery, though I still have the photograph.

Yes, the very next summer—on the longest day of the year—my binoculars were trained on Mt. Rushmore, on Theodore Roosevelt's mustache. I gasped when the shadows aligned themselves on the granite hairs under Roosevelt's nose, and a tiny Woodrow C. Lowe emerged from the mustache. The square jaw, the cauliflower ear, the scar on the cheek, unmistakable. I stared in wonder and appreciation. And within fifteen minutes, with the sun moving across the sky, Mr. Lowe's face began to settle again into Roosevelt's mustache, to wait for another year. You will see it yourself, should you be at Mt. Rushmore on the longest day of the year, and when the sun is highest in the sky.

So I returned to Boston and visited his grave at the Fenwick Street cemetery in Roxbury, where I tore up a twenty-dollar bill and let the pieces flutter onto the grass below his headstone. A few bits of the bill drifted to the nearby graves of Victoria and Zhou and Cobbler's Wax.

And then I heard the old man laugh from the beyond. That same old cackle. Or it might have been the wind in the graveyard trees.